*T*HEATRE, COMMUNITY, *and* CIVIC ENGAGEMENT *in* *J*ACOBEAN *L*ONDON

Studies in

THEATRE HISTORY

AND CULTURE

Edited by Thomas Postlewait

*T*HEATRE, COMMUNITY, *and* CIVIC ENGAGEMENT *in* *J*ACOBEAN *L*ONDON

MARK BAYER

UNIVERSITY OF IOWA PRESS, IOWA CITY

University of Iowa Press, Iowa City 52242

Printed in the United States of America
Design by Richard Hendel

www.uiowapress.org

The University of Iowa Press is a member of Green Press Initiative and is committed to preserving natural resources.

Printed on acid-free paper

Library of Congress Cataloging-in-Publication Data
Bayer, Mark, 1973–
Theatre, community, and civic engagement in Jacobean London / Mark Bayer.
p. cm.—(Studies in theatre history and culture)
Includes bibliographical references and index.
ISBN-13: 978-1-60938-039-7 (pbk.)
ISBN-10: 1-60938-039-8 (pbk.)
ISBN-13: 978-1-60938-040-3 (e-book)
ISBN-10: 1-60938-040-1 (e-book)
1. Theater and society—England—History—17th century.
2. Theater—England—London—History—17th century. I. Title.
PN2592.B39 2011
306.4′8480942109032—dc22 2011010708

For Youmna

[Plays] persuade men to humanity and good life, instruct them in civility and good manners, showing them the fruits of honesty, and the end of villainy.

THOMAS HEYWOOD

An Apology for Actors (1612)

CONTENTS

ACKNOWLEDGMENTS

This book is about how individuals and institutions built overlapping communities in a large and diverse urban environment. In writing it, I have been fortunate enough to draw upon scholarly communities that encompass numerous individuals and several institutions spanning three continents.

I am grateful for the generous financial assistance this project has received from a number of organizations. Fellowships from the Henry E. Huntington Library in Pasadena and the Newberry Library in Chicago supported archival research in the United States, while a semester's leave made possible by the William and Flora Hewlett Foundation allowed me to continue that research at the British Library, Public Record Office, and Guildhall Library in London. Librarians at these institutions and at the Folger Shakespeare Library in Washington, D.C., the Ohio State University Libraries in Columbus (especially James Bracken), and the Houghton Library at Harvard University have made conducting research for this book a pleasure.

A version of chapter 3 first appeared as "Staging Foxe at the Fortune and the Red Bull" in *Renaissance and Reformation/Renaissance et Réforme* 27.1 (2003). The first part of chapter 5 was published as "Moving UpMarket" in *Early Theatre* 4 (2001). I am grateful to the editors of those journals for permission to republish here. I have road-tested bits and pieces of the argument at meetings of the Shakespeare Association of America, Group for Early Modern Cultural Studies, and Pacific Northwest Renaissance Society. I am thankful for the attentive and helpful audiences on those occasions. Many of the ideas behind the study were first germinated in a Folger Institute Seminar in 2001, "Rethinking the *Elizabethan Stage*." Thanks to Susan Cerasano and the participants in that group for countless stimulating conversations on revisionist theatre history.

I have had the good fortune of working with several extremely talented graduate students whose research assistance has been essential in completing the project. I wish to thank Julia Mahfouz and Deema Kaedbey at the American University of Beirut, who helped in earlier stages of the project. More recently, at the University of Texas at San Antonio, Christina Gutierrez and Melissa Whitney helped with the formatting and references. Patrick Collins, whose ability with computers is truly astounding, constructed the three maps that offer a visual orientation within early modern London. And the dreary job of compiling the index was completed with alacrity by Michael Lee Gardin.

So many people over so many years have read and commented on the manuscript at various stages in its evolution. For their valuable suggestions I would like to thank Mark Allen, Richard Dutton, Christopher Highley, Jayson Iwen, John N. King, Jeremy Lopez, Joseph Navitsky, Jeffrey Turpin, Brent Whitted, Luke Wilson, Joseph Wittreich, and an anonymous reader for the University of Iowa Press. Thomas E. Postlewait, the editor of Studies in Theatre History and Culture, has helped shape the direction of the project and has challenged me through his copious comments to improve it. Holly Carver, Charlotte Wright, and the staff at the University of Iowa Press expertly guided the book into print. My copyeditor, Kathy Burford Lewis, offered incisive suggestions and brought her keen editorial eye to bear on the manuscript's inconsistencies. More than anyone else, Nick Moschovakis has commented on the manuscript at numerous stages since its inception and has helped me steadily nudge the argument in more productive directions. Finally, many thanks to Keith Owen Richards for turning my attention to the Red Bull, so many years ago in Montréal.

My parents, Tony and Judy Bayer, and my sister, Rebecca, have been a constant source of loving support during my entire life. And more recently I have benefited from the encouragement of my parents-in-law, Nuha and Ali Dbouk.

My greatest debt is registered in the book's dedication.

THEATRE, COMMUNITY, *and* CIVIC ENGAGEMENT *in* JACOBEAN LONDON

INTRODUCTION
THEATRE & SOCIAL CAPITAL

Thomas Heywood's *Apology for Actors* is well known for its defense of the public stage against its detractors. Heywood suggests that due to their "antiquity" and "ancient dignity" players have the capacity to improve the moral health of individuals who attend theatres and thereby foster a more virtuous populace. "Plays," after all, "were writ with this aim and carried with this method: . . . to show people the untimely ends of such as have moved tumults, commotions, and insurrections, to present them with the flourishing estate of such as live in obedience."[1] Unlike other humanistic appeals to the edifying powers of dramatic literature, Heywood's claim is not simply that plays can morally instruct and move individuals to virtue but that the theatre might forge a more harmonious community. The ills that he claims might be alleviated by plays are all social maladies, not private vices. Nor are the advantages conferred by theatrical activity hopelessly abstract or confined to a single group: they have the capacity to effect real social outcomes for the benefit of all citizens.

Heywood goes on to narrate an anecdote in which a company of actors, playing in Cornwall on

> the same night when certain Spaniards were landed . . . unsuspected and undiscovered, with intent to take the town, spoil, and burn it, when suddenly, even upon their entrance, the players (ignorant as the townsmen of any such attempt) presenting a battle on stage with their drum and trumpets struck up a loud alarm: which the enemy hearing, and fearing they were discovered, amazedly retired . . . At the report of this tumult, the townsmen were immediately armed, and pursued them to the sea, praising God for their happy deliverance from so great a danger. (*Apology for Actors*, G2r)

The theatre, in this view, augments social networks to the point where restorative collective action is possible in situations where it might otherwise be lacking. If we are to believe Heywood's account, the actors did not consciously intend to provide for the public defense that ultimately saved the town from the Spanish marauders; nor, obviously, were the townspeople incapable of the task. Instead, theatrical performance acted as a catalyst that warned citizens of the impending danger and mobilized them to protect their community.

Regardless of the veracity of Heywood's anecdote, it also suggests that the social meaning of plays might be properly gauged only in particular circumstances of performance. Staged somewhere else, or at any other time, the play that Heywood describes would not have resonated so forcefully for its audience. For this community, given the Spanish attack, the performance was a call to action. Other spectators would undoubtedly see it in a different light, suggesting that a historical interpretation of theatrical activity must take into account the shared circumstances of its audience. Audiences were not a random assortment of spectators but were drawn from specific communities that fundamentally affected how they attended playhouses and perceived the drama staged there. The effects of theatrical activity, moreover, extend beyond the particular audience witnessing the performance. The audience's unique response to this play saved the entire community from the Spanish, not just those who witnessed the performance.

My argument in this book is that the London theatre of the Tudor and Stuart era was an important community institution. It was enjoyed by distinctive audiences at several theatres, contributed to neighborhood economies by helping local businesses and donating healthily to charity, forged and strengthened various religious affiliations, was a meaningful source of popular education on a number of issues, offered a welcome and necessary diversion in tumultuous times, and enriched social life throughout London. Each of the theatres also contributed to a more particularized sense of community formation within the regions of the capital where the playhouses were located. Because theatre audiences were considerably more than heterogeneous and deracinated aggregates of individuals, I also argue that some of London's amphitheatres derived significant aspects of their unique identity from the types of playgoers that attended them, many of whom, not surprisingly, frequented the theatre closest to their homes or businesses.

Theatrical activity was to some extent local, and theatres like the Fortune and the Red Bull became important institutions for those living and working in surrounding and adjoining neighborhoods. Many, perhaps most, of the apprentices who frequented the Red Bull lived near that playhouse. And that may be why they reacted so vociferously when the company left the Red Bull for another venue in 1617 (see chapter 5). I want to explore these local dimensions of playgoing here even though this premise is difficult to verify, given the dearth and inadequacy of documentary evidence. My broader claim, however, will stand or fall on the premise that theatres intimately engaged with specific social communities throughout the city who witnessed their productions.

Another way of stating my thesis is that theatre enhanced social capital. The central idea behind social capital is that the density of social networks matters: they increase our sense of belonging in communities (both physical and abstract); they promote shared understanding of the needs of others; and they increase our productivity and overall happiness—often in unconscious and unintended ways.[2] Social capital calls attention to norms of generalized reciprocity that entail mutual responsibility and obligation in organizations of all kinds, from small businesses to religious groups to neighborhoods within cities. Unlike physical or human capital, which are properties of things and individuals respectively, social capital is a resource that inheres in the connections formed *between* individuals in various communities. Social capital offers a way of understanding the theatres in their urban context that situates them amid a broad range of social practices that were integral to the daily lives of the Londoners who attended them, the very people who allowed for their continued success and the expansion of the industry. I want to use the concept of social capital to help construct a sociology of the theatre from below, from the particular communities that it served and where it was most visible, rather than from broader ideological perspectives and political categories imposed from above that were at best distant from the daily experience of most playgoers. By arguing, for instance, that theatrical performance was either subversive of the social order or apologetic for it, we tend to lose sight of the more mundane and local concerns of audiences. No singular theoretical concept can fully account for such an expansive and complex social activity.

Social capital is a powerful analytic category for studying urban behavior during this period because in early modern London community was more than a callow ideal; it was a historical reality. Londoners tended to understand their place within the larger metropolis as strong overlapping communities, including (but certainly not limited to) parishes, guilds, and wards. Simply put, "belonging" mattered to residents of the capital. John Stow, the famous sixteenth-century chronicler of the city, emphasizes that the values citizens shared contributed most to the success and growth of London. For him, the age-old customs of the city and its institutions emulated the civic virtue that made the Roman Republic a model for its successors. Rehearsing the myth that Londoners shared a Trojan heritage, Stow claims:

> this city is ancienter than Rome, built of the ancient Trojans and of Brute . . . and therefore useth the ancient customs of Rome. This city, even as Rome, is divided into wards; it hath yearly sheriffs instead of consuls; it hath the dignity of senators in aldermen . . . I do not think that there is any city wherein are better customs, in frequenting the churches and serving God, in keeping holy days, and giving alms, in entertaining strangers, in solemnizing marriages, in furnishing banquets, celebrating funerals and burying dead bodies.[3]

The institutions Stow discusses were not reserved for a wealthy elite, as they were so often in Rome, but filtered down through the pervasive guild structure that oversaw all industry in the capital to encompass the general populace, instilling some sense of civic responsibility in almost everyone and allowing all residents to partake in some form of social capital.

Many prominent figures in the period argued that the theatres contributed to the same kinds of positive civic engagement that Stow enumerates. Michel de Montaigne, whose *Essays* were first printed in English in 1603, insisted that plays promoted "common society and loving friendship." Francis Bacon, writing two years later, pointed out that "the action of the theatre . . . might improve mankind in virtue" because "the minds of men in company are more open to affections and excitation than when alone," arguing that the playhouse and other public forums could stimulate civic reform and collective action.[4] The theatre, according to Bacon, had an edifying effect on its audiences simply by bringing them together for a collective experience, regardless of the content of the plays themselves. Thomas Dekker, a figure certainly familiar with the stunning diversity of London's social spaces and the many imperfections of urban life, was even more explicit in asserting that the playhouse brings together members of disparate social groups while still managing to promote solidarity for specific factions. He links the stage to the market square, suggesting that "the theatre is your poet's Royal Exchange . . . your gallant, your courtier, and your captain, had wont to be the soundest playmasters . . . your gallant and gallery commoner buys his sport by the penny . . . sithence the place is so free in entertainment."[5] Like the marketplace, the theatre for Dekker is a place of social discourse, freedom, and mobility that allows different groups to mix even as it preserves and enhances traditional associations. At the playhouse, especially the large public houses that are the topic of this book, the gallant and gallery commoners can stick with their own, even while they intermingle.

Most contemporary scholarship on the theatre in early modern London implicitly acknowledges the social resonance of dramatic works within their urban setting. Scholars since E. K. Chambers have noted that the interplay of theatrical professionals, various levels of the municipal government, and city residents allowed the public theatres to gain an institutional foothold in the city. Sometimes, of course, the theatres promoted social dissonance rather than cohesion. In their trenchant investigation of the social topography of the theatre, other scholars have linked the stage with social elements hostile and even antithetical to dominant forms of power.[6] These arguments have greatly expanded the horizons of our understanding of the place of the theatres in London society and have opened critical possibilities for the drama staged there. Sometimes, however, these studies have attenuated our sense of the rich localized interactions of the theatre in the London neighborhoods that hosted them as well as more optimistic and progressive visions of social accord represented by the players. My intention is not to ignore the theatre's potential to promote disorder or normalize it as an uncomplicated extension or expression of the city's dominant political, economic, or religious interests. Rather, by understanding the theatre and its audiences as particular communities among other social groups in early modern London, we gain a sense of the rich and contributory social dialogue made possible by the playhouses. These theatres represented a new and in many ways unique institution, to be sure, but it was not one set apart from other forms of social exchange.

The civic engagement that I am trying to describe here is most apparent at the large public amphitheatres, the venue of choice for most of the capital's playgoers, who collectively generated millions of visits to the playhouses over the decades between 1570 and 1640. I do not significantly address the indoor playhouses. These private theatres were not viable outlets of recreation for the majority of Londoners because of their high cost. With the rising popularity of these theatres (especially by the late 1620s during the reign of Charles I) cultural consumers, mimicking courtiers' growing enthusiasm for elaborate masques, had developed more nuanced aesthetic tastes. They would flock to the Blackfriars and the Cockpit (also known as the Phoenix) out of habit and a concern for social status, setting them firmly apart from their outdoor counterparts.[7]

The players' involvement in particular communities meant different things for each of the playing companies at various times. Andrew Gurr has forcefully argued that company repertories became more specialized as the theatre industry matured, allowing for a significantly more diverse market for dramatic entertainment that appealed to the discrete tastes of various groups.[8] We must therefore avoid the temptation to homogenize what the theatre meant to the city and understand the relationships of the theatre, its audiences, and the broader urban community in particular reception contexts that changed over time. For that reason, the plays and the theatres that I discuss in this book span a period from roughly 1599 to 1625, only about one-third of the time when professional playing flourished in the city. I concentrate mainly on the Jacobean period because it was during these years that the amphitheatres became increasingly stratified, taking on stable, recognizable, and discrete identities of their own. Less preoccupied with achieving a place in the social and economic topography of the city than they had been in the first three decades of their existence,[9] the theatres by this time were not just a generic form of public entertainment. Each theatre was a unique entity with a highly particularized reputation and a diverse array of plays on offer, designed to appeal to a vast spectrum of cultural consumers and not all in the same fashion. During the late 1610s, for instance, the repertory at the Globe, featuring the tragicomedies of Francis Beaumont, John Fletcher, and John Webster, would hardly be intelligible to those used to the epic action sequences and slapstick comedy at the Red Bull.

Moreover, audiences, no longer entranced by the actors' novelty and accustomed to the availability of regular dramatic entertainment, were hardly the unpracticed playgoers that they had been in the industry's infancy decades earlier. Spectators increasingly recognized the impact that demand could have on the repertories of these dramatic troupes. Before the late 1590s companies migrated from playhouse to playhouse relatively frequently, making an identification with certain actors, playwrights, or types of plays at a single playhouse impossible. By the early decades of the seventeenth century, however, the three major Jacobean companies settled into playhouses—the Globe, the Fortune, and the Red Bull—that they would use regularly for more than a decade. This pattern changed again in the Caroline period when the market for dramatic entertainment became split between the elite private theatres like Blackfriars and the Phoenix, on the one hand, and the established amphitheatres like the Red Bull, Globe, and Fortune, on the other. By the 1630s attending the theatres became a force of habit depending on an ensemble of factors, including one's place in the social hierarchy, the social atmosphere at various theatres, and the plays themselves.

Geography was also important in the rise of the playgoing industry. One of the well-known peculiarities of all London's amphitheatres was their location: these theatres were not actually located in the city at all but were built in suburban "liberties," remnants of the monastic lands and religious orders that were dissolved in 1539 by order of Henry VIII, where London's government exercised somewhat limited jurisdiction. Legal impediments to locating playhouses anywhere in the city or its suburbs allowed for the development of two distinct theatrical neighborhoods. The first two large amphitheatre playhouses, the Theatre (1576) and the Curtain (1577), were located adjacent to one another in Shoreditch, just north of the city wall. The next three, the Rose (1587), the Swan (1595), and the Globe (1599), were built on the Bankside.[10] Consequently, the theatre became a destination for those who lived within the city walls. This suggests that factors like location and convenience, in addition to repertory and actors, had an impact on a playgoer's choice to attend a certain venue (see figure 1).

By locating playhouses in rapidly growing suburban areas, theatrical entrepreneurs also made it much easier for local populations of artisans, apprentices, and newcomers to the city (who almost always first settled in the suburbs) to attend the playhouse, unwittingly recruiting a large and stable audience that would allow them to prosper beyond their initial hopes. When James Burbage built his Theatre in 1576, Shoreditch was not yet the neighborhood of teeming tenements and shops that it would soon become. The neighborhood, in other words, did not have significant associations for many Londoners. The theatre occupied a kind of symbolic space in this community, as it would later in others, which allowed both providers and consumers of drama to orient their activities around physical locations in the city in addition to a recreational activity. Whatever the reasons for Burbage's decision to locate his playhouse in this neighborhood, others soon followed. The Curtain was built due south of the Theatre on land held by Henry Lanman, cementing Shoreditch, not the Bankside, as London's first theatrical quarter.[11]

Somewhat counterintuitive from a competitive marketing perspective, this pattern of locating playhouses close or even adjacent to one another continued for decades and is still evident in the preponderance of theatres in the modern West End. Less than a decade later, in March 1585, Philip Henslowe leased land on Bankside and built the Rose, a venue later made popular by the Admiral's Men and their leading man, Edward Alleyn, performing the unforgettable Marlovian roles of Tamburlaine and Faustus. Henslowe's venture marked a second geographical shift in London's theatrical activity. In 1595 the Swan was built to the west of the Rose, again on the Bankside, followed four years later by the Globe, about a block away from Henslowe's Rose. The Hope, which doubled as a bearbaiting arena, was the last new public playhouse built on the Bankside, in 1614, the year that the Globe was rebuilt on the same location after it was razed by fire during a performance of William Shakespeare's *Henry VIII* on 29 June 1613. Presumably the Globe had become so well established in the neighborhood over the previous decade that Henslowe and his partner, Jacob Meade, who together financed the construction of the Hope, felt that the neighborhood could again sustain a second playhouse.

The early seventeenth century marked another partial geographic shift in the location of London's theatrical industry, this time northwest of the city wall, with the opening of the Fortune in 1600 and the Red Bull sometime between 1605 and 1607. For the investors in and actors at these venues, the clustering of playhouses in certain neighborhoods took into account a complex variety of factors, including the availability of land, building restrictions, and the changing legal statutes that governed playing in the city and the suburbs. It is doubtful that the precise reasons for the location of these theatres will ever be understood with any certainty. For audiences, however, the location of playhouses in specific neighborhoods made playgoing not just a form of entertainment but a destination; not a homogeneous commodity but a location that affected the way in which playgoers related to their own local environment, allowing for affiliations with certain venues rather than the pastime as a whole. James Norwood, one of the few apprentices to leave detailed comments about his playgoing habits, writes: "I fell out with the players at the Fortune (which was the house I frequented) about a seat which they would not admit me to have."[12] This brief statement implies that Norwood felt an allegiance to a particular theatre and had forged some kind of relationship with the actors who regularly performed there. Individuals were not simply playgoers but denizens of a certain playhouse that we must assume was significantly inflected by their location.

These two playhouses northwest of London Wall, the Fortune and the Red Bull, are important in my discussion of theatre and social capital because they defy claims that the playhouses catered to audiences drawn from across the social spectrum. Both venues quickly earned a reputation for popular entertainment presented in a heroic style that firmly differentiated them from the Globe. They were poised to do so partly because of their location in and near populous neighborhoods that were home to the many artisans and apprentices who would fre-

FIGURE 1. Map of London showing the approximate location of playhouses and other sites of interest: 1, Theatre; 2, Curtain; 3, Rose; 4, Swan; 5, Globe; 6, Fortune; 7, Red Bull; 8, Blackfriars; 9, Cockpit; 10, Hope; 11, Christchurch; 12, St. James Clerkenwell; 13, St. Giles in the Fields; 14, St. Giles Cripplegate; 15, St. Saviour Southwark; 16, St. Paul's; 17, Royal Exchange; 18, Grocers' Hall; 19, Leadenhall; 20, Baynard's Castle; 21, Tower; 22, Cripplegate; 23, Aldersgate; 24, Bishopsgate; 25, Guildhall; 26, Lincoln's Inn; 27, London Bridge. This map was surveyed around 1570, more than thirty years before the period covered in this book, so the suburbs of the city would be considerably more built up and congested than depicted here. From Ralph Agas, *Civitas Londinium* (ca. 1570), scanned and corrected by Mike Calder, with locations added by Patrick Collins. Courtesy of Wikipedia Commons.

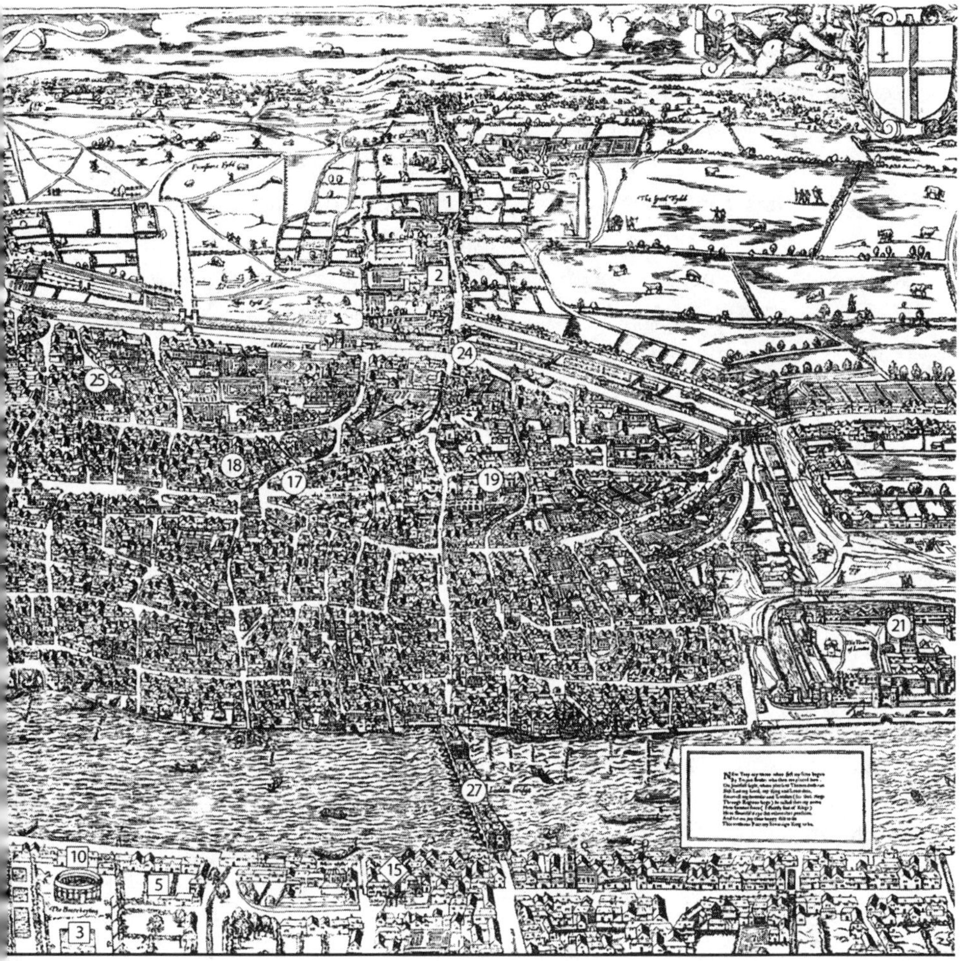

□ Theater
◇ Church
○ Point of Interest

quent them.[13] The unique characteristics of these playhouses were in part a matter of competitive positioning. Andrew Gurr, for instance, sees the Prince's Men at the Fortune as Shakespeare's opposites, arguing that the two companies "diverged from the start," developing distinct identities to capitalize on the bifurcated tastes of London playgoers.[14] I think that Gurr's assertion is correct from the standpoint of supply, but it does not suggest how fluctuations in dramatic tastes and changes in audience composition might have contributed to this development. Nor does it take account of the Red Bull, a playhouse that from its beginning was at least as notorious—and popular with paying audiences—as the other two. Gurr sees individual theatrical companies as the most important unit shaping the contours of the playgoing industry, arguing that "on the whole companies and their different kinds of plays were a much stronger factor than different venues."[15] I want to shift focus slightly by concentrating on the playhouses, especially the Fortune and the Red Bull, while of course realizing that neither factor can be completely isolated from the other.

Unlike studies of theatrical companies, my book is concerned with the *demand* characteristics of the playgoing industry, an investigation that requires us to consider the Red Bull and its unique place in the dramatic history of the period. The Red Bull looms large in this study not only because it has gone relatively unnoticed but also because the productions at that theatre tend to illuminate important relationships between the playhouse and the predominantly laboring classes that popularized it—many of whom lived in and around Clerkenwell, where the playhouse was located. By looking at this theatre, its audiences, and its local community, we can identify forms of social capital that escape our notice when we focus on the Globe, a playhouse that became a destination for Londoners from across the Thames because Southwark did not yet have a large or stable enough local population to sustain a repertory theatre without cross-river traffic. Partly due to the differences in their location—in addition to their repertory and dramaturgy—playhouses like the Fortune and the Red Bull were frequented by different kinds of audiences than the Globe, making the former two theatres especially rich sites for social interaction within specific urban communities.

Employed by modern social theorists as diverse as Pierre Bourdieu and Robert Putnam to think about and ultimately to improve civil society, the idea of social capital might seem anachronistic to a discussion of Jacobean London. Yet the general concepts it enumerates are strikingly evident in a city where bonds between individuals were unavoidable and social ties were considered the hallmark of a functioning society. Because it points to relationships between people, social capital has both a private and public face, conferring benefits on individuals as well as the broader community.[16] According to Pierre Bourdieu, social capital is a unit of value that can be appropriated and transacted with other forms of capital to the advantage of those who are able to harness their social contacts most effectively. For him, social capital is the aggregate of the connections that an individual can mobilize, a more or less tangible reserve that an agent can draw upon when needed. Like all economic phenomena, then, transacting social capital is an expression of individual accumulation. Though relatively autonomous from other, more familiar economic instruments, it is nevertheless tied up in a zero-sum game: some people have it to the detriment of those who do not.[17]

Bourdieu's economic approach suggests the potential downside to social capital. Just as it would be wrong to assume that *all* plays promoted mutual respect, civic virtue, community values, or more harmonious lifestyles, not all social networks have intrinsic value. In seventeenth-century London, economic and social pressures were often crippling to foreigners who came to the city to make a living but were ostracized from the social relationships necessary for doing just that. The cony-catching pamphlets of Robert Greene and the city comedies of Thomas Middleton and Ben Jonson, for instance, depict a type of social victim: the gentry who traveled to the city eager to use their landed wealth to earn a good reputation and purchase a cosmopolitan lifestyle. Unfortunately, all too often shrewd and predatory arrivistes used their "local knowledge" of London's social scene to hoodwink these unsuspecting provincials. Social capital is not a panacea, but its negative instantiations succinctly illustrate the extraordinary power of this kind of bonding to effect change in the community, for better or worse.

In contrast to the economic models offered by Bourdieu, Robert Putnam stresses that individual benefits are only one facet of social capital. Staying well connected affects everyone, not just those who use social ties for personal benefit.[18] Membership in one of London's livery companies accorded members enormous commercial and social advantages that would be impossible to achieve individually or in smaller associations. These guilds, premised on both professional and social relationships among practitioners of the same trade, gave their members a sense of belonging within the company and provided an entrée into city politics; only company members could earn the "freedom of the city" that conferred the right to vote and stand for office. Similarly, the wards of London frequently organized neighborhood watches to prevent crime, an initiative that made the community safer for everyone, even those who chose not to participate. Religious and secular institutions including the theatre sought to mitigate tensions between well-defined social groups like citizen and gentry, apprentice and gallant. And numerous instances of apprentices marrying up attest both to the presence of strongly defined social divisions and to their permeability.[19] These examples reveal two forms of social capital. One bonds those of similar socioeconomic status. The other bridges across previously unaffiliated individuals and groups, suggesting that social ties could be reshaped to allow for greater mobility.

Social capital, in both these variants, is a local phenomenon: in order to build strong norms of trust, reciprocity, and general amiability, people must come into frequent personal contact.[20] In London, knowing one's neighbors was a prerequisite for the trust and familiarity needed for meaningful and mutually beneficial social discourse as well as for more ambitious endeavors designed to build and rehabilitate the community. Because of mandatory church attendance, acquisition of occupational skills fulfilled and credentialed through apprenticeship that fostered one-on-one relationships with the master, and the organizational procedures that tied trades to specific company halls, social interaction was an integral part of everyday life and the key to upward mobility and a solid reputation. London was a city of overlapping communities, and its citizens reaped the benefits of strong social bonds.

During the early modern period the etymology of the word "community" evolved to include significantly broader meanings than an aggregation of people in close physical proximity. English citizens were beginning to conceive of their own communities in qualitative, almost moral, terms as a set of both tangible and intangible relationships and beliefs held in common for mutual betterment. No longer was "living in community" a geographical accident or a product of shared beliefs. Individuals were urged to maintain strong interpersonal ties for the improvement of the commonwealth. Citizens frequently cited classics by Plato and especially Cicero for the participation in social groups expected of Athenians and Romans, something Londoners were implored to emulate. In *De Officiis* (*On Duty*), by far the most frequently published and the most often translated work by Cicero in Renaissance England, he examines the relative merits of private study and contemplation against civic engagement:

> For whereas all honesty springeth forth out of four heads, whereof one is knowledge, another is of community, the third of magnanimity, the fourth of moderation; it is of necessity that in choosing of duty, these be oft compared amongst themselves. We think therefore that those duties are more agreeable to nature which . . . [originate] from community than those which are fetched from knowledge . . . Duty which is borrowed from community is the greatest. For knowledge and contemplation of nature is after a sort maimed.[21]

Due to the ubiquity of Cicero's precepts among Londoners with even a modest education, his remarks on the primacy of community were highly influential, especially because they tended to reinforce contemporary religious discourse that also preached the value of social cohesion.

For clergy in Renaissance London, concerned with both the spiritual and temporal health of their flock, St. Paul's belief that Christians participated together in the body of Christ was more than an abstract theological assertion; it was an appeal for action. "No man that hath any sense of this happy community," wrote the prolific Protestant polemicist William Fulke in 1577, "can deny [that] for being members of our common body, they must needs be partakers of the common utility."[22] Even as the community of believers was being more narrowly drawn by Protestants in terms of a personal relationship with God, advocates stressed that individual faith was most poignantly illustrated by engaging with others: "doubt not God's blessing upon thy faithful industry . . . to such a competent sufficiency as may render thy endeavors acceptable to God, comfortable to thy self, *and serviceable to the community*."[23] These writers realized that individual improvement in both a moral and material sense and advancement of the collective interest were mutually informing and mutually determining pursuits. By 1620 John Rogers had taken this belief one step further, believing that success as an individual and the future of one's soul were in large part dependent upon commitment to the temporal projects initiated by the church for the benefit of the city and its citizens: "he that scorned and disdained the Church militant, shall find no community with the Church triumphant, but shall be debarred from all comforts."[24] Personal satisfaction was intimately tied to the network of connections that one was able to forge with others.

Civic institutions and the structure of urban neighborhoods in early modern London allowed for regular interaction among citizens, frequently making social engagement the most important arbiter of advancement. London was much more than a collection of strangers pursuing their own narrow self-interests. It was a society and economy that relied on mutual interaction for its survival and for maintaining peace and civility. Stow declared that "[t]his city is glorious in manhood . . . the citizens of London, wheresoever they become, are notable before all other citizens, in civility of manners, attire, table, and talk." In addition to possessing these qualities as individuals, Londoners, he claimed, also excelled in social capital. They organized for mutual defense from foreign invaders—they could "muster 2000 armed horsemen and threescore thousand footmen serviceable for the wars." Stow frequently notes how Londoners provided bounteously to charity by establishing numerous hospitals, schools, and almshouses: London "relieveth plentifully, and with good policy, not only her own poor people . . . but also the poor that from each quarter of the realm do flock unto it." Londoners participated together in religious observances, many financing the repair of old churches and the construction of new ones. "Stored with rich merchants," the city, collectively, had the economic clout to drive "down the price of wheat from three shillings the bushel to less than half that money."[25] Although Stow often exaggerates the superiority of Londoners, his statements do show that they tended to promote the economic welfare of all, sometimes at the expense of private gain. And even though strong group affiliation also meant greater exclusion for those who were not fortunate enough to belong to one of the city's more exclusive companies, most Londoners could identify with some type of support network that would assist them in times of need.[26]

This sense of belonging was only possible when the city was subdivided into manageable units. The segmentation into wards, parishes, and suburban neighborhoods called liberties is crucial in understanding how the public theatres resonated for their audiences. Although it was possible to walk from one end of the city to the other in under an hour, the social, economic, and occupational distances traversed were significant. As Stow walked the city from east to west, along Aldgate Street, through Cornhill Street, "through the Poultry (a street so called) to the great conduit in West Cheap, and so through Cheap to the Standard . . . then by the Standard to the Great Cross . . . and to the little conduit by Paul's Gate, from whence of old time the said High Street stretched straight to Ludgate," he passed through nine wards and dozens of parishes. Each of these neighborhoods had a distinctive urban character and contained numerous specialized markets retailing everything from "fish to flesh" to luxurious fashions imported from the Continent and beyond.

Stow also described the suburbs located outside the city walls in Middlesex County.[27] These growing outlying communities like (from east to west) Whitechapel, Spitalfields, Shoreditch, Moorfields, Finsbury, Clerkenwell, Holburn, and Farringdon ringed the city and provided easy access to central London through well-traveled roads through the city's seven gates (again from east to west): Aldgate, Bishopsgate, Moorgate, Cripplegate, Aldersgate, Newgate, and Ludgate. These divisions are the organizational principle on which Stow's *Survey of London* pivots. They demarcated the neighborhoods where residents lived, worked, prayed, sought recreation, and often made their most important acquaintances.

An important clue to the abundance of social capital in the city was the trust that Londoners placed in one another. Despite the great differences among residents in both wealth and status, Stow claimed, the assorted noblemen "live in amity with the citizens, every man observing the customs and orders of the city, and choose to be contributory to charges here rather than in any part of the land wheresoever."[28] Because of the economic stability and favorable trading conditions fostered by a climate of trust and reciprocity, all citizens, he argued, reaped its benefits in one way or another. Even though Stow was not an objective recorder of historical facts and was more interested in promoting harmony in the city, he noted tendencies to act locally that were natural for Londoners. Disputes arose, of course, but Londoners frequently were able to address altercations at a local level before they got out of hand—or landed the disputants in court. Witnessing the feud between the fairies in *A Midsummer Night's Dream*, the eminently practical Bottom wonders why "some honest neighbors will not make them friends," seeking to transpose the matter-of-fact logic of ordinary townsmen to the conflict between Oberon and Titania (3.1.129–30).

Living apart on one's own, by contrast, was considered an affront to the community and the values it sought to generate. Most advice books and educational manuals of the period militated against such solipsistic behavior. Annibale in Stefano Guazzo's *Civil Conversation* (translated in 1581 and reprinted in 1586) suggests, contrary to Guazzo's desire for solitude, "[t]hat a man being a companionable creature, loveth naturally the conversation of other men, and doing the contrary, he doth offend Nature herself."[29]

Conversely, and somewhat paradoxically, "the more a man can leave himself behind him," claimed Joseph Hall, "and aspire to a care of community, the more [inwardly] spiritual he is."[30] Valentine, a disputant in another dialogue, *Civil and Uncivil Life* (1579), concurs, basing his arguments even more explicitly on the necessity of civic virtue: "continual habitation of the country . . . I utterly disallow thereof as a custom neither good for the commonwealth, neither for the gentles who use it." City dwellers, in contrast, are "persons prepared for sundry actions, not so much to serve their own turns, as their Prince and Country."[31] Wealthy gentlemen who could afford to live comfortably anywhere in the realm were expected to choose city life because of its economic advantages, the availability of educational institutions like the Inns of Court, and, above all, numerous opportunities for public service. Cities, according to Stow, are a convenient bulwark against tendencies toward isolation and inwardness: "men are congregated into cities and commonwealths for honesty and utility's sake. . . . Cities [and] towns were at the first invented that men might lead a civil life amongst themselves."[32] He thought the organization of people into cities was not an accident or a product of economic necessity but a direct result of the perceived need for greater social capital.

Social capital was also important in Londoners' recreational pursuits. Emerging in the 1570s as a commercial enterprise, playgoing had its roots in communal activities such as bearbaiting, the misrule associated with the carnivalesque tradition, and the medieval mystery plays. With the advent of purpose-built structures and plays performed every day of the week except Sunday throughout the year (except Lent), playgoing was no longer tied explicitly either to the liturgical calendar or to seasonal cycles of secular festivity. Nevertheless, commercial playing preserved and extended conditions that fostered regular conviviality as well as the opportunity, or at least the illusory perception, of alternate social affiliations that were previously unavailable to a mass audience on a regular basis. What was lost in the temporal specificity of drama was replaced by a new kind of spatial orientation around London's playhouses, which became a physical destination for citizens to meet for the same kind of collective recreation enjoyed on holidays. Despite the much different nature of the burgeoning commercial playing industry, earlier forms of drama had created certain habits that made plays a fairly natural entertainment option for Londoners and an extension of their social life.[33]

The playhouses were not merely places of entertainment or isolated businesses. Instead they became important social institutions that Londoners would flock to on a regular basis for fellowship and a reprieve from work. Just as playhouses were conspicuous features of London's geography, plays were important in the social habits of Londoners. Many early modern commentators emphasize the sheer numbers of people who attended the theatres. John Weever notes how "thousands flock to hear a poet's pen," while Thomas Platter remarks on "the great swarms" of people who resorted to the theatres. These kinds of numbers would only be possible when playgoing became routine for many residents.[34] These playgoers were participants in a rich variety of social activities that influenced their preferences for entertainment and, in turn, affected *how* they attended the theatre and perceived individual theatrical productions.

Unlike the theatre today, where the dim lights and curtain of the proscenium arch stage obscure the rest of the audience and stage business, going to the theatre in early modern London was a highly visible activity. Amphitheatres were open to daylight and conducive to mobility, meaning that the crowd was at least as aware of fellow spectators as of the actors on the stage. Attending plays in this highly social theatrical environment was both an extension of and reflection upon the very communities in which spectators participated outside the playhouse. We know, for instance, that audiences were not quiet observers of stage events; they were keen to express their pleasure or displeasure in a highly physical register through applause, hissing, and even throwing objects on the stage. Ben Jonson claimed in the prologue to *Volpone* (1607), "thus much can I give them as a token / of his play's worth: no eggs are broken." Playwrights and actors clearly took note of the crowd's reaction. William Fennor, in 1616, admitted that "clapping, or hissing, is the only mean / That tries and searches out a well-writ scene."[35] Even though the success of acting troupes was largely determined by their profitability, the approbation of spectators might have mattered just as much to the actors and been a more accurate measure of their popularity in various communities.

For most playgoers, the decision to attend one playhouse over another took into account the social environment in and around the theatre as much as the aesthetic qualities of the work onstage. Despite the paucity of early commentary on London's theatres, those who did write about their experience often mentioned a specific playhouse.[36] William Turner, in 1612, draws a stark distinction between "the fat fool of the Curtain, / And the lean fool of the Bull."[37] Actors were automatically associated with different venues, and playgoers discerned distinct house styles in all aspects of the production (in this case the comedy) at various playhouses. Indeed, Donald Lupton notes that "time, place, subject, actors, and clothes either make or mar a play."[38] All of these factors—which have little to do with the play's text—contribute to its success or failure.

I do not mean to suggest, of course, that the content of the plays was unimportant. On the contrary, plays became such important contributions to social capital precisely because they were performed before economically and culturally stratified audiences at each of the outdoor venues and resonated specifically for these audiences. Performed at the Red Bull in the northwest suburb of Clerkenwell, Thomas Heywood's *The Four Prentices of London* (1615) increased solidarity among the artisans who frequented that playhouse by tracing the heroic activity of a quartet of exalted London apprentices. The representation of these four brothers, who travel to Italy, Ireland, and Jerusalem as crusaders, is designed to engender not only nationalistic fervor but pride in one's own craft and fellowship among the laboring classes of London. Though the brothers achieve public notoriety as crusaders, they never underestimate the value of labor in one's chosen vocation and exhibit "no scorn" for "the city-trades." One of these brothers, Godfrey, wonders who

> Were that man, noble or ignoble born,
> That would not practice some mechanic skill
> Which might support his state in penury
> . . . . [and instead]
> Suck the honey from the public hive . . .
> I hold it no disparage to my birth,
> Though I be born an Earl, to have the skill
> And the full knowledge of the Mercer's trade.[39]

Feats of martial heroism are merely an adjunct to the useful and diligent performance of the brothers' ordinary occupations, the true source of their moral character and a credit to their immediate community and their country. Such plays, along with many others staged at the Red Bull, tend to engage people who share similar occupations and common values, allowing them to identify with a common purpose to galvanize already strong group identities.

But like all forms of social bonding, plays like this (known as "citizen comedies" because they endorse the values of artisans and apprentices), while increasing the cohesion of certain groups, inevitably exclude others. Perhaps the best examples of the exclusionary potential in the drama of the period are the bitingly satirical "city comedies" staged predominantly at upmarket private venues within the city walls—theatres that were the diametric opposites of the large outdoor amphitheatres. The plays staged there portray the city's various commercial and social groups as deliberately antagonistic to one another and impervious to newcomers, showing the delight that numerous Londoners took in witnessing the downfall of their neighbors. Yet even these seemingly bleak plays have a moral purpose. As commentators have noted, they tend not to single out any specific social group for their vitriol: by envisioning the city as a whole as predatory and by staging the "subtle art [that] beguiles the honest eye," they suggest that *all* citizens require considerable moral rectification.[40]

By portraying the cupidity and malevolence of numerous Londoners, city comedies intimate that the trust and neighborliness that many, like Stow, took as a hallmark of London life was on the decline by the early seventeenth century. But even statements like this suggest that enough people still cared about rehabilitating a climate of honesty to represent the dire consequences of an increasingly materialistic society onstage. Middleton himself was clearly not convinced of the inevitability of social discord and deterioration; even while he underscored London's social problems in his city comedies, he penned lavish public entertainments that celebrate London and its citizens in an obvious attempt to promote civic virtue. By alerting elites to the potentially destructive consequences of many of the practices they engage in, highly satirical plays like this might yet offer unexpected contributions to social capital.

Sometimes plays were able to bridge different social classes, occupations, and religious persuasions. The theatres offered a tangible public sphere in which various elements of society could intermingle, the views advanced by certain factions could be sifted, and various communities could be made to understand the goals and aspirations of others, even if they could not wholly endorse them. Although such interaction was not always harmonious and frequent clashes among different social factions did occur, these unprecedented opportunities for mutual recognition were also likely to dispel stereotypes rather than simply reinforce them. London had very few public venues where foreign ambassadors and the other elites in their entourage mingled with artisans and apprentices, as they did at the Fortune playhouse in 1617.[41]

Many of the plays staged during the period provide visions of a cohesive community. Comedies and romances narrate the movement from discord to social reconciliation, while tragedies force the beneficial and enlightening recognition of cultural dissonance in an obvious warning to spectators. After all, Romeo and Juliet meet their tragic end not because of their love but precisely because Verona is woefully lacking in public virtue. Following their deaths, the Prince does not indict specific individuals or groups, emphasizing instead that "all are punished" and declaring:

> . . . Capulet, Montague,
> See what a scourge is laid upon your hate,
> That heaven finds means to kill your joys with love.
> (*Romeo and Juliet*, 5.3.290–91)

It is nothing intrinsic to either Capulets or Montagues or their families but rather their "hate," or their complete denial of and resistance to social capital, that transmutes a private family feud into a tragedy that afflicts the entire city of Verona. Escalus, unaffiliated with either family, confides that he too has "lost a brace of kinsmen" (5.3.294). The Prince recognizes that he, as head of state, and all other citizens "have an interest in your [Montague's] hate's proceeding" (3.1.182).

Even as many plays of the period might exacerbate the differences and antagonisms among various segments of the populace, many others point toward social restoration through improved relations in those same urban communities where tension among competing factions was greatest. In *Henry V* all levels of society are at least temporarily united as "a band of brothers" (4.3.60) and are forced to distinguish the signal contributions made by others of different ethnic backgrounds to whom they might ordinarily be antagonistic. Moreover, Hal's gesture in the material and social context of the theatre seems more than an abstract appeal for national unity. It also suggests the collective energies necessary for a successful and, most importantly, memorable theatrical experience: the audience joins with Burbage's company, his own "band of brothers," to form a dramatic vision that itself looks forward to a more cohesive community.

Of course, theatrical professionals did not necessarily base their decision-making on the theatre's perceived contribution to social capital. While Heywood was obviously concerned about the social role of the theatres, others were inclined to understand their craft as a business. Many involved in London's theatres, including several of its pioneers, previously had been successful in other commercial pursuits and, like grocer John Heminge and joiner James Burbage, sought to parlay their business acumen, connections with the city's trades, and managerial skills into their new enterprise. The ranks of London actors were populated by many citizens free of the city's most lucrative trades (such as goldsmiths, drapers, and grocers) and included many younger members apprenticed to those same occupations, even when they were really being trained as actors.[42]

To make decisions that were good for business, Philip Henslowe, Christopher Beeston, and other impresarios and sharers in theatrical companies were forced to balance the needs of the various communities that attended plays. When companies failed to consider the tastes of their audience, they risked losing their spectators—all of them. Audiences at the Globe in 1603 found Jonson's *Sejanus* so tedious that they left the theatre en masse in the middle of the production, unlikely to return until the play onstage was more to their liking. Building social capital does not demand that participants consciously share the same goals, only that they acknowledge the complementarity of their objectives and realize that they might intersect for mutual benefit.

My aim in the following chapters is not to offer an exhaustive account of how every theatre related to each of the city's many social institutions over the seventy-year period when playgoing flourished. I want to concentrate largely on two important Jacobean amphitheatres: the Fortune and especially the Red Bull. These two theatres are often overlooked by scholars preoccupied with the Globe and Blackfriars, the playing spaces where Shakespeare's plays were performed. The social dynamic at the Red Bull and the Fortune was significantly different, making it nearly impossible to describe theatrical conditions in general by looking strictly at Shakespeare, his company, and his playhouses. Not all companies were seeking to emulate Shakespeare and the King's Men. A look at these other troupes, their theatres, and their audiences offers a more nuanced picture of the Jacobean playgoing industry that also discloses important connections with local communities that are lost when concentrating on Southwark alone.

First, I want to reexamine the relationship between early modern London and its suburbs. In chapter 1, I argue that London was heavily invested in and organized around tightly knit and well-defined communities, both physical and ideological. Londoners organized themselves into overlapping networks that centered around the local parish church, the guilds that regulated trade and industry, or simply the institutions and conventions (such as the dense collection of local taverns) that served to maintain peaceable and friendly relations in individual neighborhoods. Contrary to current scholarship that argues for a disjunction between city and suburb, I claim that the rich sense of community life within the walls also obtained in the suburbs.

In chapter 2, I look at the Jacobean amphitheatres, how they came to be built, the companies that occupied them, and the neighborhoods where they were located. Before the late 1590s theatrical companies, which were in a constant state of flux, were not yet settled at particular venues. They often moved among London's various playing spaces as opportunity and expediency permitted, making it difficult for them to acquire discrete identities based on the theatres where they performed or—because of the migration of players between companies—the actors who performed there. Once companies became settled in the same venues for longer durations, the troupes that occupied particular theatres began to form unique identities and strong reciprocal bonds with their audiences. By the Jacobean period, theatres tended to fashion themselves in specific ways to attract different types of spectators. As students of Shakespeare are well aware, the Globe offered intellectually rigorous plays that nevertheless managed to please a variety of spectators with the time and money to journey across the river for an afternoon's entertainment. Other playhouses offered less sophisticated entertainment for those who most enjoyed nostalgia, heroic characters, spectacular stage action, and more familiar types of comedy and jigs.[43] These "citizen staples" made the playhouses in the Middlesex suburbs like the Red Bull popular destinations for artisans and apprentices.[44]

London's neighborhoods were hardly identical; each had its own local color. Little surprise, then, that the neighborhood theatres developed their own distinct style and reputation based on the demographic characteristics of the people who frequented them, which probably also included many local residents. In either case, theatres were not anonymous sites of entertainment for a heterogeneous audience; their theatrical practice drew on just such a sense of community.

The next three chapters, which center on the Fortune and especially the Red Bull, offer case studies in theatre and community. In chapters 3 and 4, I discuss how certain groups of plays, reflecting and refracting a number of local concerns, resonated for specific audiences at these playhouses. In chapter 5, I examine a violent altercation in Clerkenwell induced by the move of Queen Anne's Men to the Cockpit from the Red Bull in 1616.

In chapter 3, I consider two plays based on John Foxe's *Actes and Monuments of These Latter and Perilous Days*, popularly known as *The Book of Martyrs*. Both Thomas Heywood's *If You Know Not Me, You Know Nobody* (1605) and Thomas Dekker's *Whore of Babylon* (1606) expand on Foxe's project and strive to spread the theology and politics of the Reformation effectively and polemically to the widest possible audience and to instill an ideology of reform in those elements of society not usually targeted by Protestant or Catholic religious ideologues. I argue that staged productions based on accounts from *The Book of Martyrs* reinforced a militant Protestantism in those who were uneducated or even illiterate, people who flocked to playhouses like the Fortune and the Red Bull. These were individuals who would have had difficulty deciphering Foxe's highly symbolic martyrology and were perhaps best reached by plays. By drawing on highly visible instances of Catholic insurgency like the Armada (1588) and the Gunpowder Plot (1605), the playwrights and the actors sought to solidify the tenets of the Reformation in a dramatic idiom tailored to their local audiences. Because of fears of the Jesuits' operations and apprehension prevalent in the northern suburbs due to the incomplete state of the Reformation and the widespread prejudice against Catholics, these plays by Heywood and Dekker excite latent anxieties and model how even lowly commoners participate in the religious struggle.

Thomas Heywood's five-part cycle of popular plays known as

the *Ages*, which appeared at the Red Bull between 1609 and 1611, has puzzled and even infuriated critics. Based primarily on Ovid, these plays treat Roman and mythical history from the birth of Jupiter to the end of the Trojan War, but they do so through remarkable visual effects and stage action that differentiate them from all other history plays of the period. The *Ages* and similar plays form the basis for the Red Bull's lackluster reputation for offering popular fare with little literary or dramatic merit, based on drums, trumpets, battles, and heroes. Alternate contexts for interpreting these plays arise when we understand them in light of specific historical and geographical circumstances. Appearing after years of theatre closures due to the recurrence of the plague that ravaged the city and especially its suburbs, the five plays in the *Ages* were a spectacular diversion for citizens devastated by disease. They were also a way for the company that performed them to profit from this important niche market during a turbulent period for the entertainment industry. Like the Foxean plays that adopted strategies to disseminate religious polemic to a specific demographic, the *Ages* presented humanist subjects in a form intelligible to a largely unlettered audience, tailoring the familiar precepts of Philip Sidney and others to a population undergoing acute physical and social strife.

In chapter 5, I turn again to the Red Bull, not to interpret the plays staged there in a particular performance context but to understand a riot on Shrove Tuesday in 1617. On this occasion local apprentices did considerable damage to the company's new private theatre known as the Cockpit to protest the migration of the resident theatrical troupe to this more expensive venue in Drury Lane (located in the increasingly fashionable city of Westminster). This altercation, paradoxically, tends to confirm the interplay between theatre and community that I trace throughout this book. The rioters, far from expressing an animus against playgoing in general (many apprentices were in fact frequent playgoers themselves), seem to have been incensed specifically by the company's abandonment of the Red Bull and Clerkenwell. The apprentices viewed the company's move as an odious breach of the moral economy that prevailed in the neighborhood.

In the immediate aftermath of the move, the company did not have the luxury of designing a new repertory for its new playhouse and the elites who frequented it and was forced to transfer plays and players between the two houses—a difficult prospect, given that audiences at one theatre were unlikely to appreciate drama staged at the other. One of these plays, however, Philip Massinger's *A New Way to Pay Old Debts* (ca. 1621), managed to appeal to audiences at both public and private playhouses. Audiences from very different social and economic backgrounds could be united in their opprobrium for Sir Giles Overreach, a moneylender who aroused fears of fiscal insolvency that affected rich and poor alike. The move to the Cockpit, and the ensuing riot, ultimately led to the demise of the company, again reminding us that playgoing was at the mercy of forces beyond the market.

What I hope will emerge from this study is a sense of the multiple communities that affected London's commercial entertainment industry. By focusing on the Red Bull and the Fortune, I want to recapture some of the local conditions that partially dictated why certain playgoers attended certain playhouses and why these theatres staged the plays they did. These factors have consequences for thinking about the supply and demand for various kinds of dramatic performance, for interpreting individual plays, and for writing the theatre history of the period.

Throughout the book, all quotations from early modern materials have been silently modernized. Many early modern books are not paginated, of course, so the location is noted by the signature (for example, ***3v, Mmm4r, and GGGg4v).

Untitled manuscripts from holdings at the British Library, Guildhall Library, Folger Shakespeare Library, Henry E. Huntington Library, and Public Record Office are identified by location and MS number in the text.

Where appropriate, I have expressed dates using both the old and new calendar. Throughout the sixteenth and seventeenth centuries in England the New Year did not begin until 25 March. The shifting of the New Year to 1 January came in 1751. Before that time England followed the Julian calendar, while the rest of continental Europe had made the shift to the Gregorian calendar, following the leadership of the Catholic countries. Hence in describing events in the London theatre between 1 January and 25 March it is often unclear which year is actually meant. I include both the year that early modern Londoners would have used and the year that we understand it to be today.

Chapter 1
Rethinking City & Suburb

* * * *
* * *
*

London's amphitheatres were at the intersection of overlapping communities. For actors and playwrights, the playhouses were a place of business. For audiences, they were a place of shared entertainment and a venue for social interaction. Residents and businesses in and around the theatre, though not necessarily involved in its day-to-day operations, were nevertheless keenly aware of its presence. The metropolis as a whole and especially citizens and civic leaders concerned with forging a safer, more prosperous place to live were involved with the theatre in other ways. These groups and others, whether positively disposed to the theatres or not, were part of the dynamic environment in which the players sought legal protection, acclamation from audiences, and profitability.

Given their prominent place in this urban environment, did these theatres contribute to a shared sense of community? Were they a venue for meaningful and mutually advantageous bonding rather than anonymous or incidental congress? Were the theatres an edifying force in neighborhoods and the city at large? Or were they largely antithetical to the norms that citizens, businesses, municipal politicians, and religious leaders sought to engender? Could they enhance social capital or not?

The prevailing consensus in today's scholarly climate is that they did not do so. Why were the theatres so detrimental to urban community? For decades scholars have implied that the large and well-known amphitheatres (like Shakespeare's Globe in Southwark and the Fortune and Red Bull north of the city) were located in undesirable localities and thus frequented by many insidious and highly conspicuous persons who threatened the morality of the more upstanding citizens in attendance—if they were not already corrupted by lascivious plays. The tendency to describe the early modern stage negatively, as an outside element potentially transgressive of community values, has its origins with Joseph Quincy Adams, E. K. Chambers, and many of the most influential theatre historians of the twentieth century. The general narrative that these scholars adopted long ago has continued in various forms into the present, making their conclusions familiar to almost all students of the period.

To cite just one example from "a book designed for the 'ordinary' playgoer who is sufficiently interested in drama to be mindful of its past," Donald Brook's *The Romance of the English Theatre* (1945) summarizes conditions at the public theatres in this way: "There were generally one or two pickpockets, half a dozen prostitutes, and plenty of men rather the worse for drink who were prepared to indulge in a brawl upon the slightest provocation." As the title of his book suggests, the scintillating notion of a theatre on the fringes of society, constantly struggling against an array of forces striving to stifle it, has perennially enticed us. Because of the propensity for disorder at playing spaces, Joseph Quincy Adams wrote in 1917, they were relegated to the liberties, "beyond the jurisdiction of the Common Council."[1] Much later, Steven Mullaney, among others, picked up this thread. He argues that it was not simply that the theatres fomented agitation in the suburbs but that the liberties were already "reserved for cultural phenomena that could not be contained within the strict or proper bounds of the community."[2] The theatres fit perfectly into this urban milieu by making already bad neighborhoods even worse.

Some scholars, of course, have attempted to sketch a more complex picture of the public stages and the neighborhoods where they were located. Linda Woodbridge begins her introduction to a collection of essays on early modern drama by reviewing a critical commonplace. When we think of the Bankside neighborhood, "it's easy to remember that there were brothels there"—too easy, perhaps. Prostitution, gambling, and other objectionable activities were certainly present in Southwark and the areas north of London Wall in Shoreditch where other theatres were located—as they were elsewhere, even in respectable inner-city neighborhoods. This reflexive description of theatrical neighborhoods as sites of anonymous license and criminal behavior makes it difficult to imagine what else was there. Woodbridge points out another part of south London's topography of which students of dramatic literature are seldom aware: a schoolhouse kept by John Mellis where Londoners could learn double-entry bookkeeping.[3] The Borough of Southwark also boasted the king's hospital, a market for leather goods, a mint, "many fair Inns," and an economy second only to that of London itself, in addition to various lazar-houses, prisons, and hospitals for the poor and infirm and, of course, the bearbaiting arenas and playhouses.[4]

More than just rows of tenements and cottages housing the destitute, Southwark was home to many notables, including the bishop of Winchester and the Duke of Suffolk. Stow notes that civic authorities also invested disproportionately in law enforcement initiatives in the neighborhood. From this, we might infer on the one hand that crime rates in the borough might have been higher than elsewhere in the city, but on the other that citizens were keen to assuage these problems and were neither tolerant of the offenders nor willing to let their neighborhoods devolve into ghettos for the poor and disaffected, as some critics insist.[5] The suburbs to the north of the city, London's other theatre district, displayed a similar diversity of buildings, businesses, and residents. Though Clerkenwell and Finsbury were home to Marion "Moll" Frith, Clerkenwell Bess (Joan Woodshore), the "Wisewoman" of Hoxton, and other "strapping lasses" engaged in prostitution and other unladylike occupations including theatrical performance, these neighborhoods also maintained a vibrant commercial and industrial sector that could boast wage rates 50 percent higher than in the provinces, royal households inhabited at various times by both Queen Elizabeth and James I, and an evolving aristocratic quarter.[6] Even the brothels ("stews" as they were called) in Southwark were owned by William Walworth, a former lord mayor of London, and were subject to government regulation until 1506. After that, they were grudgingly tolerated by citizens and authorities alike, much as they are today.[7]

The neighborhoods where theatres were located were significantly more complex and socially diverse than many scholars would lead us to believe. Home to active parishes as well as a number of schools, hospitals, and other public institutions, these areas were stable and harmonious communities for a number of residents, some of whom were engaged in less than desirable businesses, but most of whom were gainfully employed and reputable citizens. I argue that this underlying sense of community, frequently discounted by literary critics and theatre historians, was an important facet of theatrical enterprise and was continually alluded to and promoted in early modern plays. The prevalence of shared community values suggests continuity between the city and suburbs and their residents rather than a radical disjunction.

How has the scholarly community settled, in large part, on this less than favorable narrative concerning the public theatre's place in the community despite ample evidence to the contrary? It is sometimes easy to overlook the more respectable and communitarian aspects of the public theatres and the regions that contained them. Unlike the theatre haters who wrote frequent and passionate denunciations of the scurrility and vice that neighbored the playhouses, citizens unconcerned by the players would hardly feel the need to pen tracts and broadsides defending a healthy community. If it works, why fix it? Through the sheer mass and widespread notoriety of antitheatrical writings, we have become conditioned to accept their tendentious statements as fact. At the very least, we take antitheatrical polemic as a rough and frequently articulated description of the types of activities occurring in the vicinity of the theatres. Somewhat paradoxically, the writings of antitheatricalists have attained an important place in writing about the early modern theatre for nearly a century.

The Elizabethan Stage (1923) by E. K. Chambers has become an indispensable reference work for students of early modern drama; it has also elevated a number of conjectural hypotheses about the stage and its relation to London society so that they appear to be normative for later readers. Chambers felt that the "normal hostility" between humanism and Puritanism, a contention between a religiously motivated antitheatrical challenge and a spirited defense of the stage by men of letters, was "important . . . from the point of view of the history of the stage and of civilization." He felt it necessary to devote a significant section of his four-volume book to this controversy, even though he admits that antitheatrical polemic operated forcefully in only a handful of works over a nearly seventy-year period.[8] More than half a century later, in tracing a millennia-old trans-European "antitheatrical prejudice" beginning with Plato, Jonas Barish insists that even the most nonsensical of antitheatrical diatribes like William Prynne's *Histriomastix* (1633) represented a more or less prevalent sentiment among Londoners. "Madness tends to be culturally determined," Barish writes, suggesting that the Puritan response to the theatre was embraced by mainstream Protestants.[9]

We all recognize, as both Chambers and Barish did, that these tracts are fiercely partisan caricatures of actors, plays, and their social environment: they are short on "common sense."[10] But many later commentators also assume that their basic assumptions were accurate on some level. Admitting that antitheatrical polemic operates through substantial embellishment and ideological paranoia, Jean Howard nevertheless argues that "these tracts rendered the emergent institution of the theatre intelligible."[11] She hints that the views of the theatre's detractors, however misguided, were somehow accepted by Londoners in general, even those who did not share their puritanical zeal. The thesis that both avid playgoers and those who never attended theatres shared antitheatrical sentiments implies other conclusions about how people attended the theatre and its marginal relationship with London society.[12] While I do not suggest that *all* these postulates are wrong, I do call into question the overall narrative drawn from this evidence.

Other long-standing assumptions about London's theatres have to do with their location in the liberties, a provocative appellation for areas on the fringe of the city that has tempted Mullaney to assert that these neighborhoods were also on the fringe of civil society. What was so different about these liberties? Many recent historians and literary scholars draw a firm divide between the city within the walls and the suburbs. The city was under the strict administration of the lord mayor and his aldermen—the site of civic authority and the concentration of economic capital. The suburbs were marginally independent of the de jure channels of municipal control—the place of the stage and also of licentiousness and questionable social conduct that, according to Mullaney, was "virtually ungoverned."[13] This reading of the city as essentially a rich, sophisticated, and stable core surrounded by a poor and unruly periphery is as much a product of modern historiography as a conclusion based on primary evidence. This argument has been around for some time and might again be traced to Chambers, whose rehearsal of antitheatrical invective had ramifications for the place of the stage. In accordance with Stephen Gosson and other theatre haters, Chambers claimed that the neighborhoods containing playhouses "focused all the sin of the city."[14]

This thesis about the location of the theatres constructed by literary scholars and theatre historians bears some relation to contemporaneous studies of the city by urban historians. Seeking to revise the work of a previous generation of scholars, many historians were coming to similar conclusions regarding the character of London's suburbs. As early as 1978, in an inaugural lecture at University College London, Valerie Pearl argued that previous historians had painted a "stark and simplistic" portrait of a city in its entirety typified by poverty, overcrowding, and administrative chaos. She felt, for instance, that the "general presentation" of London in the work of Peter Clark, Paul Slack, and others, steeped in "the philosophy of doom and gloom," "places an overriding emphasis on crisis, conflict, and social polarization." While deplorable conditions existed in the suburbs, the city within the walls prospered and took its place among other great European capitals as a center for trade, manufacturing, and the exchange and consumption of luxury goods.[15] To rehabilitate the reputation of early modern London, Pearl claimed that the city encompassed *two* worlds: a world of wealth, orderliness, and civic stability surrounded by a ring of crime, scarcity, anomie, and urban blight. Interaction between the two did occur, but the basic social divisions were drawn and became more rigid as the city's population continued to expand throughout the seventeenth century.

Pearl's remarks were designed to disseminate the results of her own research and as a "scholarly work of synthesis" that attempted to crystallize the work of a previous generation of historians. Consciously or not, she annunciated the guiding paradigm for a new cadre of investigators. Many scholars of Renaissance London and its suburbs writing during the 1980s and 1990s bore witness to the popularity and success of these governing assumptions, even as they noted that the divisions between London's constituent parts did not always correspond to the wall of the city. Works like Steve Rappaport's *Worlds within Worlds* (1984), Ian Archer's *The Pursuit of Stability* (1991), Marjorie McIntosh's

A Community Transformed (1991), Jessica Browner's "Wrong Side of the River" (1994), and John Twyning's *London Dispossessed* (1998), despite their differences, portray a metropolis of deep regional variation. In these accounts, respectable and well-to-do citizens constantly struggled against marginal factions who threatened the peaceableness and order of the city and its neighborhoods during a period of enormous demographic change and expansion.

For students of early modern drama, Steven Mullaney's *The Place of the Stage* (1988) is perhaps the best-known work on the physical and cultural location of the theatres. In this ambitious study, Mullaney claims that London's periphery was an area of questionable social conduct. Like the assortment of lepers, drunkards, prostitutes, gamblers, vagabonds, and condemned criminals cast out of the city, the theatre was exiled, taking its rightful place where "the spectacle of the outcast and the marginal traditionally held sway."[16] Relying on a variety of alluring evidence, Mullaney claims that London's suburbs were a place of meager economic conditions, questionable social practices, and institutions designed for the incarceration of the sick, destitute, and criminal elements that were also represented on the public stages.

Because the theatres were also situated in these locales, Mullaney offers subversion and licentiousness as a homology for the physical place of the stage and, following other materialist critics, for its cultural and ideological contributions to civic life. The ramifications of this thesis are enormous. Mullaney suggests that the theatres, because of their proximity to a host of less than desirable social elements, were somehow "eccentric or decentered," opposed to the ethical values of traditional and harmonious communities. The playhouses trafficked the same kind of vice and spectacle to the more respectable classes from the city within the walls that attended its performances, rendering it extremely dangerous to civic authority, royal policy, and, most significantly, public morality. The whole enterprise offered playgoers and actors alike "a license to exist outside the strict confines of community."[17] Gainfully employed, upstanding, and God-fearing citizens had every reason to be wary of goings-on at the theatres and in their immediate surroundings.

Mullaney's representation of theatre and society bears a questionable relation to actual conditions in Southwark and especially the other suburbs where theatres were located. We can see that his argument about the liberties and the concomitant subversiveness of the theatre is in some ways an extension of the basic confrontation between Puritanism and humanism that Chambers and others put in place long ago. More recent and considerably more detailed analyses reveal that his description of the liberties unduly accentuates the negative elements in what was actually a rich and varied social environment in and around the theatres. Historians concerned with local conditions in specific neighborhoods stress that even "marginal" regions like Southwark were not economically homogeneous.[18] Mullaney's study is guided by a materialist understanding of culture that interprets an urban locale or physical edifice as a metaphor for various social practices, allowing a necessarily vague ideological disposition to substitute for a comprehensive survey of more tangible historical evidence. By arguing for a "dyadic opposition" between city and suburb, Mullaney reduces the nuances of community life to a power relationship that obscures the continuity between the two.[19]

I do not wish to claim that Mullaney's provocative approach fails to illuminate an important facet of the theatre's potentially ambivalent relationship to other cultural forms. I do claim that this approach forecloses on the possibility of considering the theatre as an accepted public institution. Indeed, I argue that the theatres were welcomed—albeit for many different reasons—by the diverse array of Londoners who popularized them precisely because they contributed to the community norms that citizens themselves promoted. Just as not all theatregoers were willing to abide by accepted norms of conduct, neither were they so disabused with the traditional structures of community life that they looked to the theatre as a means of subverting the status quo or challenging civil authority. Arguments that the theatres were predominantly political underestimate the sheer number of people that attended them, most of whom simply sought an afternoon's entertainment in the midst of rather mundane lives.

In contrast to those scholars who adopted a hermeneutic of subversive critique to describe the theatre and its relationship to London society, others have theorized the Elizabethan and Jacobean theatre as a more benign form of recreation. According to Paul Yachnin, the theatre was "powerless," neither involved in the defense of state ideology nor engaged in a disruptive critique of it. Playgoing was "irrelevant to the system of power," maintaining its visible and popular place in society and the support of its royal patrons precisely because it was disengaged from the world of political influence.[20] The diminished political utility of the theatres did not mean that they were devoid of social meaning for their audiences. The theatre's unwillingness or inability to influence its audiences on the larger issues of state power probably augmented its capacity to reflect matters that were more mundane, pragmatic, and resonant in the daily lives of playgoers. Yet a powerless theatre tends to be equally static. The players did occasionally partake in various—and sometimes contradictory—political and social agendas that changed with the times, as they varied by place.

Presenting the theatre either as a site of radical subversion or as largely "powerless" offers a reductive—and false—binary for the study of early modern drama that flattens the nuances of theatrical activity. Both arguments fail to account for the peculiarities of audiences and how they attended the theatres not as a homogeneous aggregate of consumers seeking to maximize entertainment value but as a collection of discrete social groups with particularized tastes. Other scholars have long recognized that accounts of the early modern stage, a complex activity forced to adapt to changing circumstances over a seventy-year period, cannot be reduced to any set of formulas. They have revisited different aspects of these standard narratives and pursued alternative readings of familiar evidence in an effort to deepen our understanding of the London theatrical marketplace.[21]

My way to recapture the rich interaction of the playhouses within various London communities is to locate the theatre's contribution to social life not at the level of state authority or the dissemination of ideology but locally, in the neighborhoods where it was most visible. Theatre in London represented those values, ideas, and anxieties shared among the groups of citizens who attended the theatres, even articulating their most optimistic visions of social accord in a city that remained closely knit despite its recent expansion. Another look at the physical place of the stage is warranted, but so is a consideration of the typical concerns and daily patterns of average Londoners, playgoers for whom power politics was at best distant and mysterious and of little or no concern to the exigencies of work, providing for one's family, maintenance of reasonably safe and prosperous living conditions, and religious observance. Recouping this context requires an account of some of the other institutions prominent in London life that were designed to promote order and sociability.

It should hardly come as a surprise that the theatre *could* function as a dynamic and vital institution in local communities, because Londoners in general were disposed to patterns of communal life that have largely vanished today. Given the enormous growth of the city and the suburbs over this period, when the population grew from 120,000 to 200,000 between 1550 and 1600, we might expect that community life became attenuated, no longer essential to average residents and the commerce that fueled the growth.[22] The institutions that had previously guaranteed community proved surprisingly durable, however, and were in fact strengthened by the pressures attending the influx of newcomers to the city and its environs. Citizens of early modern London organized themselves around their local parishes, extended families, administrative precincts known as wards, and occupations. Laboring in one's vocation engendered a sense of fraternity that transcended geographic boundaries while affirming regional identities, because many trades were clustered in specific neighborhoods.

Most Londoners did feel an affiliation with the metropolis at large but an even deeper attachment to their neighborhood and the strong communal bonds formed within it. The administrative division of the city into wards and parishes imposed a congenital distinction—even within a very small geographical area—between insiders and outsiders. London was made up of twenty-five wards as well as several boroughs outside the city walls. These wards and boroughs, in turn, were divided into 111 parishes (and an additional 11 large parishes in suburban Middlesex and Surrey), typically regarded as the most vital social unit outside of the family. The parish churches were important for the administration of civic services, for the sense of shared identity that they conferred on parishioners, and, according to Archer, for "creating mutual ties among its members, rich and poor alike."[23] The division of the city into wards and parishes made the expanding capital more manageable and less bewildering to its residents, who dispersed themselves into a collection of discrete communities, each with a unique character and identifiable history of its own yet bound together by a common leadership, commerce and industry, and a shared history.

Stow's *Survey of London* suggests just how important these divisions were. He notes that citizens operated within parish units and were inclined to spend their money locally. Individual wards even had a semiautonomous legal status in relation to one another. Arresting a citizen for a crime committed in another ward required a process of extradition that in rare instances (most often in Tower Street Ward) presented legal difficulties for those involved in civic administration. Taxes were assessed and collected at the ward level, freedom certificates (the documents that guaranteed individuals their status as citizens) were housed in ward offices, and responsibility for the nightly watch was rotated among householders within a particular ward. Those on watch were patrolling areas and citizens with which they were intimately familiar, making it easy to detect trouble. Attendance at the December wardmote meeting was compulsory for all and typically evolved (or devolved) into a day of drinking, feasting, and general celebration.[24]

Londoners were therefore *required* to interact locally. In Stow's account, they were invited to take pride in their neighborhoods and especially in the "great houses" located there, the "monuments" in their parish church as well as the noteworthy citizens and benefactors who had inhabited them in times past. In its general mode of address, Stow's massive work telescopes from a discussion of the city as a large and impersonal aggregate of people and places to a detailed treatment of individual streets and buildings with which citizens formed an intimate acquaintance. Just as one might greet a friend, Stow considers "the fair parish church of St. Mary Bow." Like all the city's edifices, this church is distinguished by its idiosyncrasies:

> [Its] bell usually being rung somewhat late, as seemed to the young men apprentices, and other in Cheap, they made and set up a rhyme against the clerk, as followeth: "Clerk of the Bow bell with the yellow locks, / For thy late ringing thy head shall have knocks." Whereunto the clerk replying, wrote, "Children of Cheap, hold you all still, / For you shall have the Bow bell rung at your will."[25]

The ringing of the bell is hardly significant; its importance lies in its small yet cherished contribution to the daily lives of the citizens of Cordwainer Street Ward, the urban lore it has generated, and the particularity it has conferred on the ward, differentiating parishioners at this church from the rest of the city's inhabitants.

Stow singles out citizens most often for their contributions to their community rather than for their individual accomplishments. "Reginald Langdon," for instance, "gave to the parsons and churchwardens of St. Mary Bow . . . for the maintenance of Bow bell." Individuals are thereby bound to their physical surroundings in the history of the city. The city is intensely personalized; even physical edifices are endowed with a human quality that connects and mediates among past, present, and future generations of Londoners. Stow suggests that the cherished buildings in their neighborhood connect citizens to the bedrock of their city's illustrious past, securing them during times of turbulent change.[26]

One of the strongest forces shaping London's neighborhoods both within and without the walls was the parish church. By law, under penalty of fine, all citizens were required to attend their local parish church on Sundays. Plays were prohibited on the Sabbath (since 1581) and during Lent (since 1579) so as not to compete with the pulpit. Because the population of most congregations was relatively small, people would undoubtedly recognize each other by sight, if not by name, making it easier to identify newcomers and those from other neighborhoods.[27] Although doctrinally the Reformed church placed considerably less importance on communal ritual and the public recital of religious faith in favor of the twin doctrines of *sola fide* and *sola scriptura* (by faith alone and by scripture alone), these values could only be instilled in the congregation through fervent and repetitive declaration in church. Attaining a truly indwelling faith and personal communion with God first required the cultivation of certain patterns of belief and habits of worship that were inculcated in a public forum to build the "community of all believers," a mission that the church and the theatre sometimes shared (see chapter 3).

The parish church was important for residents throughout the year, not just on Sundays. Clerks in each parish were charged with keeping detailed records of births, burials, and marriages and an ensemble of additional statistics. These records formed the basis for much social policy, the redistribution of wealth to the poor, and mustering the parish quota of armed men to serve king and country. The officers of the parish, however, did more than administer day-to-day church functions; they leased parish lands to residents, maintained water pumps, appointed schoolmasters, and ensured that almshouses and other local public edifices were properly maintained. Parish leaders were also a source of neighborhood information for congregants. Wardens would sometimes open their homes to entertain other church functionaries and members of the congregation with leftover communion wine. These extrareligious functions meant that the parish was a ready-made social network that mediated between private life and the larger community. According to Archer, "it was by reference to the local parish and very rarely to a ward that Londoners defined where they lived." The sense of identity that Londoners gained from their parish was augmented, and also reinforced, by their affiliations with their wards and their guilds. A parish clerk of St. Botolph Billingsgate summarized the parish's function in the life of average Londoners: as "a great many of sticks bound in one bundle will hardly be broken / So neighbors being joined in love together can never be severed."[28]

The church also played a role in dispensing popular justice, designed to maintain and promote the shared values of the community. Inspired by charivari, skimmington, and other traditional forms and ritual practices designed to register communal disapproval, the people in the suburb of Clerkenwell (home of the Red Bull playhouse) and the parishioners of St. James, like other congregations, chose to deal with public morality without recourse to the ecclesiastical courts or other legal mechanisms.[29] A letter of 1587 from John Sedell to Humphrey Masterson records one such incident in a case of adultery. Sedell claimed that Masterson and Elizabeth, the wife of one Mr. Swayne, had been living together for nine years, arguing that this is "a matter very dangerous and not to be suffered unpunished for examples' sake." The offending couple was eventually required to depart Clerkenwell. The defendants were probably happy to leave town, given the exact form of the punishment:

> I think it appropriate for examples' sake, that on the second Sunday in Lent, in the parish church of Clerkenwell at morning prayer, she [Elizabeth Swayne] stand in a white wedding dress with her red veil in her hand during the said prayer and sermon which I wish she would be made longing for these offenses, and that after the end of the sermon, humbly on her knees, humbly make penance for her offence to you and the congregation, desiring mercy of God and the congregation.[30]

Clerkenwell residents and their spokesmen, like other Londoners, apparently sought to regulate such offenses in the plain view of all parishioners in order to articulate communally held ethical values, publicly shame offenders, and deter any other congregants from similar behavior. The same fear of public shame excites Claudio in *Measure for Measure*, who seems less concerned about his arrest and impending punishment than being shown "thus to th'world," preferring to be taken hastily to prison out of common view (1.2.92). The theatres were similarly involved in the public enforcement of justice. If Nobody, in the anonymous play *Nobody and Somebody* (1606, staged at the nearby Red Bull playhouse), can be taken at his word, "somebody once picked a pocket in this playhouse yard, [and] was hoisted on the stage and shamed about it."[31] Similarly, Will Kempe notes that cutpurses were "tied to a post on our stage, for all people to wonder at, when at a play they are taken pilfering."[32] Actors—who were so often accused of instigating lawlessness—evidently were involved in maintaining order in the theatres, knowing, no doubt, that playgoers would be reluctant to attend a venue that had earned a reputation for harboring criminals.

Church penance and other forms of popular justice could only be effective in situations where citizens already knew one another and where public humiliation and the severe damage to one's reputation that attended it would have serious repercussions. This situation clearly obtained in London's suburbs, in addition to the allegedly more orderly inner-city parishes. Even when behavior was regulated through ordinary legal mechanisms, the criminal justice system proved considerably more ad hoc than the elaborate system of statutes and case law would suggest. Local magistrates and jurors were assisted in their efforts by a variety of municipal officers that extended from the lord mayor to aldermen and their deputies, sheriffs, common counselors, constables, bailiffs, scavengers, wardmotes (who conducted the annual inquest), and beadles. The sheer number and variety of officeholders meant that many citizens, from all parts of the city and including those of relatively low social and economic status, could take part in the city and its ancient customs.

The primitive transportation and communication systems also severely hindered Londoners' ability to become familiar with distant neighborhoods and their inhabitants, exacerbating an already strong tendency to interact locally.[33] Dispensing with often large and wasteful bureaucracies, local initiatives tend to be both more efficient at building social capital and more satisfying to residents, who can immediately see the results of their activities and have a personal stake in their outcome. At a time when the crown had neither the resources nor the political will to embark on far-reaching civic projects, Londoners were forced to take a local approach to various community problems: poor relief, education and training, and the enforcement of misdemeanors were all conducted at the parish or ward level.

Londoners knew their neighbors. Daily interaction between individuals in the same neighborhood guaranteed that one's actions were highly visible and probably scrutinized closely by others. And if this frequent yet informal contact was not enough, the wide array of civic and parish officeholders undertook the careful surveillance of public and private while also serving as a conduit for public opinion to reach higher-ranking officials. Escaping the notice of the inquest carried a heavy penalty; all wardmotes were instructed that at "the general court, you give afore us [the aldermen] the names and surnames of all them of your said ward that come not to your said wardmote, if they be duly warned, so that due redress and punishment of them may be had."[34] The authority granted to civic officers and their deputies was enhanced during the first part of the seventeenth century along with their numbers: in Cornhill, for instance, 118 officers served only 276 households.[35] Under such intense scrutiny, the violation of common principles of civility and order could have real and serious consequences for one's social and economic prospects. Although these measures seem draconian to us today, they were not apprehended as an onerous or invidious system of surveillance because they mandated a high degree of citizen participation in local affairs and were likely administered by familiar faces rather than by anonymous strangers. Because of the small size of each ward relative to the number of wardmotes appointed, most residents would be acquainted with their wardmote. The inquests, as Pearl speculates, were probably conducted in "the spirit of fellowship and clubbish ritual."[36]

Offenders were also punished locally. Most of the city's wards had their own pair of stocks used to discipline those who committed petty crimes within the neighborhood, such as brawling, disorder, or drunkenness. Those guilty of more serious violations might be punished at a variety of other locations. Heretics and those guilty of religious offenses were punished at Paul's Cross. "Common" criminals (i.e., repeat offenders) or more serious offenders were punished at the city's pillory in Cornhill. Convicted felons sentenced to death were executed at the city gallows in Tyburn, while the most serious felons (convicted of treason or other crimes national in scope) were beheaded at the Tower. In this way, the punishment of crimes was highly visible to local residents, suggesting that the shame involved in public exposure was at least as damaging as time spent in the stocks. Punishment also had a strong spatial component, revolving around a particular set of locations that offered a grisly alternative to other ways of navigating the city.[37]

If the multiple pressures of city government and the less formal surveillance networks that developed to complement them were not sufficient to promote civility and build community, the administrative structure of industry in London also contributed to cohesion and stability. A connection with one of the many guilds was the only legal way for individuals to obtain legitimate, skilled employment. Membership conferred the freedom of the city, the right to vote for and stand for civic office, and the opportunity to participate in the various activities that the companies sponsored. Livery companies were effectively monopolies and exerted tight control over the labor force by restricting entry to all who did not undergo the mandatory seven years of apprenticeship to a licensed member of the trade. The guilds were a superb example of bonding social capital, augmenting ties between members and contributing to a profound sense of exclusion for those who did not. Guild membership was also the qualification for partaking in much of London's social life: the companies regularly sponsored feasts, processions, and entertainments celebrating momentous dates in London's history and the life of the trade. London's companies were notable throughout the world for their exclusivity and the amount of power and wealth that they controlled. Guild life was shrouded in mystery and ceremony, much of which took place behind closed doors.[38]

Appointed to wear a special livery on numerous occasions throughout the year, higher-ranking members bore a visible marker of occupational status within their trade and social status within the city. Each company adopted a specific color scheme, usually consisting of a combination of two contrasting hues, meaning that careful observers could easily detect someone's occupation. On feast days a large proportion of the pedestrians in any given neighborhood would be wearing the same colors, because members would be clustered around the company hall. Thus the livery functioned as a kind of neighborhood uniform. The livery that members were appointed to wear also denoted their status in the company; some wore only the hood, while fully liveried members were entitled to wear the whole suit.[39] And, of course, wearing clothes above one's station was met with intense disapproval and legal sanction that could result in dismissal from office and even losing one's job. Statutes dating from the fourteenth century governed dress in uncommon detail. Both Elizabeth and James became personally involved in sumptuary matters, suggesting that the distinction afforded by dress was an issue that concerned Londoners of all degrees.[40] Those companymen who became officers of the city were especially conspicuous, allowed and invited to display their status in an even more extravagant manner: "in their violet colored gowns furred, and their violet cloaks . . . the aldermen are to bring [the lord mayor] home to his dwelling place to dinner, wearing their cloaks: and after dinner, they may take their pleasure."[41] Membership had its privileges, and guilds became communities unto themselves, superimposed upon a complementary urban landscape.[42]

The livery companies maintained a strong physical presence in local neighborhoods. The legendary company halls, renowned for their opulence, were a source of delight for inhabitants of the wards where they were located. Citizens who did not belong to the company and had little hope of ever entering the hall nevertheless took pride in these elaborate and expensive structures, which became attractions for locals and foreign visitors alike. In 1600 the Grocers' Hall on Conyhoop Lane (known popularly as Grocer's Alley) had the distinction of being the oldest building in London, complete with a garden, a bowling alley, and an armory. The premises were frequently rented out for private functions, and its lavishly furnished parlor, renovated in 1598 by Sir Stephen Soame at the high cost of £500, was used by the lord mayor, his aldermen, and gentlemen from the Inns of Court to entertain important English and foreign guests.[43] These halls were deemed such important landmarks that the expanded edition of Stow's *Survey* (1633) contains an index specifically designed so that readers could quickly locate their descriptions within the large volume.

Well-to-do companymen were also known to disperse their money locally, like "Henry Keble, Grocer" of Cheap Ward, who "gave to the seven almspeople sixpence a week forever." According to Stow, guild members occasionally bestowed funds on parishioners who were not involved in their trade.[44] Through their highly visible public edifices and activities, the guilds helped neighborhoods forge distinctive identities that were nevertheless consistent with the administrative structure of the city as a whole. Citizens of Lime Street Ward, many of them free of the Draper's Company, took pride in the guild's establishment of the Leadenhall Granary (later a market) because it affirmed their region's unique place in the history of the broader metropolis. Similarly, the action of Thomas Dekker's *The Shoemaker's Holiday* (1600) revolves around Eyre's shop, adjacent to the company hall in Tower Street Ward. The mirth and the fellowship instantiated there eventually permeate the rest of the city when Eyre becomes lord mayor and urges citizens to imitate his own dogged work ethic and good-natured relations with his fellow shoemakers.[45] Replicating a long-standing custom of friendly association with his own apprentices, Eyre announces "this day my fellow prentices of London come to dine with me too. They shall have fine cheer, gentlemanly cheer" (17.42–44). He broadens the scope of a successful, community-affirming initiative to include all London's apprentices, extending a system of social capital first tested at the local level.

Even if they sometimes failed to live up to their lofty goals, guilds were first established as fraternal organizations designed to promote community and religious involvement for all inhabitants of the city.[46] Arguably, their most visible role in the community was the administration and distribution of charity throughout the city and suburbs. Their contributions included payments to relieve the poor, donations to schools and hospitals, funds for buildings and other public works, amortized endowments to provide food for the needy, measures to safeguard the city's grain reserves, and trusteeship of lands bequeathed by the mayor and aldermen. The guilds also financed a cookery whereby "whatever multitude, either of soldiers or other strangers, enter into the city at any hour, day or night, or else are about to depart, they may turn in, bait there, and refresh themselves to their content, and so avoid long fasting, and not go away without their dinner."[47] The city, and therefore the guilds that ran it, was also charged by a royal charter of 1553 with the operation of Bedlam and Bridewell, the two hospitals established for the relief of those who were sick, destitute, or homeless, unable or unwilling to work at all. Bedlam concentrated on the mentally ill, while Bridewell attempted to rehabilitate "sturdy beggars."[48] A tract by Thomas Adams devoted to the plight of the poor, the sick, and the psychologically unstable suggests that dwellings for the infirm and the mentally ill were especially beneficial to the commonweal. He declares that "the foundation of God's tenement . . . is faith, the walls hope, the roof charity."[49] While managing these hospitals, companies were often more lenient in the application of laws that sought to punish beggars and vagabonds. The guilds could administer municipal affairs more efficiently and often more compassionately than top-heavy governments because they substituted for a complex bureaucracy that had never really existed and that authorities could ill afford to finance.[50]

Charity was seldom entirely altruistic, especially when conducted by London's guilds. Even zealous churchmen conceded this point in their efforts to integrate the rampant financial aspirations of many Londoners with the more harmonious and God-fearing spiritual community that they sought to build in the city and its environs. A sermon preached by Robert Wilkinson in 1607 suggests that charity, in addition to having intrinsic value for a properly functioning community, is an essential component of a vibrant economy. Comparing the proceeds of charitable activity to the bounty imported on a merchant ship, Wilkinson understands commerce not simply as a means to personal wealth but as an instrument to enhance public welfare. The ship "that brings her food from far away," he argues, is an equitable and harmonious symbol of economic redistribution that benefits all involved in the transaction; it is "a servant for profit *and* for uses to Godward, a spiritual instructor."[51] As early as the fourth century, St. John Chrysostom suggested that "God appointed almsgiving not only for the needy to be nourished, but also for the providers to receive benefit."[52] Far from complaining about the drain on corporate and personal income necessitated by their role as philanthropists, companies and their members relished the positive exposure in the local community that charity provided. They recognized that giving money away might, paradoxically, have a favorable impact on business.

For the livery companies, part of the benefit accruing from the decentralization of authority was legal: they were entitled to plead before the courts as a corporate entity, had monopoly control over the labor force, and could purchase land to lease for profit, a privilege that none of the company's members could achieve individually. As an intermediary between the government and the citizenry, the companies also wielded significant influence by controlling the dissemination of information. Both the queen and the lord mayor relied on masters and wardens from the guilds to read aloud proclamations and decrees to their constituents at regular meetings in the company hall.[53] This sometimes allowed the companies to circumvent royal authority. For instance, the crown's frequent attempts to stabilize prices for commodities such as beer and other victuals often proved extremely vexing precisely because they delegated the responsibility for enforcing this legislation to the companies directly affected by it. The king charged the clerk of the market to enforce the statute, who in turn enlisted "mayors, Justices of the Peace, Bailiffs, [and] Constables," all of whom were answerable to the civic authorities controlled by the companies. The companies, in turn, would annunciate the terms of the statute to their benefit.[54] Administering the city's charity would seem a small price to pay for this added authority and regulatory autonomy.

In many cases, company members did more than influence and

implement policy: they formulated it. Each year civic officeholders—including common councilmen, aldermen, sheriffs, and the lord mayor himself—were nominated, elected, and chosen from the ranks of London's elite livery companies, guaranteeing that their interests would dominate the annual agenda. Not surprisingly, the men elected by their peers to the highest offices were those who exhibited unusual magnanimity to their fellow guild members and to the community at large. In this case, the legendary and meteoric rise of Simon Eyre proved instructive for London's artisans. A good measure of his success is credited to the bounty he bestows on others. Though frequently stressing the value of a strong work ethic and excoriating the sin of idleness, Eyre nevertheless "raves in commendation" of his employees (*Shoemaker's Holiday*, 1.172), gives them "sixpences" in addition to their regular wages simply for honestly displaying "the honour of the Gentle Craft . . . the Gentlemen Shoemakers" (1.210–19), and insists that his "prentices want no cheer. Let wine be as plentiful as beer, and beer as water" (20.8–10). Through this kind of generosity, he quickly earns the adoration of his workers, other colleagues in the business community, and the king himself, allowing him to navigate the usually rigid social hierarchy easily.

Eligibility for holding charitable office was a privilege and, like the freedom of the city, could be forfeited for failing to discharge assigned duties or for residing outside London or its suburbs, "not partner to the charge of the city."[55] By establishing themselves as benefactors of the community, citizens were able to make a name for themselves in insular neighborhoods and sparsely populated parishes where reputation mattered to their well-being at least as much as personal income. Failure to discharge one's office with appropriate dedication or abuse of authority could lead to infamy and public shaming. Henry Peacham, not usually pleasantly disposed to the citizenry, notes that a true gentleman should "hold friendship and acquaintance with few" but must nevertheless be "useful to others," including occasional "discourse and converse with the meanest," in order to preserve his elevated reputation. "Lavish bestowing or giving," he claims, is "a virtue as requisite in a noble or gentleman as the care of his whole estate, and preservation of his name and prosperity."[56] Public service and success in commerce were closely intertwined. In most instances, the wealthiest individuals were the most generous donors and the most politically involved: 91 percent of London's elite held civic office or had an immediate family member who did so. One could argue that personal wealth and prominence in the business world inevitably leads to political influence and public service, as it does today. But London's elites chose to participate in city politics rather than at the national level (only 2 percent did so), which suggests that local initiative was more advantageous to those involved.[57]

Atypical of the expected conduct of firms in a competitive marketplace, corporate charity is best interpreted as an investment in social capital where immediate profits are deferred for prospective returns over the long term. By enhancing the general welfare of the community, philanthropy would improve business conditions, assure stable earnings, and guarantee mutual support in recessionary periods. Although many citizens remembered God's promise to reward almsgivers generously (Luke 12:33), companies and their members nourished the poor out of personal ambition, one-upmanship, and a fear of being ostracized by their peers, not out of any zealous sense of moral duty. In Thomas Middleton's *Michaelmas Term* (1607), Easy is easily duped into acting as a guarantor for Blastfield's bond to avoid "utter dissolution amongst gentleman forever." Easy understands his surety as a "courtesy," an act of charity among his fellows and a means of ingratiating himself to London's elites (2.3.307).

Although advocates of charity and gift-giving frequently stipulated that gifts ought to be granted without expectation of payment, with "love out of a pure heart," self-interest was endemic to this system of exchange and remuneration, both on earth and in heaven. Whether recalling God's promise to "deliver [the giver] in time of trouble" (Psalms 41:1) or noting Jesus' assurance that "the merciful . . . will receive mercy" (Matthew 5:7), liberal donors could hardly suppress the expectation of some future reward. Demonstrating personal and corporate wealth through ostentatious displays of largesse, in addition to providing an efficient means of economic redistribution and the promise of salvation, also offered a relatively benign way to compete for status that reinforced hierarchies and societal norms.[58] Even though some who received charity might have been reluctant to accept unearned or undeserved assistance, the etiquette of gift-giving obliged the recipient to accept the gift. To refuse would be shameful.

In *Twelfth Night*, Olivia's sarcastic and uncharacteristically caustic reaction to Viola when she refuses to accept her purse illustrates the degree to which failure to adhere to these protocols was considered an insult to those of higher rank and an egregious breach of civility:

> "What is your parentage?"
> "Above my fortunes, my state is well:
> I am a gentleman." I'll be sworn thou art!
> Thy tongue, thy face, thy limbs, actions, and spirit
> Do give thee fivefold blazon. (1.5.259–63)

Refusing to participate in this manifestation of the guest-host relationship was the sign of a poor upbringing and tantamount to the abdication of one's place in the social hierarchy, which first alerts Olivia to the possibility that Viola is not the servant she appears to be.

Another perceived breach of the norms of charitable conduct discloses just how important these conventions are in the play and how ingrained they were in London's theatre audiences. Antonio is incredulous when Viola (as Sebastian) fails to return his generosity. His anger centers on the hypocrisy of those who would fail to participate in the economy of benevolence:

> But O, how vile an idol proves this god!
> Thou hast, Sebastian, done good fortune shame.
> In nature there's no blemish but the mind.
> None can be called deformed but the unkind. (3.4.330–33)

Not to participate in the spirit of charity was not just "unkind" but unnatural, a kind of social death that reveals how important philanthropy was to the economic prospects of Londoners.

London's guilds also promoted their own form of playgoing. They staged frequent entertainments to celebrate holidays, the annual installation of the new mayor, and other momentous events in the city's history. Usually performed for an exclusive audience of city dignitaries but enjoyed by the community as a whole, these plays were not confined to audiences consisting only of company members. Such performances are designed to promote the guild and its activities to the general populace, not unlike their involvement in charity. Perhaps the most conspicuous features of these productions were their forceful—some might say heavy-handed—emphasis on public morality and their commitment to representing the city and its leaders in the best possible light.

The pageants delivered this message as they progressed through the city, linking disparate neighborhoods under the singular authority of the mayor.[59] Although the precise route of the annual lord mayor's progress evolved from year to year, the newly elected leader attempted to traverse through as many parts of the city as possible to bind the city together as one community, enjoining citizens to forget—at least momentarily—the many issues that divided them. The mayor first traveled by water from the Guildhall to Westminster (to swear the oath of office to the king), allowing ample opportunity for residents of wards along both sides of the Thames to view his lavishly decorated barge. From there, he returned on the river as far as Baynard's Castle (just inside the walls in Farringdon Ward), moving north to St. Paul's, east along Cheapside, back to the Guildhall for feasting, again to St. Paul's for church services, and finally to Leadenhall (in Lime Street Ward, to the northeast) for a final speech.

The mayor's shows are most often remembered for the text of the staged vignettes that punctuated his movement through the city but the elaborate movements of the opulently dressed group between the hastily erected stages would have captured the imaginations of the assembled residents. The crowd would focus on the regally attired mayor, who, despite his elevated position and finery, had emerged from their ranks, underscoring the inclusive message of the pageants. This kind of public display was especially important for those who remained relatively distant from the corridors of power. Orazio Busino, in the entourage of the Venetian ambassador, recalled that during the progress of George Bolles on 29 October 1617:

> Looking below us onto the street we saw a huge mass of people, surging like the sea, moving here and there in search of places to watch or rest . . . It was a chaotic mixture . . . especially of that race

> of apprentices . . . berriboned serving wenches; lower class women with their children in their arms . . . A perpetual shower of firecrackers rained from the windows onto the seething crowd, popping mischievously . . . It really was splendid spectacle.[60]

Evidently, this was the kind of drama that the whole city could comfortably support. These public spectacles instilled pride in one's occupation, community, and city—the fixtures of daily life for Londoners from all walks of life. By drawing on these same local dynamics, purpose-built structures might achieve a similar degree of positive civic engagement.

These pageants emphasized city values that the guilds jealously guarded and sought to disseminate throughout their membership and the broader population. Mayoral entertainments and company pageants were frequently written by consummate theatrical professionals, including Thomas Middleton, Thomas Heywood, Ben Jonson, and Thomas Dekker, who threw themselves into the glorification of the city as fervently as they represented its vices and satirized the pretensions of its citizens in other plays designed for the commercial stage.[61] Their commissions as pageant writers might seem a complete reversal from their regular occupation as professional dramatists, their panegyrics to the city and its leaders a radical departure from the pugnacity and materialism displayed by the characters of city comedy. But their civic entertainments evince the same complex reflexivity, a nuanced understanding of systemic problems, and the importance of reciprocal bonds, that permeates their more familiar professional drama. Thomas Dekker's *Troia-Nova Triumphans*, performed for lord mayor John Swinnerton in October 1612, recognizes that many citizens might regard the elaborate spectacles that greeted each new mayor as an unnecessary and even wasteful allocation of public funds when so many Londoners languished in poverty and suffered from annual visitations of the plague. The high cost of the pageants is justified as "a debt paid to time and custom" in the expectation that the expenditure of monetary capital will build social capital among citizens:

> Because yourself [the mayor] being generous of mind, have met with men and with a company equal to yourself in spirit. And upon

as fortunate a tree have they ingrafted their bounty; the fruits whereof shoot forth and ripen, are gathered, and taste sweetly, in the mouths not only of this city, but also our best-to-be beloved friends, the noblest strangers . . . And I make no doubt, but many worthy companies in this city could gladly be content to be partners in the disbursements, so they might be sharers in the glory.[62]

Other companymen and the citizenry at large will emulate the bounty of the mayor, his government, and the company from which he is chosen to the mutual advantage of all. Just as the cony-catching of strangers in so many city comedies is the direct result of the avaricious tendencies of Londoners, virtuous living and generosity might also beget an ethos of productivity, education, and mutual respect. Dekker's entertainment personifies these attributes: "*Wisdom* sets *Desire* aburning to attain to *Virtue*, and that *Burning Desire* begets *Industry* . . . And all these (together) make men in love with *Arts*, *Trade*, *Sciences*, and *Knowledge*."[63] In both cases, the decisive conduit between material bounty and greater civic engagement is the affective power of theatre and the understanding that viewers will seek to mimic the actions observed onstage.

The parish church and the livery companies were the most conspicuous city institutions charged with regulating two of the most important aspects of life, religion and industry. These institutions bound Londoners to their local communities through a series of economic dependencies and by encouraging loyalty to one's neighborhood and its residents. Conformity and community in London were also maintained in less regimented ways. Gossip was a powerful form of social exchange with the ability to shape behavior while offering a welcome diversion, as it is today.[64] The steady din is a sign of viable social networks and a measure of their extension to all members of the community. Samuel Rowland's fictional dialogue *A Whole Crew of Kind Gossips* (1609) attests to the pervasiveness of gossip and to the social discourse it made possible. Gossip "hath very nimble wings . . . It flies about the town from ear to ear," a natural sociable breeze to assist in everything from commerce to courtship, making distant parts of the city as familiar as one's own.[65]

An early seventeenth century woodcut entitled *Tittle-Tattle* (see

FIGURE 2. A broadsheet satirizing the habits of housewives, which shows the remarkable ease and fluidity with which information can travel from one location to the other. *Tittle-Tattle, or, The Several Branches of Gossiping* (London, 1603). Courtesy of the Trustees of the British Museum, London, England.

figure 2) fascinatingly illustrates the remarkable permeability of gossip through various social elements of the city and its ability to generate cohesiveness for particular factions. Designed as a satire on the social habits of housewives, the broadsheet depicts women in several very different domestic and social locations, including the "child-bed," church, market, and public bath—aspects of a functioning city all contained within an allegorical house. What binds these diverse locations together is the constant chatter and rich social interaction that provides a constant accompaniment to the women's daily routines. Gossip circulates throughout the community with surprising ease and rapidity, spreading as individuals move from one social circle to another and soon informing the entire populace of the day's news, even those who do not venture beyond their own block. Men, of course, had ample opportunities to partake in similar forms of gossip at their shops, the guildhall, or the local tavern. Unlike most forms of communication and civic organization, gossip simultaneously functions as a form of social bonding and, like the branches on a tree that connect its various parts, bridges groups unfamiliar with one another.

This exchange of information received a kind of infrastructure through the network of taverns and alehouses that dotted nearly all city streets. Peter Clark has determined that by the early seventeenth century England had perhaps 50,000 or more licensed and unlicensed drinking establishments, with thousands in London and its environs (306 in Finsbury alone in 1630). Thomas Dekker claimed in 1638 that in London "a whole street is in some place but a continual alehouse."[66] John Taylor, in an alternative to Stow's description of London, moves through the city and suburbs, surveying its many famous drinking establishments (excluding, of course, the smaller alehouses that had not attained local notoriety). What is striking about this early modern pub crawl is the sheer number of victualing houses within relatively small neighborhoods, even on the same street, suggesting how important they were in the daily lives of residents: "we are commonly accompanied with wine . . . [that] kindly accompanies us all our life . . . Thousands of people do live by it."[67]

The number and diversity of these establishments suggest that they were hardly short on patrons but also beg the question of stratification. With so many options in relatively close proximity, why would an individual choose to frequent one alehouse over another? It appears that some kind of victualing house catered to every clientele. Large inns provided superior lodgings, lavish meals, and fine wines for the well-to-do; taverns served less elaborate meals and a variety of beverages; significantly more modest alehouses served beer, cider, and only the lightest provisions to accompany the drink. Even within these official categories alehouses varied significantly. Certain establishments apparently tended to cater to certain groups according to geographical location, occupation, class, age, and the forms of entertainment provided, which ranged from dice, cards, and board games to prostitution. These establishments were also important in advertising plays. Patrons might expect to find playbills advertising the latest offering at the public theatres both inside and outside taverns, raising the possibility that players, knowing something about the clientele at certain alehouses in specific areas, could selectively target plays to certain social segments.[68] Alehouses, open to all and frequented by travelers and newcomers, also bridged social cleavages, offering strangers a way of integrating themselves in new neighborhoods. Conflicts between newcomers and local residents did occur, but on the whole denizens of the neighborhood alehouse tended to be more tolerant, even welcoming, of strangers than we might expect.[69]

The alehouse and the playhouse share a similar place in modern historiography. Drawing on the rhetoric of more conservative religious and municipal authorities, some early modern commentators suggest that both institutions were places of ill repute, drunkenness, and disorder, inimical to the maintenance of community values and a God-fearing society. Thomas Thompson preached in 1608 that "drunkenness . . . is an undecent behavior" that results in "beastliness which is a troublesome loathfulness . . . so odious unto God," potentially resulting in "riot," "quarrelling and fighting," and "disobedience to the king's laws." Thompson argued that drunkenness was a sin with both moral and social ramifications, especially given the ubiquity of "taverns and alehouses." Thomas Adams went further, suggesting that these establishments threatened patrons' spiritual health, comparing "the serpent in the fens [to] the man at the alehouse."[70] The narrow and obviously biased perspective of these religious ideologues is echoed by Patricia Fumerton (in 2002), who claims that "alehouses . . .

partook of the very essence of vagrancy, constituting a threat to stability throughout the realm and especially in the capital."[71]

Alehouses, however, were important institutions within local neighborhoods that complemented the parish church and the guild. In 1619 William Cornwallis felt that he could not "find out a more honester harbor" than at an alehouse, noting the hypocrisy of those who railed against them: "methinks a drunken cobbler and a mere hawking gentleman rank equally."[72] And though some alehouse keepers were presumably dishonest, those found guilty of mendacious behavior were required to "forfeit ten shillings to the use of the poor."[73] Keenly aware of the charge that time spent at the alehouse was time spent away from work, justices mandated that "any Innkeep or Alehousekeep shall suffer any person dwelling in the town, village, or hamlet where said Inn or Alehouse is, to remain and continue drinking there [away from] laboring and handiwork for [only] one hour at dinnertime."[74]

In addition to being places of recreation, alehouses were a venue for a variety of business transactions, dowry negotiations, marriage contracts, and resolution of disputes among various parties. Their keepers were a source of local information (especially concerning employment), sellers of ballads, and, in many cases, the creditors of last resort for local residents, often providing an essential service for the lower orders. The ensemble of functions fulfilled by local watering holes suggests that they were central to the community, sometimes serving as an alternative to the parish church. Later commentators have argued that taverns were therefore subversive of community values, places where unruly popular culture was celebrated, seditious ideas might spread, and drunken and disorderly lifestyles threatened pious and hardworking ones. Alehouses, however, complemented the church and other local institutions rather than substituting for them and fulfilled roles that were not possible elsewhere. Gathering at taverns allowed groups to bond along more narrow interests that were not necessarily geographic, religious, or occupational. Perhaps the best evidence that victualing houses of various kinds did not provide serious competition to the church comes from clergymen themselves, who often resorted to alehouses to fulfill parish functions such as reconciling parties involved in disputes.[75] As with the playhouses, the unwholesome place of the alehouses in English society has been significantly exaggerated, obscuring their functional role in London's communities.

The theatre also functioned as a source of news and as a site for the exchange of local information. The large public amphitheatres, though hardly an anonymous and completely heterogeneous forum, drew together a broader and more assorted constituency than any other regular gathering place in London. The parish church certainly was frequently attended and functioned as an essential community institution, but on a much smaller and more parochial scale, where interaction with those outside the congregation was sporadic at best. The marketplace, which many commentators both past and present have likened to the theatre, offered a much larger and more fluid social venue, but it too was limited to a particular stratum of the population. Most Londoners not engaged in the exchange of commodities or in the purchase of household goods would have little reason to visit on a regular basis. As a social institution and a gathering place, the playhouse was the alehouse writ large.

Those antagonistic to the theatre most recognized and most feared its unique capacity to influence its constituents both individually and collectively. Just as one might allegedly be corrupted by spending too much time at the local tavern, regardless of the company or the parsimony of one's drinking habits, attending the theatre was debauched regardless of the play onstage. The common theme running through Stephen Gosson's copious *Plays Confuted in Five Actions* (1582) is the automatic and unmistakable transference, as if by osmosis, between the characters and events portrayed onstage and the demeanor and behavior of the audience: "when anything is represented by players upon the stage, it is openly blown into the ears of many . . . 'til they be settled in the mind and immovable in affection."[76] While acknowledging the powerful effect the theatre had on playgoers, Heywood and other theatrical professionals drew a different conclusion. Just as alehouses sometimes fulfilled a positive function in individual neighborhoods, theatres might instill thoughts and actions beneficial to the community norms that contributed to long-standing practices in London designed to promote social capital. Thomas Overbury notes how the theatre was able to weed out those same vices that many antitheatricalists accused it of aggravating: "the playhouses," he proclaims, "only keep him sober; and as it doth many other gallants, makes him an afternoon's man."[77]

The city, with its long and rich history and relatively confined parish units, seemed uniquely susceptible to the formation of strong and lasting social bonds. But what of recently developed areas outside the walls, home to a significantly more transient population and lacking the rich sense of tradition nurtured over many centuries? Did the assiduous governance of civic behavior by both the lord mayor and other ad hoc mechanisms organized by citizens also prevail in the suburbs? Many Londoners who lived within the wall claimed that this was not the case. In 1604 Henry Petowe, a cloth worker residing in St. Michael's Wood Street, argued that "the filthy froth of sensual beastliness [was] expelled from the inner parts, and as I may say, the heart of the city [into] the outmost skirts and appendant members thereunto."[78] Many historians and literary critics, including A. L. Beier and Steven Mullaney, have taken Petowe and others like him at their word. Ian Archer, however, reminds us that we should not necessarily imagine a city divided based solely on this evidence. Condemnations of the suburbs by residents inside the walls may have been more self-serving than true, a way of diverting attention from the shortcomings of the city by blaming all its sins on its suburbs.[79]

The reason most often given for the greater lawlessness and immorality in the suburbs, as well as for the natural gravitation of the playhouses to these neighborhoods, is that they were beyond the rigid control of London's governance. Although the jurisdiction of the lord mayor in the liberties was neither as absolute nor as effective (lacking the wardmote inquest and some other instruments of the constabulary) as it was within the walls, the civic authorities continued to exercise some degree of dominion in these areas that was augmented by other local bodies.[80] The mayor was still considered the "lord" of the Manors of Southwark and had considerable legal influence, especially since the city purchased the rights of the crown in the suburb on 9 May 1550.[81] This charter significantly tightened the city's control of the borough, implying that in law, if not in practice, Southwark was just another part of the city: its residents enjoyed the same rights and privileges—and were punishable by the same laws—as those within the walls.[82] Even if this charter did not automatically elevate administrative efficiency and living conditions in the Bankside to those of the city, it illustrates a general tendency in the neighborhood toward greater accountability and deference to local authorities; both criminal and civil actions now could be adjudicated in city courts. The 1550 charter signaled greater integration with the city of London, rather than increasing marginality. By the time the players arrived in the 1580s, Southwark and its citizens were becoming less profligate, not more so.

The situation was somewhat different in the regions to the north of the city that were also the home to theatres. Legal directives in this region were nevertheless consistent with the well-governed community that Londoners sought to enact throughout the metropolis. Shoreditch, Finsbury, Clerkenwell, and the other liberties to the north of the city were all located in Middlesex County. The antiquarian and cartographer John Norden noted in 1593 that Middlesex, unlike other "shires," was "under the high officer of the City of London, the Mayor, who by force of the same charter, yearly constituteth a sheriff who also is accountable unto the city for all matters appertaining to his said office," according to a charter enacted by King John in 1204.[83] The lord mayor did indeed hold sway in Middlesex, but indirectly through the sheriff and the justices he appointed, who governed not from the Guildhall in London but from Westminster. Residents of the suburbs could seek redress for their grievances from a number of sources. They might petition authorities in London proper, the justices of Middlesex and Surrey, local institutions administered by the parish, the manorial courts that previously had held sway in the region, or in some cases the royal courts responsible for adjudicating matters of national importance, such as the regulation of commerce and industry—not exactly a dearth of mechanisms charged with maintaining public order and morality.

Steven Mullaney argues that this overlapping jurisdiction must have resulted in administrative chaos. Frequent bickering among various regional and national authorities would have rendered all three bodies impotent and exacerbated an already keen tendency toward lawlessness.[84] As a practical matter, however, all governmental bodies worked together on issues of mutual concern, especially the fundamental tasks of maintaining the peace, suppressing crime, and controlling the plague. They reinforced one another rather than languishing in an internecine power struggle. "Contrary to what might be expected," argues Jeremy Boulton, "local government [was] a significant institution in neighborhood life which lent structure and coherence to the society."[85] Overlapping jurisdiction in Middlesex led to the development of a more complex, empowered, and competent bureaucracy than that which existed in the city itself.

Legal control in the outlying neighborhoods was shared among the lord mayor, the justices of Middlesex and Surrey, and the Privy Council, with no entity emerging as an unquestioned authority. All levels of government sought to improve administrative efficiency in suburbs that had developed a reputation for disorder since the Middle Ages. Their efforts seem to have had the desired effect. Throughout the sixteenth century, Londoners were accustomed to blaming the suburbs and the illicit activities of their residents for visitations of the plague, believing that God was punishing the city for the actions of a handful of iniquitous suburbanites. As observant Londoners gradually realized that this strict dichotomy between a model city and disorderly suburbs was unfair and probably self-serving, tracts that indicted the city as a whole gradually replaced those inveighing specifically against the suburbs. In 1603 Henoch Clapman urged that "we have sinned together, and the hand of God hath come upon us together: let us therefore humble ourselves together before our Lord." He believed that "[i]t is not a change of place, but [a] change of life that must help us."[86] Londoners increasingly stressed the unity and continuity between the city and the suburbs, understanding the city as an integrated whole. Despite regional variation, the suburbs did not compromise the moral integrity of the metropolis.

To make the case for the lack of effective government in the liberties, theatre historians have been preoccupied with the supposed conflict between the city fathers and the theatres ever since E. K. Chambers focused on the issue of the "control" of the stage. Scholars have noticed the frequent differences of opinion between the lord mayor and the Privy Council, noting that the former's constant attempts to suppress plays were in many instances overridden by the latter. The two bodies were opposite poles in efforts to regulate the players: one representing the extreme pursuit of law and order, the other an emerging humanist ethos. Andrew Gurr, for instance, argues that the players had an indispensable ally in the Privy Council, noting that many councilors were also patrons of theatre companies. He suggests that "three or four leading patrons led the fight against the city authorities' opposition to playing," eventually giving the industry a foothold in the city.[87]

Although this narrative does capture the give-and-take between city and state that characterized the management of drama and other forms of entertainment, it posits the relationship between the two as a polarity. This viewpoint underestimates the degree to which the two bodies worked together and relied on one another for the implementation of sound policy. Neither body's jurisdiction was absolute; nor was the Privy Council the unabashed defender of the theatre against the puritanical zeal of the mayoralty. In 1583 lord mayor Edward Osborne petitioned Francis Walsingham, an influential member of the Privy Council, to support the city in its efforts to suppress plays. Osborne claimed that "it availeth not to restrain [the players] in London, unless the like orders be in those places adjoining to the liberties," seemingly admitting to his inability to police the suburbs beyond the walls. Walsingham's reply, however, suggests that the crown could not unilaterally enforce its will: "I pray your Lordship therefore that from hence forth you will suffer them to have the benefit of this liberty"; he asked the mayor for "your especial license to be granted to this end."[88] The Privy Council relied on the lord mayor to do its bidding in an area where the crown held sway but had little practical jurisdiction to enforce its will. The city government also stood to gain from the players (see chapter 2).

Those who argue for the licentiousness of the liberties have urged that these exchanges between the city governance and the Privy Council are evidence that both levels of government sought to wash their hands of these neighborhoods that were forever out of control. The evidence does imply that neither crown nor corporation could effectively control the suburbs without the support of the other. Because both sides enacted mechanisms to enforce playing and expected the other to follow suit, their debate over the presence of the theatres must be understood within the larger context of the collaborative development of policy designed to establish and guarantee order and prosperity. The dialogue between the two was only minimally about the theatres. Regulation of the theatres, moreover, evolved over time and took into account complex political, economic, and historical factors that cannot easily be reduced to a static binary between city and court or Puritanism and humanism. Richard Dutton has shown that policy on the licensing of plays changed significantly, depending on the personnel in the Revels Office, various domestic and international political crises, and power struggles within the Privy Council, matters that had almost nothing to do with the players.[89] Although suppressing theatres in a given locality and censoring a given playscript may appear to be motivated by a singular and unchanging preoccupation with stability, a more detailed understanding emerges when we locate the control of the stage in more localized and dynamic historical contexts.

A final reason frequently given for the poor government and questionable moral character of the suburbs has to do with the lack of regulation of industry and trade, the failure of the venerable guild structure to infiltrate the suburbs. Although the guilds are often understood as inextricably and exclusively tied to the city within the walls, their reach regularly extended to communities outside London proper, including the neighborhoods that hosted the players. Because of the rapid population expansion and the increasing number of persons seeking employment in these communities, the livery companies quickly recognized the benefits of overseeing industry outside of their traditional domain and gradually sought to expand their authority. Laws approved throughout the Elizabethan and early Jacobean period affirmed the guilds' rights to inspect work and control the labor supply for several miles beyond the city walls.

Many individual companymen employed in the city but lured by more space and lower housing costs chose to make their home in the suburbs, transplanting the corporate culture that prevailed within the city to newly developed areas. By 1616 roughly one-third of tilers and bricklayers worked in precincts that were legally outside of the jurisdiction of the lord mayor.[90] Henslowe, himself a resident of Southwark, preferred to deal with these local artisans. His *Diary* frequently mentions the "ironmonger in Southwark at the Frying Pan," an establishment where he purchased the supplies necessary for the upkeep of the Rose.[91] To compete in a constantly changing city, the companies had to adopt their modus operandi to suit the changing topography and new economic climate, demonstrating a flexibility that many previous historians were reluctant to ascribe to them.[92]

The guilds' ability to foment social bonding among companymen led to alienation among noncitizens, many of them foreigners or newly arrived in the city from the provinces. This sense of exclusion might, paradoxically, have increased the cohesion of newcomers to the suburbs. Resistance to the livery companies was a source of solidarity for those journeymen who were excluded from the guilds and therefore prohibited from practicing their trade. Southwark in particular was a catchment region for immigrants from the Low Countries, who often engaged in victualing, retailing food and drink, and transporting goods throughout the south of England. Newcomers unaffiliated with livery companies often availed themselves of opportunities for employment on the Bankside that may not have been available within the city.

Many of these poorer residents also worked at a number of different occupations over the course of the year, making it difficult to pinpoint someone's trade with any accuracy while also offering an alternative to membership in a single guild.[93] For these flexible and possibly desperate individuals, their search for a respectable living offered an implicit challenge to the rigid structure of the guilds, bonding them not so much along occupational lines but through shared economic circumstances and their common aversion to traditional labor practices. The overall result was a net increase in social capital, but of a type that often failed to connect across specific affiliations, creating and perpetuating antagonisms among various groups. Though this may highlight an important source of discord and rivalry within London society, it does not follow as a general rule that those suburban residents who lived and worked outside of the recognized guild structure were derelicts, a bane to harmonious living and community in the liberties. These unlicensed journeymen were probably forced to work harder, for longer hours, and for less pay because they existed beyond the protection of the guilds and other regulatory bodies, hardly leaving them the time to cause the kinds of trouble that some have alleged.

This general picture of the cohesion between established inner-city neighborhoods and the expanding out-parishes provides a more complex and productive basis for interpreting the place of the stage and its role amid other institutions in the community, whether religious, occupational, or recreational. Thinking about the role of the theatres in the daily life of Londoners forces us to probe deeper into those neighborhoods where playhouses were located for a better understanding of their competitive positioning, their audience base, and the drama performed there. How did playhouses capitalize on characteristics of the local community to gain the legal approval of civic officials and earn the loyalty (and financial support) of audiences? Why, for instance, did the Red Bull in Clerkenwell develop such a reputation for bombastic "drum and trumpet plays" as opposed to the more refined reputation of the Globe on the Bankside, a neighborhood that was arguably worse off economically and more unruly than the northern suburbs? The answers to these questions, I believe, cannot be found only by interrogating theatre companies, playwrights, and the thematic content of the drama. We might more fully grasp these issues by understanding audiences, their preferences, local demographics and tastes, and how certain plays resonated in these more specific performance contexts.

Chapter 2
THE PUBLIC THEATRES & THEIR COMMUNITIES

Londoners circulated locally, in communities focused not on the metropolis as a whole but on more narrow occupational, neighborhood, and personal concerns. The anonymous ballad *London's Ordinary* (ca. 1605?) notes:

The gentry went to the King's Head,
The nobles unto the Crown;
The knights went to the Golden Fleece,
And the ploughmen unto the Clown.

The farriers will to the Horse,
The blacksmiths unto the Lock;
The butchers unto the Bull will go,
And the carmen to the Bridewell Dock.[1]

The atmosphere at each of these alehouses apparently was more suited to the tastes and expectations of certain groups, and eventually these drinking establishments came to cater to a particular demographic and develop specific reputations based on their patronage. Londoners, not surprisingly, attended the theatres with this same localized focus and strong tendency toward social stratification. William Turner (in 1612) claims:

The players of the Bank side
    The round Globe and the Swan
Will teach you idle tricks of love,
    But the Bull will play the man.[2]

Londoners chose what theatres to attend based on the type of drama staged there and the types of people they tended to attract. The "idle tricks of love" at the Bankside theatres, which may recall Shakespeare's love comedies, suggest a more sophisticated, perhaps leisured, audience that reveled in more intricate plots on certain subjects. The Red Bull in Clerkenwell catered to those with more popular tastes, who enjoyed the bombastic style and heroic plays that that theatre was notorious for. Turner's brief verse underscores significant differences in audience composition and repertory, an important feature of the playgoing industry during the Jacobean period.

Attending to the social capital inherent in theatrical activity therefore requires a survey of community relations in greater London as a whole and a reevaluation of those neighborhoods that were home to playhouses. Suburban neighborhoods differed from the city within the walls, but not always as commentators on the early modern stage have assumed. An accurate sociology of the theatre must attend to relationships among theatres, actors and proprietors, and local residents and businesses, all of which are best understood in the context of specific neighborhoods and patterns of local behavior.

The first, more global, issue that I want to address is the frequent charge that the theatres adversely affected the ethical character of neighborhoods. Although it is nearly impossible today to assess early modern public morality empirically, and equally misguided to take the obstreperous comments of biased theatre haters and often paranoid civic authorities at face value, it seems safe to assume that property values would deteriorate and other economic indicators would worsen in theatrical environs if the players were truly detrimental to communities. Although citizens in the parish of St. Saviour Southwark—home to four theatres at various times, including the Globe and the Rose—were not the wealthiest in the city, they were certainly not destitute and included many families rated at or above £5. As William Ingram has shown, many of these wealthier citizens lived in the immediate vicinity of the playhouses and chose to stay in these lodgings well after the theatres opened. People affluent enough to reside virtually anyplace in the city elected to live, raise families, and even relocate to dwellings adjacent to playhouses, which suggests that the theatres were not themselves a significant source of urban decay.[3]

Perhaps the most compelling evidence for the immanently tolerable living conditions in theatrical neighborhoods comes from the players, many of whom, despite their wealth earned as sharers in lucrative joint-stock companies, chose to live near their place of employment even after their retirement. Players seem to have preferred to live close to the theatres in which they acted, as witnessed by their tendency to move to new parishes shortly after their troupes migrated to new venues.[4] Like most residents of the capital, actors apparently preferred to avoid having to travel too far to their place of employment.

Theatres were a boon to local finances in several ways, as city fathers had always recognized, at least implicitly. For reasons that probably had more to do with public health and welfare than with a concern for the deterioration of public morality, the lord mayor and his aldermen frequently strove to suppress if not eradicate the theatres. Several municipalities in and around London followed suit and resisted the encroachment of players and playhouses, but again the arguments against them had little to do with the ethical degradation of the community. Citizens claimed instead that discretionary spending on plays was ill advised when the local poor wanted relief. In 1573, when the commercial entertainment industry was in its infancy, the Corporation of the City of London refused an offer to hand over licensing to a certain Holmes, maintaining that the city fathers were exploring options more profitable "to the relief of the poor in the hospitals."[5]

Since 1552, licensing by municipal governments had proved an expedient way of channeling revenues from the rapidly expanding alehouse trade toward poor relief. Both proceeds from the sale of licenses and fines for operating an establishment without a license went toward this cause, partially mitigating the taverns' alleged negative social impact. Regulations on drama followed a similar pattern, stipulating that some of the profits from the public staging of dramatic entertainments must be routed to the indigent. Directives from city authorities, of course, were not as binding in the liberties such as Halliwell and Shoreditch, where the first commercial theatres were built, but this did not mean that the acting companies were free to keep all their profits. In another example of cooperation between levels of government, an unsigned letter of 1587 to Francis Walsingham (then secretary of state) petitioned the Privy Council to intervene with local magistrates and force companies to make regular weekly contributions to the poor in exchange for permission to ply their trade.[6]

While we do not know if Walsingham followed the suggestions of his anonymous correspondent, considerable evidence suggests that conditions for playing in the liberties were stipulated on a local and parochial level. The vestry of St. Saviour Southwark petitioned the Privy Council in 1598 for the closing of the Swan and the Rose, but by 1600 it was content to allow playing if the community could derive material good from it. Churchwardens were ordered to "talk with the players for tithes for their playhouses and money for the poor,"[7] clearing the way for an expansion of theatrical activity in this region with the construction of the Globe and later the Hope.

Other neighborhoods did not bestow their favor so grudgingly. In April of 1600 a loosely organized group of parish authorities and other concerned citizens signing themselves as the "Inhabitants of Finsbury" solicited the Privy Council to permit the construction of the Fortune. Their reasons were threefold. First, they argued that since the site for the projected theatre was so far removed "from any person or place of accompt," no one could legitimately complain that its operations interfered with normal business. Next they adduced the benefits for the community:

> [B]ecause the erectors of the said house are contented to give a very liberal portion of money weekly, towards the relief of our poor, the number and necessity whereof is so great that the same will redound to the continual comfort of the said poor.

Most surprising, though, is the third reason. Contrary to a recent act of Parliament, the justices of Middlesex had not "taken any order, for any supply out of the country" to relieve the parish poor. Because the parish could not meet their needs locally, and higher government bodies were not fulfilling their obligations, the "Inhabitants of Finsbury" were compelled to seek help from the players.[8]

A few years later the adjacent suburb of Clerkenwell also stood to gain from the construction of a local theatre, and the neighborhood would benefit from the Red Bull well after revenues from playing had dried up for other communities following the closing of the theatres in 1642. Just one year before the Restoration would clear the way for renewed legal theatrical performances, Edward Shatterall was bound over for appearance before the Sessions of the Peace for staging illicit "enterludes" at the Red Bull. In his defense, he argued that he had behind him the local government of Clerkenwell, who hired out the theatre for 20s a day to anyone who was willing to risk a theatrical venture and who would furthermore contribute "towards relief of their poor and repairing their highways."[9]

Much earlier, the Red Bull's conversion from an inn into a full-time theatre also appears to have been conditional upon contributions to the neighborhood from the company occupying the playhouse. In the spring of 1605 Martin Slater, an itinerant player who had been selected to assemble a company of players to perform under the patronage of the Duke of Holstein (the brother of Queen Anne), wrote to James I asking him to lift the prohibition on renovations and new building in Clerkenwell so that a permanent house for the company that would eventually become Queen Anne's Men could be completed. In support of this application was a petition giving the "consent of the parish" to the players in exchange for contributions of 20s a month toward poor relief and an astonishing £500 for highway maintenance.[10] Even a much lesser sum for highway repair would have injected a sizable amount of money into the local economy and provided work for many of Clerkenwell's unemployed. More likely than not, the money was spent locally. Road repair is labor intensive, and the area had a ready population for such industry. Work on the highways would build upon a comparative advantage that the neighborhood had enjoyed for centuries as an important transportation hub. Since 1170, St. John Street had been a major packhorse route to the city and to Smithfield market that brought numerous merchants, butchers, and their attendants through Clerkenwell and Finsbury, where they undoubtedly patronized local businesses.

The players could expect in return the loyalty of local residents, especially when their theatrical practice and their repertory drew on a vision of the community that seems tailored to the values of the artisans and apprentices who resided there. While gentrified playgoers complained about the "drum and trumpet" plays common at the Fortune and the Red Bull, many others, including a sizable local population, thronged to the performances, allowing this region northwest of London Wall to supplant Bankside as the city's theatrical center in the early seventeenth century. We sometimes underestimate the importance of this theatrical neighborhood today because the majority of early modern commentators on the theatre (the majority of them well-to-do) attended the Globe and the private theatres and frequently maligned the Red Bull and the Fortune. Because of their unmistakable class bias, this group does not represent anything close to a cross section of London's playgoers, the thousands of daily spectators who kept the theatres afloat.

Although city authorities were not delighted with the construction of purpose-built structures to expand playing, they were lured by the prospects of revenue from it, like investors. The new public theatres were nominally within the city's jurisdiction, which raised the possibility of licensing, and municipal authorities were keen not to miss an opportunity to regulate this growth industry. Enforcing orders requiring theatrical ventures to contribute to poor relief would prove far less troublesome when fees could be levied directly against theatre owners rather than against the innkeepers who rented out their yards for occasional dramatic performances. Magistrates were even more enthusiastic, because the tax revenue generated from the playhouses would be earmarked for local charity and other neighborhood projects.

The municipal government recognized, albeit in a rather grudging and calculating way, that the theatre might enhance social capital. The already significant concessions on the part of acting companies were often duplicated by the philanthropy of individual players. Many, including William Sly, William Shakespeare, Henry Condell, and John Heminge of the King's Men, bequeathed part of their estates to charity. This money was also spent locally, either in parish efforts to assist the less fortunate or to fund hospitals and other institutions in the community. Other theatre people were involved in the distribution of wealth at an administrative level: Philip Henslowe was at various times a churchwarden and overseer of the poor at St. Saviour Southwark; Henry Condell occupied the same posts at St. Mary Aldermanbury; and John Heminges was a sidesman (or usher) at the same parish.[11] Edward Alleyn was especially active in London's charities. In addition to joining Henslowe as overseer of St. Saviour, Alleyn also assisted the poor in St. Botolph's Bishopsgate (the parish where he was born), regularly provided loans to his fellow actors, contributed to the establishment of Chelsea College by Samuel Jeyens in 1610, incorporated the Hospital of the Poor in St. Saviour, and established a row of almshouses in Finsbury (near the Fortune playhouse where he acted). His philanthropy culminated in building and endowing the College of God's Gift in Dulwich in 1613 at the phenomenal cost of £802 7s 9d.

These kinds of building projects were especially conspicuous in the community and of the many charitable activities available to Londoners would offer the most public recognition and acclaim. This would be especially important to actors, eager, perhaps, to rehabilitate their less than immaculate reputations. Henslowe and Alleyn also contributed a total of £35 to a loan to King James in 1616, an advance probably granted without the hope of repayment but with the expectation that the crown would continue to support their theatrical endeavors.[12]

The playhouses also contributed to community formation in less tangible ways. Accurately describing their role in suburban life necessitates not just a consideration of the economics of parishes but a close look at the thorny question of audiences. We at least need to estimate who attended what theatre and why. Like London itself, entertainment was increasingly stratified. Groups of playgoers attended different theatres based partially on location but (related to this and probably most importantly) also on the repertory, dramaturgy, audience composition, and behavior at the different venues. In an effort to stress Shakespeare's popularity among all population segments, many critics have assumed that all of London's theatres were remarkably heterogeneous institutions catering to the full social range from aristocrats to apprentices. We have very little evidence for this claim after the 1590s, however, and the idiosyncratic reputations developed by individual theatres throughout the early seventeenth century suggest that they were becoming more specialized rather than more diverse.[13] These differences go beyond the obvious ones between large, outdoor "public" theatres and their much smaller, enclosed, considerably more exclusive "private" counterparts.

Contemporary allusions to playgoing repeatedly insist that amphitheatre playhouses differed among themselves. These differences encompass the plays performed there: the "musty phrases from the Bull" opposed to more intellectually challenging "pathetique tragedy" at the

Globe. Perhaps most importantly, the amphitheatres differed in the social makeup of the crowds that attended them. Outdoor playhouses ranged from the "infamous" Curtain, "in which no good citizen or gentleman would show his face," to the "fair-filled Globe," popular among gentlemen and law students.[14] Such diversification in the market led to strong reciprocal ties between theatres and audiences. Characteristics of the plays and performances of a single company built a stable audience from a particular social stratum, which further encouraged the company to specialize in the performance of plays of that type. On the one hand, we need to avoid tendentious assumptions that economic status was an indicator of artistic taste and that plays not staged by Shakespeare's company at the Globe were worse because of their socially "inferior" audience. On the other hand, certain groups clearly preferred certain types of plays and adjusted their playgoing habits according to the dramatic fare available at different theatres.

We can therefore identify the rough contours of distinguishable theatrical communities, a market for entertainment varied enough to accommodate diverse tastes that were not always compatible. The theatres in some ways mimicked the division of the city itself into interrelated units, where citizens from different parts of the metropolis disagreed on some matters but nevertheless cohered around shared goals and values. The playhouses took on some characteristics of their local neighborhoods while still drawing a larger pool of spectators based on audience tastes.

The Jacobean playhouses, especially those in the northern suburbs like the Fortune and the Red Bull, were located within growing neighborhoods and uniquely positioned to cater to the demographics of these communities. In contrast, playhouses on the Bankside, lacking a large and stable local market, were probably forced to draw on the more diverse population of the city as a whole. These theatres in Southwark were poised to take advantage of (and probably came to depend on) cross-river traffic to fill their galleries. Hence they were undoubtedly a boon to the shops lining London Bridge and were crucial to the prosperity of ferrymen who transported "such great concourse of people" across the river "by water." Watermen came to rely on the theatre traffic for their livelihood. John Taylor, the "water-poet," asserts in his "Suit against the Players" (ca. 1614) that traffic from playing accounted for "the greater half" of ferrymen's income. "It is an infallible truth," he claims, "that had they [the companies] never played there it had been better for watermen by one half of their living, for the company is increased more than half by their means of playing there in former times."[15]

Though the residents of Southwark no doubt attended local playhouses, the neighborhood's relatively small and transient population meant that the Bankside simply did not have enough potential local playgoers to sustain the daily performances of one troupe, let alone several. Perhaps only in the 1610s and 1620s, as the population of the borough continued to expand, did a second theatre become economically viable, allowing the Hope (built in 1613–1614) to fill this demand for performances in the neighborhood while also generating a stable revenue from bearbaiting. If cross-river traffic was largely sufficient to support an entire industry along with secondary and tertiary businesses, clearly playgoers who traveled across the Thames were spending more than the penny admission for their afternoon recreation. Playgoers willing and able to make the trip across the river were probably better off than those who attended the theatres closer to their homes, whose disposable income quite possibly allowed them only the cost of admission and mandated that they reduce travel time and expense.

By financing the construction of the Rose in 1587, Philip Henslowe first moved the permanent, commercial playgoing industry out of its very narrow geographical confines in Shoreditch. Thus he added demographic complexity to the commercial theatres, changing the way both the producers and the consumers of drama approached these concerns. The prospect of licensing, taxation, and Henslowe's promise to repair the bridges and wharves in St. Saviour parish first attracted Southwark's municipal leaders to the project.[16] What attracted the entrepreneurial Henslowe, however, to locate a playhouse in the neighborhood? At that time, little evidence suggested that London could sustain a third playhouse, especially one separated from the city by the Thames. The Theatre and the Curtain in Halliwell had monopolized the industry for more than a decade even while various inns around the city continued to host regular theatrical performances.

A number of reasons for Henslowe's gamble are possible. Perhaps the most likely is that Henslowe lived in Southwark. His knowledge of the local market would have alerted him to the availability of property fit for development bounded to the south by Maiden Lane and to the west by Rose Alley. On 25 March 1585 Henslowe leased the property for twenty-one years from the parish of St. Mildred, Bread Street, which had the land bequeathed to it by a widower, Thomasyn Symonds.[17] It might strike some as ironic that land on which a theatre was erected was obtained from a parish church. Its willingness to lease land to Henslowe reminds us that only a vocal minority of religious extremists opposed the players. By the same token, Henslowe's actions display some charity by taking control of land that the parish was probably ill equipped to administer (see figure 3). Although it is impossible to know, it is tempting to speculate that his decision to embark on theatrical enterprise was a product of a previous connection with actors, perhaps Alleyn himself. The two might easily have crossed paths in the 1580s, given the extensive and overlapping social and family networks that both families cultivated for generations with nobles in Sussex and beyond.[18]

To operate a permanent successful playhouse in an untried area of the city, Henslowe illustrated the shrewd business acumen he is noted for. He also generated considerable social capital with partners whose financial and other contributions were essential. One was John Cholmley, a grocer, who agreed to a partnership with Henslowe at the Rose that contractually obliged Cholmley to pay £816 in quarterly installments of £25 10s. He was charged with the upkeep of the premises in exchange for half of Henslowe's share of the gallery receipts and the exclusive right to provide theatregoers with food and drink.[19] Because Cholmley's takings from the gallery alone were never likely to recoup his large initial investment, operating a tavern on the property to provision patrons was clearly profitable. Gilbert Rocket, a waterman and Henslowe's neighbor, was another partner. With his company, Rocket petitioned the lord admiral to lift the restraint on playing on the Bankside, arguing that "we your said watermen have had much help and relief for us our poor wives and children" and that "you [the Privy Council] should do a good and charitable deed but also bind us all according to our duties."[20] The watermen claimed that playgoing

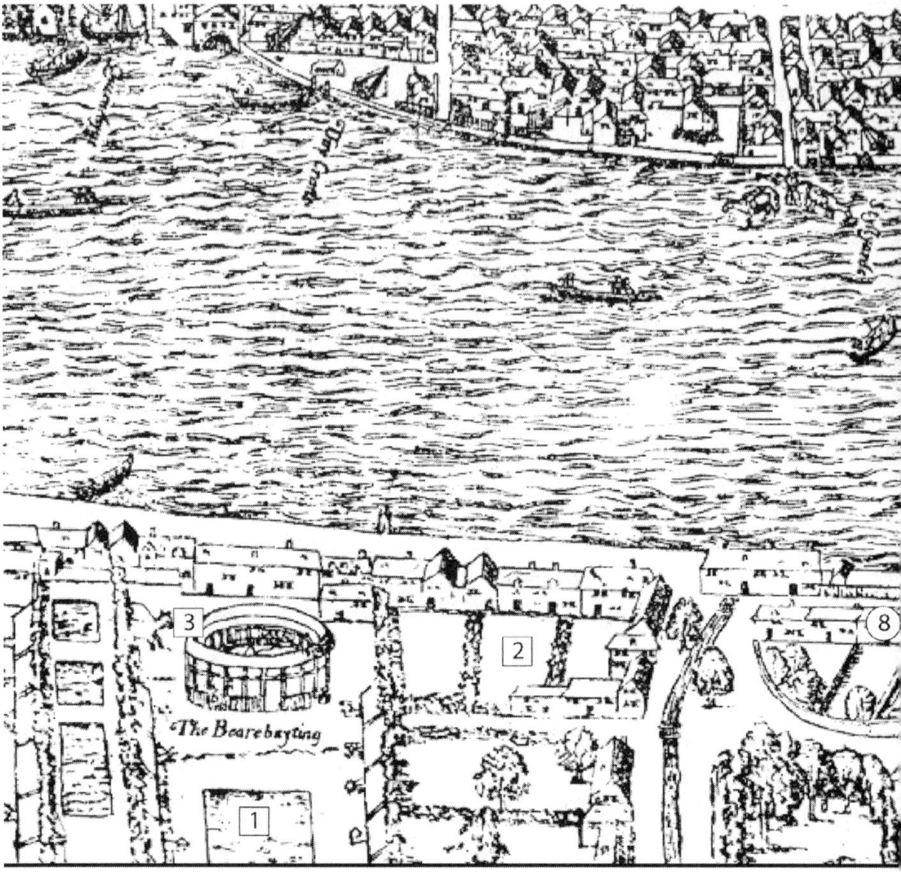

FIGURE 3. Southwark, showing the approximate location of the Globe and the Rose and other sites of local notoriety: 1, Rose; 2, Globe; 3, Hope; 4, St. Olave Southwark; 5, St. Saviour; 6, St. Thomas Hospital; 7, London Bridge; 8, Clink Prison. Detail from Ralph Agas, *Civitas Londinium* (ca. 1570), scanned and corrected by Mike Calder, with locations added by Patrick Collins. Courtesy of Wikipedia Commons.

London bridge
7
4
5
6
Theater
Church
Point of Interest

would serve local interests and forge a more financially stable, less disorderly, and more law-abiding community. John Griggs, the carpenter who built the Rose, also earned Henslowe's trust and respect. Edward Alleyn, who almost certainly heard about Griggs through Henslowe, employed the carpenter to work on his own residence in 1592. Henslowe bound his niece Mary to Griggs's wife as an apprentice in 1595 after the death of Edmond (his brother and Mary's father), preferring to see his family newly come to London from their ancestral home in Surrey locate themselves somewhere in the neighborhood.[21]

Due to the Shakespeare-centric narratives that have dominated much theatre history, Henslowe has received a bad rap. As early as 1845 John Payne Collier claimed that "Henslowe was an ignorant man, even for the time in which he lived, and for the station he occupied."[22] Believing that aesthetics and commerce should not converge, Collier was the first in a line of commentators who looked on Henslowe with derision, as an enemy of the theatre that thrived despite his best efforts to make actors and playwrights subservient to his capital. Norman Nathan even believed that Henslowe was the model for Shakespeare's Shylock.[23] More recent assessments (beginning with Bernard Beckerman's in 1971) suggest that Henslowe was considerably more concerned with the players he employed, neighborhood residents, and local businesses.[24] Beckerman reviews Henslowe's transactions both inside and outside the playhouse without the previous bias against his nontheatrical activities to reveal a fairly typical Elizabethan entrepreneur with myriad business interests whose theatre dealings must be understood in light of his overall career.

As a citizen and dyer, Henslowe, like Burbage before him, would have been intimately familiar with the social and professional mechanisms of the guild system. His career shows a willingness to forge connections both inside and outside his trade. He owned land in the liberty of the Clink (in Southwark) and collected rent on nearly thirty properties, including a tavern, the James's Head, and the Bear Garden that was rebuilt as the Hope Theatre in 1614. As a residential and commercial landlord, Henslowe would have dealt with countless local matters and had considerable personal and financial interest in improving the neighborhood in order to maintain property values and the goodwill of his tenants. This is suggested by the numerous public offices he acquired throughout his career: Groom of the Chamber under Elizabeth, Gentleman Sewer and Master of the Game under James, tax assessor for Southwark, collector for the poor in St. Saviour, and governor of its free grammar school, all offices that merged an interest in local matters with broader civic and national concerns. In the words of S. P. Cerasano, Henslowe was "a valued member of the Elizabethan court," not the shady financial operative that many have described.[25]

Henslowe's extensive dealings in Southwark suggest an alternative interpretation of his decision to locate his theatre project where he did and of the ethical trajectory of his career. Contrary to generations of historians who have seen his business aspirations at odds with his participation in civic projects, we need to understand the continuity between them, how investments in social capital served both private and public interests. Perhaps it was not just Henslowe's familiarity with Southwark and his neighborhood connections that led him to locate his theatre there but a conscious desire to inject revenue into the neighborhood, the possibility of making Bankside a destination for city traffic with money to spend. The Rose would generate revenue for local residents, some of them Henslowe's tenants, and increase property values in the process. Henslowe recognized an important feature of social capital: improving local conditions and providing opportunities for associates and local residents would contribute to his own aspirations.

The same is true of Henslowe's frequent loans to players and other associates, which Frederick Fleay argued were a strategy to maintain financial control "by lending them money and never allowing their debts to be fully paid off."[26] These loans might just as well have amounted to a desire to assist colleagues in need. Henslowe readily accepted the risk of default as a necessary investment in his theatrical business. His success depended not just on the accumulation of a single individual but on the well-being of all, which was especially true of his numerous dealings, financial and otherwise, with his son-in-law, Edward Alleyn. Failing to placate the leading man is the surest way to undermine a production. Henslowe's loans include advances to playwrights for forthcoming plays and advances to his playing companies to buy properties and other equipment necessary to perform them. His money also extracted playwrights and company members from legal trouble; he "lent unto Robert Shaw the 10 of March 1599 to lend William Haughton to release him out of the Clink." Henslowe loaned money to his nephew Francis in June 1595 "to lay down for his half share with the company which he doth play with."[27]

In all of these cases, Henslowe appears to be making a conscientious and collegial effort to benefit his associates, which would certainly further his own interests. His actions seem rather generous and do not indicate the kind of financial bondage that later commentators have accused him of. Most of his loans were interest free and came only with the expectation of repayment within a reasonable time. They occasionally represent considerable sums (as in one loan of £23 to William Bird on 11 July 1601). Taken together, his loans amount to a veritable fortune for the period, suggesting that these theatrical enterprises could never have come to fruition without a creditor of such means.[28] A more altruistic account even of Henslowe's dealings as a pawnbroker is possible when we glance at the period when he operated in this capacity. According to the *Diary*, the height of his activities as a pawnbroker was between mid-1593 and late 1594, during and immediately after the worst of the Elizabethan plagues. Henslowe may have provided an important service to community members facing hard financial times after the pestilence.

The detailed records in Henslowe's *Diary* provide an insight into the Rose (at least from 1594) that is simply not available for other playhouses. Perhaps the most striking feature of its repertory was its diversity. Popular comedies like Robert Greene's *Friar Bacon and Friar Bungay* (ca. 1589) and the anonymous *Knack to Know a Knave* (ca. 1592) featured the antics of William Kempe. But the Rose also featured some of the early history plays of Shakespeare and the legendary Marlovian roles of Edward Alleyn. Attesting to the dramatic range spanned by productions at this venue, the prologue to Marlowe's *Tamburlaine the Great* (1590) promises Rose playgoers that they will witness everything

From the jigging veins of rhyming mother-wits
And such conceits as clownage keeps in pay
We'll lead you to the stately tent of War,
Where you shall hear the Scythian Tamburlaine

Threat'ning the world with high astounding terms
And scourging kingdoms with his conquering sword. (ll. 1–6)

Henslowe also undertook major repairs and alterations to the Rose. In 1592, to prepare for the arrival of the Admiral's Men, he spent £105 to enlarge the playhouse, build a roof over the stage, and erect a shed adjacent to the tiring house.[29] In 1595 he used the break in playing during Lent to overhaul the premises at a cost of £105 19s. And he made numerous smaller repairs over the years. Ensuring that the Rose kept abreast with the latest stage technology, on 4 June 1595 he "paid [£7 2s] for carpenters work & making the throne in the heavens."[30] Henslowe's decision to locate his first theatre project in Bankside and his pattern of expenditures during its fifteen-year history confirm that the Rose expanded the physical boundaries of the stage beyond Shoreditch as well as broadening the intellectual and dramatic horizon of the plays performed. Does this make the Rose a useful model for theatrical practice in general?

The Rose was vitally important for the development of London's commercial theatre industry, demonstrating that theatres could thrive in different parts of the city. Its records are also instructive for the business practices adopted by theatrical professionals. Management and playgoing habits at that theatre, however, are not necessarily indicative of the competitive patterns and spectator allegiances that were to develop in the following decades, when playhouses earned specific reputations and attracted audiences to match. Unlike the triumvirate of the Globe, the Fortune, and the Red Bull that emerged in the next two decades (consistently featuring drama written for and performed by companies patronized by King James, Prince Henry, and Queen Anne, respectively), the Rose, at least until 1594 or 1595, played host to a progression of companies, including the servants of the Lord Admiral, Lord Strange, the Earl of Derby, the Earl of Sussex, the Earl of Worcester, and the queen herself.

This panoply of companies would have prevented the Rose from acquiring a distinct identity based on a specific group of actors or a predictable repertory. These companies were not yet stable units and were frequently formed, disbanded, reconstituted, and merged, migrating from one venue to another. Even if certain troupes acquired specific followings, that reputation could not have been attached to a particular playhouse until later in the 1590s, at the earliest. During this decade the Chamberlain's Men played at the Theatre, the Curtain, the Swan, and Newington Butts, nearly all the available playing places in London. The Admiral's Men were not settled as the permanent tenants of the Rose until 1595, only five years before they would again move to the Fortune.[31]

This is not to say that London's playgoing industry was not yet competitive but that specific venues, as the reliable home to the same companies with relatively little turnover in personnel, were not yet the locus of that competition as they would be in years to come. Commentators from these years, rather than centering on a specific theatre, tend to focus on individuals. In *Pierce Penniless* (1592), Thomas Nashe notes that "not Roscius nor Aesop, those admired tragedians that have lived ever since before Christ was born, could ever perform more in action than famous Ned Alleyn."[32] His gushing praise for Alleyn ignores the supporting cast of the Admiral's Men. By the end of the decade, however, when the Rose had emerged as the permanent London home of the Admiral's Men, the relationship between acting troupes and specific theatres provided a model of practical convenience and profitability that set a standard for the industry, beginning with the Chamberlain's Men.

During the halcyon years of the Rose in the 1590s other theatrical entrepreneurs were drawn to the neighborhood, possibly to emulate Henslowe's success. The first was Francis Langley. Amid the usual protests of the lord mayor against constructing new playhouses, he built the Swan in 1595 or 1596 on the northeast corner of the Paris Garden estate that he had purchased in 1589, several hundred yards west of the Rose and directly across the river from Blackfriars. According to contemporaries, the Swan was the largest and most visually impressive of all the playhouses that had yet appeared in the city. It was occupied by a succession of troupes, most notably the Earl of Pembroke's Men in 1596, who appeared to have poached some of the Admiral's Men for their company.

The Swan venture was short-lived. A Privy Council order of 28 July 1597 forced all playing spaces in London to close for the rest of the summer, quite possibly due to the Pembroke's Men's performance of the apparently seditious *Isle of Dogs* by Thomas Nashe and Ben Jonson.[33] When playing resumed that autumn, the Swan stood empty. Langley was unable to obtain a license for his playhouse, presumably because of the continuing legal troubles surrounding Pembroke's Men. Many of that troupe's members returned to Henslowe and the Rose and never went back to the Swan, despite Langley's threat to sue. Although the theatre remained in existence through the 1630s, it was home to only sporadic playing during that time. We might speculate that the Swan, with several of Langley's other enterprises, failed at least in part because of the ill will against him that had built up in the community. The churchwardens of St. Saviour in Southwark were continually forced to petition Langley for the tithes he owed to the parish; unlike the generous philanthropy of Henslowe, Alleyn, and others involved in the playgoing industry, Langley was singularly recalcitrant in many of his community dealings.[34]

The success of the Rose and, for a time, the Swan was clearly one factor in the decision by James Burbage's sons Cuthbert and Richard to reorganize their company and relocate to Bankside in 1599 (their father had died in 1597). The Burbages had failed to settle on new terms on the lease of the Theatre from its landlord Christopher Allen after years of negotiation, and their current venue, the Curtain, was nearly twenty-five years old and showing its age. The troupe was forced to look beyond Shoreditch for a suitable venue.[35] More has been written about this new venture, the Globe, than about any other London playhouse of the period. Scholars have shown a lingering desire to make the playhouse that Shakespeare wrote for and acted in representative of his age. Although the Globe has become more widely known than other theatres, its immediate association with early modern drama has rendered claims made about it normative for all early modern playhouses.

Though the Globe drew some playgoers from all walks of London society, the Chamberlain's (later the King's) Men may have succeeded in cultivating a more discriminating audience than the other large public amphitheatres, especially by the first decade of the seventeenth century, when the dramatic market became more specialized. By this time the Globe, the Fortune, and the Red Bull (amphitheatres approximately similar in size) had become the regular home of the servants of the king, prince, and queen, respectively. James Wright claims that "the last two were mostly frequented by citizens, and the meaner sort of people," hinting at a somewhat different theatrical environment at the Globe, the only theatre in continuous use on the Bankside for nearly fifteen years from the turn of the century.[36]

We might surmise the unique nature of the Globe and its audience based on the interplay of two basic factors: its location and its repertory. Despite the long-standing myth of the heterogeneity of Shakespeare's audience and his theatre's affordability and accessibility to all Londoners, the Globe was probably not all that convenient for those in the northern wards of the city and its suburbs. Because of its location across the river, traveling to the Globe across London Bridge would have been a significant walk for the average citizen, about a mile and a half from St. Paul's, two miles from Finsbury, and two and a half miles from Clerkenwell, along some of the most crowded thoroughfares in the realm. Playgoers taking time off from work to see a play would be forced to consider this time and distance when determining which playhouse to attend. The long and unpleasant journey might have seemed manageable when playing on the Bankside was the only show in town; but with the opening of the Fortune and the Red Bull early in the seventeenth century, it could well be viewed as too great a sacrifice. Traveling by water, while considerably cutting down on both time and distance, would have represented an extra expense for those for whom the price of admission was something of a luxury.

Those who had the time and the means to make the regular journey across the Thames were rewarded with the drama of Shakespeare, Jonson, and others. Globe plays tended to stimulate audiences at a more abstract level, often deliberately eschewing the sonorous battle scenes, hyperbolic rhetoric, and slapstick humor expected by "vulgar" audiences at other theatres. Hamlet famously elaborates on how the vast majority of city audiences cannot appreciate "good" theatre. He realizes sadly that more subtle, intellectually engaging productions are "caviary to the general" (2.2.397). John Heath notes that playgoers at the Globe approached the performance with a "judicious eye" as opposed to those at the Fortune and the Curtain.[37] Ben Jonson's plays especially, though not always as popular with audiences at the Globe as their author would have liked, presuppose a level of literacy and learning that repudiates the myth of the heterogeneous audience. His plays require a considerable degree of "application," the capacity swiftly to discern and intuit a variety of topical allusions. Gallants, courtiers, and Inns of Court students could readily apprehend and take pleasure in these references, while the lower orders of society were unlikely to grasp them.[38]

Jonson's claim that most playgoers sought what pleased the eye rather than the ear implies that most audiences were not up for intellectual refinement while suggesting that the audiences he wrote for were more talented and experienced listeners. Not surprisingly, Jonson frequently wrote for the King's Men at the Globe but never for the Fortune or the Red Bull, even though he did occasionally write for Henslowe at the Hope. John Webster, like Jonson, fancied his plays more suited to an educated audience. After complaining about the "ignorant asses" in attendance at the Red Bull, who were apparently less than enthusiastic about *The White Devil* in 1612, he sold his next work, *The Duchess of Malfi* (1614), to the King's Men.[39] Webster thought that his plays would be received more favorably at the Globe and at the Blackfriars.

The precise circumstances under which Will Kempe, known internationally for his jigs and improvised clowning, left the Lord Chamberlain's Men in 1599 are unclear. Robert Armin, a much more pensive and cerebral clown, soon replaced him.[40] David Wiles argues that Shakespeare's company no longer had any use for Kempe's onstage antics, his trademark farce, or his traditional and improvisational approach to comic acting. The troupe members began to position themselves as the providers of more literarily satisfying plays driven by plot and character, substituting greater authorial control for individual showmanship. The theoretical framework for this argument is the familiar opposition between the carnivalesque misrule embodied by Kempe and the order and rational control over the playscript wielded by Shakespeare, Jonson, and other playwrights.[41]

Wiles's conclusions are more persuasive when read in the less politicized context of the competitive positioning of theatrical companies around the turn of the century and their increasing tendency to seek out more specialized niche markets. In seeking to integrate even their comedy with a marketing strategy designed for a more sophisticated clientele, the Chamberlain's Men arrived at a formula suited to the talents of their leading actor (Burbage) and their leading playwright that left little scope for Kempe and his antics. Kempe next appears on the public stage with the Worcester's Men (a precursor to Queen Anne's) at the Curtain, where his traditional approach to the clown's role was more appreciated. The timing of Kempe's departure, immediately after the Chamberlain's Men moved to the Globe, suggests that the new playhouse gradually attained a reputation that differed from that of its predecessors and its competitors because of the emerging artistic aspirations of its tenants. The theatre was not built with the *intention* to showcase more sophisticated dramatic material and upstage its neighbors at the Rose. The desire of the members of the Chamberlain's company to enhance their status and that of their audience may have been a strategic goal for a few years, a move first signaled in their aborted attempt to acquire a private theatre at Blackfriars in 1596.

Changes in the staging practices of Shakespeare's company also signal a move away from its own previous practices and those of its competitors. Andrew Gurr notes that the convention of performing a jig to end the day's performance gradually dwindled at the Globe (perhaps due to the departure of Will Kempe) and died out entirely around 1612, possibly as early as 1601. By the 1620s the prologue to Thomas Goffe's *The Careless Shepherdess* notes: "I'll go to th'Bull or Fortune and there see / A play for two pence and a jig to boot" (B4v), suggesting that jigs were alive and well on the London stage but only at the theatres he mentions. Gurr speculates that the often bawdy and overtly satirical subject matter of these jigs, which Wiles has labeled "a form of soft commercial pornography," was incongruous with the more sophisticated subject matter of the plays that the King's Men performed, especially the subtle tragedies and romances of Shakespeare and Fletcher.[42]

Due to an ensemble of financial, legal, and artistic decisions over a few years, the Globe may have attained a certain degree of "authority" as a destination for wealthier and more educated Londoners from across the river.[43] Ann Jennalie Cook claims that after 1603 leisured or "privileged" playgoers sought to attend the same dramatic performances witnessed by the nobility at occasional court performances by flocking to the Globe to see the troupe patronized by James I himself.[44] Rather than describing the playgoers at the Globe, she extends this argument to characterize audiences at all theatres. Martin Butler has suggested that this claim is implausible, given so much evidence indicating that theatre audiences were anything but privileged.[45] London and its environs simply did not contain sufficient numbers of "privileged" individuals to generate the phenomenal number of daily visits needed to sustain such a large-scale theatrical industry. Cook's conjecture might apply to some playgoers; if so, the audience at the Globe would seem closer to her description than spectators at the Fortune and the Red Bull. The range of plays staged at the Globe coupled with the versatility of Shakespeare's plays in performance meant that the Chamberlain's Men could still appeal to a fairly large segment of the population even as they positioned themselves at the artistic vanguard of London's theatre industry.

Assuming that playing was fundamentally an aesthetic practice whereby theatrical professionals vied with one another to improve their status and reputation in polite society, Alvin Kernan argues Cook's point from the standpoint of supply. He claims that playwrights (especially Shakespeare) composed plays with the court and leisured gentlemen in mind. Public playing was a mere dress rehearsal for transacting more serious ideological business at Whitehall or Hampton Court. Kernan contends that the company's frequent attendance at court and presumed connection to the royal family imply that His Majesty's Servants sought to cultivate the kind of courtly audience at the Globe that they entertained in the presence of the king. Providing edifying entertainment for the broader London community was at best a secondary concern.[46]

We know that many of London's notables and notable visitors, including Thomas Platter (1599), the ambassadors of Florence, Venice, and France (1607?), Prince Frederick of Württemberg (1610), Sir Thomas Lake (1624), and the Duke of Buckingham (1628), attended and apparently preferred the Globe. Thus it is conceivable that more pompous and upwardly mobile audiences frequented performances of the King's Men, as they did those of the boy companies. They perhaps believed that attending these playhouses conferred some kind of social status or entrée into gentlemanly society. During the years

1600 to 1610, when the dramatic marketplace was undergoing crucial changes, only five true members of the gentry are positively known to have attended the playhouses; all of them went to either the Globe or Blackfriars. Even the slim records we possess trace a believable pattern whereby most playgoers of any repute attended the Globe (and the private theatres), significantly fewer went to the Fortune, and almost none ventured to the Red Bull.[47]

Despite a smattering of inconclusive yet intriguing evidence, it is ultimately difficult to tell how much the practice of the King's Men at the Globe differed from that of other companies, how significant these differences are in marking a unique direction for that company, or how views like this are clouded by a lingering desire to elevate the status of Shakespeare and his colleagues above the commercial playgoing industry as a whole. Yet even if Shakespeare's company was aesthetically and socially a notch above the other public theatre companies, it does not follow that this troupe and its audience were representative of the theatrical trade as a whole. Shakespeare's troupe emerges as the best from the perspective of later commentators because it achieved a theatrical target that other companies were not aiming for. Understandably, this has proved nearly impossible for modern readers to grasp, because our experience with this drama is almost always through reading it as a literary text. By positing a model audience of "gentlemen" of varying degrees, Cook, Kernan, and others render the theatrical field more uniform than it actually was, obscure local differences in audience composition, and fail to account for the obvious cultural stratification suggested by the plays themselves and repeated by so many early playgoers. The King's Men were able to sustain their business on audiences drawn from all over the metropolis, but this does not imply that all troupes would, could, or indeed wished to follow a similar business model. In fact, Andrew Gurr convincingly argues that the Admiral's Men were successful by doing exactly the opposite of their rivals.[48]

Productions at the Globe certainly resonated with the community and sought to transact social capital, but it was a community that lacked some of the local inflections at other playhouses. Shakespeare's nonhistorical plays (with the exception of *The Merry Wives of Windsor*) are potentially instructive in this regard, because they are set in foreign and often exotic locales. Dramatists like Dekker, Heywood, and Middleton, by contrast, often set their plays in particular London neighborhoods, making the drama intimately familiar to audiences. The marketing strategy pursued by the King's Men at the Globe was certainly not the only way to build a stable base for commercial entertainment, as Henslowe, whose moves seem motivated by strategic calculation rather than by logistical necessity, seemed to grasp. By playing in the northern suburbs, acting companies—wittingly or not—had identified and occupied specific niches in the market for cultural goods that ensured their economic survival and were to prove a new and exciting institution in these neighborhoods. The actors capitalized on the social patterns of a large, vocal, and influential group of playgoers. These troupes situated their dramatic offerings within the cultural traditions and the socioeconomic demographic of particular communities. What were the tenets of such a business model? And how can we perceive the demand for drama in geographical terms?

The Fortune and the Red Bull, simply by virtue of their location, were more accessible to artisans and their apprentices regardless of where they lived in London, eliminating the need to cross the river. Many artisans had shops either in these suburbs or in the northern wards of the city and could attend a performance with a relatively minimal absence from work, spared the time and expense of traveling to Bankside. Walking from one end of the city to the other along tangled, crowded, and often poorly maintained streets was arduous and time consuming, requiring people to traverse numerous physical and social obstacles along the way. Londoners, who tended to circulate locally, crossed these barriers only with some trepidation.[49] The practical desire to attend a local theatre gradually became force of habit. Playing companies were not attracted to specific liberties because they provided anonymous sites for license, subversive political statement, or the dissemination of any particular ideology.[50] Instead they sought to draw upon a large population inclined to seek entertainment locally, within easy reach of their homes and businesses. These playgoers might have been uncomfortable in venues that were farther afield, in parts of the city with which they were unfamiliar (see figure 4).

Even if Southwark had garnered a reputation in certain quarters for

- Theater
- Church
- Point of Interest

FIGURE 4. Northwest London and its suburbs, showing the approximate location of the Fortune and the Red Bull along with the parish churches, company halls, and notable sites in the surrounding neighborhood: 1, Fortune; 2, Red Bull; 3, St. Andrew Holborn; 4, St. James Clerkenwell; 5, Priory of St. John's of Jerusalem; 6, St. Sepulchre; 7, St. Bartholomew the Great; 8, St. Bartholomew the Less; 9, St. Botolph's Aldersgate; 10, St. Giles Cripplegate; 11, St. Mary Staining; 12, St. John Zachary; 13, St. Anne and St. Agnes; 14, St. Martin's le Grande; 15, St. Alphgale; 16, St. Mary Adermanbury; 17, St. Alban Wood St.; 18, St. Michael Wood St.; 19, Christchurch; 20, Barbers' Hall; 21, Bowyers' Hall; 22, Curriers' Hall; 23, Plasterers' Hall; 24, Brewers' Hall; 25, Haberdashers' Hall; 26, Wax-Chandlers' Hall; 27, Embroiderers' Hall; 28, Goldsmiths' Hall; 29, Butchers' Hall; 30, Cooks' Hall; 31, Smithfield; 32, Charterhouse; 33, Cripplegate; 34, Aldersgate; 35, Newgate; 36, Christ's Hospital; 37, Counter. Detail from Ralph Agas, *Civitas Londinium* (ca. 1570), scanned and corrected by Mike Calder with locations added by Patrick Collins. Courtesy of Wikipedia Commons.

relaxed morality and greater festivity—a dubious proposition, given numerous attempts by municipal leaders to bring that neighborhood in line with the rest of the city—modern accounts of theatrical activity there do not necessarily delineate the situation at the theatres north of the city. The Fortune and the Red Bull were situated in viable communities where playgoers and players actually resided and formed meaningful social bonds.[51] For residents in and around these neighborhoods, the theatre was not necessarily a destination to travel to but a local institution that provided on a larger scale the same kind of reprieve as a local tavern or bowling alley. Clerkenwell and Finsbury quickly became a competing center for public entertainment in London, partially due to the emergence of a large local audience for plays in this rapidly growing region northwest of the wall.

We know very little about individual playgoers, especially those of a lower social status. But nearly all of those few named as having attended the Fortune or the Red Bull were artisans or apprentices, and many lived within a very short distance of the theatre. On 28 February 1611, for instance, three playgoers are mentioned in the Middlesex County Records for "causing tumults and outrages at the Fortune." John Shaw, a butcher, lived in Grub Street (about 300 yards from the playhouse); another butcher, John Lynsey, was a parishioner at St. Andrew Undershaft, just to the east within the city; and Gilbert Borne lived on Whitecross Street, mere steps from the Fortune. Edward Brin, John Fryne, Thomas Williams, Alex Fulsis, Edward Purfet (all feltmakers), William Tedcastle (yeoman), and John Gill (an unspecified apprentice) were involved in a similar scuffle at the Red Bull. The feltmaker's trade, along with a number of other components of the cloth-working industry, was centered on Aldersgate, a short walk from that playhouse via Farringdon Road and Newgate Street.[52]

The remarkable growth of London in the late sixteenth and early seventeenth centuries was even greater in the suburbs, where the growth rate outpaced that of central London by about 15 percent.[53] Seeking to alleviate overcrowding, the spread of contagious disease, and the ghettoization that coincides with periods of rapid population growth, authorities urged Londoners to disperse themselves throughout the city and suburbs.[54] Although many of the newcomers were unemployed, at times hampering local parishes' ability to provide adequate alms, the prospects of finding a job were higher in London than elsewhere in the nation and higher in the suburbs than anywhere in London.[55] Londoners of all sorts trumpeted the commercial success and comparative advantage achieved through greater population density in the growing metropolis; Stow, for one, claimed that "London is a mighty arm and instrument to bring any great desire to effect."[56] He recognized that London's current status both in England and abroad would have been impossible without rapid growth and the construction necessary to accommodate it, even if he sometimes waxed nostalgic for simpler times.

Growth in the northern suburbs meant a steady influx of potential playgoers. Many of the newcomers were young men and women in their late teens and early twenties seeking career opportunities as artisans, unburdened by family obligations and banned from marrying during the term of their apprenticeship. Naturally, they sought frequent and affordable entertainment in the neighborhoods in which they lived. Easily identified by their woolen caps, apprentices represented a significant and vocal social group, accounting for at least 10 percent and probably as much as 17 percent of the city's population during the late sixteenth and early seventeenth centuries.[57] Although they were sometimes the perpetrators of mob behavior and other forms of civil unrest, these young people were hardly a formidable threat to stability. While some, like the pamphleteer Samuel Rowlands, condemned their conduct on the streets of the city, claiming that a "certain band of Ragamuffin Prentices about the town . . . will abuse any upon the smallest occasion," other observers lauded the "exemplary practice (in general) used among London Prentices which might worthily be wished that it were in some record drawn into custom in all Christians."[58] After their seven-year apprenticeship, with prospects for gainful employment secure, these young people who occasionally displayed rebellious tendencies became established, upstanding, and conscientious members of their communities and, even more importantly, the largest group of consumers in London. The playgoing habits developed in their adolescence made them a hedge for future theatrical profits.

We cannot overestimate the importance of this large and constantly replenished collection of apprentices in fueling the expansion of the entertainment industry in early modern London. Despite controversy over the real ability of apprentices to fill the coffers of various public entertainment concerns, documentary evidence confirms that this group did attend the theatres, often in large numbers. Attending a performance at one of the amphitheatres cost two pence for a seat in the galleries or only a penny if the playgoer did not mind standing in the yard, a price that only excluded the poorest of Londoners with absolutely no income and little chance of obtaining one. Most apprentices had at least some spending money, especially in the later stages of their seven-year terms when they enjoyed more responsibility and the trust of their masters and were often rewarded with some kind of unofficial wage. Apprentices' highly visible presence in the yards of London's amphitheatres suggests that the playhouses and their offerings were much more than a pastime: they served as a place of resort, a cultural service to be enjoyed collectively.[59] Apprentices were a highly conspicuous group representing an important pocket of social capital, whose cumulative influence was formidable. As frequent consumers of entertainment and vocal commentators on popular culture, they could significantly influence both the commercial health and the social reputation of a given theatrical endeavor. Perhaps to solidify the Red Bull's reputation as the playhouse most favored by apprentices, Heywood wrote a play lionizing them. *The Four Prentices of London* (1615) not only displays astonishing feats of heroism by apprentices but is also dedicated to those "brave spirited prentices . . . [who] have their courage and forwardness, their noble fates and fortunes."[60]

Most apprentices favored the Fortune and later the Red Bull, playhouses in the northern suburbs located closer to the places where they lived and worked. The Fortune, at the intersection of Golding Lane and Whitecross Street in Finsbury, was positioned to draw citizens and apprentices from these rapidly expanding suburbs and the city just to the south. The playhouse was also easily accessible to residents of Westminster and other points west along one of two major thoroughfares, Holborn and the Strand. Competition, cultural differentiation, and the reciprocal engagement between the theatre and its community were all clearly important considerations for Edward Alleyn when he first conceived the project during his brief retirement from

1597 to 1600, settled on terms to lease suitable land on 22 December 1599, negotiated with local authorities for permission to play in the neighborhood, and drew up plans for the new playhouse. The Admiral's Men's decision to relocate from the Rose has generated significant debate. Their move north has spawned two basic narratives that have little to do with the theatre's location and are instead based on assumptions about competition with Shakespeare and the Chamberlain's Men, who had moved to the brand new Globe a year earlier. The current venue of the Admiral's Men, the Rose, had been in constant use for nearly fifteen years and was increasingly in a state of "dangerous decay"—it would most certainly pale next to the Globe, just a stone's throw away on Maid Lane.[61]

One long-standing hypothesis suggests that the Admiral's Men's move to the Fortune was predicated on the need to diffuse the relentless competition from rivals at the Globe to whom they would ultimately succumb. Theatre historians beginning with Edmond Malone have argued that the company must have viewed the Globe as the superior venue because the indenture of Peter Street, the contractor hired to build the Fortune, instructs the carpenter to emulate the Globe no less than four times.[62] Competition with Shakespeare's company posed such a threat to their future prospects that the Admiral's Men were compelled to move to the other side of the city less than half a year after the Globe was completed. Their new building, the Fortune, was modeled on their competitor's theatre in nearly every respect. This narrative sounded plausible enough to theatre historians for generations who shared the assumption that Shakespeare's company was preeminent and that rivals could only hope to emulate their success somewhere else, not compete with them on their own turf.

Two important pieces of evidence call this thesis into question. First, the decision to commission Peter Street to build the Fortune was probably not a direct result of his work on the Globe but evolved over time. As early as 13 December 1599, about a month before the contract to build the Fortune, Henslowe "paid for building of my house upon the bankside . . . with Mr. Street carpenter." Alleyn chose Street because he had acquitted himself admirably in previous work for Henslowe, in addition to his work on the Globe.[63] Rather than making a desperate attempt to keep pace with their rivals, Alleyn and

Henslowe made their own careful consideration of Street's abilities and assessment of the Globe. The Globe had been completed some months earlier, so the Admiral's Men could have begun work on the new playhouse much earlier if they were so desperate and probably would not have invested in any repairs on the Rose at that time. Second, the receipts recorded by Henslowe during the 1599–1600 playing season at the Rose show no significant decline from previous years. If the opening of the Globe did have an impact on the Admiral's Men, it was not as immediate as some have suggested and actually continued a reduction in income that started some years earlier.[64] Andrew Gurr argues that the Admiral's Men's move to the Fortune was part of a larger competitive strategy that had begun much earlier with the emergence of the duopoly around 1595—they were not capitulating to the Chamberlain's Men but solidifying their rivalry.[65]

S. P. Cerasano and Roslyn Knutson, seeking to revise this Shakespeare-centered account, lend greater weight to Henslowe's own claim that the Rose had fallen into disrepair. Any savvy theatre owner would realize that the venue needed to be replaced or at least extensively remodeled.[66] Far from finding the competition from Shakespeare and the Chamberlain's Men stifling, they claim, two adjacent playhouses might in fact reap the benefits of "cluster marketing," the ability of both theatres to capitalize on a massive influx of playgoers traveling daily across the river seeking entertainment.[67] The move north might not have been the best financial decision, because healthy competition between the two playhouses might have benefited both. Due to the planning, financing, and permissions necessary to build a new playhouse, it is likely that the decision to move to Finsbury was made much earlier, probably during Edward Alleyn's retirement and potentially as early as 1597.[68] Building a theatre was certainly a capital-intensive enterprise; but this money, once raised, could be allocated to any site. Neither the contract with Street nor negotiations with local authorities began until January 1599/1600.

Both of these accounts posit theatrical enterprise as a closed system, a set of internal financial and artistic relationships dictating decisions that were relatively impervious to the larger social dynamics of city life. Given that the majority of Londoners identified themselves with particular regions of the city, traveled infrequently to different neighborhoods, and organized themselves into discrete social and cultural units, the Admiral's Men's move to the Fortune seems a natural response to local market conditions. The Fortune was located in the parish of St. Giles Cripplegate, just outside of the city walls. As its name implies, Cripplegate had a reputation for poverty and was relatively underdeveloped when the Fortune was built in 1600, allowing Alleyn to lease the plot of land where the theatre would be built for a mere £12 per year. Neighboring parishes in Aldersgate and Bishopsgate were significantly more affluent, however, and the region as a whole contained a large—and growing—number of potential playgoers.[69] Building the Fortune in Cripplegate was a way of reaching an expanding market in one of the fastest-growing regions of London rather than a concession to competitive pressure exerted by its rivals. Just as the Globe became the newest and most technically advanced playhouse on the Bankside, so the Fortune would immediately gain preeminence in the north, where the Curtain (nearly twenty-five years old) would pale in comparison.

In the move to the Fortune, Henslowe and Alleyn relied on the social capital that they had accumulated in Southwark and in their other endeavors throughout the city. The partners were involved in a number of lucrative enterprises that ranged from bearbaiting and playing to real estate. They also maintained an important place in various branches of the civil service, making both men known in a number of social and business circles.[70] The implementation of any new playhouse project required extensive negotiations involving the players, municipal leaders, and local residents and necessitating concessions on all sides. In this case, however, the negotiations went fairly quickly. Alleyn first seems to have been able to capitalize on his connection with the lord admiral, Charles Howard, now Earl of Nottingham, who defended the proposed playhouse in a warrant dated 12 January 1599/1600 on the grounds that

> my servant Edward Alleyn . . . in respect of the acceptable service, which my said servant and his company have done and presented before her Highness to her great liking and contentment; as well

> this last Christmas as at sundry other times is graciously moved towards them [the Admiral's servants] with a special regard of favor in their proceedings.

Howard entreated local magistrates and justices of the peace in Middlesex (over whom he had considerable influence as a commissioner for the peace of both Middlesex and Surrey) "to permit and suffer my said servant to proceed in the effecting and finishing of the said new house, without any let or molestation towards him or any of his workmen." He also recognized that Finsbury was an optimal location for the theatre for the same reasons that Henslowe and his company of players were drawn to the neighborhood: it was "very fit and convenient of the building" and the regular "resort of people."[71]

Apparently Nottingham's letter was not enough. Two months later (on 9 March) the Privy Council upheld an injunction to stop construction initiated by Lord Willoughby on behalf of the parishioners of St. Giles without Cripplegate. Willoughby's appeal cited the usual reasons: the theatre could lead to social unrest and "breed increase of base and lewd people and diverse other disorders." Eventual clearance to complete the project came not from the Privy Council overriding the wishes of local magistrates, as was ordinarily the case, but from local residents themselves. Twenty-seven signatories representing "the inhabitants of Finsbury" petitioned the Privy Council to overturn the injunction, noting that the influx of the players would assist with poor relief and that the new playhouse would not amount to a net increase in theatergoing because the Fortune would be replacing the Rose.[72]

Although the assistance of the players would certainly augment poor relief, as it had in other neighborhoods where playhouses were erected, it is difficult to believe that this was the sole reason for their petition. Perhaps residents came to believe that the playhouse would be a boon to the local economy. The Fortune would provide opportunities for services in the neighborhood, not to mention a ready source of recreation for the growing mass of local residents—just as Henslowe's previous project, the Rose, had proven profitable to residents and businesses of Southwark for more than a decade. The presence of a local theatre might generate a level of prosperity in the community that would lessen its reliance on charity. Convincing the local population of the benefits of the new theatre might have been easier for Alleyn. The actor was raised in St. Giles Cripplegate, a local boy made good, and had been a benefactor of the parish for many years before the Fortune was even conceived.[73] The Privy Council acceded to local demands and overturned its previous injunction a month later, on 9 April 1600.

A song at the beginning of Dekker's *The Pleasant Comedy of Old Fortunatus* (1600), almost certainly the first play staged at the new playhouse, perhaps speaks to the hopes for the Fortune of both local residents and the Admiral's Men:

> Fortune smiles, cry holiday, . . .
> With our song let heaven resound,
> Fortune's hands our heads have crowned
> Let us sing merrily, merrily, merrily.[74]

The opening of the Fortune brought recreation and "holiday" in the form of regular playing to Finsbury. But it is possible also to detect in this song the desire and the expectation that the theatre might bring greater material benefit, a literal "fortune," to the community.

In the same play the Admiral's Men seem to signal a departure from playgoing on the Bankside, acknowledging that their move north afforded unique challenges and a different set of opportunities. Outdoing the Chamberlain's Men would require not just an outstanding repertory but the loyalty of audiences:

> Behold you not this Globe, this golden bowl,
> This toy called world at our imperial feet?
> This world is Fortune's ball wherewith she sports,
> Sometimes I strike it up into the air,
> And then create I emperors and kings . . .
> Circled about with wonder of all eyes,
> The shouts of every tongue, love of all hearts. (A4v)

Fortunatus promises to regale audiences with "emperors and kings" while the Chamberlain's Men, in their "wooden O," could muster only princes and monarchs. Rather than understanding the Admiral's

Men's move as the result of competitive pressure from the Chamberlain's Men when they occupied the Globe a year earlier, it is perhaps best to think of the building of the Fortune as the beginning of a competitive arrangement that would obtain for the next two decades. The crown had begun to limit the number of theatrical companies allowed to play in London, an order that would continue in various forms into the reign of James. The differences in the acting style and repertory of the two troupes were now mirrored in the physical location of their playhouses, at opposite ends of the city.

The Admiral's Men's move to the Fortune capitalized on a growing local demand for theatrical entertainment. The Fortune also became a popular destination for artisans and apprentices from other neighborhoods seeking "lowbrow" yet edifying dramatic productions. In addition to the rapidly growing market in the northwest suburbs, the Fortune was poised to cater to theatregoers in Cripplegate, Aldersgate, Farringdon, and other wards immediately within the city walls, greatly reducing what would be a lengthy journey first across town and then across the river by bridge or ferry. These wards, though not as affluent as some in London, were highly populated by a diverse assortment of artisans and apprentices, merchants, civil servants, and religious figures (including John Foxe). The vibrant economies of these neighborhoods, which contained many shops and businesses, meant that they were spared the devastatingly high unemployment and penury that was beginning to distinguish London's worst regions to the south and east.[75]

The numerous company halls (no less than seven—the Haberdashers, Pinners, Plasterers, Brewers, Curriers, Wax-Chandlers, and Bowyers—were located in Cripplegate) attest to the thriving industry in these wards and the close proximity of persons eager and able to pay regularly for an afternoon's recreation at the playhouse.[76] Records also indicate that residents of Cripplegate, both within and without the walls, though residing in modest dwellings, sought to forestall the urban decay that had ravaged other neighborhoods in the growing metropolis. With an eye to increasing property values, landlords took pains to ensure that their holdings were kept in good repair, even upgraded, by their tenants. In October 1615 one Joanna Turner initiated a proceeding in Chancery against her tenant, Robert Smith, not for defaulting on the rent but for failing to "sufficiently maintain and repair" the adjoining "orchard yard" in Golding Lane (just down the street from the Fortune). Neighborly conduct and home improvement were important in the community even though some still lacked either the desire or the means to subscribe to these shared values.[77]

The parish of St. Giles Cripplegate encompassed areas both within and without the walls, lending it both urban and suburban qualities. It contained a collection of venerated edifices like "one fair house" on Whitecross Street built by Henry V, more modest dwellings recently built during the period of more rapid expansion, and a number of almshouses, which indicate that Cripplegate was not one of the city's more affluent regions.[78] The multiplicity of residents in the surrounding communities was mirrored somewhat in the Fortune's audience and reflected in the theatre's eclectic repertory, which ran the gambit from citizen favorites like Dekker's *Shoemaker's Holiday* (1600) to Samuel Rowley's intricate history of Henry VIII: *When You See Me You Know Me* (1605).

Only a few years after the Admiral's Men (who became known as Prince Henry's Men after 1603) first began staging plays at the Fortune, another large amphitheatre opened in Clerkenwell, just to the northwest. This theatre, the Red Bull, has become more notorious than any other playhouse after the early 1600s, largely because of the number of apprentices that frequented it and the popular drama that it staged. Home to a succession of playing companies beginning with Queen Anne's Men, the Red Bull (which opened around 1606 or 1607) operated to the mutual benefit of citizens and theatrical professionals well into the Restoration—even during the interregnum, when plays were ostensibly banned. The players provided Clerkenwell residents assistance in financing their poor relief and capital to repair highways and support other local improvements. More importantly, the citizens of Clerkenwell and those who ventured to the neighborhood for afternoon performances were entertained by the kinds of bombastic plays they enjoyed most.[79] The Red Bull, which has not been scrutinized by scholars to the same degree as many of London's other playhouses, provides an especially vivid and instructive example of the interaction between a local community and the theatre that allows us to examine the reciprocal relationships and obligations of playgoers, players, and neighborhood residents.

The first years of the seventeenth century saw Worcester's Men (the precursor to Queen Anne's Men) playing variously at the Rose, the Curtain, and the Boar's Head, all considerably inferior venues compared to the newly built Globe and Fortune. Because of their financial constraints around this time, after a long theatre closure from March 1603 to April 1604, the company could ill afford to finance an entirely new structure. In 1604 members of the troupe and other investors in the project eventually obtained favorable terms on the lease of what was apparently a decrepit inn-yard that had fallen into disuse on the upper end of St. John Street adjacent to Clerkenwell Green. The inn was located on property that belonged to the Seckford Estate, obtained by the family during the dissolution of the monasteries in the reign of Henry VIII. The current administrator of this estate, one Henry Seckford, was at this time Master of the Tents, a post closely related to the Revels Office. That probably made him more amenable to the construction of a playhouse on his property, especially given the proceeds that would accrue to the neighborhood and to him personally.[80] One of his lessees, the actor Martin Slater, apparently claimed joint tenure on a lease of this property with a non-playing investor, Aaron Holland, and petitioned the Privy Council in June 1605 to renovate the inn into a playhouse. Holland claimed that he had "altered some stables and other rooms . . . to turn them into galleries."[81] The council had previously denied this request but overturned its previous decision in response to Slater's letter.[82]

With the legal impediments temporarily circumvented due to the actors' promise to contribute to poor relief and highway repair, the investors, led by Holland, emulated a variant of the joint-stock sharer system employed successfully by the King's Men at the Globe six years earlier to finance their new venture. Holland's instrument for financing the theatre consisted of eighteen shares of £25 each, which entitled investors to a proportionate share of the proceeds from the galleries (usually allotted to the owners), a scheme that would have raised £450.[83] The sum for converting the Red Bull to a full-time theatre was not significantly less than the cost of building the Globe (£700) and the Fortune (£520) from scratch, suggesting that the venue was probably just as well appointed as its competitors. The residence of Queen Anne's Men at this playhouse was to forge numerous reciprocal bonds between the players and their community and allowed for the emergence of a specific type of urban playgoer for whom plays were communal entertainment to be consumed en masse rather than an artistic form to be contemplated privately.

Located northwest of London Wall, along a heavily traveled thoroughfare leading out of the city, Clerkenwell was in some ways very typical of London's growing fringe; but its rich ecclesiastical history, many opulent buildings, and venerable traditions also lent it the flavor of a well-established city neighborhood. Clerkenwell was not immune to the ravages of poverty, and St. James was certainly not one of London's wealthier parishes but was not destitute. Modest new businesses and trades flourished there, demanding a force of both skilled and unskilled labor earning low but sustaining wages.[84] The butcher's trade, centered in nearby Smithfield market, ensured a stable demand for labor and supported several secondary and tertiary businesses. The Red Bull's name testifies to the prominence of this local industry.

The neighborhood seems to have been spared the worst of the penury, perhaps owing to the unique circumstances attending its growth. Property was more available there than elsewhere around London because Clerkenwell had been relatively unpopulated until the mid-sixteenth century. The neighborhood contained the priory of St. John's and other monastic lands that were procured from the crown at attractive prices when the monasteries were dissolved in 1539. Many prominent London families subsequently established their estates there, including James Byatt in 1585 and Lord Cobham sometime in the early 1590s, according to a 1598 manuscript by one of Cobham's descendants, Thomas Thyne.[85] By the beginning of the seventeenth century, Clerkenwell boasted three teeming residential neighborhoods around the Charterhouse, St. John's Priory, and Clerkenwell Priory.[86] Despite the population growth and worsening crime that prompted the establishment of a prison known as Hick's Hall in the east end of Clerkenwell by Middlesex authorities in 1610,[87] Clerkenwell did not suffer the same degree of overcrowding as nearby Aldersgate, Newgate, and other suburbs immediately without the city wall. The small but noticeably affluent population that had previously taken advantage of the dissolution of the priory lands sought to imbue the growing community of artisans and apprentices with an ethos of mutual trust and civility.[88]

The influx of prominent new residents precipitated a demand for the greater provision of goods and services in the community (such as the roads that the monies from the Queen Anne's Men were earmarked to provide), attracting artisans, apprentices, and journeymen who relocated to the neighborhood in search of employment. Migration to the neighborhood, in turn, stimulated new jobs for even lower-order workers and those engaged in the service industry, spurring population growth and leading to a neighborhood with an eclectic blend of "middling" residents. Although some complained about certain "lewd persons . . . rogues and vagabonds" who frequently descended on the community, such denouncements were probably an overreaction to the arrival of generally honest people seeking work.[89] If not for the possibility of employment, vagrants and other newcomers would have bypassed the neighborhood altogether. Mobility between jobs and masters (officially referred to as "vagrancy") was a natural feature of working life in early modern England, and these vagrants were a considerable segment of the workforce.[90] Transience among the working population does not mean that these people represented the threat to order and civility connoted by the term "vagrant" and repeated—and exaggerated—in complaints by civic authorities. Nor does the incidence of vagrancy mean that the communities where they settled (often on the fringes of the metropolis) became tainted by their allegedly lax morals and disruptive behavior. Local authorities were keen to manage the growth of the suburb. In an attempt to attract responsible newcomers interested in improving the community, the Middlesex authorities enacted a statute in 1544 that enabled residents who improved the roadway in front of their homes to deduct the cost from their rent. By 1633 "St. John's Street [was] (on both sides) replenished with buildings up to Clerkenwell."[91]

The generosity of the neighborhood's freeholders indicates that Clerkenwell was a remarkably cohesive community (despite divisions based on wealth and status), especially for the frequently changing suburbs. Stow recounts how William Herne, a cloth worker and yeoman of the guard, "gave lands and tenements" in trust to his company in 1580 in order to "pay yearly forever fourteen pounds to the churchwardens of Clerkenwell." Thomas Holford replicated Herne's charity in 1606. Despite being a parishioner of "Christchurch, near Newgate," Holford dispensed all his freeholdings in the northern suburbs to "the parish of St. James Clerkenwell."[92] The voluntary relief provided by these inner-city donors corresponded to the City of London's mandated solution to local poverty, which stipulated that richer parishes must subsidize poorer ones.[93] Much of the land in Clerkenwell was acquired cheaply during the monastic breakup, which might account for the generosity of its landowners. The type of charity exhibited by Clerkenwell freeholders was less common in other inner-city parishes, where lingering debt fomented by the perennially high price of property prevented the vigorous and voluntary exercise of this kind of philanthropy.

Prior to the Reformation, in addition to being a relatively harmonious and tightly knit neighborhood, Clerkenwell was a noteworthy site for public entertainment and other leisure pastimes for its own residents and visitors from its more populous southern neighbor. Moorfields, just north of the wall, was drained between 1514 and 1521 and became London's first public park. This community predisposition toward recreation seems to be partially a product of its long and close association with several venerable institutions of the Roman Catholic Church. The Nunnery of St. Mary, the Priory of St. John's of Jerusalem, and the Charterhouse monastery, all well-established in Clerkenwell for hundreds of years, sponsored the performance of miracle plays and dramatic renditions of saints' lives throughout the medieval period. All three of these Catholic institutions flourished in this ideal location, within easy reach of the city yet far away enough from the overcrowding and stench of the river to facilitate pious religious contemplation.[94] After only a century of existence, St. John's was "acknowledged as the richest priory in Christendom" due to the bounty of its Norman benefactors. The priory generated funds for the crusades, and the Knights of St. John were conspicuous participants in these expeditions.[95]

The parish of St. James (originally St. John's, rededicated sometime during the reign of Henry VIII) was established on Easter Day 1175. It soon gained regional notoriety when it was selected by the parish clerks of London as the location for the annual exhibition of sacred drama. Rolling hills and grassy fields made Clerkenwell a felicitous site for mystery plays performed over the course of several days.[96] Rather than marking a radical change in the neighborhood, the construction of the Red Bull in the early seventeenth century suggests continuity with Clerkenwell's past as an important performance district. From 1560 until 1608 the Revels Office was also located in Clerkenwell, which made the neighborhood an almost natural choice for the location of a full-time theatre and might have made the regulation of drama easier.

Given the availability of open land, the community was also home to sledding and ice-skating in winter, May Day festivities, "leaping, dancing, shooting, wrestling, casting of the stone and ball . . . and [other] merry disports."[97] The annual wrestling bouts held during Bartholemew Fair drew even the lord mayor and his aldermen to Clerkenwell. The neighborhood was well equipped to provision residents and playgoers alike, boasting a number of popular taverns in addition to countless smaller alehouses catering to numerous tastes. The more well-known establishments included the St. John's of Jerusalem; the Sun on Old Street; the George and the Christopher on Turnbull Street; the Crane, the Hart, and the Prince's Arms in Hoxton; and the George, the King's Head, the Miter, and the Nag's Head, all on St. John Street. And where better to stop for a pre- or post-theatre beverage than the Bull Red, also on St. John's Street?[98]

The Red Bull playhouse continued a long tradition of public entertainment in Clerkenwell by providing amusement for artisans and apprentices, who had some money to spend at the theatre despite their modest means and limited education. In exchange for their hard-earned money, they sought entertainment that resonated with their social position. By all accounts, the Red Bull delivered. Extant commentary from people at all ends of the social spectrum suggests that the Red Bull's audience was more homogeneous than audiences at other playhouses.

Citizens and apprentices made up the majority of the spectators. The first reference to the theatre, in fact, comes from a fictional apprentice in Beaumont's *The Knight of the Burning Pestle* (ca. 1607) who complains that a given play is "stale [because] it has been had before at the Red Bull" (4.1.43), beginning a tendency to ridicule the playhouse for its downmarket plays that has continued ever since.[99] The theatre's repertory featured a panoply of heroic dramas that catered to the preferences of artisans and apprentices, including a number of plays that featured the noble exploits of artisans. Plays like John Day's *Travels of the Three English Brothers* (1607), Samuel Rowley's *A Shoemaker, a Gentleman* (1608), Thomas Heywood's *Fortune by Land and Sea* (ca. 1608), John Cooke's *Greene's Tu Quoque* (ca. 1611), and Thomas Dekker's *Match Me in London* (1611) stand in marked contrast to the more familiar repertory at the Globe and its lineup of plays by Shakespeare, Jonson, and later Fletcher. Understood in the context of the Red Bull and its community, plays like these allowed audiences to take pride in their professions and their contributions to civic life. Occasionally, plays staged at the Red Bull featured citizens not as characters but as actors. Wentworth Smith's *The Hector of Germany* (ca. 1614) was "publicly acted at the Red Bull . . . by a company of young men of the city," not by Queen Anne's Men, the theatre's usual occupants. The play's dedication to John Swinnerton, the lord mayor in 1612 (and possible relation to Thomas Swinnerton, a player with the Queen Anne's Men),[100] remarks that "this play, entitled The Palsgrave, being made for Citizens, who acted it as well, I deemed fit to be patronized by a citizen."[101] The Red Bull consciously specialized in entertainment for this large and stable group of consumers.

Not surprisingly, patrons of London's more venerable playhouses cast aspersions on the unfashionable and outmoded repertory at the Red Bull and the outlandish behavior of its audiences—opinions that have shaped that theatre's reputation to this day. An association with the Red Bull became something of an insult in gentlemanly society. George Wither, for instance, dismisses the pretensions of a would-be poet, claiming:

> His Poetry is such as he can cull
> From plays he heard at the Curtain or the Bull,
> And yet is fine coy Mistress Mary Muff,
> The Soonest taken with such broken stuff.[102]

People who were willing to imitate verses uttered at the Red Bull or were taken in by them must certainly have been foolish and naïve, outcasts from polite society. Or were they? Another fictional lover, Trincalo, in Thomas Tomkis's *Albumazar* (1615), woos his mistress with similar verses, apparently to great effect: "then will I confound her with complements drawn from the plays I see at the Fortune and the Red Bull, where I learn all the words I speak and understand not."[103] One person's drivel could be extremely persuasive when addressed to interlocutors who did not share the same biases and pretensions. A young man from Cornwall is utterly alienated at the theatre: "To St. John Street to the Red Bull I went, / Where I the roaring Rhymer saw, / And to my face was made a daw."[104] Although probably inclined to enjoy the roaring Rhymer, the poor youth is isolated because he is marked as an outsider, not part of the regular playgoing crowd that frequented the venue.

These three observations indicate that the Red Bull elicited extremely powerful and polarized reactions from spectators. Impressions of the theatre varied primarily according to the observer's social and occupational status within London, suggesting that the playhouse generated a remarkably keen sense of shared identity, welcoming some and excluding others. Reflecting the community to which it catered and, to some degree, the neighborhood where it was located, the Red Bull was clearly on the opposite side of the artistic spectrum from the Globe. Though many seventeenth-century commentators on the Red Bull betray a marked class bias, their collected remarks have remained the basis of its reputation. G. E. Bentley notes that "the Red Bull was the subject of more sneers than any other playhouse of the time." In a section of *The Jacobean and Caroline Stage* devoted to "The Reputation of the Red Bull," he concludes that the playhouse earned a reputation for "ignominy."[105] Bentley's assertion has been repeated ever since by scholars who have tended to judge the Red Bull retrospectively, according to the standard set by Shakespeare and the Globe.

Some more recent theatre historians and literary critics have attempted to rehabilitate the reputation of the playhouse. Noticing that many Red Bull plays in print seem designed to appeal to a more educated and upwardly mobile readership, Marta Straznicky argues that a "'low' or popular theatrical repertory is not sufficient evidence of the social or educational make-up of its audience." Similarly, Tom Rutter suggests that thematic similarities among plays staged at the Red Bull, Globe, and Fortune indicate that they keenly competed for each other's spectators and that the three playhouses were not therefore socially or artistically distinct from one another.[106] These arguments allow us to entertain alternate possibilities for the Red Bull, its audience, and its repertory that challenge generations of received assumptions. While the Red Bull was probably not a viable alternative for audiences who preferred the Globe (much less the private theatres), neither was it a place of disrepute simply because it was typically patronized by artisans, apprentices, and other "unlettered" residents of the city and suburbs. On the contrary, the reputation of that theatre suggests that it was an important community institution and source of social capital for its audiences, who were not adequately served by other venues for staged entertainment. The reputation of the Red Bull has been constructed from above by early modern elites predisposed to inveigh against any kind of popular entertainment to highlight their own class distinction and by more modern commentators interested primarily in the literary merit of the plays performed there. Instead I want to reassess the social character of this theatre from the perspective of those who frequented it on a regular basis and made it profitable.

The Red Bull and the Fortune are often grouped together as the purveyors of "citizen staples" designed to please an unsophisticated audience. Their more discriminating detractors dismissed the actors at both houses as "terrible tear-throats." And their repertories become virtually interchangeable by the 1630s: the King's Revels Company and Prince Charles's Men swapped venues between the Red Bull and the Fortune in 1631 and again in 1637.[107] The two playhouses are also closely associated in the dramatic history of the period for the greater number of petty crimes and disturbances committed in their confines, events that even when exaggerated tend to conflate the reputations of the two theatres. Incidents like these have led to the frequent and perhaps misleading generalization that "[t]he Fortune and Red Bull . . . provide[d] popular theatre for a down-market clientele."[108]

Though both were large amphitheatres, evidence suggests that their social dynamics may have differed significantly: while the Red Bull was known for its distinctive house style replete with broad acting, frequent battle scenes, and numerous stage effects popular among citizens, the Fortune seems to have catered to a more diverse and less easily discernible demographic mix. To some extent, the quality of its productions seemed more to the tastes of elite theatregoers like Busino, a Venetian visitor to the Fortune in 1617 who witnessed "such a crowd of nobility, so very well arrayed that they looked like so many princes, listening as silently and soberly as possible."[109] Londoners would hardly expect this kind of atmosphere at the Red Bull. Other notables who might seem more at home at the Globe or one of the private houses also attended performances at the Fortune, including Count de Gondomar, the Spanish ambassador and his entourage (who banqueted with the players afterward), the scholar Richard Norwood in 1612, and even the young John Milton in 1621. We know of no such visitors to the Red Bull.

The Fortune's repertory was built on old favorites like Marlowe's *Tamburlaine* and *Doctor Faustus* and Thomas Kyd's *The Spanish Tragedy*, which were mainstays at the theatre until it closed in 1642. These plays, like many others staged at the Fortune, feature prominent heroes, ample stage action, and special effects that were always popular with citizens. These same elements became even more dominant at the Red Bull, which eventually exceeded its neighbor in appealing to this segment of the audience. Where plays like Heywood's *Ages* at the Red Bull proceed almost entirely through fireworks, battle scenes, and intricate choreography, Fortune plays use stage action to accentuate already compelling dialogue and plot, suggesting, perhaps, that the Prince's Men refused to give themselves over entirely to spectacle.

The story of Dekker's *If This Be Not a Good Play, the Devil Is in It* (ca. 1610) might usefully exemplify the subtle differences in the strategic organization of the two companies' repertories. Dekker brings devils, demons, and other ghoulish characters to life in the play, using a variety of pyrotechnics and other special effects that might seem at home at both the Fortune and the Red Bull. When the Prince's Men at the Fortune rejected the play, perhaps feeling that it took spectacle a bit too far, the Queen Anne's Men immediately took it and performed it at the Red Bull. In the 1612 quarto Dekker dedicates the play to the Queen Anne's Men, stating that "when Fortune (in her blind pride) set her foot upon this imperfect building, you gently raised it up (on the same columns) . . . To you therefore is the whole frame consecrated."[110] At the Red Bull, Dekker's "building" joined a repertory that at this time probably included Heywood's *Golden Age*, *Silver Age*, *Brazen Age*, and *Fortune by Land and Sea* along with Cooke's *Greene's Tu Quoque* and Dekker's *Match Me in London*. Red Bull playgoers could revel in spectacle, the slapstick antics of the clown, or both.

We might say, then, that the Fortune, while leaning toward a popular audience of citizens and apprentices, exemplified more of the heterogeneity that we often associate with the early modern theatre generally than the other two amphitheatres did. Both socially and artistically, it appears to have been somewhere in between the two poles represented by the Globe and the Red Bull. Those living in the immediate vicinity of the playhouse, on Golding Lane and Whitecross Street, spanned the occupational and social spectrum. The immediate neighborhood boasted an eclectic mix of residents that included the vicar of the local parish, several cloth workers, two butchers, a goldsmith, and many (occupations not specified) who dwelled in tenements owned by the neighborhood's well-to-do residents.[111]

Spectators at the Fortune seem also to have been a mix of diverse social elements. Sir Alexander Wengrave, in Dekker and Middleton's *The Roaring Girl* (1611), a play that itself parades a cast of characters drawn from all ranks of urban life, proudly gestures to his eclectic portrait gallery, often taken as a description of the galleries at the Fortune during a typical performance. His remarks show that different social groups intermingle with surprising amity while still firmly aware of their individual identities:

> When you look into my galleries,
> How bravely they are trimmed up, you shall swear
> Y'are highly pleased to see what's set down there:
> Stories of men and women mixed together
> Fair ones with foul, like sunshine in wet weather;
> Within one square a thousand heads are laid
> So close that all of heads the room seems made;
> As many faces there, filled with blithe looks,
> Show like the promising titles of new books
> Writ merrily . . . (1.2.14–23)

The prologue to the play attests to the remarkable diversity of the Fortune's audience and highlights the skill of the playwright, who must negotiate the tastes of such an assortment, "each one [of whom] comes / And brings a play in's head with him" (ll. 4–5). Different playgoers, though approaching the drama with their own interpretive lens, can nevertheless respond collectively with their applause, which may make the Fortune a promising model for harmonious interchange among very different classes of Londoners.

Perhaps alluding to the numerous altercations mentioned in the records, Sir Alexander concedes that the theatre's audience did contain some troublemakers: "Here and there, whilst with obsequious ears / Thronged heaps do listen, a cutpurse thrusts and leers / With hawk's eyes for his prey" (1.2.25–27). He implies, however, that such an active audience might in fact serve to enliven—and even enrich—the social environment and the sensual experience of spectators, forcing playgoers not just to be aware of the action onstage but to survey nervously the volatile crowd around them. The overall impression is of an astounding public experience where audiences are swept away by their collective engagement with the dramatic spectacle, influenced at least as much by their fellow spectators and the environment inside the playhouse as by the actors onstage: "The very floor, as 'twere, waves to and fro, / And like a floating island seems to move, / Upon a sea bound in with shores above" (1.2.30–32).[112] Audiences at the Fortune took part in a unique theatrical culture that was hardly identical to that at other venues although similar in some ways, illustrating once again that playgoing in Shakespeare's London cannot be reduced to a singular description that adequately accounts for the nuances at individual venues.

The complex divisions within London society, the highly regimented and traditional patterns of everyday life to which citizens were accustomed, the tendency of the theatres to draw identifiable groups of playgoers, and the unique but hardly debased flavor of local neighborhoods where different theatres were located strongly urge us to reconsider the playgoing industry in London. The market for theatrical entertainment in the city was more than an abstract and uniform aggregate of companies and playgoers observing the laws of supply and demand in a competitive marketplace; it was a set of subcultures that mirrored the diversity and regional variation of the metropolis that it served.

However strategic their location in London society, and however great their financial contributions to the neighborhoods and parishes in which they were located, the theatres could do little to contribute to social capital over the long term without a product that resonated with audiences, whether homogeneous crowds of apprentices or an eclectic and cosmopolitan audience drawn from all ranks of life. Any playhouse venture, especially in such a highly saturated and competitive environment, could hardly sustain itself without audiences who attended not just once or twice but regularly over a period of years and even decades. The prologue to John Cooke's *The Two Merry Milkmaids*, performed at the Red Bull in 1619, entreats the audience to reward the players with their applause but more importantly asks that "as ye like it, pray know the House again" (A4v).[113] In a market where the average playgoer went to the playhouse twenty times a year, repeat attendance at the same theatre was absolutely essential for continued success.[114]

Occasionally the players would poll the audience to determine the next day's production. Some audiences apparently were not just loyal to a playhouse but inclined to attend almost daily.[115] Ensuring that theatregoers returned frequently to the same house required a repertory that interested them not as a deracinated aggregate but as members of discrete communities with their own theatrical tastes, economic positioning, and social aspirations. The following chapters show how certain theatres and the plays they staged reflected decidedly local concerns, giving the Red Bull and the Fortune a large and fiercely loyal following that is difficult for modern commentators (used to the more subtle and cosmopolitan drama of Shakespeare) to understand and appreciate.

Chapter 3
RELIGIOUS COMMUNITIES AT LONDON'S NORTHERN PLAYHOUSES

* * * *
* * *
*

Religious communities, many of them vehemently antagonistic, were a conspicuous feature of the social and ideological landscape in Jacobean London in the aftermath of the largely unsettled Protestant reformation. John Foxe characterized the devotional life during this period—even among Protestants—as one of "unbrotherly division."[1] According to Henry Ainsworth, the city was populated by "a misceline multitude of believers and infidels, holy and profane."[2] John Robinson in 1610 thought that Londoners, as a spiritual body, had embarked on "perplexed paths . . . [and a] suspicious course,"[3] the temporal mirror of a larger metaphysical struggle between "true" and "false" churches so prevalent in the period's ecclesiastical discourse. Like most aspects of London life, religious issues were sifted locally, inflected by differences in class, occupation, and education. Religious conflict affected all Londoners, but it did not impact their lives in the same way. To understand how the public stage dealt with topical theological controversies and how theatres might have influenced the religious affiliation of Londoners, we must do more than gloss Protestant themes and allusions to contemporary religious issues in the plays. We need to think about early seventeenth century drama in the context of its audiences and their communities, recognizing that all approaches to religious controversy were neither effective nor appropriate, given an increasingly stratified theatrical market.

In this chapter I consider how London's two northern amphitheatres, the Fortune and the Red Bull, adapted material from John Foxe's *Book of Martyrs* to address matters of local religious significance, seeking to spread the tenets of the Reformation in neighborhoods and parishes where religious allegiance was especially fraught. Thomas Heywood's *If You Know Not Me, You Know Nobody* (1605) and Thomas Dekker's *Whore of Babylon* (1606) present Foxe's polemic in an idiom intelligible to audiences largely composed of artisans and apprentices, who were not usually targeted by religious ideologues, Protestant or Catholic.[4] Just as *The Book of Martyrs* saturated Elizabethan religious culture, these plays brought religious issues of national and international import in contact with local neighborhoods and the much more parochial concerns of their residents. Many of these playgoers did not have the time, intellectual capacity, or desire to acquaint themselves with the tedious theological and historical nuances of ecclesiastical controversy but were nevertheless vitally concerned—even fearful—about the outcome.

Clerkenwell, Finsbury, and the parish churches in and around them (St. James Clerkenwell, St. Giles Cripplegate, St. Botolph's Aldersgate, St. Andrew Holborn, St. Sepulchre Newgate, St. John Zachary, St. Mary Staining, St. Martin's le Grande, St. Anne and St. Agnes, and St. Bartholomew the Great and the Less) had a long history of internal religious conflict. As in other localities within the city and throughout the nation, the progress of the Reformation in these neighborhoods was slow, constantly fluctuating, and fraught with dissension. Residents were constantly bewildered in matters of faith. In the 1540s chantry priests from the recently dissolved monasteries were recruited to assist with additional (Catholic) masses at St. Botolph's Aldersgate. One of its congregants, John Mayler (a grocer and a printer), was presented to the authorities for declaring the Eucharist a "baken god" and stating that "there is more abomination in the Mass than in all other things that is [*sic*] spoken of."[5] Congregants at the same church were vehemently conflicted, threatening to destroy the very community that parishes were supposed to instill.

Foxe also describes a case a few years later, during the reign of Mary (the exact date is not specified), in the neighboring parish of St. James Clerkenwell that was to become the home of the Red Bull playhouse:

> [T]here was one John Fetty, a simple and Godly poor man, dwelling in the parish of Clerkenwell and was by vocation a Taylor, of

> the age of 42 years or thereabout, who was accused and complained of unto one Brokenbry a priest and parson of the same parish *by his own wife* for that he would not come to church and be partaker of their idolatry and superstition.

After Fetty was placed in the stocks for fifteen days, his eight-year-old son asked a bishop's chaplain about his father's whereabouts. He was told that his father was a heretic. But the boy, "being of bold and quick spirit, and also Godly brought up and instructed by his father," accused the priest of heresy and was, according to Foxe, "most shamelessly and without all pity, so whipped and scourged . . . that he was all in a gore [of] blood." Both father and son were presented to Edmund Bonner, bishop of London, "who turned the poor man about and thinking to deface him, said in mocking wise: what have we here? A Player?" Both were eventually released, but the boy died from his injuries two weeks later, making him one of thousands of martyrs for the Protestant cause.[6]

Nearly seventy years after Fetty's incarceration, and over fifty years after Elizabeth's accession supposedly set England on a Protestant course, religious controversy continued to impinge on life in Clerkenwell. In March 1627/1628 authorities discovered a dwelling housing a college of Jesuits, along with a number of priests, their lay supporters, their relics, altars, and other accoutrements. As Father Henry More recounts:

> A day had been appointed for the renewal of the vows of some [of the Jesuits], and for the solemn profession of others. The matter was conducted so cautiously but that the neighboring Protestants observed an unusual quantity of provisions and necessaries carried in, which excited suspicion. The envy too of the adjacent shopkeepers helped it on, for the extra supplies were procured from a distance to avoid suspicion, and not from their shops.[7]

Those discovered were taken to Newgate for questioning, and one priest was executed. The matter was fiercely debated in Parliament, with many members arguing that the government had become lax in its prosecution of recusancy. Henry Foley, who narrated this and other accounts of Jesuit activity in England, interpreted the event as a dramatic presage of a more widespread conflict that was to come. He argued that this discovery was "an occurrence of trifling import in itself, but the origin of much bitter political strife."[8]

These events, and countless others like them, disclose the deep divisions within neighborhoods, parishes, and even families evinced by the Reformation. Social capital played a considerable role in the ongoing turmoil in these communities as church leaders attempted to use preexisting social networks to spread rival religious ideas. Fetty would never have been presented to Bonner, and his son never beaten to death, without the cooperation of his wife and other members of the congregation. The Jesuit conclave was not discovered by the concerted investigation of the authorities but through the surveillance of local residents and business owners aroused by individuals who failed to shop locally. Despite the emphasis that Protestants placed on indwelling faith and a personal approach to spiritual matters, religious convictions only occasionally superseded traditional loyalties to parishes, occupational groups, and neighborhood communities. Religious zeal varied greatly from place to place, and even from street to street, in the densely populated city and its suburbs.

Fetty's incarceration and the discovery of the Jesuits in Clerkenwell also disclose a theatrical context. Bonner's chiding accusation that Fetty was "a Player" and Foley's exaggerated claim that the discovery of the Jesuits' safe house was "the origin of much bitter political strife" suggest that the overblown dramatic energy of the theatre was somehow (metaphorically or otherwise) enlisted to support religious causes. By turning matters of local religious notoriety into such highly charged, fanciful, and melodramatic narratives and by likening their participants to the actors in stage plays, commentators both magnified the significance of local events and suggested that they were appropriate—even necessary—subjects for wide public deliberation. The theatre, with its ability to reach vast numbers of Londoners across traditional social cleavages, would seem an ideal vehicle to disseminate religious ideology, especially to those in less well-to-do neighborhoods not usually at the vanguard of the ongoing controversy. These citizens required something considerably more dramatic than abstruse theological doctrine to pique their interest.

How could the theatre, an institution so frequently maligned by many religious factions, help to galvanize London communities around a single unified religious vision, when so many other outlets fell short? Many of the issues posed by dramatic productions were understood differently, depending on one's place in the city's social, economic, and occupational hierarchy. In some cases, the theatre reinforced and modeled various conceptions of a national Protestant congregation for specific audiences at certain playhouses who might otherwise lack any kind of thoroughgoing education in the permutations of topical ecclesiastical controversy. While most discussions of theatre and religion focus on the content of the plays themselves and posit a homogeneous audience reacting to them, I propose to examine how Heywood and Dekker's dramatic versions of Foxe resonate for a more specific audience by looking briefly at the religious history of the communities in which they were performed.[9]

As we have seen, Henslowe's move north to the Fortune and the opening of the Red Bull a few years later offered theatrical professionals a business model different from the model for playing on the Bankside and allowed them to target their drama to specific audiences based in part on their location within the city. These troupes, the Prince's Men and Queen Anne's Men, had also migrated to neighborhoods where religion remained a highly contested issue, probably to an even greater degree than in other areas of the city where parish churches and their smaller and more stable congregations were more uniform in their confessional landscape. Drawing on local populations in these suburbs and the surrounding neighborhoods, these two playhouses, even more than the Globe and the other theatres on the Bankside, tended to be willing purveyors of popular low culture entertainment for often raucous audiences of artisans, apprentices, and the working poor.[10]

Considerable religious division existed within the neighborhoods of north London. Many parishes, including St. Botolph's without Aldersgate near the Fortune, enthusiastically returned to Catholicism even before the order from Archbishop Bonner in 1554 and only reluctantly conformed to Protestantism again under Elizabeth. St. Martin's Lane, also in Aldersgate, was home to a "fair and large college of a dean and secular canons and priests" that had existed since 1056 and had long "claimed great privileges of sanctuary and otherwise." The building was destroyed in 1548 during the reign of Edward VI, but many of its Catholic leaders were not apprehended.[11] The venerable Catholic history of these regions suggests that a significant recusant population remained in the neighborhood into the seventeenth century or, at the very least, that many in the parish were not nearly as zealous about reform as its Protestants hoped.

Fear of mounting Catholic activities was even more worrisome in Clerkenwell, home since 1185 to the erstwhile priory of St. John's of Jerusalem and Nunnery of St. Mary. Henry VIII confiscated the estates of this priory in 1546,[12] but as a result of nearly 400 years of intimate ties to the Church of Rome, members of this community probably maintained Catholic allegiances longer than the general London populace—which distressed their Protestant neighbors.

Indeed, a disproportionate number of those cited for recusancy and "failing to attend church" in the Session records of Middlesex County were parishioners at St. James Clerkenwell. Fears of Catholic insurgency in the community were confirmed in 1590 when a Catholic missionary, Anthony Middleton, was seized in a house in Clerkenwell and subsequently tried and executed in Clerkenwell Green in 1599.[13] Catholic activity in the parish did not cease. On 14 March 1627/1628, as noted, authorities raided a clandestine Jesuit College located in a mansion belonging to the Earl of Shrewsbury adjacent to St. John's.

Protestants reacted as expected. One penned a short tract called *The Rat-Trap* (sometimes attributed to Heywood) that was eventually published in 1641. The author argued that, like the Gunpowder Plot and other examples of Jesuit treachery, the discovery of the Jesuits in Clerkenwell was the "presage of a future . . . of damnable plots and practices."[14] Whoever wrote the tract took great delight in detailing the excruciating ways in which convicted papists were tortured for their various crimes throughout Europe (see figure 5). Subsequent investigations revealed that this Clerkenwell brotherhood of ten priests was well funded and well supplied with utensils, relics, and books containing the emblem of the Society of Jesus. This group had evaded persecution through the patronage of influential members of the nobility, civil service, and perhaps municipal authorities.[15] The conclave was

FIGURE 5. A Jesuit priest captured. Note the "eye of providence" in the upper left, a frequent component of Gunpowder Plot and other anti-Jesuit propaganda. From *The Rat-Trap, or, The Jesuits Taken in Their Own Net* (London: John Oakes, 1641), sig. A1r. Wing R294. Courtesy of the Henry E. Huntington Library, San Marino, California (shelfmark: 105676).

in existence at least by 1614, if not much earlier, and may have been organized shortly after the dissolution of the many Catholic establishments in the neighborhood earlier in the sixteenth century. Regardless of the date when the college was established, the decision to locate it in Clerkenwell suggests that at least some members of the community maintained Catholic sympathies. *The Whore of Babylon*, perhaps in an effort to alert its audience of the close proximity of the Jesuit threat, alludes to the existence of these Catholic safe houses, claiming that some "fill our rooms . . . to watch our entrance, / And arm all against us" (1.1.179–81).

Later accounts attest to the anxieties aroused by this discovery. Sir John Elliot, in the Parliament of 1628, exclaimed that "here is a ground laid for a new religion, and a foundation for the undermining of the State."[16] In a quasi-fictional religious "vision" set in early Stuart London entitled *Messis Vitae* (1886), John Stuart Blackie expresses anxiety that "In St. John's at Clerkenwell / Subtle Jesuits are training / Simple English youths for hell!"[17] The fear is not merely that Jesuits are active throughout England as a whole but that the "simple" and relatively uneducated "youths" of Clerkenwell are especially susceptible to their influence.

Players, too, were implicated in the religious controversy. Religious divisions plagued the Queen Anne's Men, the resident acting troupe at the Red Bull that first staged Heywood's play. Although Thomas Greene, Heywood, Swinnerton, and other sharers in the company apparently were firm proponents of Protestantism, Christopher Beeston (who became the troupe's manager), despite his outward conformity, maintained Catholic allegiances. Beeston's wife, Jane, was cited for recusancy on nine separate occasions, and the family may have been victims of popular persecution because of it.[18] One of Beeston's descendants, Heathcliffe Beeston, in a manuscript letter to Shakespeare scholar John Quincy Adams dated 12 December 1932, elaborates on the actor's religious affiliations and the hardships they imposed on the otherwise successful impresario. He suggests that both Christopher and his brother William (also an actor) "labored under extraordinary difficulties throughout their lives because they were staunch 'papists and recusants' in times when to be suspected of leaning in this direction was to court fines, imprisonment, and often death."[19]

This, Heathcliffe suggests, is what forced Beeston to assume the alias "Hutchinson." Beeston's recusancy illustrates how religious controversy permeated all aspects of social life, even within outwardly cohesive organizations like playing companies.

It would be wrong, however, to assume that the northwest of London was a hotbed of recusancy and residual Catholic sentiment. These neighborhoods also contained large numbers of prominent Protestants, heightening the religious conflict within a small geographical area and suggesting that religious tensions ran especially high in these communities. John Foxe himself lived in Moorfields, just outside the city wall, and attended St. Giles Cripplegate, whose parishioners erected a monument to him in 1587.[20] Foxe spent much of his time and received his mail at the shop of another notable local Protestant, John Day, who undertook the massive task of manufacturing and financing *The Book of Martyrs*. He operated out of a shop in a gatehouse in Aldersgate below St. Martin's le Grande, nearly adjacent to the erstwhile Catholic Priory on St. Martin's Lane.[21] Upon his death in 1584, the business along with several of his most lucrative monopolies passed to his son, Richard Day, who was trained as a clergyman. The younger Day continued his father's practice of printing staunchly Protestant titles until his own death in 1606, when the business fell to Richard's widow, who operated the press until 1614.[22]

Day's large shop (which operated three presses simultaneously) and its prodigious output of religious material over such a long period would have become something of a landmark in the neighborhood. Day was one of a number of stationers located in Aldersgate, including Bernard Alsop, John Beale, John White, Gregory Seaton, John Hammond, Thomas Este, and Martin Clerke. Day's shop was singularly impressive, however, both in its prodigious capacity to print intricately typeset and complexly organized volumes and in its physical presence. Stow notes that "on the east side [of the gate] is the addition of one great building of timber, with one large floor paved with stone, or tile, and a well therein curbed with stone of a great depth, and rising into the said room, which is two stories high from the ground . . . John Day stationer, a late famous printer of many good books, in our time dwelled in this gate, and builded much upon the wall of the city towards the parish church of St. Anne."[23] Day retailed his publications on the ground floor of the shop, making Aldersgate an important distribution point for Protestant propaganda. In a sense the printer's shop was physically reoccupying space that had previously been occupied by a venerated Catholic edifice, demonstrating that religious battles were waged on a number of planes, from the abstract and spiritual to the streets and buildings of the city.

Local clergy worried about the threat to religious orthodoxy well into the Jacobean period. They entreated their flocks to remember their deliverance from the Church of Rome, urging them not to stray from the "true" path. John Andrews, preacher at St. James Clerkenwell, in a sermon on 31 December 1620, compared "the inconstancy and ingratitude of that people [the Israelites in the time of Moses], ever whining, ever complaining, never contented" with "[m]any nowadays either fainting under the cross, or grown wanton with too much happiness and prosperity, [who] do bark against heaven and complain because they are freed from Romish tyranny insomuch as they open their mouths against God, his gospel, his messengers and ministers, as if they were the originals of all the evils and curses that ever happened to this land."[24]

This shrill commentary and invocation of "Romish tyranny" suggests that the same ecclesiastical issues that excited reformers in the sixteenth century were still present in the seventeenth century, that the hold of Protestantism was not yet as absolute as many had hoped, and that congregants had a tendency to relapse due to their lack of fervor and vigilance. The presence of Jesuits and recusants in the midst of outwardly conforming neighborhoods was even more troublesome. Reformers were in need of any galvanizing pressure to solidify popular support for the new religion and to repair the divisions exacted upon families and communities, divisions that go largely unnoticed by historians interested in canvassing the beliefs of the city or kingdom as a whole.

Certainly the most potent and well-known attempt to clarify this state of religious confusion—to define the principles of the Reformed church, celebrate the return to Protestantism under Elizabeth, and demonize Catholics' vicious persecution of Protestants under Mary—was John Foxe's polemical history of the English church, *The Actes and Monuments of These Latter and Perilous Days* (1st ed. 1563). This massive book, popularly known as *The Book of Martyrs*, disseminated the ideology of Reform in an effort to maintain and complete that project. The sponsors of this massive book also tried to stave off the threat of a Counter-Reformation and thwart a return to the massive and violent persecutions of Protestants under Mary. True to Foxe and Day's goal of reaching the widest possible audience, *The Book of Martyrs* was effectively distributed and financed, making it more affordable to sections of the reading public that could not otherwise purchase such a capacious folio volume. The third edition of 1576, often known as the "cheap" edition, is smaller, is printed on a poorer quality of paper, contains fewer typefaces, and generally uses smaller type to conserve the amount of paper required for each volume.[25] It also reprints many features, initiated in the 1570 edition, designed to ameliorate the book's daunting complexity among a lower class of readers—the same kinds of people who regularly attended the Red Bull and the Fortune. The book also contains numerous appendices, tables, and indexes, which assist the reader in finding specific accounts by year, author, or martyr.[26]

Artisans, apprentices, the destitute and the dispossessed—in short, the uneducated—make up a substantial portion of Foxe's intended audience. In "The Epistle Dedicatory to the Queen's Majesty," he states that "though the story being written in the popular tongue serveth not so greatly for your own peculiar reading, and for such as be learned . . . [it is] in the necessity of the ignorant flock of Christ committed to your government in this Realm of England."[27] Despite this desire for inclusiveness and interpretive coherence, Foxe still must rely on his audience's ability to read and decipher religious controversy according to given theological models. Like the individual episodes that it relates, *The Book of Martyrs* is presented in terms of an Augustinian dichotomy between the visible and invisible church, interpreted by Reformers as that between the false Roman church and its true, Reformed counterpart. Semiliterate theatergoers would have considerable difficulty with this presentation of religious material. Even the iconographic elements that Foxe designed to accomplish this objective require considerable interpretive acumen. In particular, readers are forced to decipher diametrically opposed approaches to worship by comparing depictions of the rituals sanctioned by both churches on the work's title page (see figure 6), a task undoubtedly beyond the reach of many in Foxe's intended audience.

Plays based on episodes from *The Book of Martyrs* offered a way of extending Foxe's message to an even broader audience. Drama, of course, was a method of delivery that many Protestants were reluctant to embrace. Some Reformers, however, were beginning to see the potential value of the popular theatre in cementing Protestant beliefs. John Gee, despite the usual misgivings of those inclined to Puritanism, actually implicated the failure of the theatres in the sluggish spread of the Reformation and the growing insurgency of the old religion: "the Jesuits being or having actors of such dexterity, I should see no reason that they should set up a company of themselves, which will surely put down The Fortune, Red Bull, . . . and Globe."[28] Gee's argument is not that the theatre is inherently papist but that Catholics have been much more adept at manipulating theatrical resources to promote their cause. Jesuits, like poets who play on the emotions of their readers, "well knew that deep passions, especially affright and astonishing admiration, do for the time bereave and suspend exact inquiring discourse." Protestants, he felt, might use the theatre to replace some of the sanctity eradicated in the turn away from transubstantiation, the performance of miracles, adulation of the saints, and other "fabulous tricks" by using the emotional dimension of playgoing to alert the audience to the error intrinsic to these abandoned practices. Gee wanted to use the very things that were reminiscent of Catholic ritual to "shake off [our] gracious grand-fathers the priests and Jesuits, and so to bid . . . the Roman Religion farewell."[29]

Preaching in 1609 at St. Botolph's Aldersgate, in a neighborhood near the Fortune and Red Bull, William Holbrooke probably understood more than many of his peers the dynamic interplay between the church and the playhouse that had developed over the preceding decades. If the pulpit was in fact competing with the stage for the attention of Londoners, nowhere was this competition more acute in 1609 than at St. Botolph's. Holbrooke was no ally of players; in fact, he sought to eradicate plays entirely. Perhaps because of the location of his congregation, however, he was willing to understand the argument between the two in a more pragmatic way and to forward a novel solution:

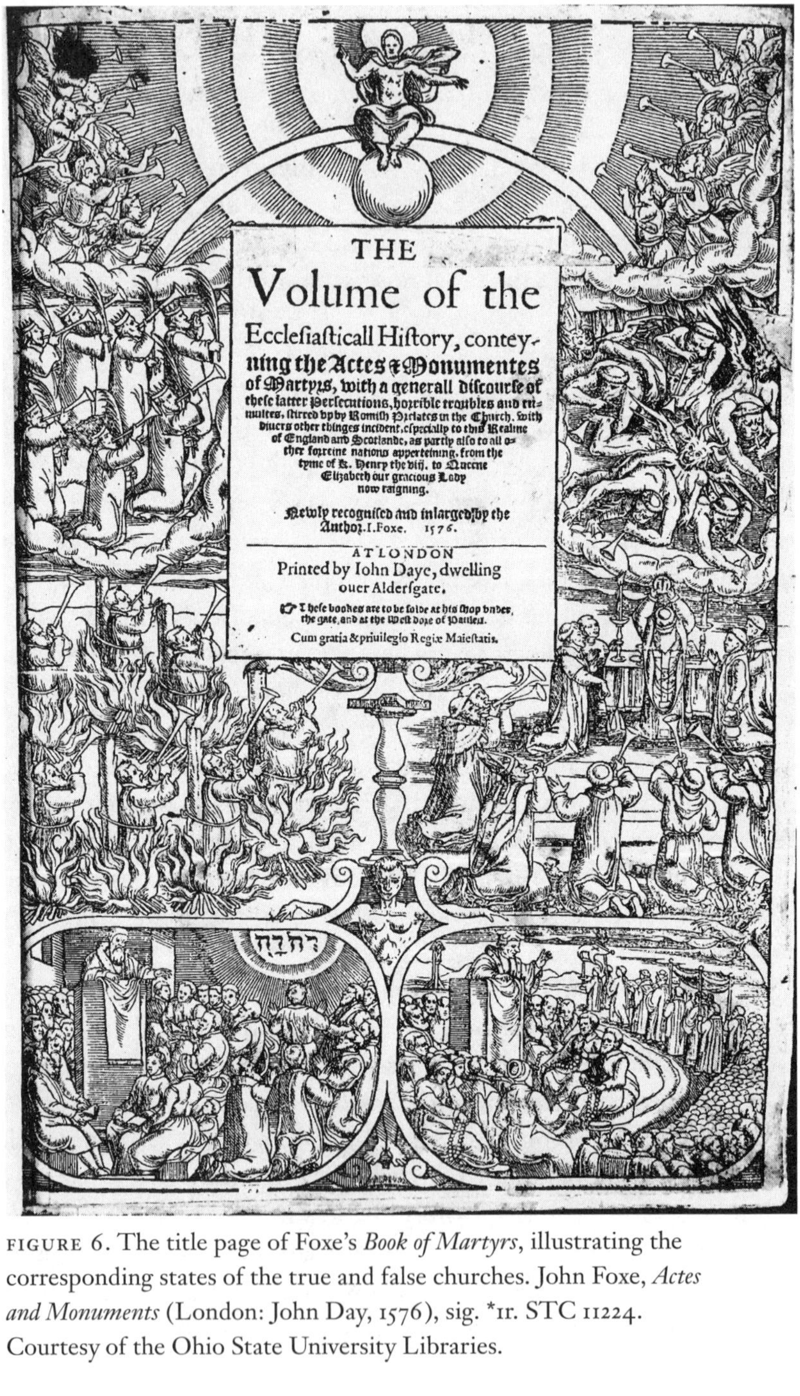

FIGURE 6. The title page of Foxe's *Book of Martyrs*, illustrating the corresponding states of the true and false churches. John Foxe, *Actes and Monuments* (London: John Day, 1576), sig. *1r. STC 11224. Courtesy of the Ohio State University Libraries.

> Christians must not only reject, and show their dislike to the carnal and unsavory speeches of the wicked, but also learn and reach good out of the same. I do not mean nor teach hereby that Christians are willing and usually to intrude themselves into such companies and places as stage-plays, taverns, bawdy houses, and the like, where they may have occasion offered hereof . . . but if occasionally and unwillingly they hear such, then this doctrine is for direction unto them . . . as it appeareth in [Paul's] epistle to the Romans that they might do evil that good might come thereof.[30]

Holbrooke was unwilling to condone the practice of playgoing in theory, although he was willing to concede that some positive benefit might eventually accrue from attending the theatre. He recognized the appeal of plays and other allegedly ungodly pursuits for his congregation and reasoned that those who choose to attend the theatre sporadically would ultimately see it as an unwholesome influence. People who attended plays would gradually turn away from them, "so that godliness changeth the discontented will of man" (C5v). Attending plays, paradoxically, might be the best path toward their eventual elimination, especially if the drama underlined a Protestant message.

Many Protestants did recognize the utility of the theatre, of course, and Protestant heroes were regularly lionized on public stages throughout the period. W. S.'s *Thomas, Lord Cromwell* was dramatized at the Globe in 1600. The same actors who performed *The Whore of Babylon* at the Fortune staged the two-part *Sir John Oldcastle* in 1599 and 1600, undoubtedly capitalizing on the Chamberlain's Men's miscalculation in depicting a roguish figure of the same name negatively in Shakespeare's *Henry IV*. During their years at the Rose and the Fortune, the Admiral's/Prince's Men developed a form of "elect nation" drama, a type of history play inflected with a degree of militant Protestantism not evident in Shakespeare's histories based predominantly on Raphael Holinshed's *Chronicles*.[31] Another play, *Captain Thomas Stukeley* (ca. 1597, quite possibly by Heywood), like *The Whore of Babylon*, consistently portrays the Catholic forces of Spain, Portugal, and Ireland as wholly incompetent and effective only through treachery and duplicity.[32] Protestants recognized that the playhouse was often perceived as a welcome alternative to tedious sermonizing and that the theatre was a natural analogue to the catechism, which strove to distill essential religious principles into a form that the ignorant could readily grasp.[33] Decades later, plays seemed to be having the desired effect. Thomas Jordan's retrospective prologue to Robert Daborne's *Poor Man's Comfort* (1655), a play staged at the Red Bull in 1617, notes the positive changes produced by popular drama. He suggests that "players are turn'd [religious] phanaticks" and "the Red Bull where sports were wont to be, / Is now a Meeting-house" in which "actor and auditor" alike are "inspired" with "mutual fire."[34]

If You Know Not Me first appeared amid this tense religious climate. The play, based on the account of the "Miraculous Preservation of Princess Elizabeth" in *The Book of Martyrs*, shares Foxe's general goal: effectively and polemically spreading the theology and politics of the Reformation to the widest possible audience and instilling an ideology of reform in the artisans and apprentices who made up the majority of the Red Bull's audience. Its performance at this theatre, in fact, could extend bellicose Protestant ideology to those who were completely illiterate. Heywood's drama not only incorporates but also enhances and extends the martyrologist's unique techniques of popular appeal, rendering the rhetoric of reform in language readily intelligible to playgoers. Heywood's play transforms the abstracted theological and historical minutiae of Foxe into a palpable dialogic interaction in which Clerkenwell audiences are invited to fashion themselves among the persecuted and thereby become participants in Elizabeth's plight. The playwright, according to Kathleen McLuskie, attempts to "naturalize the politics of Protestantism" by placing religious concerns within a more "human" agenda.[35]

According to its 1639 prologue, *If You Know Not Me* was so popular "[t]hat some by stenography, drew / The plot" and printed it without authorization from the players or the playwright eight times between 1605 and 1639, forcing "the Author to vindicate that wrong" decades later. The play's popularity in print was mirrored in performance, where it was constantly revived throughout these decades. Heywood attributes the play's notoriety to its having been "well perform'd" among the plebeians at the Red Bull, who "did throng the seats, the boxes, and the stage." Its audience, he hoped, left the theatre with a more intimate knowledge of the princess than any written work could convey.[36]

Elizabeth's story is an example of godly perseverance. The narrative presents a queen who provides the basis for a Protestant version of national history, starkly juxtaposed against her antithesis, Mary Tudor, one of the obvious targets for the vitriol in Foxe and in both this play and Dekker's *Whore of Babylon*.[37] Returning audiences to the reign of Mary would have triggered a disturbing cultural memory shared by all English Protestants: playgoers might have recalled the activities of local Catholics like Anthony Middleton who sought to undermine the achievements of Reformers like Foxe and Day.[38] In *The Book of Martyrs*, Mary's reign is judged to be the lowest point in the history of the English church, due to that monarch's papistry and "the utter destruction of the Realm which indeed afterward came to pass."[39] In Foxe's narrative of Elizabeth's deliverance, Mary and the bishop of Winchester, Stephen Gardiner, are singled out as culprits. Both characters in the play, especially Gardiner, take a much more active role in endangering the life of the princess: Mary, rather than a subordinate, explicitly gives the order to commit Elizabeth to the tower, shunning all appeals for mercy (ll. 111–32). Even after Elizabeth's release, Gardiner vows to charge one of Elizabeth's servants "upon suspicion, of some treachery, / Wherein the princess shall be accessory" (ll. 133–35). He continues a private vendetta against Elizabeth even on his deathbed.

The choice of Winchester as archvillain serves a dramatic purpose. True to exaggerated dramatic conventions, especially popular with the Queen Anne's Men at the Red Bull, Heywood provides his audience with an antagonist reminiscent of the vice figures in earlier Protestant drama by John Bale, R. Wever, and others.[40] The reported dialogue in Foxe is rendered onstage as a rancorous condemnation of ideal Christians like Elizabeth and her supporters. Under a veneer of civility to her person, the deceptive bishop reports to Mary that Elizabeth is "saucy" and pursues the execution of the princess with a haste not warranted by the queen or her officers. Gardiner's duplicity and acrimonious tone in the play may be intended to rile the audience against a traditional stage villain. Like Richard III, Barabas, and other stage machiavels, the bishop orchestrates the political intrigue and deliberately urges the queen to manipulate her supporters and accuse her half-sister falsely, suggesting that "she [Elizabeth] in Wyatt's expedition, / And other insurrection lately quelled was confederate" (ll. 100–102).[41] Whereas Foxe's demonizing of Gardiner evokes an apocalyptic context relying on scriptural typology, beast fables, and broadsheets such as William Turner's 1555 *Hunting of the Romish Wolf*, Heywood places this villain firmly within dramatic conventions that would be immediately intelligible to all avid consumers of the public theatre.[42]

Many elements in the Foxean narrative appear to be nothing more than artful embellishments designed for a plebeian audience. Among these are the seemingly superfluous role played by Elizabeth's servants, a little boy who brings Elizabeth flowers, and a chorus of impoverished onlookers who greet Elizabeth on her various journeys. In keeping with the task of popularizing history for a specific group, the play stages these vignettes instead of the nuances of the council scenes that form the centerpiece of Foxe's account. These councils are represented through a series of rapidly executed dumb shows which depict the entrances, exits, and deliveries of various petitions to and from various nobles—dialogue that an audience of apprentices might find difficult and unengaging. After all, the audience at the same theatre in 1612 reproved Webster's *White Devil* for the overuse of unintelligible—not to mention boring—court dialogue and complicated intrigue.[43] Apart from providing expedient narrative devices, the dumb shows have the added benefit of heightening the dramatic spectacle. They incorporate supernatural elements not mentioned in Foxe but expected by this audience, who enjoyed fantastical "drum and trumpet" plays such as John Day's *Travels of the Three English Brothers* (1607) and Heywood's *The Four Prentices of London* (1600), *Fortune by Land and Sea* (ca. 1608), and numerous *Ages* (1610–1612; discussed in chapter 4).[44]

In one dumb show, for example, Heywood introduces the prominent device of the English Bible as symbolic of the truth and faith embodied by Elizabeth. Rather than alluding to the typological relationship between the English Bible and Book of Truth by referring to Matthew 24 (as Foxe does),[45] Heywood silently depicts Gardiner, Barwick, the Constable of the Tower, and other Friars entering along with two angels "at the other door . . . the Friar steps to her [Elizabeth], offering to kill her: the angel drives them back . . . The Angel opens the Bible, and puts it in her hand as she sleeps" (ll. 1050–53, stage direction). When she wakes, Elizabeth finds the Bible open to Proverbs 29:25 ("whoso putteth his trust in the Lord shall not be confounded") and, upon learning that none of her ladies-in-waiting placed the book in her hand, exclaims "then 'twas inspiration, heaven I trust / With his eternal hand will guide the just" (ll. 1062–63). The book—even more than the princess—becomes the focal point of the audience's gaze, asserting the primacy of the Word, the spiritual power of basic symbols, and the intervention of providence (see figure 7). Even Gardiner grudgingly admits that Elizabeth's "life is guarded by the hand of heaven," a line with no analogue in Foxe's account (l. 1150).

By simplifying complicated theological issues for an audience who might not be intimately familiar with particular passages of the Bible, these scenes emphasize Elizabeth's commonality, the trials of faith, and the signal importance of the vernacular scriptures in the religious experience of all Christians.[46] All Protestants were inclined to believe that God was intimately involved in protecting the elect. But the miraculous simplicity of these supposed acts of providence allowed these "visible sermons" to animate those who could never be moved by words alone.[47] In the introduction to his popular *Book of Christian Prayers* (1578), Richard Day (the book was also printed by John Day and reprinted three times in a twenty-year period) notes not only the singular importance of prayer but also its relative ease and convenience for average working Christians: "And because God understandeth, pray not thou therefore in a language which thou understand not . . . and pray not with much babbling or vain repetition."[48] In keeping with one of the principal tenets of Reformed theology, and in stark contrast to Roman Catholic ritual, both the play and the works from which it is derived insist on simplicity and accessibility.

The familiar tropes of time, truth, and the Bible as aids to the princess also recall Elizabeth's triumphant entrance into the city prior to her coronation. This event became part of the enduring cultural memory of this and subsequent generations of Londoners, who would witness it annually, on a reduced scale, with the installation of the lord mayor. A pageant erected by citizens at the Little Conduit in Cheap, narrated in Richard Mulcaster's *The Queen's Majesty's Progress through the City of London* (1558), provokes Elizabeth to note: "'Time hath

FIGURE 7. Princess Elizabeth with a Bible. The corresponding text makes it explicit that this is a vernacular Bible: "And because God understandeth, pray not thou therefore in a language which thou understand not" (*2v). The prominence of the English Bible in Heywood's play *If You Know Not Me* draws upon this and other woodcut illustrations depicting the future queen with the Bible. From Richard Day, *A Book of Christian Prayers* (London: Richard Day, 1578), sig. *iv. STC: 6429. Courtesy of the Henry E. Huntington Library, San Marino, California (shelfmark 143488).

brought me hither' . . . When Her Grace understood that the Bible in English should be delivered unto her by Truth, which was therein represented by a child, she thanked the city for that gift and said she would oftentimes read over that book."[49] As in Foxe and Heywood, the emphasis upon iconic figures and symbols in Mulcaster's text is designed to forge a triangular linkage of Elizabeth, the citizens of London, and the Protestant faith as represented by the vernacular Bible. By foregrounding these memorable events in London's recent past, both Mulcaster's popular text and Heywood's play lend the familiar narrative a more local appeal designed to evince nostalgia for Elizabeth specifically in residents of the capital.

The princess's interactions with those of lower rank in *Actes and Monuments* are amplified in the play to emphasize Elizabeth's amity and charity toward her poorer subjects. Despite a massive gulf in rank and status, Elizabeth and playgoers at the Red Bull share the same spirit of community. After a young child is questioned because he brought flowers to the princess, Elizabeth "smiled, but said nothing." Recalling Fetty's son's intervention in his father's examination, the boy here underscores the surveillance visited on all those who sympathize with those imprisoned for their faith, regardless of age or station. After the boy is examined by various authorities for purportedly delivering a letter from the Earl of Devonshire to the imprisoned princess, the narrator in Foxe commends "the discretion of the child, being yet but four years of age." The play expands the boy's interaction with the princess:

> *Eliz*. Welcome sweet boy, what hast thou brought me there?
> *Boy*. Madam, I have brought you another nosegay,
> But you must not let it be seen, for if it be,
> I shall be soundly whipt, indeedla, indeed I shall.
> *Eliz*. God a mercy boy, here's to requite thy love. (ll. 781–85)

Foxe's version diminishes the magnanimity of the boy's gift: though he did "bring her grace flowers," he "did likewise to the other prisoners that were there."[50] At the Red Bull, where this boy and the boy playing Elizabeth would most likely be of the same stature, an audience would be able to view her verbal interaction with the admiring child as an expression of the monarch's solidarity with a plebeian community.

Perhaps Elizabeth's most significant encounter with commoners, at least from the perspective of lower-class playgoers, occurs en route from the Tower of London to Woodstock. In *The Book of Martyrs*, though her loyal followers "were very desirous to see her," Elizabeth reportedly said: "yonder I see certain of my men: go to them and say these words from me: tamquam ovis [like a sheep led to the slaughter]" (see Isaiah 53:7).[51] These Latin words, though potent in a book aimed at a learned audience, would be lost on the majority of the crowd at a raucous public theatre like the Red Bull. Though the play preserves these words, they are followed by a brief exchange between some of these characters, whose misprision of Latin terminology satirizes the unintelligibility of the Roman Catholic service of worship:

> *1 Poor Man*. Tanqus Ovrus pray what's tanqus Ovrus, neighbor?
> *2 Poor Man*. If the priest were here he'd smell it out straight.
> *Cook*. Myself have been a scholar, and I understand
> What tanquam Ovis means.
> We sent to know how her grace did fare,
> She tanquam Ovis said, even like a sheep
> That's to the slaughter led.
> *1 Poor Man*. Tanqus Ovrus, that I should live to see, Tanqus Ovris.
> *2 Poor Man*. I shall n'ere love tanquam Ovris again for this trick.
> (ll. 889–97)

Aside from the satire, this interchange is likely a realistic portrayal of an uneducated populace forced to decipher Latin phrasing. "Tanqus Ovrus" is gibberish, of course, but the poor men do not understand the nuances between the two phrases, even after explanation, and instead tend to view the entire discourse as some kind of sham perpetrated by the Catholic authorities persecuting Elizabeth. The poor men's failure to comprehend this phrase illustrates the necessity for more popular forms of religious instruction. These two seemingly insignificant characters in Foxe's version stand as important models of the average Christian for a Clerkenwell audience. The ordinary, albeit amusing, parlance of these familiar figures fosters religious awareness and conviction and fuels anti-Catholic sentiment, in a way that written words could not.

Not all plays revolving around this Foxean narrative rendered its religious message transparent to less-educated Londoners. Like Heywood's drama, John Fletcher and William Shakespeare's *All Is True* (*Henry VIII*) (1613) is heavily invested in a Foxean providential model of history in which past events are interpreted teleologically, as conditions underlying the emergence of a unified Protestant nation under Elizabeth and maintained by James I. With very few exceptions, *Henry VIII* does not feature a prominent role for average citizens and takes place firmly within the circumscribed world of Henry's court. The differences between *Henry VIII* and *If You Know Not Me* seem to be a function of the different audiences that the authors were seeking to attract. Although *Henry VIII* was performed three times at the Globe, including the famous performance that brought down the house in 1613,[52] it was apparently commissioned for the King's Men's private winter home at Blackfriars.[53]

Unlike Heywood's play, *Henry VIII* is directed toward the educated social elites at the private theatres and deliberately distinguishes itself from the usual fare offered on the public stage. The prologue grants that the play might appeal to those who seek merely the entertainment associated with theatrical spectacle, "[t]hose that come to see / Only a show or two, and so agree / The play may pass" (ll. 9–11). But it flatly dismisses the kind of playgoer for whom gross entertainment value is the primary arbiter of dramatic taste, suggesting that this play's appeal lies in its ability to engage its audience intellectually:

> . . . Only they
> That come to hear a merry bawdy play,
> A noise of targets, or to see a fellow
> In a long motley coat guarded with yellow
> Will be deceived. (ll. 13–16)

The play's authors signal a desire to target more educated playgoers, admitting: "'Tis ten to one this play can never please / All that are here" (Epilogue 1–2). By writing *Henry VIII* as high culture, Shakespeare and Fletcher demonstrated that they were adept at isolating and catering to their troupe's upwardly mobile market segment, a fact of life in the increasingly stratified Jacobean dramatic marketplace that required different reenactments, even of the same material, for different communities.

If You Know Not Me seeks to disseminate Protestant ideology through the sentimental rendering of a specific historical manifestation of the struggle between the two churches, placing the story directly within the affective horizon of its audience. Even more urgently, *The Whore of Babylon* capitalizes on anxieties resonant in the daily lived experience of the burgeoning Protestant nation, especially given the successful and disturbingly unnoticed infiltration of Catholics into outwardly conforming local communities. While *If You Know Not Me* merely suggests the many potential incursions lurking to disrupt the steady ascendancy of English Protestantism, *The Whore of Babylon*, staged almost immediately after the Gunpowder Plot (5 November 1605), focuses on the potentially disastrous attempts to destabilize the English state. The play was likely performed in repertory at the Fortune during the spring and summer of 1606, entered in the Stationer's Register on 20 April 1607, and published shortly after by Nathaniel Butter (who also printed *If You Know Not Me*).

Despite drawing on immediate controversy, *The Whore of Babylon* is not anomalous in the repertory that the Admiral's/Prince's Men constructed at the Fortune. We can discern a slight but noticeable shift in the drama of this troupe after the move north, toward chronicle history plays that feature heroes like Robin Hood and Richard Whittington (a fifteenth-century mayor noted for his charity, especially to apprentices)—figures known for their civic engagement. Many of these plays continue a pattern begun with *The Shoemaker's Holiday* and treat the city and its neighborhoods in rich topical detail by tracing the exploits of some of its more colorful residents. These plays, now lost but mentioned in Henslowe's accounts, include William Haughton's three-part *Blind Beggar of Bethnal Green* (1601), the two-part *Six Clothiers* (1601), Richard Hathway's *Conquest of Spain by John of Gaunt* (1601), Thomas Middleton's *Randall, Earl of Chester* (1602), and Thomas Heywood and Henry Chettle's *The London Florentine* (1603).

Perhaps most striking in this company's repertory during these years is the unprecedented number of plays on religious history that highlight Protestant themes. For whatever reason, these topics were of special interest to the company and the new audience that it courted in Finsbury. The company dramatized the life of biblical figures in *Judas* (1601), *Tobias* (1602), *Jephthah* (1602), *Sampson* (1602), and *Joshua*

(1602) and looked back at the religious history of England in previous centuries in *Sir John Oldcastle* (1600), Henry Chettle's *The Life of Cardinal Wolsey* (1601), *Philip of Spain* (1602), *The Family of Love* (1602), and Rowley's *When You See Me You Know Me* (1605, on Henry VIII). The company's preoccupation with militantly Protestant history plays continued until 1624, when Thomas Drue's *The Duchess of Suffolk* became the last new play performed at the Fortune by the Palsgrave's Men (successors of the Admiral's and Prince's companies). This preponderance of plays on religious themes is probably not accidental and may indicate some kind of agenda on the part of this company that coincided with its move to the Fortune.[54]

In addition to contributing to Henry's Men's preoccupation with religious themes, *The Whore of Babylon* exploits the frenzied climate in the city at a time when tracts denouncing the Gunpowder Plot flourished. The event was frequently discussed and alluded to in sermons, woodcuts, and broadsheets, forging it in the popular imagination.[55] Dekker's play attempts to reinforce the founding ideological tenets of Protestantism and—more importantly—to maintain them in the face of an active Counter-Reformation. In addition to documenting instances of treacherous Jesuit activity, his play readily confronts the fractional hold of Protestantism in England, especially for those removed from the locus of debate and therefore more susceptible to the efforts of Catholic insurgents. The First Cardinal initially acknowledges that in England "the stream of ceremony / Is scarcely settled," imploring his colleagues to "trouble it more" so that "Babylon / And all we are, is not driven clean from thence" (1.1.197–203). Titania (this play's Elizabeth figure) also laments the threat to the emergent Protestant order in England posed by Jesuit "leopards" who "build caves / Even in our parks" (4.2.132–33). These statements forcefully bring the play's concern with international religious politics within the purview of Dekker's audience by suggesting that individual Protestant communities must shoulder the blame for not maintaining faithful guard against Catholic incursions, many of which could be witnessed locally and were expounded at length in nearby parish churches.

The Gunpowder Plot did much to alert Londoners of the threat against the emergent Protestant regime. Nearly everybody, it seems, understood the capture of Guy Fawkes as a sign of "special providence" for England, even while people became even more paranoid about future popish plots. A number of the play's critics suggest that Dekker's overtly allegorical representation of little-known Continental figures makes for an unintelligible and ultimately unsuccessful play, especially given its performance at the Fortune before an audience unfamiliar with historical minutiae. For these scholars, the play's indebtedness to Foxe's apocalyptic pattern and its consistent rehearsal of commonplace antipapal tropes amounted to an indecipherable piece for the public stage.[56] Allegory was not a natural dramatic mode for many, and the style of this play (though not its subject) is different from that of others in the repertory of the Prince's Men at the Fortune during these years. Looking at the play in a local context, however, *The Whore of Babylon* harnessed popular animosity toward various Catholic forces by offering figural representations of momentous events like the Armada, assassination attempts against the queen, and the well-publicized actions of Jesuits. For playgoers at the Fortune in 1606 and the following years, the allegory was close enough to the surface to preclude the interpretive difficulties encountered by later generations. Though it is unlikely that the behind-the-scenes orchestrations of the Marian regime against Elizabeth, nearly fifty years before, would be a vivid part of the living memory of audience members, the Armada—not to mention the Gunpowder Plot—certainly would. This play and others like it seem to have succeeded in fomenting anti-Catholic and anti-Spanish sentiment among their audiences to the extent that the Spanish ambassador, Count de Gondomar, attended the Fortune on 16 July 1621 in what Andrew Gurr thinks was a "diplomat's publicity stunt" calculated to combat the prejudice that had built up among artisans and apprentices over the previous decades.[57]

Many, in fact, were inclined to view the Gunpowder Plot in dramatic terms. William Barlowe's sermon preached before a large and no doubt rabid crowd at Paul's Cross on 10 November 1605, only four days after the apprehension of the perpetrators, suggests that the plot itself was a "tragi-comical treason."[58] Barlowe implies that the dramatic form might usefully capture and explicate the events of 5 November just as it was employed to describe other apocalyptic subjects, including the Book of Revelation. Dekker's emblematic mode of representation, easily enhanced through costuming and stagecraft, frees the playwright from the constraints imposed by a linear narrative. Dekker blends several events into a unified dramatic whole, synergistically registering the cumulative effect of all Catholic plots, both foreign and domestic. The result is a dizzying bombardment of Catholic devices, all designed to tempt and coerce England back into the Catholic fold.

Francis Herring's account of the Gunpowder Plot, *Mischief's Mystery* (1617), similarly details how the combined actions of English recusants, foreign Jesuits, and Spanish invaders deploy a multifaceted attack upon individual and isolated Protestants (see figure 8). Like this tract and much other printed propaganda, Dekker's play suggests that all Protestants, however lowly, are responsible for building and maintaining the true church in their local communities. Plebeian audiences who might otherwise feel removed from the arena of conflict are asked to participate in the spiritual struggle and apprehend their role in maintaining the stability of the English nation and its Protestant church. The play invites its audience members to relive the Gunpowder Plot and hyperbolically alerts them of the potentially disastrous consequences of Catholic control of England even if (as in the case of the Gunpowder Plot) the nation is saved from the brink by the end of the drama. For Protestants, exaggerated presentations of the consequences of Catholic insurgency confirmed previously held religious convictions and increased religious zeal in plebeian communities, "raising the temperature" in previously tepid individuals, to use Patrick Collinson's metaphor.[59]

The *Whore of Babylon* implicates its audience in religious controversy by underscoring religious affiliation as a choice between competing ways of life and visions of society. Dekker suggests that political and religious authority among Catholics coalesces centripetally around a central figure, the Empress of Babylon, who dictates and coerces her subject's obedience. The negative portrayal of that church's dictatorial and corrupt global leadership shows an autocratic regime unaware and unresponsive to local concerns and unconcerned with promoting and maintaining the cohesion of traditional neighborhoods. The difference between the two faiths amounts to a question of agency. Where the Roman Catholic powers rely on an entrenched hierarchy to assert control over the flock, agency in Protestant En-

FIGURE 8. Clouds of Ignorance, Fear, Rome, Hell, Spain, and three other Roman Catholic personages threatening England. From Francis Herring, *Mischief's Mystery* (London: E. Griffin, 1617), sig. A4v. STC: 13247. Courtesy of the Henry E. Huntington Library, San Marino, California (shelfmark 61407).

gland is distributed among large segments of the populace, drawing strength from individual members of the community who function collectively to effect outcomes.

Early in the play, Plain-Dealing illustrates to Titania the different conceptions of individual action under both churches. He claims that "in some games of chess, knights are better than pawns, but here a good pawn is better than a knight" (2.1.96–97). The nature of the "game" is fundamentally different in England, especially in London, where individual "pawns" are expected to develop their own sense of indwelling faith and religious obligation. Plain-Dealing exhorts Titania to "let them [citizens] cure themselves first, and then they may better know how to heal others: then have you other fellows that take upon them to be surgeons" (2.108–9). His remarks emphasize the importance of cultivating an individual response to religious matters through personal devotion and the reading of scriptures, and he distrusts any authoritarian apparatus that seeks to coerce religious opinions. Determining the religious sentiments of average citizens is difficult, especially in a nation incompletely reformed and infiltrated by Jesuits: "If I give you a copy of the City's countenance, I'll not flatter the face, as painters do; but show all the wrinkles in it" (2.1.124–25). Plain-Dealing warns Titania to beware of Catholic insurrection within London and to ignore the kind of flattery which permeates the court of the Empress and will eventually lead to her downfall.

The play's concern with the "city's countenance" mirrors contemporary sermons involved with determining the religious and political loyalty of Londoners. These sermons argue that the religious and spiritual health of individual citizens in various isolated communities necessarily must precede a robust nation-state and the effective operation of foreign policy. In a sermon preached in 1608 at Hampstead in Middlesex County, in close proximity to Clerkenwell and Finsbury, William Bailey compares the dangerously volatile religious situation in London with the period when the Ten Commandments were revealed to Moses and the wandering Israelites. Due to some dissimulating leaders, Londoners, like the Israelites, "could not, or would not, distinguish between the sign and the thing signified."[60] Bailey assesses religious controversy as essentially a problem of interpretation, suggesting that history—of biblical times or contemporary events—

must be read diachronically and typologically in order to determine whether a given sign is true or false. Interpretation, according to this author, is a process of accumulating facts from scripture. Familiarity with scripture and the history of the church provides a hermeneutic key developed through the ages that offers individuals protection during turbulent periods, when the proper course of action is not readily apparent or is disguised through treachery. This approach enables the exegete—and invites the congregation—to apprehend current events in terms of the ongoing religious struggle.

Similarly, the physical and spiritual action of *The Whore of Babylon* revolves around the "discovery" of the names and hiding places of those who sow religious discord, whose true identities are obfuscated through their feigned service to the Fairie Queene. Like the legion of clandestine Jesuits, Catholic insurgents are expressly instructed by the Empress to "turn your selves then to moles, / Work underground and undermine your country . . . Fly with the bat under the eyes of night / And shift your nests" (3.1.150–59). English Jesuits were well known for their ability to change residences frequently and utilize a vast network of sympathizers to avoid detection. Thomas Browne, a noted recusant, admitted to staying at eight different houses over the course of just over a month.[61] Because of the subtle ways in which Catholics were able to infiltrate the Protestant regime and elude authorities, the figure of Plain-Dealing is obsessed with issues of proper identification and interpretation, asking Truth, "how shall I know thou art the right truth?" (3.3.1). Truth's response suggests that his plain aspect signifies his truth, which is in marked contrast to the "strange ugliness" of the Empress of Babylon. Plain-Dealing argues that true Christians' consciences must match their plain apparel and demeanor in a way that implicitly condemns multiple social groups within the city for their lack of outward modesty and its concomitant reflection of inward humility: "I saw no more conscience in most of your rich men than in tavern faggots: nor no more soberness in poor men than in tavern spigots" (3.3.38–40).

Dekker's play, along with sermons preached in local parishes, posits a fundamental distinction between the structure of conscience among Protestants and Catholics. John Andrews, preacher at St. James Clerkenwell, addresses the fiercely contested issue of the sacraments in the two churches in exactly these terms, claiming that "they are signs, yet not bare signs, but moral instruments and means by which God doth confer those graces really and truly upon us that those signs do represent . . . I mean an outward and visible sign of an inward and spiritual grace, given unto us ordained by Christ himself."[62] Outward signs are empty; they are only activated by individual believers and generate meaning for the community only by private devotion. *The Whore of Babylon* similarly presents England, and London more specifically, as a collection of dispersed, free-thinking individuals, as opposed to the hierarchical structure of the Catholic church and the nations under its sway, especially Spain.[63]

The primacy of indwelling faith guarantees the importance of "pawns" in England, like the artisans and apprentices that flocked to theatres like the Fortune. Titania's court is a discursive and consensus-building forum where her decisions are constantly tempered by the advice of her councilors. The Empress and her followers soon recognize that a single unilateral strike against "Fairieland" or an assassination attempt against the Fairie Queen herself will prove unproductive, because power in Titania's realm does not reside solely within a single agent. The First Cardinal realizes that "to fell down their queen is but one stroke / Our axe must cleave the kingdom, that's the Oak" (3.1.246–47). As monarch, Titania is a leader among fellow soldiers, each of whom retains decision-making authority and responsibility. Each soldier individually exhibits the attributes necessary for success in this martial and spiritual endeavor. Audiences appreciate how religion operates within local communities, recognizing their role in maintaining a national faith that might otherwise seem beyond their purview.

By contrast, the Empress of Babylon compels the submission of her followers; her Herald summons her forces to arms in the name of

> her who hath power given her to make the backs of stubborn kings her foot-stools, and emperors her vassals . . . no captains generals of armies, generals of squadrons, admirals, colonels, captains, or any other officers of her magnificent, incomparable, formidable, and invincible Armada . . . shall presume to set one foot on shipboard, till her sacred hand hath blessed the enterprise by sealing

them all on the forehead, and bowing their knees before the beast. (4.3.29–40)

The Empress, riding onstage on a beast evocative of the one depicted in Revelation 17, uses the "sacred" and mystical "power" allegedly granted her directly from God to exercise complete psychological control over her followers, whose autonomy has atrophied within the rigid hierarchy and ritual observance demanded by the Catholic regime. Protestants would likely notice the biblical allusion to Revelation (or more recently to Edmund Spenser's *Faerie Queene*: 1.4.36–38). Habitual theatregoers would recognize the parallel with Marlowe's *Tamburlaine*, a popular play frequently in repertory at the Fortune, where the title character makes Bajazeth his footstool and later yokes the kings of Trebizond and Soria to drive his chariot (I: 4.2.14 and II: 4.3). The ugliness of the "damnable harlot" and her grotesque mount onstage is not just a metaphorical association but provides audiences with palpable visual reinforcement of the rhetoric.

As with Heywood's depiction of the role of ordinary citizens within the overall religious struggle, Dekker demonstrates the structural importance of individual faith and the localized actions of community members in preserving a healthy state. All members of the audience were encouraged to take partial credit for the numerous victories celebrated in the play precisely because they possess virtues of truth and plain-dealing. Dekker invites playgoers to recognize that they are essential components of a growing religious community despite their lowly social status. Although Dekker, like most dramatists, was hardly an apologist for either the church or the state, he could nevertheless recognize the value in affirming a set of beliefs that could unite Londoners, thus enabling greater civic engagement for the benefit of local neighborhoods and for the metropolis at large.

The topicality and polemical Protestantism of *If You Know Not Me* and *The Whore of Babylon* are self-evident through even a cursory reading. Understanding their local circumstances of production at large public amphitheatres amid a turbulent religious climate in the growing Middlesex suburbs both elaborates on and subtly differentiates between the more general messages they offer. These two plays obviously continue the didactic project initiated by Foxe and other

Elizabethans to instruct a large segment of the populace in the importance of scriptural authority, justification by faith, discerning the true church from the false, and other tenets of the Protestant religion. Beyond this, the plays situate the potentially factional audience directly as vital defenders of the faith, along with monarchs, soldiers, and diplomats. Although we can never know to what extent religiously motivated plays like these influenced playgoers or changed their minds on ecclesiastical matters, understanding them locally highlights an important dimension of the drama's appeal and suggests another way in which it engaged with a specific constituency. In an urban environment that revolved around parish life and where many frequented the playhouse, it is hardly surprising that the church and the theatre shared jurisdiction over many things, even people's souls.

Chapter 4
THE SPECTACLE OF HISTORY AT THE RED BULL

In the midst of one of the worst visitations of the plague in a decade, Thomas Dekker conjures a harrowing image of life outside London's walls:

> Death hath pitched his tent in the sinfully polluted suburbs . . . Toxin rings out for life, and no voice heard but kill, kill . . . In this pitiful (or rather pitiless) perplexity stood London forsaken like a lover, forlorn like a widow, and disarmed of all comfort . . . so hungry is the Estridge disease that it will devour even iron . . . They that rode on the lustiest geldings could not outgallop the plague.[1]

Like most of London's suburbs, the neighborhood of Clerkenwell—home to the Red Bull playhouse—and its immediate environs were dreary, drab, and depressed, its residents apprehensive and fearful. In addition to enduring the perennial struggles of daily life and work during a prolonged inflationary period, Londoners had recently survived recurring outbursts of the plague every year since its truly cataclysmic outbreak in 1603, "when these miserable calamities entered in . . . thy gates, slaying 30,000 and more as thou heldst them in thy arms."[2] Because of the crowded physical conditions and a larger transient population, the plague hit the suburbs harder than parishes within the walls, exacting a severe toll on nearly every family and leaving residents anxious that large-scale and life-changing disease was never far away.

In stark contrast to the horrifying plague, this series of stage directions accompanies the climax of Thomas Heywood's *The Brazen Age*, staged at the Red Bull around 1610 or 1611, just after a long series of theatre closures due to the disease:

> Enter Hercules from a rock above, tearing down trees . . . All the princes break down the trees, and make a fire in which Hercules placeth himself. Jupiter above strikes him with a thunder-bolt, his body sinks, and from the heavens descends a hand in a cloud that from the place where Hercules was burned, brings up a star and fix it to the firmament.[3]

In addition to Jupiter's thunderbolts and the earth-shattering immolation of Hercules, this play and the five-part cycle known as the *Ages* also depict centaurs, sea monsters, magic snakes, raging bulls, the seven planets, nymphs, amazons, satyrs, furies, fates, ghosts, dragons, Cyclopes, giants, and perhaps most spectacularly the Trojan Horse. The plays also stage countless battles between foes both mortal and immortal in settings that range from the heights of Olympus to the depths of hell, from Egypt, to Troy, to all parts of Greece and the seas in between. Such elaborate and versatile choreography, exotic settings, stage violence, otherworldly characters, and staggering pyrotechnics, remarkable for their time, permeate these plays (ca. 1609–1613).[4] They treat mythical history, as told by Ovid, "from Jupiter and Saturn, to the utter subversion of Troy, with a faithful account of all these Princes of Greece, who had hand in the fate thereof."[5]

"Drums, trumpets, battles, and heroes."[6] This simple description, repeated in almost all discussions of the Red Bull and its repertory, has become the basis for that theatre's identity. For those who regularly attended the Red Bull, bombastic plays like Heywood's *Ages* were a hit; the first of this group, *The Golden Age* (ca. 1609), spawned four sequels; during these years the Red Bull became extremely popular among the artisans and apprentices who typically resorted there. These plays have not met with the same approval of theatre historians and literary critics from the seventeenth century to the present, who tend to condescend toward the Red Bull and its audience, which apparently delighted in little more than "loud clamors" and "daily tumults."[7] To refer to the "drum and trumpet" fare at the Red Bull has become something of an insult.

Yet the juxtaposition of these spectacular plays with the gloomy social environment in which they were first performed begins to suggest an important local context in which to interpret the popularity of the Red Bull and the *Ages*. For those struggling through recurrent visitations of the plague and its aftermath, the *Ages* were a welcome—if brief—reprieve from daily hardships. For the Queen Anne's Men, the troupe that performed them, these plays meant steady profits and a loyal audience during a period of financial instability due to the interruptions to daily performances.

How and why did this particular set of plays resonate so dynamically for the audience at the Red Bull during these difficult years? Certainly, their elaborate physical staging of familiar mythical events would have distinguished them from the many plays on similar topics staged by other companies, allowing audiences to witness in an extremely visceral manner what other productions could only deliver verbally. The Red Bull surpassed its competitors in special effects. An exhaustive study of staging at the playhouse by George F. Reynolds notes several features called for in Red Bull plays that set it apart, including a front and rear stage (or simply a larger stage) to allow a greater depth and range of action, additional stage doors in the tiring house and trapdoors in the floor, a sophisticated deus ex machina for flying characters above and around the stage, and of course abundant fireworks and elaborately choreographed battle scenes. In contrast to the extensive use of properties and effects at the Red Bull, where some type of extralinguistic device was used in nearly every scene, 80 percent of the scenes in Shakespeare's plays could be performed without any props on a completely bare stage.[8]

The staging of the *Ages* at the Red Bull allowed the Queen's Men to appeal directly to the histrionic tastes of artisans and apprentices, capitalizing on this important niche in an increasingly specialized dramatic market. In addition to these plays' social function as entertainment for an audience very much in need of some kind of reprieve from the plague, Heywood hints at a more familiar humanist agenda, something that critics seldom associate with the Red Bull. Speaking the epilogue to *The Brazen Age*, the narrator Homer underscores both the purpose and the intended audience of the play, suggesting that the players were

> Striving to illustrate things not known to all,
> In which the learned can only censure right:

The rest we strive, whom we unlettered call,
Rather to attend than judge: for more than sight
We seek to please. (L3v)

Through these eye-catching productions, the Queen Anne's Men sought not just to entertain but to inform and improve their largely "unlettered" audience. The action was more than a mere pleasing "sight," embodying purposes both moral and communal. Heywood and the players embraced lavish spectacle as a profitable way of differentiating their plays from those of other companies but also as a calculated way of adapting classical works to a particular clientele. Understanding the *Ages* plays as spectacular entertainment infused with some genuinely humanistic aspirations helps us see how the Red Bull and the drama staged there constituted a social capital investment in the local community. The stakes of that investment can be judged by imagining how spectators appreciated these plays' fantastical Ovidian narratives of immortal gods and heroes in contrast to the dire scene immediately around them, marked by ferocious disease and mortality.

Theatre historians and literary critics frequently point out the importance of the plague to the dramatic history of the period, noting that the frequency of the disease proved a considerable challenge to the economic stability and repertory management of theatrical companies. The plague's effects on theatre audiences, on the demand for dramatic performance, have received less attention. If the plague was a challenge for actors, for citizens of London (especially the disadvantaged) it challenged their ability to survive. Recurrent visitations of the plague in the early seventeenth century were horrendous: tens of thousands out of a total population of approximately two hundred thousand, more than one-fifth of all residents, lost their lives to the pestilence in the first decade of the seventeenth century. Over three thousand perished in a single week in August 1603 alone, and 29,083 during that calendar year. Each of the major outbreaks of the disease was nothing short of a holocaust, with yearly eruptions in succeeding years that were only slightly more benign. The extremely high number of casualties meant that everybody in the city would have known a family member or friend who succumbed to the disease.

The extreme threat forced even those not infected to modify their daily routines drastically. For them, the closure of the theatres was only the beginning. All residents were subject to a strict set of orders, gradually imposed by the Privy Council and the various branches of the city government, that covered multiple facets of civic life in an attempt to assuage the severity of the plague. Although they were modified slightly over time, the London plague orders of 1583, consisting of twenty-one interrelated instructions, sought to regulate everything from public gatherings to domestic procedures for dealing with the dead and the infected to sanitary procedures to be practiced by all Londoners. Responsibility for enacting the orders fell to the aldermen and their constables, who were subject to increasingly harsh punishment for dereliction of duty as the plague continued to reappear annually despite the best efforts of the city government.[9]

Yet the plague did not affect all Londoners equally. As with most calamities, the brunt of the epidemic was borne by the poor. Thomas Lodge noted during the worst of the pestilence (in 1603) that "where the infestation most rageth there poverty reigneth among the commons, which having no supplies to satisfy the greedy desire of those that should attend them, are for the most part left desolate and die without relief." The plight of the poor was exacerbated because the rich tended to leave town without "leaving nor sending any succor for the poor . . . [leaving] in a manner none but the poor to relieve the poor." Given the disparity in wealth between city and suburb, those dwelling in the suburbs suffered more than those living in more affluent inner city parishes: "for, go we into the suburbs, what do we hear but the lamentable voices and cryings of the visited poor."[10] Infection varied with urban geography to such a great extent that one pamphlet, entitled *Lachrymae Londinenses*, draws a "map of the city's misery," sketching a city where the plague was not spread evenly, aggravating its effects and spawning conflicts among residents.[11] Not only were suburbanites unable to afford the wide assortment of (largely ineffectual) treatments on the market, but the rapid growth of suburban areas meant the deterioration of sanitary conditions, greater overcrowding, and, of course, greater risk of infection. Just as many Londoners were inclined to understand the plague as God's scourge for etiolated values and lascivious living, many—noticing the higher incidence of the plague on the outskirts of the city—tended to blame the suburbs for the plague and to extrapolate from this that the suburbs were in some way morally degenerate.

The fairly detailed surviving records kept by the Company of Parish Clerks attest that the brunt of the sickness was indeed borne by outlying parishes. St. James Clerkenwell, St. Saviour Southwark, and St. Giles Cripplegate (the parishes that contained the Red Bull, the Globe, and the Fortune, respectively) were more populous than many inner-city parishes, so we might expect a correspondingly greater mortality rate. The casualty figures in these out-parishes, however, were astronomically higher than within the city proper, entirely incongruous with their respective sizes. Of the 24,504 people who perished throughout the city from the plague in a five-month period (from 14 July to 15 December 1603), 15,033 (61.4 percent) died in the twenty-three parishes outside the city walls, either in the liberties or in the out-parishes. The ninety-six smaller and less populous parishes within the walls recorded deaths at a much lower rate.

Because the parish was the most important unit of social organization and day-to-day community life, we need to think through these local statistics to get a more comprehensive understanding of the affects of the plague on suburbanites, especially in Clerkenwell and its environs. In St. James Clerkenwell and St. Giles Cripplegate, the death tolls over these same months were 617 (2.5 percent of the city's total) and 1,443 (6 percent), respectively. During some particularly devastating periods, the death rate at St. James reached almost 100 and at St. Giles slightly over 200 in a single week. For several weeks the death toll in these parishes alone accounted for over 10 percent of the total for the entire city of London, compared with a mere twenty-three deaths in all of Cornhill Ward (perhaps the wealthiest in the city) and eight in St. Olave's Silver Street, where Shakespeare was residing at the time. Those in these suburban parishes seeking solace at Sunday services at either of these churches—one form of public gathering that was not proscribed—would face the grave reality that many of their neighbors and fellow congregants would not be there in one week. The effects of the plague in and around Clerkenwell not only were worse in numeric terms but were sustained over a longer period. By October, when the weekly death toll in many inner-city parishes had dwindled to a handful, the death toll at St. James and St. Giles remained in the dozens or higher.

Anecdotal evidence confirms these statistics. In his report of the disease in the ironically titled *The Wonderful Year* (1603), Thomas Dekker describes just how horrible conditions were:

> [I]n the . . . suburbs the plague is muster-master and marshall of the field; burning fevers, boils, blains, and carbuncles, the leaders, lieutenants, sergeants, and corporals; the main army consisting of a mingle-mangle of dumpish mourners, merry sextons, hungry coffin-sellers, scrubbing bearers, and nasty grave-makers. . . . Fear and trembling (the two catch-poles of death) arrest everyone.[12]

Dekker's militaristic metaphor is not simply a play on the name of many of these suburban parishes ("in-the-fields") or merely designed to emphasize the scope of the plague's invasion of the suburbs and the suffering it caused; it is a reference to the fact that the suburbs, in addition to being the hardest-hit neighborhoods in London, were in the vanguard of the disease. Plague visitations almost always began in the suburbs, spreading throughout the outskirts of the city before moving inward.[13] This was a familiar pattern in later years, meaning that suburbanites, and especially those in the northern suburbs, had no warning of an outbreak, unlike inner-city parishioners.

The plague recurred every year until 1609. Thankfully, casualties did not reach the appalling levels of 1603 again until 1625. This proved to be of little consolation to Londoners. Residents of the capital were subject to immense psychological trauma exacted by the pestilence: a pressure often overlooked by those who concentrate on the admittedly shocking statistics alone. One of the characteristics of the plague that struck London in the early years of the seventeenth century was its regularity. It reappeared slowly in the summer and reached endemic levels by the autumn every year.[14] Unlike sporadic outbreaks of disease that remained dormant for decades, despite high death tolls and extreme civil strife, Londoners were continually worried about bubonic plague and its predictable recurrence, wondering if this might be the year when they or a family member finally succumbed. Attesting to this extreme psychological terror, the ordinarily sardonic Dekker narrates how "a freezing horror sucks up the rivers of my blood, my hair stands on end with the panting of my brains, my eye balls are ready to stand out, being beaten with the billows of my tears" when he recalls the devastation caused by the 1603 plague, a fear made even worse in the anticipation of future outbreaks for those reading the tract later in the decade.[15]

The plague cast a shadow of fear and uncertainty over almost every aspect of life in the city, making it a frequent, almost obsessive, topic of conversation and debate that centered around its causes and its prevention. Dozens of tracts, appearing at an average of nearly two a year over a period of almost forty years, promised both physical and spiritual remedies for the pestilence. They either offered useless medical advice or rehearsed long-standing theories that the plague was an instrument of divine wrath—neither of which did much to reduce uncertainties that festered over decades.

Adding to the dread, the plague was a highly visible disease. Those infected developed large swelling wounds called bubos that were known in the Renaissance as "tokens . . . whereby we are put in mind of those horrible torments that follow after death and the fire of hell."[16] Oozing wounds like these attested to the seriousness of the disease and were no doubt disgusting to look at and smell, especially when encountered on a person's own body, prognosticating worse to come. "Those marks or tokens," writes John Taylor, "show them they must die."[17] Almost as frightening as the physical pain and mental anguish they caused, tokens were a form of social signification, informing the community that the individual in all likelihood would perish (four-fifths of those who fell ill died within eight days) and posed an extreme risk of contagion while still alive. We can only imagine nervous Londoners obsessively checking themselves for signs of the disease, fearing for their lives and realizing that their open wounds would surely bring social death and unknowable hardship for their families and loved ones even if they did manage to survive. The mildest fever or blemish on the skin could conceivably evince extreme psychic trauma. Little wonder that the disease brought about hypochondria on a massive scale. The plague was thereby inscribed in the memories of all Londoners and remained a topic of morbid conversation for years.

Some felt that the various public health measures undertaken by the municipal government, including the establishment of plague houses for the afflicted, were pointless in the face of such a horrible disease. These measures had the untoward effect of splitting up families and shutting off sources of assistance within local communities even if they minimally lowered the risk of contagion. Most saw the key to good health in the air citizens breathed. Londoners were instructed "to perfume the whole house and chambers with the fume of rosemary, juniper, the parings of apples, sorax, benjamin, incense, dried roses, lavender, and such like, both evening and morning."[18] This caused a run on herbs: Dekker reports that "the price of flowers, herbs, and garlands, rose wonderfully, in so much that rosemary, which had wont to be sold for twelve pence an armful, went now for six shillings a handful."[19] Residents of Clerkenwell and other suburbs could ill afford such dear remedies, whether preventative or curative, just as they could not afford to flee to the countryside. Perhaps more significantly, the enormous publicity that accompanied these imagined cures would intensify the sense of doom and heighten the depression and paranoia among those unable to afford them, again illustrating how the plague became a psychic and social malady in addition to a physical one.

Many Londoners, perhaps the majority, saw medical treatment and epidemiological measures as equally misguided, reading the plague instead as a spiritual affliction, the mark of an angry God. "There is no plague but for sin," Anthony Anderson reminded his congregants, "and the lion roareth not, without his prey." The only natural recourse to this kind of divine malady was repentance for a variety of sins, notably for "inward contempt and outward disdain, each one of other"—for a failure to live in community with their fellow citizens.[20] Lest Londoners put too much trust in the power of prayer and amending their lives, Thomas Hastler reminded them that "time . . . should yield us (in these our contagious and deadly times) a strong persuasion of a timely return unto the right way: we are all out by sin, and therefore we must begin again by repentance, that we may regain our peace with God *in time*."[21] Londoners could take little immediate comfort, even in religion.

If preachers, officers of the city, and medical authorities were able to isolate various causes of the plague and means for its redress, it was up to more subtle commentators to diagnose its invidious social consequences, which a presentation of medical facts and statistics has often obscured. T. C. recognized that one of the worst effects of the plague was the inconsolable fear wrought among individuals and groups in once harmonious communities, where neighbors came to distrust one another, even blaming each other for the calamity. The plague was so fearful, he writes, "because that it taketh away the people very suddenly, unlooked for and unawares: And therefore then followeth strife, lawing or business among sinners, and of the commonwealth, as every man by himself can lightly perceive and understand. Therefore it is also an horrible punishment . . . which concerneth both them that die, and them that are left alive." Unlike many other preachers who discussed the virtues of faith and righteousness as biblical abstractions, T. C. advocated charity, seeing the values that once prevailed in neighborhoods as perhaps the best defense: "And at the last shall He save him, that continueth not without fruit, but breaketh out with right love and faithfulness towards his neighbor."[22]

The plague also proved a considerable challenge to London's entertainment industry, especially the actors who depended on regular playing for their livelihood. We cannot know how the players weathered the plague. Some, like Edward Alleyn and his family, escaped the epidemic relatively unscathed.[23] Others did not. Robert Browne, a player at the Boar's Head who was associated with a number of companies, including most recently Worcester's Men (the precursor of Anne's Men), succumbed in October 1603.[24] But with this exception actors seem to have emerged from the years of pestilence with comparatively few casualties, perhaps owing to their greater mobility and ability to relocate to less-infested parts of the country. Sporadic mention of the King's Men over this period implies that they stayed away from London as much as possible.[25] Queen Anne's Men spent August 1604 at Durham House, but their whereabouts during other outbreaks of the plague cannot be determined with the same precision. It is possible that many in the troupe, which did not receive its official patent until 19 February 1604/1605, were forced to move to or remain in Clerkenwell around this period due to the negotiations surrounding the conversion of the Red Bull to a full-time playhouse, hoping to begin using their new venue as soon as conditions permitted.[26]

Though the plague apparently did not gravely affect the physical survival of the players, as it did with so many other citizens of London, it severely hampered their financial prospects: theatres in London were closed for seventy-three out of the ninety-six months from 1603 to 1610.[27] Seasonal court performances (perhaps more than usual, as the crown provided some kind of modest compensation to the struggling players) and sporadic touring when the plague was in remission offered a modest source of income when the London playhouses were closed.[28] The loss of day-to-day revenues would have placed companies in a dire financial predicament, severely limiting their ability to acquire new plays, stage properties, or costuming. When an actor is asked, in a fictional dialogue of the Caroline period, why he performs only tragedies and not comedies "in this heavy and contagious time of the plague in London," he responds that it is because "my purse each day doth perish most tragically."[29]

Because the plague was so detrimental to the theatrical industry during this period, we need to reconsider the companies' repertories and their competitive practices in the crucial years after 1609, when the plague subsided and daily playing resumed. The financially burdened companies were now pressed to generate the revenue necessary to stay in business and recoup six years of losses.[30] With only one six-month period of uninterrupted playing (from April to September 1605), it is improbable that any new plays could have completed a full repertory cycle or reached profitability until the theatres reopened for complete seasons after 1609. By this time, all companies undoubtedly had a large inventory of new plays waiting to be performed for the first time or to complete their stage runs.[31]

In this climate of impending disease and even greater anxiety, residents in and around Clerkenwell, player and playgoer alike, sought to begin the fledging theatrical venture at the Red Bull. By 1603 the King's Men and Prince Henry's Men both had relatively new venues, the Globe and the Fortune, in which to perform. Queen Anne's Men, however, were still using the outdated Curtain in anticipation of the conversion of an innyard in Clerkenwell into the theatre that would become the Red Bull. The plague further delayed the already troubled theatre project, forcing the troupe to play at inferior venues until at least 1605 and perhaps as late as 1607.[32] Regardless of the date of their debut at the Red Bull, performances in the first years of the playhouse were sporadic at best due to the mandatory plague closures. Queen

Anne's Men were unable to settle into a regular cycle of performing at their new venue until 1609, when the plague subsided and the theatres remained open for full seasons. The year 1609 and following years would provide a crucial test for the company's new venture, suggesting that the *Ages* were pivotal in the history of the company and the success of the Red Bull.

Playgoers, too, were eager for regular playing to resume, both for the sense of normalcy that it represented and for the psychological distraction from the extreme pressure evinced by the plague and the dislocations that it caused in their daily lives. The terror no doubt remained for some time. In hindsight, we know that the plague slackened in the years after 1610. Londoners had no way of knowing this, and it is only natural that the endemic fear generated by the plague continued unabated. Actors with the Queen Anne's Men, even if they did not suffer severe losses to members of their profession, were nevertheless participants in the shared struggles of the community, just as prone to uneasiness and dread of what might lie in store. Members of the company would no doubt be reminded of the death of Browne, a loss that was to prove even more influential for the company when his widow, Susan, married Thomas Greene, a sharer in the troupe and a long-time resident of Clerkenwell. Many of the players were parishioners at St. James, including Greene, John Duke, Robert Lee, and Heywood himself, all likely traumatized by the devastation to the parish and its congregants.[33] Participating in this shared struggle would have allowed them to forge even more intimate ties to the local community. Within Clerkenwell, these players were significantly more than anonymous purveyors of a cultural product and would no doubt have had personal relationships with many of the playgoers concerning matters that had little or nothing to do with the theatre.

The *Ages* responded to a string of turbulent years in theatre history and in the social history of Clerkenwell as well as the larger metropolis. These blockbusters would have been popular with the Red Bull crowd as a temporary reprieve from current hardships, satisfying playgoers' desire for diversionary entertainment and putting the company on a somewhat more stable financial footing. The plays also might have represented, at least for some playgoers, a response to the plague and the social strife it caused. Almost everyone involved in the crisis (from members of the city government who took seriously the challenge posed to public welfare to religious and secular commentators who documented the plague's physical destruction and mental duress) realized that something was needed that could inspire the courage to confront the plague even in residents of the most devastated neighborhoods, bolster severely weakened spirits, and restore communal bonds that had been frayed almost beyond repair.

Numerous models of heroic behavior were available, but perhaps none so notorious as the larger-than-life heroes of classical history and myth—characters whose stories already had considerable purchase on the imagination of Londoners who believed, or at least imagined, that they were the Trojans' descendants. These plays therefore might be understood as part of a communal struggle to make an unparalleled social crisis intelligible and controllable. The playgoers' desire for grandiose entertainment and the players' desire to gain competitive advantage and turn a profit combined to shape a set of plays that satisfied both. Yet the plays also intimated the moral precepts encoded in this mythical history to a community still suffering. Whether playgoers thought of the plays as moral education is debatable—and perhaps unlikely—but is beside the point. Humanists, including Heywood, thought that presenting classical material could move readers or viewers to virtue even if they were not cognizant of a didactic agenda. As with many other forms of social capital building, playing and playgoing could yield positive community outcomes as their unintended result.

Classical history was nothing new on the Renaissance stage, even if its previous incarnations looked or sounded nothing like the *Ages*. One of the fiercest arenas of competition among theatrical concerns was in history plays, a staple of company offerings since the opening of Burbage's Theatre in 1576. Just as English chronicles had been the rage during the 1590s, so history plays in the years after 1600 mirrored a trend that had penetrated literary prose and verse years earlier. The theatres adapted Plutarch's *Lives*, Livy's *Roman History*, and Ovid's *Metamorphoses*, staging the fabulous exploits of figures such as Jupiter and Hercules or the supposedly real deeds of Greek and Roman leaders such as Achilles and Caesar. English poets, statesmen, and chroniclers, all keenly aware that their own lineage could be traced to the Roman occupation and to Caesar's legendary building of the Tower of London, had long celebrated classical learning and Roman history. London, they assumed, was originally "Troynovant," the new Troy. Humanists also saw Rome and its history as an important part of the English present. Troy and its Italian reincarnation in Rome were understood as a "cultural parent." The history of these cultures and the virtue displayed by their leaders were often taken as a model for the ideal organization of social and political life in England.[34]

Heywood absorbed these intellectual currents and entitled his own verse mythical history (a more scholarly and literary precursor to the *Ages*) *Troia Britannica* (1609),[35] rehearsing the popular Troynovant legend as he does again in the *Iron Age*. In the play's second part Hector prognosticates to Aeneas:

Thousands shall issue from thy sacred seed
Cities more rich than this the Grecian spoil.
In after times shall thy successors build,
Where Hector's name shall live eternally.
One Romulus, another Brute shall rear,
These shall nor honours, nor just rectors want,
Lumbardy's Rome, Great Britain's Troy-novant.[36]

Unlike more learned accounts of the legend (and deviating significantly from Shakespeare's cynical treatment of the same events in *Troilus and Cressida*), Heywood invites his audience—the descendants of Priam, Hector, and Aeneas—to identify with the Trojans, both in their valor and in their shortcomings. By their very presence in the playhouse, audiences are participating in the millennium-old project of enshrining the memory of Hector and the other valiant Trojans, spreading the virtues they embodied, and reestablishing this ancient and revered community in London.[37] Although the ubiquity of the Troynovant legend in both learned and popular culture meant that most Londoners—even the unlettered at the Red Bull—were aware of their supposed Trojan heritage, this information could do little to forge a more harmonious community for those who knew very little about Troy in the first place. *The Iron Age* was a lowbrow version of the Trojan story as told in George Chapman's *Iliad*, *Troia-Britannica*, *Troilus and Cressida*, and many other contemporary variants. It offers an entertaining introduction to the legend, emphasizing its similarities to London and offering an example of the fate that could befall even a venerated city like Troy when its citizens do not live in amity with their neighbors.

General interest in classical history led to a related captivation with myth. In ways that are often unsettling to later generic classifications, Renaissance authors and historians viewed mythology as a close subdiscipline of history, partially explaining the strong supernatural content that permeates the *Ages* and other history plays of the period. George Puttenham's influential *The Art of English Poesy* (1589) suggests that "histories were of three sorts, wholly true and wholly false, and a third holding part of either, but for honest recreation, and for good example were they all."[38] Adherence to the historical record was immaterial from a strictly moral perspective. Because of its didactic content, the Ovidian material that Heywood incorporated in the *Ages*—despite its deified characters and otherworldly settings—was considered a legitimate and illuminating form of history.[39]

In the preface to his translation of *The Metamorphoses* (1567), Arthur Golding demonstrates how a familiarity with mythical characters and their exploits can move us to virtue:

> By Jove and Juno [we] understand all states of princely sort;
> By Ops and Saturn ancient folk that are of elder sort;
> By Phoebus young and lusty brutes of hand and courage stout;
> By Mars the valiant men of war who love to fight it out;
> By Pallas and the famous troup of all the muses nine,
> Such folk as in the sciences and virtuous arts do shine (C1v).

The characters that populate these fables instruct precisely because they are so real, fully encapsulating the virtues and vices so familiar to those in all periods—"a mirror for thyself thine own estate to see" but malleable enough to be applied to a variety of particular historical circumstances.[40] Heywood's dedication "To the Reader" of *The Iron Age* purposefully disintegrates traditional generic boundaries in the same way: "I shall presume the reading thereof shall not prove distasteful to any, first in regard of the antiquity and nobleness of the history: next because it includeth the most things of special remark which have been ingeniously commented, and laboriously recorded by the muse's darlings, the poets, and Time's learned remembrancers, the historiographers."[41] The poet and the historian were essentially up to the same thing. Both sought to educate and enlighten their audiences to improve public virtue.

Of course the vogue for classicism, the frequent allusions to Rome in chronicle histories, and the rising humanist tide cannot themselves account for the widespread popularity of mythical and Roman history even among uneducated Londoners. Most playgoers (especially, from what we are told, those who frequented the Fortune and the Red Bull) were not the beneficiaries of a humanist education. They did not have access to Roman authors in their original language and were forced to rely on translation or oral accounts of these historic events. Yet by the early seventeenth century even these audiences could claim a growing familiarity with these subjects, partly because new printing technologies had rapidly increased the availability of Roman history in translation. Knowledge of classical history was extending to segments of the population that had little previous access to these narratives.[42] Translations of Roman history were not intended solely for a learned readership; Thomas North's dedication to Queen Elizabeth, reprinted in Stuart editions, entreats "the protection" of the monarch's patronage so that "the common sort of your subjects shall not only profit themselves hereby, but also be animated to the better service of your majesty."[43] Citizens were educated not only in the intricacies of the historical record but in the virtue and civility necessary to forge a more harmonious community.

Attempting to merge the intellectual rigor and educative capacity of humanism with the affective power of the stage, Heywood's *Apology for Actors* forges a triangular relationship of drama, history, and didacticism. He argues that witnessing dramatic productions might have the capacity to inspire. "Why," he asks, "should not the lives of these [classical] worthies, presented in these our days, effect the like wonder in the princes of our times?"[44] Like Sidney, for whom the historian provided instruction but lacked the means to inspire readers to moral probity like the poet, those in the Renaissance concerned with spreading humanism to the larger populace recognized a problem with history as a written narrative. They realized that the mode of representation must allow people to apprehend the noble deeds of classical heroes viscerally to gain a true appreciation for the magnitude of their virtue and, most importantly, imitate them in their own lives. Unlike chronicle history, "wherein our forefather's valiant acts . . . have lain long buried in rusty brass and worm-eaten books," Thomas Nashe writes that "there is no immortality can be given a man on earth like unto plays."[45]

Like Nashe, Heywood felt that words on a page were insufficient. Something was even lacking in the visual arts: "a description is only a shadow received by the ear but not perceived by the eye; so lively portraiture is merely a form seen by the eye, but can neither show action, passion, motion, or any other gesture to move the spirits of the beholder to admiration."[46] Drama contained both rhetoric pleasing to the ear and visual elements pleasing to the eye, all within the coherent narrative structure favored by the historian replete with the linguistic artifice and imaginative vigor of the poet. Plays also contained something more: action. And, depending largely on the audience, some dramas relied on this extralinguistic appeal more than others. Rather than "hearing a play," as Hamlet proposed to the audience at the Globe, the less-educated audiences at the Red Bull—"ignorant asses," according to John Webster—seemed more interested in seeing the drama, a desire satisfied by the *Ages*.[47]

Because the unlettered could readily apprehend staged drama, Heywood felt that history plays could educate and even ennoble those who lacked refinement; they could "unlock the casket long time shut / Of which none but the learned held the key."[48] The spectacle in plays, even more than their language, was viscerally appealing in a way that allowed audiences to apply the events onstage to their individual and collective circumstances. While some playgoers sought political intrigue, literary artistry, or rhetorical skill, others required something else. For the hard-working residents of Clerkenwell, ambivalent about the future, plays had the capacity to "refresh such weary spirits as are tired with labour . . . to moderate the cares and heaviness of the mind, that they may return to their trades and faculties with more zeal and earnestness, after some small, soft, and pleasant retirement."[49] The need for recreation did not vitiate other agendas like education and moral improvement; it simply meant that these projects had to be incorporated discreetly into the plays. "Men come not to study at a playhouse," wrote Edmund Gayton, "but love such expressions and passages which with ease insinuate themselves into their capacities."[50] If the right "expressions and passages" were used, audiences would absorb even the most unfamiliar material.

Drama, then, became an important vehicle for appeasing the general public's growing appetite for Roman culture and for an educative agenda approved by both Elizabeth and James. Due to the costly effects that differentiated the *Ages* from other drama of the period, including plays by rival companies on similar subjects, these plays must also have entailed significant risk from the perspective of the company that underwrote them. Over the long term, investing in spectacle certainly paid off for the troupe financially, but what of the loftier goals of civic engagement that Heywood had in mind for history plays and for theatre in general? Only by gauging these plays' effects on this worried audience, with its outlook shaped for so long by the plague, can we begin to recognize how these plays resonated so forcefully—shoring up the traditional values that were under stress in these communities.

We must first accept that these plays are very different from the early modern drama that we are used to and realize that these differences might have been their greatest asset. The *Ages* lack the evolving narrative structure typical of early modern drama (especially the plays of Shakespeare) that we are familiar with. Each is a multigeneric spectacle, incorporating elements of comedy, history, and tragedy along with song, dance, lavish costuming, stage effects, and pyrotechnics unprecedented on the public stage. Recounting the episodes in Ovid's *Metamorphoses*, they progress as a series of vignettes, each act telling a story functionally and chronologically connected to the others but with its own plot and thematic structure. The *Ages* have more in common with civic entertainments than with the more familiar plays of the period. A rowdy audience of artisans, late for the performance or temporarily absorbed in their own banter, could quite easily miss an entire act of the play and still leave entertained. Unlike other presentations of the same material, the dense classical allusions that might otherwise prove a significant barrier to comprehension were rendered intelligible through the special effects that more recent commentators have sneered at.

Just as the plague had both a social and psychological component, the presentation of mythical history in the *Ages* effectively mediates between the deeply personal resonance of myth and the particular historical circumstances (especially the perennial struggle with the disease) shared by everyone in the audience. In an episode from *The Silver Age*, Hercules journeys to the underworld, a place where "barking groans shall make the brazen towers / Where ghosts are tortured echo," to confront Pluto and death itself. He "undertake[s] what neither Jupiter, / Neptune, nor all the gods dare make their task," a fit endeavor for the son of Jupiter or the son of God.[51] The obvious biblical overtones in this rendition of his quest are highlighted in the play's physical descriptions of the underworld. Audiences, after all, were accustomed to listening to sermons that warned of the "dreadful horror of hell, the place of darkness and devils, having in it continual flames of intolerable and unquenchable fire eternally tormenting the souls and bodies of the damned."[52] For others in the audience at the Red Bull, Heywood's description of the underworld might conjure more immediate memories of the squalid plague hospitals, so gruesomely portrayed in tracts by Dekker and others. Replete with three-headed Cerberus and his hellhounds, "Pluto, with a club of fire," "flashes of fire," and "fireworks all over the house," the play treats the audience to a literal "holiday in hell," as Homer (the play's narrator) describes it.

The torments that Hercules undergoes at the hands of Pluto and his minions provide the audience with a vivid image of Christ's suffering and that of those unfortunate enough to be damned or struck down by the plague. Pluto warns:

> . . . my flaming Crown
> Shall scorch thy damnèd soul with infernal fires.
> My vassal furies with their wiry strings
> Shall lash thee hence, and with my Ebon club
> I'll ding thee to the lowest Barathrum.[53]

Heywood taps a number of available descriptive codes and current phobias in his ghastly portrait of the underworld, all to illustrate an ultimate spiritual triumph that preachers claimed might also emerge from Londoners' experience with the plague. Thomas Pullein used the example of Jeremiah to argue for perseverance in the hope of deliverance. He claimed that "insomuch that the Lord having laid his heavy hand upon . . . this city, and is like to proceed further . . . for great sins procure great punishments, and great punishments are never without great sorrow and lamentation . . . the sorrow that is great cannot be long [and] weeping itself must needs have an end . . . He hath not left us without hope."[54]

Like Christ's resurrection and the eventual abatement of the plague, the victory of Hercules over his stygian tormentors is not an individual triumph; nor does it simply rescue Proserpine (the ostensible purpose of the journey). Hercules "dissolves [the] torments" of "all the ghosts" who are interred there. He promises to deliver hell's captives from "the weight of the world / And the huge earth's mass," language reminiscent of the "cares of the world" evoked in the gospels (Matthew 13.22; Mark 4.19). Heywood, moreover, had at his disposal special effects that even the most eloquent parish priest could only dream of to ensure the rapt attention of playgoers.

If *The Silver Age* narrates a spiritual message familiar to any audience, *The Iron Age* provides an even more poignant vision of community, far less abstracted than the fires of hell. The play is an imaginative reenactment of the Trojan War and the events leading up to it and offers a glimpse at the internal relations in both the Greek and the Trojan camps. The Trojan heroes who populate this play are afflicted by the same all too human maladies that Heywood and other Londoners might recognize in their own city and their social relationships that had become strained over the previous decade. Its message is simple: especially during times of war and extreme social dislocation, a functioning community is integral for success in battle and for the long-term survival of the nation. This sense of shared mission is something that the Greeks are able to maintain and that the Trojans lack.

Before Paris's mission to Sparta to abduct Helen, the Trojans are internally divided. Priam and Paris encourage the expedition, feeling that some sort of decisive move is needed to recoup the city's honor after twice being subdued by Hercules (depicted in *The Brazen Age*). Hector, however, cautions that "[i]n mine opinion we have no just cause / To raise new tumults, that may live in peace" (B1v). When Paris returns, Helen, clearly an outsider, is not integrated into Trojan society and laments that she has "left [her] King, [her] brothers, subjects, friends / For strangers" (H2r). Helen's unease in Troy exacerbates the internal divisions that have already begun to rupture the national unity that Priam desperately seeks to inculcate among his subjects. As the siege of the city wears on, support for the battle wavers and then disappears entirely. Troilus's zeal for combat wanes when Cressida wonders if the city must perish over the foreigner Helen; Andromache (Hector's wife) urges her husband to stay at home rather than risk his life in mortal combat with Achilles; and Priam defies Paris's desire to see Hector fight, charging Hector "by thine honor stay / Go not this day to battle" (H1v). Hector's death leaves the Trojans in shambles and dissolves any sense of communal accord to the point where Paris breaks a code of honor that binds Trojan and Greek alike when he assassinates Achilles with an arrow through the heel. Priam promptly disowns him: "Degenerate Paris, not old Priam's son, / Thou never took'st thy treacherous blood from me" (K1r).

The Greeks, by contrast, display remarkable cohesion throughout the play (which subsequently breaks down in *2 Iron Age*, when the war ends). When the prospect of attacking Troy is first broached, the Greeks unanimously support the mission and prepare for the invasion, without the internal dissension that plagues the Trojans. Achilles, so reticent to join the combined force in other versions of the story, immediately vows to "march into the town courageously," while Menelaus quickly accedes to his rival's suggestion to settle the dispute with Paris by forcing Helen to choose between her suitors (E2v). Later in the play Achilles, believing that his honor and social reputation are at stake, is easily persuaded to rejoin the battle and confront Hector—a contrast with the convoluted stratagems of Ulysses and Nestor to coax the hero to fight that dominate Shakespeare's version of the same events in *Troilus and Cressida*. Success in Heywood's play seems to depend on a congruity of interests, open channels of communication, and the ability to quell intramural disputes swiftly—in short, on social capital. Paris's selfish desire for Helen, Hector's obsession with martial valor, and the regard for individual fame over the well-being of the community have caused a breakdown of communal accord in the city. The discord among the Trojans alerts Londoners, the new Trojans, of the consequences befalling those who would wantonly pursue their own success at the expense of their neighbors.

Notwithstanding the intrigue of these classical narratives, outstanding visual effects were the most conspicuous feature of the *Ages* and their greatest asset in delivering classical history. In a very short time the Red Bull earned a reputation for innovative staging and marvelous effects. More than any other theatrical professional of his era, Heywood, a sharer in the company and the resident playwright, knew what it took to bedazzle audiences. His long career as a dramatist and actor at large public amphitheatres and his later success as a pageant designer attest to his understanding of the multiple ways in which audiences might be manipulated, educated, and, most importantly, entertained through nonverbal aspects of performance.[55] Nearly every resident of the city would have been familiar with the pageants accompanying the installation of the mayor each November, and Londoners were drawn to them year after year by dazzling visuals that clearly overshadowed the dialogue.[56] The *Ages* offered Londoners an opportunity to witness that kind of spectacle throughout the year.

The bravado characteristic of productions at the Red Bull struck a negative chord with some dramatists (not to mention several modern critics), who were perhaps envious of their success. Contemporaries disapproved of Heywood's "huge bombasted plays, quilted with mighty words to lean purpose" and "this fashion of play-making," incredulous that so many would flock to "gather musty phrases from ye Bull."[57] How did the Red Bull come to be singled out for this kind of spectacle, captivating some while piquing the ire of others? By no means unique to the Red Bull, certain basic structural features designed to enhance the production visually had been used to great effect at London's amphitheatres for decades, allowing Faustus to be carried down to "hell," Romeo to court Juliet on the balcony, armies to confront each other from both sides of the stage, and monarchs and deities to descend from the "heavens" (as the roof over the stage was known). Such spectacle was only possible outdoors, at sizable venues.

The Queen Anne's Men developed stage techniques and technologies of their own that allowed the Red Bull to differentiate itself from the other public theatres and to capture an important niche market. For one thing, more people were involved in the production. Scholars generally assume that a Jacobean acting company included about ten people, with a few additional hired men to round out certain scenes.

Many scenes in the *Ages* require more than this number onstage at the same time, even though the speaking roles of the characters are minimal. In the final scene of *The Brazen Age*, Omphale narrates the entrance of twelve princes, two priests, and Hercules, who are later joined (without anyone leaving the stage) by Lichas, Jason, Tellemon, and Nestor—twenty characters in all (K3v–L1r).

In addition to having a larger stage to accommodate so many actors, the Red Bull also had a larger, curtained discovery space for use with larger stage properties (like the Trojan Horse) and a third—and perhaps larger—door onstage to allow for "Pluto, his chariot drawn in by devils" (*Silver Age*, G3v). Wentworth Smith's *The Hector of Germany* (1615) calls for a railing around the stage (perhaps for safety, given the spectacle). If the Red Bull did indeed have a railing, it was the only outdoor venue of its era that employed this particular feature. It also seems that the playhouse had more than one trapdoor to facilitate several entrances and exits from below the stage simultaneously.[58] Where Faustus is dragged to hell at the Rose, damnation happened on a much larger scale at the Red Bull.

What most separated the Red Bull from its predecessors and contemporaries was the magnitude and frequency of its stage effects, especially at a time when many other venues in the city were moving away from spectacle to emphasize dialogue and character.[59] The intricate battle scenes that punctuate the *Ages* and other Red Bull plays in such great quantity would be extremely difficult to choreograph. In a battle involving Jupiter, Enceladus, and their armies in *The Golden Age*, the characters "combat with javelins first, and after with swords and targets." The two groups of characters must rush across a crowded stage to confront their opposite numbers twice while regrouping in between and exchanging weapons. Unlike Shakespeare's history plays—where physical conflict, when it occurs at all, is usually a brief and symbolic affair between two characters representing two armies—Queen Anne's Men staged complete battle scenes with many combatants again and again, even in the same play.[60] And sometimes the very identities of combat participants imply the use of special effects, as when "Hercules kills the sea monster" (*Brazen Age*, F1v). Battles, moreover, are frequently combined with further effects to produce even more stunning visual images. In "a confused fray" in *The Sil-*

ver Age, "with stools, cups, and bowls . . . the centaurs are beaten" and later are "all dispersed and slain" (H3r–v). Two actors presumably played centaurs, one portraying the human part, the other in equine costume. Nessus—the only centaur to escape—is involved in another intricate scene in *The Brazen Age*, where he is killed by an arrow shot by Hercules.[61]

But battles were not the only way in which Queen Anne's Men excelled in stage action. Reminiscent of the detailed orchestration of civic pageants, the plays also contain a dance featuring Diana, "six satyrs, after them all their nymphs [with] garlands on their heads, and javelins in their hands, their bows and quivers" (*Golden Age*, D3v). Another scene calls for the intricate and ordered movement of numerous characters at once: "exeunt three ways: Ceres, Theseus, Philoctetes, and Hercules dragging Cerberus. Pluto, hell's judges, the fates, and furies [descend] down to hell. Jupiter, the gods and planets ascend to heaven" (*Brazen Age*, F1v). The characters leave the stage simultaneously, using all three stage doors, the trapdoors below the stage, and the rope mechanism employed to move characters to the "heavens" (*Silver Age*, L1r).

Vivid costumes and other key effects complemented Heywood's inventive and expansive use of the whole stage and the full dramatis personae in such elaborate scenes. Audiences are treated to Neptune riding his seahorse (*Golden Age*, K2v), Jupiter "in his glory under a rainbow," "Proserpine attired like the Moon," and "Pluto, his chariot drawn by devils" (*Silver Age*, F1v, G3r, and G4v). These set pieces challenge our understanding of staging practices in the public amphitheaters, suggesting that it could be significantly more elaborate and involve considerably more participants and more space than many better-known plays suggest. The set pieces steadily increase in both number and complexity as the cycle progresses, which may imply that they constituted one of the plays' most popular features.

The visual and auditory stimulation provided by so many effects would have been especially striking for suburban playgoers, who had never experienced anything of the sort in their lives. Near the conclusion of both *The Silver Age* and *The Golden Age* winds "appear" and devils "rise . . . at every corner of the stage," brandishing torches at the resounding fireworks, whereas in *The Brazen Age* Hercules sinks "with flashes of fire . . . [and] several fireworks" (L2v). This massive pyrotechnic display and the ghoulish uprisings from below the stage, making use of several trapdoors at once, would have provided a real sense of spiritual possession not only in Hercules but also in members of Heywood's largely unlettered audience, who were inundated with folktales that warn of the dangers of demonology. For some, effects like these were too close for comfort. Thomas Middleton reports that audience members at a production of *Doctor Faustus* were deeply distressed "in their uncertainty as to whether all the devils on stage were real or not."[62]

Audiences were especially captivated by combat between the plays' heroes. In *The Iron Age*, while Priam, Hecuba, Helen, and others observe the action from the walls of Troy (the upper stage), the Myrmidons of Achilles kill Hector. The scene is accompanied by such a dizzying array of martial action and "alarums" that the audience would apprehend the declamatory speeches of the heroes as considerably more than empty (and expected) rhetoric. When (to quote the stage direction) "Hector falls slain by the Myrmidons, then Achilles wounds him with his lance," the audience, which had actually witnessed Hector's heroic exploits and was seething from an almost uninterrupted sequence of battles, experienced his death emotionally as a work of treachery. For one playgoer, the murder of Hector by Achilles was a dastardly act that could not be tolerated. According to Edmund Gayton:

> [O]ne butcher of our nation, . . . seeing Hector over-powered by Myrmidons, got upon the stage, and with his good baton took over the true Trojan's part so stoutly, that he routed the Greeks, and railed upon them loudly for a company of cowardly slaves to assault one man with so much at odds. He struck moreover such an especial acquaintance with Hector, that for a long time Hector could not obtain leave of him to be killed, that the play might go on.[63]

This butcher apparently got caught up in the physical spectacle to such a great degree that he could not allow the presumed injustice to continue. His antics also suggest that he was not expecting Hector to die or Achilles to act so shamefully, that he was inclined to judge the play based on popular notions of honorable behavior rather than its fidelity to any previously known story. Nor was the butcher the only audience member to get involved in stage action at the Red Bull. In 1620 an apprentice sitting on the edge of the stage to rest his legs from standing in the yard challenged one of the players to a duel when the actor accidentally grazed him with his sword.[64] While such energetic reactions say something about the type of playgoers that flocked to the Red Bull, the flamboyant staging surely had some role in provoking the audience to mimic the players.

Special effects, providing an exhilarating visual counterpoint to the dialogue, are nonetheless integral to the plays' broader humanist project. They "suit the action to the word," as Hamlet advises, and also conform the medium of delivery to the audience addressed, as so many rhetoricians of the period stipulated. Unlike numerous Renaissance plays that demand explication through the characters' running commentaries on their own and each other's actions, the techniques at the Red Bull must have been believable on their own; its characters rarely narrate their own actions.[65] The same goes for scenery: whereas Shakespeare's Edmund conjures the cliffs of Dover for the benefit of audience members who must use their imaginations (*King Lear* F: 4.5.11–23), *The Iron Age* alludes to "Troy's high bulwarks" and a Trojan Horse that are physically present on the stage. This horse was more than a small-scale replica. It is "discovered," apparently in an alcove at the rear of the stage, and its "huge bulk" is such that "Pyrrhus, Diomedes, and the rest leap from out the horse," initiating yet another loud battle scene and the eventual destruction of the city (C4v) (see figure 9).[66]

Some of the most spectacular—and most dangerous—effects utilized at theatres during the period were those that involved fire. In the *Ages* these include fireworks that punctuate the performance, torches carried by the characters, and other fiery effects, including Pluto's burning cloak, the "flames of hell," and "burning staves."[67] With "fireworks all over the house," as one stage direction mandates, the Red Bull clearly excelled in flame.[68] Although pyrotechnics were hardly unknown on the public stage—and torches were used as an integral property in a host of plays—the vast majority of the multiple plays calling for fire, fireworks, burnings, or fireballs were performed by Queen Anne's Men at the Red Bull.[69] The use of fire at the Red Bull

FIGURE 9. "Ajax and Hector" and "The Trojan Horse." The two woodcuts adorning the title pages of *The Iron Age* may be designed to allow readers to recall the play's spectacular staging at the Red Bull, reminding them of the "luster" that dazzled audiences (A4v). From Thomas Heywood, *The Iron Age* (London: Nicholas Oakes, 1632), sig. A1r (in both parts). STC 13340. Courtesy of the Henry E. Huntington Library, San Marino, California (shelfmark 81538-9).

is noteworthy because it is seamlessly integrated with other stage machinery to compound the spectacle, not just to punctuate an occasional scene.

After Semele is seduced by Jupiter in *The Silver Age*, she dies in a lightning-induced fire: Jupiter "toucheth the bed, it fires, and all flies up, Jupiter from thence takes an abortive infant."[70] To execute this scene, some device was needed to light the bed, presumably located in the middle of the stage. At the same time, Jupiter must descend from the heavens with "his thunderbolts burning" and then the bed must rise rapidly with Semele still inside. As Jean MacIntyre notes, the bed must be properly counterbalanced with ropes to keep it level while it "flies up," so that the actor (while suspended above the stage) does not fall out or slip toward the area of the bed that is on fire.[71] *The Brazen Age* showcases perhaps one of the most elaborate uses of flame onstage: "two fiery bulls are discovered, the [golden] fleece hanging over them, and the dragon sleeping beneath them: Medea with strange fiery works, hangs above in the air in the strange habit of a conjuress" (G2v). This scene would require the controlled use of more than one "fiery" effect on multiple levels of the stage while managing the onstage movement of numerous characters and a dragon. Safe use of these pyrotechnics on a regular basis would have meant a considerable investment of money and time. Fireworks would need to be replaced for each show, and the actors would have to spend hours to rig the stage before each performance. The troupe would not or could not continue to employ such effects if it was not rewarded by the repeated visits of numerous spectators.

As part of a coherent strategy to appeal to a specific group of playgoers, the Queen's Men monopolized pyrotechnics on the London stage through their tenure at the Red Bull. They were certainly not the first company do so, perhaps acquiring a niche occupied years earlier by an Elizabethan company, Strange's Men, that seems to have cultivated and refined the use of fire onstage, often for depicting immolation.[72] French plays as early as the late fourteenth century used a variety of fiery effects, which soon found their way to England and were employed in the sixteenth century, most prominently in the annual lord mayor's shows. To achieve such pyrotechnics onstage, theatrical professionals used a series of paper tubes called squibs, lines doused in alcohol, and various mixtures of gunpowder to control the rate of burn and explosion to produce effects that were quite sophisticated, even by today's standards.[73]

We can safely assume that on a gray London afternoon, flames and fireworks would provide a stark visual contrast to the otherwise dull surroundings, especially when coupled with the loud sound effects. Flames would constantly focus attention on the action when even the bombastic dialogue became prosaic and tedious. In one of his many prologues, Homer realizes just how important variety was to these playgoers, who clearly did not have the same attention span as audiences at the Globe: "Loath are we," he claims, "to cloy / Your appetites with viands of one taste." He entreats any potentially bored spectators to witness the action-packed finale: "lest it tedious grow, / What is too long in word, accept in show."[74] Heywood and the players evidently struck upon a formula that would make these kinds of classical legends profitable, palatable, and instructive to playgoers at the Red Bull.

Finally, how might these extralinguistic features—so ridiculous to many of Heywood's contemporaries—have made these narratives and the ideas they project resonate for the unlettered playgoers that Heywood had in mind? One way is suggested by the synergy of the effects, the dialogue, and the plays' thematic message. In a battle between Ajax and Hector in which both characters lose their weapons, the combatants uproot a tree and dislodge a boulder in order to continue fighting, maintaining that their martial strength is "equal in spirit"—the arena of spiritual combat. Spectacular and, perhaps more important, auditory effects stimulated an audience's awareness and to this extent motivated it to focus on a play's themes. And unlike the illusionistic stage devices that would be used to enhance realism in later centuries, the spectacle at the Red Bull stood in stark contrast to the everyday life of theatregoers: audiences could only associate such sights with the theatre. Placing the audience in the middle of the action, engulfed and astounded, the Red Bull offered its less privileged patrons a total (albeit temporary) escape from difficult lives.

Heywood, as we have seen, firmly believed that the unique allure of stage performances was primarily extralinguistic. Spectacle was so important to the success of the *Ages* that their eventual publication evoked considerable anxiety in him, precisely because the dialogue was stripped of visual enhancement. In his dedication to the first printed edition of *1 Iron Age* (1632), he voices his fear that "the grace they had then in the acting [might] take . . . away the expected luster hoped for in the reading."[75] Without the adornment, the "luster" afforded by lavish stage effects and pyrotechnics at the Red Bull, the dialogue alone might fail to beguile a reader, especially one who had witnessed a performance. Knowing that *The Golden Age*, published in 1611, "hath already passed the approbation of auditors," Heywood is concerned "with the general censure of readers" who are forced to evaluate the work strictly on its literary merits.[76] The book, though a durable and tangible commodity, lacks a main source of the play's original impact. Perhaps for this reason, both parts of the printed play are illustrated with intricate title-page woodcuts that allow the reader to recall or imagine the spectacle of these heroic figures doing battle onstage many years before (see figure 9).

The *Ages* were not for everybody, as their history of critical drubbings makes abundantly clear. Their popularity no doubt had something to do with an auspicious convergence of time and place, in a neighborhood burdened by struggles with the plague and welcoming any escape from present circumstances. The plays' success, even amid a spate of others treating similar themes, attests once again to the stratification of the theatrical market. Dramatists and actors alike sought to appeal not to a heterogeneous playgoing audience from across the culturally and economically diverse London population but to particular communities whose tastes could be more readily gauged, in turn making the plays' profitability easier to ensure. Such a marketing strategy successfully merged the audiences' values with the company's financial aspirations, resulting in an institution that benefited consumers and producers alike.

Occasionally, however, this equilibrium was lost—usually when the company sought to augment its profits at the expense of loyal, locally rooted playgoers. The ensuing violent reaction of an aggrieved community is the subject of the following chapter.

Chapter 5
THE CLERKENWELL RIOT & ITS AFTERMATH

* * * *
* * *
*

We have seen how a number of companies developed complex and mutually beneficial ties with their audiences and local neighborhoods. What happens when the purveyors of popular drama abandon, or at least are perceived to abandon, their constituent community? Late in 1616 the Queen Anne's Men transferred their theatrical operations from Clerkenwell's Red Bull to a recently refurbished private playhouse known as the Cockpit in the fashionable Drury Lane west of the city.[1] Though economic considerations and a desire to emulate the King's Men's move to the Blackfriars seven years earlier precipitated their move to a more profitable private theatre, Queen Anne's Men did not anticipate the vocal and violent reaction of their former audience. On Shrove Tuesday (4 March 1616/1617) a large group of apprentices, many of them from Clerkenwell, registered their dissatisfaction with the company's move in a riot that caused severe damage to the new theatre and forced the company to return temporarily to the Red Bull. The altercation on Shrove Tuesday exemplifies a different, yet no less instructive, form of civic engagement than those I have been looking at so far. The riot forces us to consider the operations of theatrical companies not only as autonomous firms in a competitive marketplace but as fixtures in the local community. Despite their destructive ends, the violent reactions of Clerkenwell apprentices and Red Bull theatergoers represent an important strain of social capital, one that was, ironically, consolidated by the very theatre and actors they were now determined to attack.

The events of 4 March dramatically illustrate the loyalty and civic responsibility demanded of the Queen Anne's Men by their audience.

A letter of 5 March from the Privy Council to the lord mayor and aldermen reports that on the previous day "a Rout of lewd and loose persons apprentices and others" committed "tumultuous outrages . . . in attempting to pull down a Playhouse belonging to the Queen's Majesty's Servants." Their attempts were not unsuccessful, as a letter of 8 March confirms: "Though the fellows defended themselves as well as they could, and slew three of them with shot, and hurt diverse, yet they entered the house and defaced it, cutting the players' apparel into pieces, and all their furniture, and burnt their playbooks, and did what other mischief they could." The rioters gathered at the Fortune in nearby Finsbury and moved to the Red Bull and the Cockpit with a clear design to cause damage to the newly occupied playhouse. The group was large, homogeneous, organized, and intent on achieving its goals. In the aftermath of the event a contemporary writes:

> the prentices on Shrove Tuesday last, to the number of 3 or 4,000 committed extreme insolencies . . . a justice of the peace coming to appease them, while he was reading a proclamation, had his head broken with a brick bat. The other part, making for Drury Lane, where lately a new playhouse is erected, they beset the house round, broke in, wounded diverse of the players, broke open their trunks and what apparel, books, and other things they found, they burnt and cut in pieces.[2]

The sheer number of apprentices involved in this altercation proved a force too large for either the players or the municipal authorities to deter. The fact that plays were presented at neither house for several months suggests that the attack successfully registered the rioters' grievances.

An event that failed to happen a year after this first altercation sheds more light on the intent of the Clerkenwell protestors. By that time Beeston and his company had resumed playing at the Cockpit, known after its renovation as the Phoenix. The apprentices, unfortunately, appeared unwilling to grant this particular Phoenix the long life accorded to its mythical namesake. They organized a second riot the following year, despite the fact that "such of [the crowd] as were taken his majesty hath commanded shall be executed for example's sake."[3] This time the authorities were warned of the apprentices' plans. A letter of

12 February 1617/1618 from the Privy Council to the Lieutenants of Middlesex cautioned that a large number of apprentices planned "to meet at the Fortune," which they would again use as a staging ground, "and after that to go to the Playhouses the Red Bull, and the Cockpit, which they have designed to raze, and pull down."[4] Apparently authorities took adequate preventative measures to ensure that these plans did not come to fruition.

The disgruntled residents of Clerkenwell did not confine their expressions of anger to damage against playhouses. Christopher Beeston, the troupe's manager and the instigator of their move to Drury Lane, himself became a target. On 20 March 1617/1618, two weeks after the riots at the playhouses, Henry Baldwin and Christopher Longe, both of Clerkenwell (occupations not specified), along with several unnamed accomplices, were arraigned "for a riotous assault and spoil done upon the dwelling house of Christopher Beeston." Baldwin pled not guilty but was "taken in irons for a year" and forced to pay a fine of £6 13s 4d. Longe, who pled guilty, received a lesser sentence of three months' imprisonment and a fine of 40s.[5] Several citations for recusancy against Beeston and his wife (Jane) may already have made him and his family conspicuous members of the community; absconding with the local theatrical troupe would only have incensed residents more, marking the beginnings of a private vendetta against the hapless impresario. Perhaps because of the violence against him and his company, he soon moved with his family from Clerkenwell to the parish of St. Giles in the Field—an area close to Drury Lane "so full of Catholics as to be called Roma Parva."[6]

Still a relative newcomer to theatrical enterprise in 1617, Christopher Beeston looms large in the history of the Queen Anne's Men and in the arc of later Jacobean and Caroline theatre more generally. From humble beginnings in 1598 as a journeyman actor with the Chamberlain's Men and Worcester's Men, Beeston (who often used the alias "Hutchinson") became a sharer with the Queen Anne's Men and began managing their financial affairs around 1612, after the death of the popular clown Thomas Greene. He went on to a career as one of the most important impresarios in early Stuart London before his death in 1638.[7] His venture at the Cockpit continued for over twenty years; he controlled every company to play in that theatre, organizing several of them himself and owning a two-thirds share in the successful Queen Henrietta's Men. Along the way, Beeston is mentioned in dozens of lawsuits and depositions, usually as the defendant, suggesting that his dealings with his colleagues, though shrewd, were not necessarily honest. The riot in 1617 was only the first time that Beeston's corporate aspirations ran afoul of the local community.

The full scope of Beeston's mendacious business practices would not come to light for several years, and it would probably be wrong to attribute such large-scale collective action to the dealings of a single individual. We might therefore interpret the actions of these rioters in several different ways. March 4 was Shrove Tuesday, the traditional day of license for apprentices in the city that was often punctuated by various acts of civil disobedience. Twenty-four riots are recorded in Elizabethan and Jacobean England on this holiday alone, many of them involving damage to theatres. Shrove Tuesday brought with it a panoply of carnivalesque practices that included dancing, burlesque jousting, singing, and feasting in parodic imitation of the great companies. These activities occasionally ended in some sort of altercation.[8] By the early seventeenth century these celebratory tumults had become larger, as the number of apprentices increased, and centered in and around the rapidly growing suburbs, where the majority of apprentices resided.[9] Even young children, if not involved in riotous activity, nevertheless participated in the carnivalesque spirit of the holiday: "Every year also on Shrove Tuesday . . . the schoolboys do bring cocks of the game to their master, and all the forenoon they delight themselves in cockfighting."[10] Just as Simon Eyre and his employees and apprentices are comfortably integrated into the political hierarchy in Dekker's *The Shoemaker's Holiday*, Shrove Tuesday celebrations did not pose a serious threat to order or to the traditional governing bodies of the city. They were not riots in the minds of most civic authorities and did not have the homogeneity, organization, or common purpose to inflict serious damage to persons or property. By 1617, in the wake of some kind of apprentice uprising every year since 1604, mild altercations on Shrove Tuesday had become so commonplace that authorities had come to expect some kind of mild disturbance. Understood in this light, the Clerkenwell riot was just another Shrove Tuesday celebration that got out of hand.

One also could argue, with Alfred Harbage, that the strike against the Red Bull and the Cockpit, like attacks on playhouses generally, has "no especial place in dramatic history." He argues that, because playhouses were "conspicuous and public," they became frequent targets upon which young apprentices might vent their aggressions: "riotous collegians now de-trolley street cars and destroy goal posts, expressing thus no general pique against public transit or the game of football."[11] Harbage is correct in insisting that all acts of destructive behavior need not be read as evidence of organized hostility directed at strategic targets. Theatres were not the only target of Shrove Tuesday riots, which frequently concentrated on brothels and the dousing of whores and occasionally on prisons, to free those the apprentices believed to be incarcerated unjustly. London's mayor and aldermen consistently expressed anxiety over these riots, not out of concern over harm to specific individuals and institutions but because any act that might be construed as evidence of widespread or chronic civil disobedience posed a threat to the general law, order, and peaceableness of the city. A manuscript letter dated 13 October 1606 suggests that James himself became concerned over the "oftentimes tumult" in the liberties in and around the Tower of London that impinged upon "his majesty's staff royal."[12] In this case, the rioters did not damage any property belonging to the royal household but merely constituted an unwanted annoyance to the king's servants that derogated the tranquil public face of city life that James was eager to maintain.

Other branches of government echoed the concern of the royal family. Edward Coke's *Institutes* provided the model for judicial thinking on this matter, describing a riot as "three or more [participating] in any unlawful act, as to beat any man, or hunt in his park . . . or take possession of his land, break down hedges or pales, or cast down ditches."[13] Coke's precedent was frequently reformulated on the local level, where magistrates often slackened the criteria to label a gathering a riot and stipulated more severe punishment. A manuscript entitled "What a Justice of the Peace May Do" (1627) consists of a calendar of quasi-official statutes that form the basis for the execution of practical justice in local communities. The section on "Riot, Rout, and Unlawful Assembly" encourages the justice to exercise broad discretionary powers in determining what constitutes unlawful assembly and in punishing the perpetrators. It mandates that "to make a riot, rout, or unlawful assembly, 3 persons at the least must be gathered together." If the justice determines that this small group is gathered with "the intent to do any unlawful act with force or violence," he is obliged to deal with the offenders "in that matter and form as is contained in the statute of forcible entries." Any subsequent offender automatically "shall be 3 months imprisoned."[14]

From this it would seem logical to infer, with Harbage, that, given the pervasiveness of riot, any disorderly act might be read as symptomatic of larger patterns of social behavior rather than as a situation-specific protest against isolated targets. The threshold for prosecuting any kind of gathering as a riot was so low, and the invocation of this law so frequent, that the device was frequently used as a legal fiction to indict any number of offenders for myriad crimes, making it difficult to determine from legal records alone whether a riot, in the conventional understanding of the term, actually occurred.[15] And it is important to note that most Shrove Tuesday altercations did not meet this threshold. Understandably, the civic authorities' frequent paranoia over acts of civil unrest has made later historians reluctant to label a certain conflict a riot. Is this reticence justified? Is it correct to theorize the Clerkenwell riot as just another unlawful assembly without clear direction, arising from the hyperactivity of local apprentices on their day of license, to which authorities were perennially overreacting?

Although the popular protests of apprentices find their origins in a generalized ethos of Saturnalian misrule, many of these altercations were animated by a desire for social justice and the improvement of local communities. Apprentices often rioted to protest a rise in food prices or the imprisonment of those they believed to be interred unjustly. Even the frequent attacks on theatres were not indiscriminate acts of violence directed at the purveyors of popular entertainment or the content of stage plays. Roger Manning's assiduous study of apprentice riots in London during this period describes one such event at a playhouse in 1584 "provoked when a serving-man wounded an apprentice with his sword at a theatre door [and] subsequently drew a crowd of near a thousand people."[16] This riot led to the temporary closure of all playing places in London. The apprentices were taking it upon themselves to police matters of concern to the local community.

I believe that this context best explains the remarkable altercation at the Red Bull and the Cockpit as a specific and strategic rebuttal to the actions of the Queen Anne's Men. The attack on the Cockpit was extraordinary for the amount of damage done to the theatre and the extent to which the players went to protect their livelihood. These rioters' actions were not directed at theatres in general but aimed directly at a single company. Although they gathered at the Fortune, the apprentices made no attempt to damage that theatre; nor was there any evidence of violence directed at any persons other than Queen Anne's Men. The Fortune seems to have been an appropriate staging ground for this event because of its convenient geographical proximity to the Red Bull and to large apprentice populations in the parishes close to London Wall and to the north of the city. The choice of the Fortune was also symbolic, sharpening the focus of the attack on the Cockpit by deliberately choosing not to damage the company's closest competitor.[17]

The altercation on Shrove Tuesday 1616/1617 was not the action of an unruly mob that posed an unfounded or unreasonable threat to stability or the authority of the mayor and the crown but a complex and end-directed action best understood in a local context. The riot was designed to register the specific grievances of the community that were not always given a fair hearing in the deliberations of civic authorities, much less in those of profit-taking businesses. Symptomatic of a considerable accumulation of social capital and solidarity around a specific set of issues, the apprentices' actions constitute a particular kind of exchange that E. P. Thompson labels a "moral economy." Focusing his observations on bread and grain riots in the eighteenth century, Thompson argues that the frequent riots following price inflations were specifically designed to register the crowd's displeasure over what they felt were unfair business practices: the rioters were defending traditional rights and practices against the onset of an increasingly impersonal and mercantile means of exchange. The consensus of the crowd outweighed their fear and deference to local authorities.[18] The moral economy of the Clerkenwell apprentices conflicted with the market-driven model followed by the troupe, which was motivated by profitability and the accumulation of cultural capital. This riot is instructive both in dramatic history and in the history of civic unrest in Jacobean London precisely because the apprentices, animated as they often were by a desire to enact social justice, found a specific and clearly identifiable outlet for their grievances in the economically motivated actions of the troupe.

Clerkenwell apprentices certainly had numerous grounds to view the company's move to the Cockpit as an affront to the principles of fair-dealing they shared. The most obvious is that residents could no longer enjoy dramatic entertainment in their own neighborhood. Although the new playhouse was barely a mile distant from the Red Bull, the twenty-minute walk along unpaved streets—muddy from frequent rain and smell from the lingering odor from open sewers—was anything but pleasant. By all accounts, walking the streets of London—and especially its suburbs—in the early seventeenth century was something of an ordeal. Streets were crowded with pedestrians, carts, and wheelbarrows that often collided with the people. Thoroughfares were loud, not just from the heavy traffic but from the loquacious antics of passersby and the incessant barking of stray dogs. Much of the "paving was ankle-twistingly bad," and injuries to pedestrians were frequent.[19] Walking one mile to the Cockpit would represent not only a commitment of time but something of a physical challenge.

Monetary considerations were even more pressing. Most apprentices could hardly afford the drastically higher price of admission: instead of paying a penny, playgoers would now have to hand over sixpence for a seat in the top gallery, one or two shillings for a better vantage in the middle and lower galleries respectively, and two and a half shillings (a veritable fortune) for a seat on the stage or in a private box.[20] For many apprentices as well as artisans, this sum would be prohibitively expensive, representing a significant portion of their weekly earnings at a time when many artisans brought home as little as 1s 2d a week.[21] Some artisans and apprentices, in the interests of social status, fondness for particular plays, or a desire to participate in or mimic the conspicuous consumption of their social superiors, undoubtedly would be willing to pay the higher price at the private houses. Even this dear price of admission was potentially within reach of those apprenticed to wealthy or particularly generous masters in lucrative trades. Apprentices were, after all, better off than the large segment of the population who were prohibited from earning a livelihood by practicing a trade because they lacked even an apprentice's credentials.[22] Many apprentices, despite the social stigma attached to their occupations and frequent criticism for their unseemly social pretensions, came from families of decent pedigree who supplied them with modest amounts of spending money. Quicksilver in Ben Jonson, George Chapman, and John Marston's *Eastward Ho!* (1605) declares that he is "entertained among gallants" and, because he frequently brokers loans for his boss, "may use his recreation with his master's profit" (1.1.16–17, 31–32).

Cost and proximity were not the only factors in the company's move that angered local apprentices. The new venue was also socially distant from the familiar confines of Clerkenwell. The liberties where the public theatres were located, though not as degenerate as some historians claim, were far from the urbane sophistication of the fashionable West End.[23] Westminster, already the seat of law and government, was beginning to develop a distinctive urban character of its own by the 1610s, one in sharp contrast to the city and its other suburbs. By the beginning of the seventeenth century, Stow noted "a continual new building of diverse fair houses" to complement the "hostelries and houses for gentlemen and men of honor" that were already there, suggesting that Westminster was the neighborhood of choice for many wealthy sojourners from the provinces eager to take advantage of the bountiful amenities of the growing metropolis.[24] In Thomas Middleton's *A Trick to Catch the Old One* (1606) Harry Dampit urges Theodorus Witgood, one of the provincial arrivistes who populate Middleton's city comedies, to have his "feet stink about Westminster Hall [to] see the galleons, the galleasses . . . of the time" (1.4.43–46). Even the outlets for recreation, "divers fair tennis courts, bowling-alleys, and a cock-pit, all built by King Henry VIII," betrayed the aristocratic pedigree of the neighborhood.[25]

One of the main features that differentiated the environs around Drury Lane from most of the rest of the city, at least from the perspective of apprentice playgoers, was the absence of a significant working-class population. Many inner-city parishes were certainly as well off as Westminster, but its denizens were successful merchants and artisans—though wealthy, they often came from much humbler beginnings and were nevertheless integrated within the institutions of government and guild that had structured London life for centuries.

For apprentices, theatres like the Fortune and Red Bull were attractive precisely because they were located in suburban neighborhoods that embodied what they felt to be a more familiar, down-to-earth, and comfortable atmosphere than that which prevailed in other London neighborhoods. The Red Bull celebrated the same values and ideals that apprentices took to be axiomatic. Contrary to claims that licentiousness and perversion were what attracted the working classes to the theatres, we might easily theorize the social space of the theatre in reverse: Clerkenwell apprentices likely refused to attend performances of their former troupe at the Phoenix precisely because of the different theatrical atmosphere and the unfamiliar location of the new private theatre. Playgoers at theatres like Blackfriars and the Cockpit, as Martin Butler explains, developed complex networks of friendship and kinship that would have made that environment intimate and familiar to habitual attendees but extremely alienating to outsiders, especially those of a humbler socioeconomic background.[26] The regular and harmonious crowds in Clerkenwell would be radically out of place and intimidated in Drury Lane, unable to carry on their usual banter or continue their vocal responses to the onstage action in the decorous confines of the Phoenix and roundly chastised for doing either.[27]

The Phoenix, and its audience, differed markedly from the Red Bull. It was an environment that would be positively estranging to most apprentices. The Cockpit was close to Lincoln's Inn (one of the Inns of Court) amid the fashionable houses of the wealthy, who would typically arrive at the theatre by coach and attired in finery.[28] Little wonder that a lone apprentice would feel intimidated arriving at the Cockpit's grand entrance on foot, fresh from the shop and a few refreshing beverages at the local alehouse. Even with a familiar play imported from the erstwhile Red Bull repertory onstage at the Phoenix, the production and general theatrical ambience would hardly be recognizable to those accustomed to the troupe's former venue. Because it was indoors, the Cockpit's artificial lighting offered a radically different perspective on the stage action; the spectacular pyrotechnics that typified several popular Queen Anne's Men plays would be too dangerous; and the diminutive size of the hall did not provide scope for the stage effects and broad acting style of the "terrible tear-throats" at the Red Bull.

Our hypothetical apprentice would almost certainly be ridiculed by the elite crowd at the Phoenix and by his fellows upon his return to Clerkenwell. Though some apprentices had pretensions to gallantry, it was probably best to keep these ambitions to themselves around their master and more sullen fellow laborers. Far from being a "liminal" entertainment zone that trafficked in subversive ideas, the liberties were a comfortable and familiar home for their residents. Artisans and apprentices from Clerkenwell and other regions of the capital would view the "civilized" West End with the same trepidation that Londoners traveling to Clerkenwell, Finsbury, or Southwark for dramatic performances might feel in these unfamiliar neighborhoods. Because more commentary from upwardly mobile playgoers has survived, we have lost sight of the perspective of the larger segment of theatre audiences.

Long-standing antagonisms persisted between apprentices and youthful artisans, on the one hand, and young gentlemen and Inns of Court students, on the other—if not the two largest then certainly the most vocal groups of playgoers. Because theatrical companies were hard-pressed to cater to both at once, they usually sought to target either one or the other. Apprentices tended to frequent public theatres, while euphuistic students and city gallants resorted to the private houses. The overlap might have been more frequent than companies and their playwrights anticipated, however, limiting the players' ability to satirize the dramatic fare of rival troupes.

Just such a convergence, and the inability of the Children of the Queen's Revels to gauge their audience accurately, may have led to the failure of Beaumont's *Knight of the Burning Pestle* at Blackfriars in 1607. That play, through the running commentary of George and his wife, is a parody of the usual characters and themes of citizen comedy and disparages the repertory at the northern public theatres. The boy in *Knight of the Burning Pestle* remarks that the popular *Four Prentices of London* is "stale [since] it has been had before at the Red Bull"

(4.4.31). Apparently the elites expected to be in attendance either were not present or did not readily apprehend or approve of the barbs directed at rival theatrical productions. Walter Burre, the publisher of the first quarto edition of the play (in 1613), claims that the audience members missed "the privy mark of irony about it," perhaps because they viewed it as straight citizen comedy rather than satire, prompting Andrew Gurr to label it "a complete flop."[29] The case of *The Knight of the Burning Pestle* demonstrates that some degree of audience overlap existed between private and public theatres and that audiences loyal to one theatre (or one type of theatre) were fully aware of the kinds of plays staged by their rivals as well as the kinds of playgoers who were likely to patronize them. The Queen Anne's Men's choice to target this particular demographic over another, thereby breaking an implicit social contract with their local community, proved to be a dilemma not usually present in a normal competitive marketplace where an appeal to one target group does not actively dissuade another group of consumers.

Playgoing, like all economic enterprises, is a type of exchange; the theatrical experience—like the production itself—is a tangible commodity. This economic model successfully captures the essential mercantile elements of this industry but raises serious difficulties when we seek to determine what precisely is being exchanged or try to assign value to these amorphous goods.[30] For theatrical companies, the mark of success was monetary, leading in many cases to immense financial gain for sharers and investors. The Queen Anne's Men, however, were forced to consider intangible factors like audience loyalty and a safe operating environment en route to long-term fiscal prosperity. Playgoers were paying for more than a dramatic performance. They were buying a social experience that incorporated more than the play itself, its performance characteristics, and its literary merit. In this transaction, the venue at which a play was staged affected its perceived entertainment value, depending on the demographic in question. For an apprentice, a play staged at the Red Bull would quite conceivably be considered more valuable than the same play performed at the Phoenix, despite its lower monetary cost. The Red Bull allowed for a more satisfactory and inclusive social experience than the unnerving atmosphere that might greet an apprentice indoors.

The public face of the troupe in the community was not limited to its performance onstage. Its actions also violated principles of fair-dealing in more easily quantifiable ways. The cessation of regular performances at the Red Bull had a detrimental effect on many other local businesses that relied on the daily increase in pedestrian traffic in their neighborhood to augment their trade. One such establishment, an unnamed "tavern on Clerkenwell Green," was a frequent haunt for actors and theatregoers both before and after performances at the Red Bull, probably one of many similar taphouses catering to the theatre crowd.[31] Similarly, those local grocers who provided provisions to the Red Bull's patrons stood to lose a significant and reliable source of income.

The lucrative concessions that the troupe made to the Clerkenwell community at the start of its tenure at the Red Bull, which included regular payments to relieve the parish poor as well as to repair local highways, came to an abrupt halt. In October of 1617 the Sessions of the Peace in Middlesex charged Christopher Beeston for being in arrears on his highway contributions.[32] Beeston's company was not actually using the theatre at this time and argued that it should be exempted from making these payments. Without capital underwriting from Anne's Men, the roadwork ended, along with the employment of many local residents—many of them likely regular visitors to the Red Bull. In addition, the company transferred its poor relief to St. Giles in the Fields Westminster, whose 1623 assessment book records that "Mr. Beeston, as from the Cockpit" had paid £10 7s "toward the building of the [new] church," forcing the congregation of St. James Clerkenwell to seek other means to deal with local poverty.[33] The Queen Anne's Men removed an important source of social capital by ceasing to provide regular entertainment in an otherwise bleak neighborhood. They abandoned the community financially by discontinuing all charitable endeavors.

We can easily guess why the company decided to move indoors. Marginal profits at private houses were significantly higher, and entrepreneurs like Heminge, Condell, Burbage, and Beeston realized the potential for nearly boundless returns at these venues. Henslowe, recognizing the opportunity for great financial gain, repeatedly attempted to acquire a stake in a hall playhouse. His efforts to replace the Whitefriars with a private house in the same area in 1614 were prevented by a staying order, as was his attempt to finance the building of the Porter's Hall in Puddle Wharf, which was again thwarted by the opposition of local residents. Both projects remained unrealized upon his death in 1616.[34] Because attendance at the hall playhouses offered a highly visible marker of social status and upward mobility, private theatre performances were conspicuous consumption goods, which have positive demand curves due to their extrinsic qualities or "snob appeal." As the price of admission increases, the desire to attend also rises, making performances at private theatres virtually insensitive to fluctuations in price. For upwardly mobile audience members, the entertainment value provided by the dramatic performance was negligible compared to the social desires satisfied by attendance and their ostentatious visibility to their peers. Participation in this social ritual and concomitant entrée into a more refined peer group, however, required attendees to demonstrate pecuniary strength and the gross consumption of overinflated goods; failure to do so was considered a mark of demerit.[35] Membership in this elevated social echelon came only at significant cost.

In hindsight we can perceive that Queen Anne's Men's decision to move to a new venue took into account a number of factors quite different from those worrying local residents. By aligning its repertory with the tastes of the Red Bull audience, the company had achieved enormous popularity and a stable audience base and thrived as a community institution. But the innovations in stagecraft that led to success at the Red Bull were costly, and the bottom-line revenues at this theatre were nothing like those available at a private house. Ascertaining the daily revenues of theatrical companies based on estimates of attendance is a notoriously dubious exercise, especially given that no daily record of earnings exists for the Red Bull, unlike Henslowe's companies at the Rose and Fortune. We might estimate the revenues at the Red Bull by comparing it with the Fortune, a theatre of about the same size. Harbage calculates the capacity of the Fortune to be 1,526 in the galleries and an additional 818 standing in the yard for a total of 2,344, generating £16 2s 6d when the theatre was filled to capacity.[36] Many historians, however, believe that Harbage's estimate is unreasonably high. Revising this figure downward accords more closely with Heywood's testimony in Chancery (3 October 1623) that on prosperous afternoons "there hath been eight or nine pounds in a day received at the doors and galleries" of the Red Bull.[37] Outdoor playhouses were rarely, if ever, filled to capacity, so these daily attendance and revenue estimates should be lowered for a typical business day. At the Cockpit, however, with only 400 spectators but drastically higher admission prices, daily receipts could have amounted to £19 6s 6d.[38] And of course it is likely that the Phoenix would be at or near capacity on a more regular basis, because it took fewer people to fill it. The company was willing to accept a loss in the impressive number of spectators who attended the Red Bull each day in exchange for an improvement in the bottom line.

Playing at the Cockpit, Beeston and his company could turn a greater profit than at the Red Bull—if it could continue to draw audiences. Here the company confronted a more fundamental question. How could the Queen Anne's Men fashion a repertory consisting of newly commissioned plays as well as Red Bull stalwarts that appealed to the dramatic tastes of a more pretentious and discerning audience at the Cockpit? We have seen how the character of the neighborhood and the composition of the audience heavily influenced both the plays staged by companies at different theatres and the prevailing atmosphere at these venues. A highly successful play at one theatre might fail at another—especially at a private playhouse. A change of venue would necessitate a radical rethinking of the repertory. The linguistic density and thematic complexity of many of Shakespeare's late plays, for instance, suggest that they were written with the more sophisticated playgoers of the Blackfriars in mind, as opposed to the more heterogeneous audience at the Globe. Many plays, designed either for public theatres like the Red Bull (like the *Ages*) or private theatres like Blackfriars (like *The Knight of the Burning Pestle*), succeeded precisely because they invoke stereotypes designed to assign and affirm cultural stratifications along class and occupational lines. Because they were forced to occupy both the Red Bull and the Cockpit simultaneously (rather than the summer/winter arrangement that the King's Men adopted at their two playhouses), Queen Anne's Men did not have the luxury of designing discrete repertories at the two different venues. The troupe was forced, through a combination of its own poor financial health and the damage to its theatres and stage property caused by the rioters, to transfer plays and players between the Red Bull and the Cockpit by dividing into more than one company.[39]

Notwithstanding the obvious differences in the composition of audiences at different theatres, theatrical professionals had long recognized that their greatest challenge was to appeal to multiple and stratified audiences simultaneously. They realized that the tendency of groups of playgoers to attend certain playhouses was neither absolute nor fully predictable. Despite discernible and important similarities in their composition, audiences were ultimately a collection of individuals. The prologue to Middleton's *No Wit, No Help Like a Woman's* (1612) wonders "how is't possible to suffice / So many ears, so many eyes?" He recognizes that specific audiences prefer certain types of plays but that the motivations that bring different individuals and social groups to the playhouse differ markedly:

> Some for mirth they chiefly come,
> Some for passion, for both some;
> Some for lascivious meetings, that's their arrant;
> Some to detract and ignorance their warrant.

Companies therefore tried to turn tragedy into comedy and comedy into tragedy, to satirize certain groups and their values while also endorsing and even valorizing them, depending upon the perspective of the individual witnessing the play: "yet I doubt not . . . We shall both make you sad and tickle ye" (prologue, ll. 1–14). The prologue does not simply disclose the remarkable diversity of theatrical products on offer throughout the city as a whole or even within the repertory of a single company. It implies that some plays—the types of plays that the Queen Anne's Men desperately needed—have a kind of protean appeal able to cross ordinarily rigid social boundaries of collective taste.

To recognize how drama might appeal to two very different audiences at once, the citizens of the Red Bull and the socialites at the Cockpit, we must consider not only the literary attributes of the playtext but the shared concerns of different communities of playgoers. We must focus not just on the many issues that divided and differentiated them but on those few issues that they had in common. By the seventeenth century, London had developed very distinctive social and economic niches. The gulf between rich and poor was wider than ever, to the point where the luxurious lives of the wealthy and the laboring struggle of many artisans and apprentices during a period of rapid inflation were becoming mutually unintelligible, even within a guild system that ostensibly united them.[40]

Despite the widening social and economic gap among Londoners, a merchant at the Cockpit and a butcher at the Red Bull could still see eye to eye on some matters. Perhaps the most salient—and the most obvious—of these was money. Whether aspiring to buy the latest fashions from the Continent, attempting to woo the prettiest woman on the block, or struggling to feed a family fallen on hard times, Londoners constantly seemed to need more money. William Rowley's hilarious story aptly entitled *The Search for Money* (1609) narrates the pursuit of "the wandering knight, Monsieur l'Argent." In the collective quest for money in Rowley's tale, "there would be left then scarce so many behind as there were undrowned in the deluge."[41] Richard Barnfield attests to the profligate spending habits of Londoners when he describes the multitude of suitors of Lady Pecunia: though few "could ever gain her: / Or if they did, she soon was gone again, / And could with them but little time remain."[42] The desire to spend did not respect class boundaries.

The expansion of the economy that allowed for this growing disparity was largely fueled by the availability of credit, meaning that rich and poor alike were constantly in debt. Even apprentices, whose economic futures were intricately tied to the fortunes of their master and who sometimes used debt to emulate the spending habits of more prodigal young gallants, were not immune from the impact of fluctuating credit relations. Imprisoned in the Counter (London's foremost prison for debt in Cheapside), forced to say "farewell [to] fellow prentices all," Quicksilver in *Eastward Ho!* learns the hard way to

> Shun usurers, bawds, dice, and drabs;
> Avoid them as you would French scabs.
> Seek not to go beyond your tether,
> . . . .
> So shall you thrive by little and little,
> Scape Tyburn, Counters, and the Spital.[43]

The would-be gallant realizes that all his hardships stem from a single vicious circle: the availability of money at interest readily satisfied greed and financed vice, leading inevitably to bankruptcy. Indeed, all facets of the economy were becoming more and more interrelated, with reliance on credit functioning as the common denominator among all social classes.

The continued availability of credit injected an unprecedented degree of liquidity into the economy, allowing the rich to finance the ever-growing consumption of luxury goods, artisans to establish and expand their shops, and theatrical professionals to build new venues for performance and extend their offerings in increasingly specialized ways. Greater financial speculation led others to suffer. Many from all walks of life faced foreclosure and the humiliation associated with an inability to pay their loans. Litigation for bad debt increased dramatically over the period, causing financial duress and extreme social pressure precisely because standing within the community hinged on the ability to secure credit.[44] Credit, however small, was a sign that an individual had made it at least somewhat above the poverty line. In this respect it was an experience shared by most—if not all—of London's playgoers.

The widespread social resonance of this issue made it an ideal candidate for theatrical representation at a variety of venues and before markedly different audiences. Philip Massinger's *A New Way to Pay Old Debts*, staged at both the Red Bull and the Phoenix,[45] circumvents the mutual exclusivity that ordinarily divided audiences at public and private playhouses by singling out a target of nearly universal opprobrium: the moneylender. Sir Giles Overreach, even more than Shylock, whose vilification is partially dependent on his religious identity, is the quintessential usurer. Because all audiences could comfortably unite against a moneylender, Overreach was unambiguously a villain. Other stage villains of the period might well seem heroic to some audiences. No doubt some would-be cony-catchers at private theatres would secretly applaud the deeds of someone like Quomodo in Middleton's *Michaelmas Term* or Jonson's Volpone.

Overreach was different. These other villains preyed on specific social groups: "gentry is the chief fish we tradesmen catch," admits Quomodo.[46] Overreach's usury negatively affects everyone, however, whether nobleman, tradesman, or yeoman. Like "Mammon" himself, he professes "the art of undoing men," revels in foreclosure, and covets monopoly power whereby he will "have all men sellers, / and I the only purchaser."[47] Because of his wealth, Overreach can effectively manipulate the flow of credit among the other characters in the play, exercising significant control over domestic and social relations in Nottingham. He abuses his capacity to lend money and enlists both the legal (Justice Greedy) and social (Marrall and Tapwell) apparatuses of communal authority to aid in the extortion of even more wealth to solidify his usurious position and perpetuate the indebtedness of those to whom he has lent money. Only when the rest of the play's dramatis personae—from all social groups—triangulate around the usurer are they able to bypass the credit crunch and exact their revenge on Overreach.

Reliance on credit and its manifold effects on interpersonal relations impinge upon everyone in Massinger's play, just as they permeated all aspects of Jacobean society. Moreover, extensive borrowing and insolvency had enormous ramifications for one's reputation. Securing a loan, regardless of the amount, depended on the potential borrower's trustworthiness as measured by lenders, friends, kin, and the courts alike.[48] Paradoxically, however, trustworthiness was generally predicated upon the ability to secure credit: insolvency meant the loss of one's good name as well as the ability to secure the financial capital necessary to rehabilitate it. In *A New Way to Pay Old Debts*, Wellborne's deteriorating financial situation has cast him as a "son of infamy" and forced him to rely on "the fair fame" of Lady Alworth's reputation to alleviate his financial straits (1.3.80, 93). When Tapwell berates Wellborne because his "credit is not worth a token," he refers to his financial insolvency and his diminished reputation, both the result of the "foolish mortgages, statutes, and bonds" that were forfeit to Sir Giles (1.1.50, 54). Marrall later uses the same logic in his attempts to persuade Wellborne to commit suicide: "pray you hang yourself, / And presently, as you love your *credit* . . . If you not like hanging, drown yourself, take some course / For your *reputation*" (2.1.106–19; emphasis added). Wellborne, though eponymously born with the seemingly unassailable credit rating that his title affords, has fallen victim to vice and poor money management; he has lost his good name and, along with it, access to the ready loans that he had previously relied upon to support his profligate habits.

Poorer characters are no less immune to Overreach's usury than Wellborne and the Alworths. Tapwell is a social climber. From his humble beginnings as the "under-butler" at the Wellborne estate, he, with "some forty pounds or so, bought a small cottage, / . . . [and] gave entertainment" (1.1.60–62). Unlike Wellborne, Tapwell has invested his money wisely:

> . . . The poor income
> I glean'd from them [his customers] has made me in my parish,
> Thought worthy to be a scavenger, and in time
> May rise to be overseer of the poor. (1.1.65–68)

To an audience of apprentices and common laborers, Tapwell's modest social advancement, built on an accumulation of social capital among his patrons, would be regarded as a significant achievement, certainly worthy of emulation. Within the microcosm of society that existed within parishes like St. James Clerkenwell, the rank of overseer would be enough to command the respect of one's peers just as wealth and titles would in the larger kingdom. Tapwell's success is contingent upon a £40 loan from Overreach that he used to purchase the alehouse in the first place.

Tapwell's predicament—striving for social advancement but reliant on others to achieve it—would resonate for playgoers at the Red Bull, many of whom were suffering financially because of the asset mismanagement of their landlords or employers, over which they themselves had little or no control. For artisans, the credit crunch had more serious consequences. Where a merchant or nobleman might be forced to surrender his reputation, property, or ability to secure future loans, artisans and their apprentices, reliant upon the financial stability of their employers and customers, stood to lose their livelihood and the ability to provide for themselves and their families. Given this play's presentation before financially stratified audiences, candid interchanges like this might promote mutual understanding among social classes. United in their disdain for the usurer, more affluent audiences at the Cockpit might sympathize with the plight of the frequently exploited lower orders, while plebeians at the Red Bull, witnessing the fiscal duress of Wellborne, Alworth, and Lady Alworth, might come to recognize circumstances shared by their more affluent fellow citizens. This is one of the few topics in the 1620s that could work at the Red Bull and the Cockpit, probably the most socially distinct of London's playhouses.

More than simply disclosing the risks of credit and its penetration throughout the social order, *A New Way* draws on long-standing popular tropes to describe and demonize usurers. Overreach and especially his sidekick Justice Greedy are often described using porcine imagery. Nearly every scene features these characters overindulging in food and drink. Furnace reports that "Sir Giles feeds high" (2.2.110), and Overreach does not mind that "my dressers crack with the weight / Of curious viands" (3.2.1–2). Conforming even more closely to this stereotype, Greedy (as his name implies) boasts that "my belly's braced like a drum" (3.2.23) and spends the play devouring a cornucopia of rich and decadent food while others starve. Usury, for Greedy, is clearly a way of funding his wanton lifestyle. "Why," he wonders, "[i]s't a time to talk / When we should be munching?" (3.2.215–16).

This is precisely the image of the usurer propagated in popular tracts like John Blaxton's *The English Usurer* (1634), a treatise that moves freely from scholastic disputation to corporeal imagery in order to appeal, like the play, to an audience encompassing both rich and poor. For Blaxton,

> The usurer is like a pig, for while he liveth, he is good and profitable for nothing, for he will be ever rooting up the earth, running through, . . . eating and devouring up good corn, beans and peason, so likewise does the wicked swinish usurer whilst he liveth: but when the pig is dead, then there cometh profit by him to many. So the usurer, when death taketh him, then the poor may have some profit.[49]

The woodcut on the tract's title page compares the usurer's outward appearance (in the right panel) with his inward deformity (on the left): demons prey constantly on his mind. The inevitable connection between an overindulgent lifestyle and spiritual damnation is echoed in the play when Overreach realizes that "he who bribes his [Greedy's] belly, / Is certain to command his soul" (2.1.8–9) (see figure 10).

FIGURE 10. The "usurer" as "pig." Frontispiece from John Blaxton, *The English Usurer* (London, 1634). Courtesy of the Henry E. Huntington Library, San Marino, California. STC 3129 (shelfmark 96503).

The ending of the play—where everyone's debts are paid in a new way—comes about through the good graces of Lord Lovell. Lovell has earned his reputation in the wars and therefore stands outside the local system of accreditation engineered by Overreach. But Lovell is a fantasy. As Theodore Leinwand notes, "it would have been more difficult to imagine an unfettered Jacobean nobleman than a creditor like Sir Giles."[50] The play's ending, then, is a wish fulfillment for audiences at both the Red Bull and the Cockpit, which allowed all spectators to displace their latent aggressions onto the larger-than-life loan shark.

It is perhaps fitting that insolvency ultimately undid the Queen Anne's Men, just as it had (or would) so many of the individuals who witnessed *A New Way to Pay Old Debts*. Unfortunately for the troupe, it did not have a Lord Lovell to bail it out. The micromanagement of Queen Anne's Men during this transitional period in their history reflects fundamental changes in their corporate policy and commercial objectives, largely due to the private aspirations of Christopher Beeston. Beeston's decisions amounted to a blatant disregard of the commercial value of social capital. For Beeston, as for many other members of the company who were residents of Clerkenwell and parishioners at St. James (in some cases even before the troupe located its playhouse there), part of the original attractiveness of playing in Clerkenwell must have been the large population of artisans and apprentices who lived in or around the region, from which a loyal audience might easily be recruited. The sharers in the theatrical concern apparently were also able to draw upon local connections to negotiate favorable terms on the lease of the Red Bull from Aaron Holland. Holland had leased the land from Christopher Beddingfield, built the theatre, and incorporated the business. The company's sharers paid a mere £17 10s annually as well as a modest share of the profits to Holland to lease the building. According to the terms of this arrangement, a player, Thomas Swinnerton, stood as the gatherer, responsible for collecting the daily box-office receipts, for which he was entitled to an additional one-eighteenth of the proceeds.[51]

In February 1608/1609, however, a new agreement was drawn up, presumably on the same terms, making Philip Stone (who bought Swinnerton's share) the gatherer. Stone was not a member of the company and evidently saw an opportunity to make a ready profit on his investment in the increasingly popular theatre. In 1612, needing money, he sold out to a merchant, Thomas Woodford, who left a fiduciary, Anthony Paine, solely in charge of this aspect of his financial affairs.[52] Woodford's interest in the company was speculative. A resident of St. Dunston's in the West, he had been involved in the Paul's Boys in 1600 and financed the troubled private theatre in Whitefriars from 1607 to 1614. Woodford viewed the theatres as a "source of easy wealth" and frequently turned to the courts to recoup losses from risky investments.[53] For his part, Paine proved a less than capable financial agent. Three months after the transaction, Paine failed to pay his employer's share of the rent on time, prompting Holland to enter a case in the Court of Requests demanding the payment of back rent and a renegotiation of the terms of the original lease that would make him the gatherer:

> if . . . [Woodford and Paine] [sh]all satisfy and pay all such sums of money as he the complainant [Holland] . . . claims have unjustly detained or caused to be detained from him, he is well contented to make a new indenture unto the complainant in his own name, under such covenants, articles, provisos, conditions, & agreements as are contained in the said indenture formerly made by him to the said Philip Stone.[54]

The wording of the document clearly indicates Holland's willingness to take this opportunity to renegotiate along the same lines as the Woodford/Stone agreement, which gave him access to more of the theatre's profits by way of the lucrative gatherer's share.

The lawsuit also attests to the popularity of the Queen Anne's Men, suggesting that Holland had underestimated the company's earning potential in 1605. He now believed that the playhouse had grown more profitable than the building's rent reflected.[55] Shares in the Red Bull had doubled in value between February 1608/1609, when Philip Stone paid Swinnerton £25 for a share, and June 1612, when Stone sold the share to Woodford for nearly £50. At the same time, however, the new agreement diminished the company's net profits by effectively increasing operating costs and prescribing the amount of money that could be allocated to day-to-day expenses. The troupe, in essence, was forced by the court to relinquish a percentage of its future earnings without the immediate capital infusion of a normal equity transaction. With the benefit of hindsight, this agreement, by preserving and enhancing the bonds between the theatrical enterprise, the local community, and the audience, might have proved lucrative over the long term, eventually outweighing the advantages of moving to the Cockpit. But, as on so many other occasions, Beeston seemed oblivious to social cost, concentrating solely on short-term financial gain.

These negotiations were not the only concern troubling Beeston and his company. Beginning in 1609, Thomas Swinnerton, in an effort either to augment his personal income or to alleviate his company's financial predicament, used a duplicate patent while touring the provinces with a hastily pulled together group of actors. This patent allowed the troupe to play in two places at once, which, though lucrative, was also illegal. In 1616 Swinnerton was apprehended by the Norwich authorities, who, fortuitously, did not inform the lord chamberlain (who had the authority and obligation to revoke the company's patent) of the offense.[56]

Whether Beeston genuinely wished to rescue his company from its escalating debt or, as Andrew Gurr puts it, to "siphon its cash" for his other enterprises, he secured for the troupe £95 in loans from Susan Baskerville, the widow of Thomas Greene. Formerly an actor-sharer in the concern, Greene eventually acquired nine of the eighteen shares in the Red Bull.[57] Far from ameliorating their financial crisis, Beeston's excessive borrowing from Greene and his estate opened new antagonisms among company members, their families, and their constituent community, which once again landed them in court. Greene, who was buried at St. James Clerkenwell on 7 August 1612, was a resident of the neighborhood. His will enumerates a number of close contacts and friendships among local clergy and businessmen. His popularity as a clown, evident in John Cooke's enormously successful *Greene's Tu Quoque* (1611), written expressly for the troupe's leading comic actor, was partially responsible for the rapid growth in the popularity of the Queen Anne's Men during their tenure in Clerkenwell. In his will, Greene shows a clear interest in the continued success of the company, bequeathing money to many of its members. But his financial support seems to have been contingent on the troupe remaining in Clerkenwell. He gives "to the fellows of the house of the Red Bull forty shillings to buy gloves" and other gifts (a normal enough bequest), but only to those who were also St. James parishioners.[58]

Beeston was unable to make arrangements for a lump-sum purchase of Greene's former share from his wife, Susan (now remarried to James Baskerville). After negotiations in June 1615, he agreed on a large amortized payment to Greene's widow of 1s 8d a day, six days a week, as long as the company was playing and Susan and James Baskerville lived. The company did not—and probably could not afford to—live up to its end of the bargain. It drew up another arrangement whereby Queen Anne's Men would pay an additional pension of 2s to either Susan or her son from a former marriage, Francis Browne, in exchange for a further investment of £38. The company again defaulted and was also behind in wage payments to several of its hired actors, including William Browne, another of Susan's sons. By this point, the company was playing at the Cockpit and appeared to be ignoring its obligations and debts in Clerkenwell. When the Cockpit was sacked, though, the company had to return to the Red Bull and renegotiate with the Baskervilles. A third settlement was reached in Chancery by which the pensions were reassigned to William Browne in the event of Susan's death. Once more Beeston and his company were unable or chose not to honor their agreement. They returned to the Cockpit, possibly hoping to sidestep accountability in this as in other matters in their former neighborhood.[59] Not surprisingly, Susan, who now controlled her husband's stake in the company, felt betrayed, realizing that Beeston's chronic borrowing was being used to build the Cockpit and move the troupe to Drury Lane, against the apparent wishes of her late husband. More importantly, according to the testimony of Thomas Basse and Richard Perkins, Susan may no longer have had a claim on the company's earnings at the Cockpit.

William Browne also had a claim on the company for arrears on wages payable to him as a hired man. Other nonsharing actors suffered a similar fate through what C. J. Sisson described as Beeston's "heads we win, tails you lose" policy on the payment of wages.[60] According to this system, actors were paid a fixed rate of no more than ten shillings a week when the troupe was prosperous but were forced to accept a reduction in wages adjusted to the company's earnings during less-profitable periods:

> If at any time it should happen the gettings of the company to be but small and to decrease, that then I should not have my whole wages agreed to be paid unto me but to bear my part of the loss thereof as well as the company and to have a part proportionable only to those gettings.[61]

In a further Chancery Suit of 1623, an action that finally broke the company, Susan again sued Beeston and two other remaining sharers from the 1617 settlement for arrears in the various loan payments and the pensions to be paid according to the terms of the will.[62]

Andrew Gurr interprets the troupe's financial and legal difficulties during this period as the story of a company chronically short of cash and prone to gross mismanagement.[63] Through loans secured from his fellow sharers, Beeston raised the funds to build the new theatre. Unlike Henslowe and his companies, Beeston did not have the capital to finance the company's daily operations; nor was he successful in consolidating individual shares, as Heminge and Condell were with the King's Men. Although Gurr's analysis astutely interrogates the internal dynamics of the company's governance, he fails to consider their policies within the larger moral economy. The personal affronts to Greene and his family, compounded with the loss of their local theatre, were likely contributing factors in the apprentices' decision to destroy the Phoenix. The Greene family was well liked and established in Clerkenwell: the actor's ancestors had resided there for over a century and were descended from Sir Thomas Dacra, a prior of St. John's of Jerusalem and in 1504 the grand prior of England. Greene's associations with important Clerkenwell business interests made him and his company a welcome addition to neighborhood commerce.[64] His acting style was especially appealing to the audience at the Red Bull. As Heywood notes in his preface to *Greene's Tu Quoque* (1614), no actor was "more applauded by the audience . . . or of more general love for the city" than the late Greene.[65] Greene was sorely missed both by Queen Anne's Men, who had difficulty replacing his talents, and by the numerous playgoers who reveled in his performances.

None of these factors alone would likely be sufficient to precipitate such a violent, collective, and organized reaction. Nevertheless, the severity of the Shrove Tuesday riot was aggravated by the "resentment by Clerkenwell [residents] for . . . the injustice done to Susan in a matter of local notoriety," according to Sisson.[66] The same might be said for the injury done to Aaron Holland, the landlord of the Red Bull, who found himself without tenants and without prospects of finding players to replace them due to the restrictions placed on the number of acting companies under James. Holland, if not the shrewdest of businessmen, was well respected in the community and was appointed constable for Clerkenwell in 1613, placing him in the ambivalent position of having to prosecute apprentices who, at least to some degree, were protesting on his behalf. Earning only £48 in annual revenues on the Red Bull, Holland would not have been able to profit on his original investment by 1616.[67] Beeston's less than savory reputation would have exacerbated grievances against the company, which were finally catalyzed by the move to the Cockpit.

The fierce reaction of the Clerkenwell populace must have made the company members feel like victims of their own success. The money that they made in Clerkenwell afforded the funds and attracted the necessary financing needed to build the Cockpit, and it was probably their success at the Red Bull that led them to contemplate moving in the first place. Not only did the sacking of the Cockpit disrupt their London playing season, but the burning of playbooks, props, and costumes (many of which were likely procured expressly for use in the new venue) represented a significant capital loss for the company. The total value of the contents of a Jacobean company's tiring house was anywhere from £500 to £1,000.[68] With no place to play, no revenues from production, and no properties to furnish their performance, Queen Anne's Men were unable to pay their debts to actors and community members alike. While the gradual manufacture of social capital stimulated the success of several theatrical enterprises and occasioned their rich engagement in the daily fabric of London society, neglecting their social obligations could just as easily result in their demise.

The Clerkenwell riot and its aftermath illustrate an unusually immediate and passionate connection between London's theatres and its constituent communities. Most interactions between the two were significantly more oblique, requiring us to contextualize the plays not just temporally, in Jacobean England, but spatially, within London and its various urban and suburban neighborhoods. The success of acting companies and the plays they performed varied according to the wealth, occupation, religion, and expectations of the playgoers who witnessed them. Producers and consumers realized, for better and for worse, that the theatre was a mobile business and that operations could be relatively easily relocated somewhere else in pursuit of greater profits. Mobility, however, came with associated challenges. The loyalty of audiences could not be guaranteed. Furthermore, companies had to adapt a preexisting repertory that was designed with a specific demographic in mind for a much different audience in a markedly different physical and social milieu. Occasionally, as in *A New Way to Pay Old Debts*, the theatre could appeal to many of these groups, even simultaneously, strengthening the ties between residents from many different walks of life. In most cases, however, plays appealed to more particularized groups, and performers had every reason to be wary of the reactions of their audiences.

EPILOGUE

AFTER 1642

Histories of the early modern stage end approximately twenty-five years after Beeston and his company first moved to the Cockpit in 1616. On 2 September 1642 Parliament ordered the theatres closed. Members reasoned that because England was

> threatened with a Cloud of Blood, by a Civil War, [we] call for all possible means to appease the Wrath of God appearing in these judgments . . . and whereas public sports do not well agree with public calamities, nor public stage-plays with the seasons of humiliation, this being an exercise of sad and pious solemnity, and the other being spectacles of pleasure, too commonly expressing mirth and levity: It is therefore thought fit, and ordained by the Lords and Commons in this parliament assembled, that while these sad causes and set times of humiliation do continue, public stage-plays shall cease and be forborne.[1]

Parliament argued that public gatherings like stage plays posed a threat to stability at such a dangerous time. Some argued that the content of some of the plays staged was seditious, amplifying partisan rancor. These are essentially the same reasons given by more recent commentators who have argued that the early modern theatre in general was detrimental to community. The theatre, in this view, had always been disruptive, immoral, and dangerous. Parliament, now dominated by Puritans, finally used the political crisis as a cover to ban playing entirely. Rick Bowers summarizes prevailing opinion on the 1642 closure, claiming that the ban ushered in a "dark age of Philistinism"—using the perpetual conflict between Puritanism and humanism so important to Chambers and other theatre historians to characterize the events of 1642.[2]

Yet performances continued periodically even after the parliamentary ban. A glance at where these performances took place and the audiences they drew tends to confirm the relationships of theatres, spectators, and their constituent communities that are the subject of this book. Although the 1642 ban applied to all performance spaces, the government seemed especially concerned with the private playhouses. *The Actor's Remonstrance or Complaint for the Silencing of Their Profession* (1643), a tract representing actors and management at "the private houses of Blackfriars, the Cockpit, and Salisbury Court," actually acknowledges that these three theatres may have been involved in seditious activity. In exchange for allowing these theatres to reopen, the authors of the tract promise to "purge our stages from all obscene and scurrilous jests such as might either be guilty of corrupting the manners, or defaming the persons of any men of note in the City or Kingdom."[3] The private theatres were so worrisome because the political satire contained in the plays performed there had real potential to sway their elite spectators, many of whom had political influence. Although some actors were willing to defy the law and continue playing indoors, they were swiftly and forcibly suppressed:

> In the winter before the King's murder, 1648, they ventured to act some plays with as much caution and privacy as could be at the Cockpit. They continued undisturbed for three or four days, but at last . . . a party of foot soldiers beset the house . . . and carried them away in their habits . . . to Hatton House, then a prison.[4]

The situation was somewhat different at the large public amphitheatres. Plays continued to be staged—and even tolerated to some degree—at the outdoor theatres throughout the period. Because the lower-class audiences at these playhouses were less likely to perpetrate treason, and probably attended the theatre more for honest recreation than for political intrigue, government authorities were more willing to turn a blind eye. Perhaps they even thought that performances might serve to relieve social tensions during such a turbulent period, seeing plays as a distraction from weighty political matters. Plays continued at some amphitheatres longer than at others, but most of the playhouses eventually closed. The Globe was pulled down in 1644, the Fortune and Salisbury Court met a similar fate in 1649, and Blackfriars was destroyed on 6 August 1655. Although the Cockpit was not torn down, after the fracas in 1649 it was converted to a schoolhouse and did not host a theatrical performance until the Restoration—much to the dismay of William Beeston (Christopher's son), who invested £200 to repair the theatre in 1651.

The Red Bull was the only theatre left standing. And nobody really seemed to care. Francis Kirkman wrote that "I have seen the Red Bull playhouse, which was a large one, so full that as many went back for want of room as had entered."[5] Even when the authorities did interrupt performances at the Red Bull, the consequences were not particularly grave, as this account in the 1655 *Weekly Intelligencer* describes:

> This day proved tragical to the players at the Red Bull, their acting being against an Act of Parliament . . . it never fared worse than the spectators at this present, for those who had monies paid their five shillings apiece, those who had none to satisfy their forfeits, did leave their cloaks behind them . . . all which their poverty being made known, and after some check for their trespasses, were civilly restored to the owners.[6]

Although some playgoers did pay the official five-shilling fine, many spectators were regularly exempted from the penalty, especially if they could prove that they were in fact indigent.[7] Despite the harsh condemnation of plays and the claims for the success of the government's stern policy against actors and playgoers, this report actually confirms the failure of the authorities to eradicate playing or to diminish its popularity among a large and diverse audience of artisans and apprentices. Leslie Hotson claims that at the Red Bull "actors were safer from the soldiers than they were from themselves."[8]

Why were the authorities less concerned about the Red Bull than about other theatres? For one thing, the operators of the Red Bull continued to contribute to local charities. In 1659 the authorities detained Edward Shatterall for staging illicit plays at the theatre. Shatterall had received permission to play from local magistrates, however, in exchange for contributions to relieve the poor at St. James Clerkenwell and fund the repair of local highways, exactly as earlier troupes at the Red Bull had done.[9] Another reason for the apparent indifference of the authorities stems from the kinds of plays performed at the Red Bull. "All that we could divert ourselves with," writes Kirkman, "were these humorous pieces of plays" and drolls with no serious political or intellectual import. Bowers suggests that "these emasculated performances that were generally permitted at the Red Bull during this time seem to be something of a punishment in themselves."[10] Although perhaps not as intellectually engaging as the plays presented at other playhouses, these drolls and comedies were hardly dissimilar to those that Red Bull audiences had enjoyed for decades. This is exactly what made the Red Bull less subversive in this climate than its competitors. Authorities were less concerned with prosecuting artisans and apprentices, who, after all, were only attending the same kinds of relatively benign performances that they had always liked, continuing a pattern of life in the community that had existed for fifty years. While we do not know exactly what plays were performed at the Red Bull during the civil war, if its repertory immediately after the theatres officially reopened is any indication, they may have been exactly the same plays that had been popular there for generations. The Red Bull's repertory in 1663 featured *Greene's Tu Quoque*, William Rowley's *All's Lost by Lust*, Thomas Heywood's *The Rape of Lucrece*, and *The Two Merry Milkmaids*, all plays that had debuted in Clerkenwell in the 1610s and 1620s.[11] Nothing much had changed over the years. The Red Bull proved a remarkably durable community institution, even if it was not aesthetically adventurous.

The frequency of performance at the Red Bull during the crisis of 1642–1660 suggests alternatives to standard narratives concerning the closure of the theatres, just as the activities at that theatre during the Jacobean period reveal patterns of civic engagement not evident at the Globe and other playhouses of that era. The early modern theatres each meant something different to the London communities they served, and an accurate sociology of the theatre of this period requires us to treat each of these playhouses and their communities discretely. But in the end the exact permutations and effects of this social exchange are probably secondary to the fact that so many Londoners from so many different backgrounds (and on both sides of the stage) availed themselves of this exciting and dynamic forum, channeling theatrical energy into civic engagement. What playgoers and players had in common, after all, along with Londoners who never attended the theatres, was the necessity of living together and the challenge of fashioning a more harmonious community.

NOTES

INTRODUCTION

1. Thomas Heywood, *An Apology for Actors*, F3v.

2. Robert Putnam, *Bowling Alone: The Collapse and Revival of American Community*, 19.

3. John Stow, *A Survey of London . . . Enlarged by the Care and Diligence of A. M[unday] in the Year 1618, and Now Completely Finished by the Study and Labour of A. M[unday], H[umphrey] D[yson], and Others, This Present Year 1633*, 66.

4. Michel de Montaigne, *The Essays or Moral, Political, and Military Discourses of Lord Michel de Montaigne*, 87; Francis Bacon, *The Advancement of Learning*, book 2, chapter 13.

5. Thomas Dekker, *The Gull's Hornbook*, B2r.

6. Steven Mullaney's *The Place of the Stage* (see the discussion in chapter 1) is perhaps the best-known study in this vein. It is indicative of a wide range of more specific studies that concentrate on that which was marginal, subversive, or disruptive about early modern English drama.

7. On the "elite" character of the private theatres, see Martin Butler, *Theatre and Crisis, 1632–1642*.

8. Andrew Gurr, *Playgoing in Shakespeare's London*, 60–73. Gurr's general claim is that individual playing companies were integral in controlling the supply of new plays and therefore in determining the contours of the market for staged drama. He maintains this position in his work on London playgoing generally and, perhaps most illuminatingly, in his studies of individual playing companies. See *The Shakespearian Playing Companies*; *The Shakespeare Company, 1594–1642*; and *Shakespeare's Opposites*.

9. Douglas Bruster, *Drama and the Market in the Age of Shakespeare*, 2.

10. Another playhouse, dating from around 1580, was located in Newington Butts, about a mile south of the river, making it inconvenient for Londoners. The short-lived Hope was the last theatre to be built in the neighborhood, around 1614.

11. E. K. Chambers, *The Elizabethan Stage*, 2:401.

12. Quoted in Charles Whitney, *Early Responses to Renaissance Drama*, 172. This is obviously an isolated example, but we must assume that other playgoers (perhaps many of them) had personal relationships with the actors both inside and

outside the theatre. This possibility is even more tantalizing because so many players lived near their place of employment and would have interacted with local residents on a regular basis.

13. On the repertory and the acting style at these northern amphitheatres, see John Astington, "Playing the Man: Acting at the Red Bull and the Fortune," 137–40.

14. Gurr, *Shakespeare's Opposites*, 4–5.

15. Andrew Gurr, *The Shakespearean Stage, 1574–1642*, 173.

16. In its contemporary variants, social capital has been understood in various ways, from its highly abstract valence in the writings of Pierre Bourdieu, who attempts to place a specific economic valuation on social networks, to Robert Putnam's view of social capital as a means of diagnosing the health of civil society. See Pierre Bourdieu, "The Forms of Capital"; and Putnam, *Bowling Alone*, 19–26.

17. Craig Calhoun, "Habitus, Field, and Capital: The Question of Historical Specificity," 68.

18. Putnam, *Bowling Alone*, 33–38.

19. Ira Clark, *Comedy, Youth, and Manhood in Early Modern England*, 15.

20. Robert Putnam, *Better Together: Restoring the American Community*, 9.

21. Marcus Tullius Cicero, *The First Book of Tully's Offices*, 304–7. *De Officiis* was reprinted twenty-seven times between 1580 and 1630.

22. William Fulke, *Two Treatises Written against the Papists*, 198.

23. Robert Sanderson, *Ten Sermons Preached*, 438–39 (emphasis added).

24. John Rogers, *A Discourse of Christian Watchfulness*, 248–49.

25. Stow, *Survey of London*, 86, 700, 88.

26. Joseph P. Ward, "Imagining the Metropolis in Elizabethan and Stuart London," 26.

27. Stow, *Survey of London*, 46–47.

28. Ibid., 70.

29. Stefano Guazzo, *The Civil Conversation*, A4v. See Lena Cowen Orlin, *Locating Privacy in Tudor London*, 10.

30. Joseph Hall, *Contemplations on Principal Passages of the Holy Story*, 127.

31. *Civil and Uncivil Life*, B3r, B4v.

32. Stow, *Survey of London*, 692.

33. Michael D. Bristol, *Carnival and Theater*, 46; Robert Weimann, *Shakespeare and the Popular Tradition in the Theater*, 24.

34. Quoted in Gurr, *Playgoing*, 222–23.

35. Quoted in ibid., 46.

36. Some 65 percent of the title pages of printed playbooks after 1600 also mention the theatre where they were performed. Alan Farmer and Zachary Lesser, "'Vile Arts': The Marketing of English Printed Drama, 1512–1660," 82.

37. William Turner, *Turner's Dish of Lenten Stuff, or, A Galymaufery to the Tune of Watton Towns End.*

38. Donald Lupton, *London and the Country Carbonadoed*, F3r.

39. Thomas Heywood, *The Four Prentices of London*, B1v–B2r. Godfrey's brothers are a goldsmith, haberdasher, and grocer; each therefore represents one of the most well-established livery companies in the city.

40. Thomas Middleton, *Michaelmas Term*, 1.1.84. See Gail Kern Paster, *The Idea of the City in the Age of Shakespeare*, 158.

41. Gurr, *Shakespearean Stage*, 217.

42. David Kathman, "Grocers, Goldsmiths, and Drapers: Freemen and Apprentices in the Elizabethan Theatre," 4–7. For the persistence of the guild structure in the organization of playing companies, see Roslyn Knutson, *Playing Companies and Commerce in Shakespeare's Time*, 23.

43. Astington, "Playing the Man," 141; Mark Bayer, "The Red Bull Playhouse."

44. Gurr, *Playgoing*, 151.

1. RETHINKING CITY AND SUBURB

1. Donald Brook, *The Romance of the English Theatre*, 9, 23; Joseph Quincy Adams, *Shakespearean Playhouses*, 26.

2. Mullaney, *Place of the Stage*, vii.

3. Linda Woodbridge, ed., *Money and the Age of Shakespeare: Essays in New Economic Criticism*, 1.

4. Stow, *Survey of London*, 444. See Mullaney, *Place of the Stage*, 38–39; and William E. Carroll, *Fat King, Lean Beggar: Representations of Poverty in the Age of Shakespeare*, 26.

5. Stow, *Survey of London*, 444; Mullaney, *Place of the Stage*, 21.

6. W. I. Pinks, *The History of Clerkenwell*, 4–11; for the early history of Clerkenwell and Finsbury, see also Richard Tames, *Clerkenwell and Finsbury Past*, 23–30. For a discussion of Marion Frith's public activities in the neighborhood and at the Fortune playhouse, see Stephen Orgel, *Impersonations: The Performance of Gender in Shakespeare's England*, 139–53.

7. Stow, *Survey of London*, 448.

8. Chambers, *Elizabethan Stage*, 1:236–37.

9. Jonas Barish, *The Antitheatrical Prejudice*, 87–89.

10. Chambers, *Elizabethan Stage*, 1:253.

11. Jean E. Howard, *The Stage and Social Struggle in Early Modern England*, 22.

12. See Thomas Postlewait, "Theatricality and Antitheatricality in Renaissance London," in *Theatricality*, ed. Tracy Davis and Thomas Postlewait, 100–103.

13. Mullaney, *Place of the Stage*, 21. Christina Eccles echoes Mullaney, claiming that Southwark was "a law unto itself." Eccles, *The Rose Theatre*, 8.

14. Chambers, *Elizabethan Stage*, 1:255.

15. Valerie Pearl, "Change and Stability in Seventeenth-Century London," 1–5.

16. Mullaney, *Place of the Stage*, 26.

17. Ibid., 31.

18. Along with a high population of underemployed aliens, the Bankside also "attracted a large number of wealthy retailers." Jeremy Boulton, *Neighborhood and Society*, 69. These historians stress the uneven distribution of wealth and occupation in the borough. Since skilled and unskilled laborers might reside only a block apart, generalizations about the social or economic character of the neighborhood are highly suspect.

19. Daniel Fischlin, "Theatre, Theory, and the Shaping Fantasies of Early Modern Criticism: A Review Essay," 241.

20. Paul Yachnin, *Stage-Wrights: Shakespeare, Jonson, Middleton and the Making of Theatrical Value*, 2–13.

21. The works of Richard Dutton (on licensing and control), Douglas Bruster (on drama, the market, and society), Andrew Gurr (on playing companies and audiences), William Ingram (on the economics of playgoing), Roslyn Knutson (on repertories and company management), S. P. Cerasano (on Henslowe and his relationship to the theatres), and David Bergeron (on civic pageantry) listed in the bibliography all offer a more expansive way to understand theatre in relation to urban life.

22. For statistics on the city's growth during the period, see the tables in Roger Finlay and Beatrice Shearer, "Population Growth and Suburban Expansion," 39.

23. Ian Archer, *The Pursuit of Stability*, 92.

24. Ibid., 83.

25. Stow, *Survey of London*, 126, 269.

26. Edward T. Bonahue, "Citizen History: Stow's *Survey of London*," 62.

27. Finlay and Shearer, "Population Growth and Suburban Expansion," 53, 77.

28. Archer, *Pursuit of Stability*, 83–85.

29. Such practices were hardly unique to Clerkenwell. See Michael D. Bristol, *Carnival and Theater*, and "Shameless in Arden: Early Modern Theater and the Obsolescence of Popular Theatricality," 284–91.

30. E135/9/20, National Archives (formerly Public Record Office), Kew, UK.

31. *Nobody and Somebody*, I1v.

32. Will Kempe, *Kemp's Nine Daies Wonder*, B1r.

33. Jeremy Boulton, *Neighborhood and Society*, 210.

34. Stow, *Survey of London*, 669.

35. Boulton, *Neighborhood and Society*, 262.

36. Pearl, "Change and Stability," 17.

37. See Stuart Minson, "Public Punishment and Urban Space in Early Tudor

London," 1–4. Criminals were often paraded through the city along appointed routes that varied according to the offense.

38. Steve Rappaport, *Worlds within Worlds: Structures of Life in Seventeenth-Century London*, 193.

39. Robert Blackham, *The Soul of the City: London's Livery Companies*, 34–37.

40. Susan Vincent, *Dressing the Elite: Clothes in Early Modern England*, 117–18.

41. Stow, *Survey of London*, 652.

42. Boulton, *Neighborhood and Society*, 60.

43. John Benjamin Heath, *Some Account of the Worshipful Company of Grocers*, 8–13.

44. Stow, *Survey of London*, 275.

45. These two stories are related, for it was Simon Eyre, actually a merchant and a draper, who established Leadenhall. His trade is changed in the play to emphasize his connection with Shrove Tuesday, a holiday associated with the shoemakers. Although *Shoemaker's Holiday* was first performed in 1599, it was not published until the following year.

46. Blackham, *Soul of the City*, 5; George Unwin, *The Guilds and Companies of London*, 201.

47. Stow, *Survey of London*, 711.

48. Carroll, *Fat King, Lean Beggar*, 97–111. These institutions, though funded through the charity of the city, were more like penal institutions for vagrants, who represented a major source of anxiety for the government at all levels. Joanna Innes sees these types of institutions as "[o]ne product of the creative governmental enterprise of this period," not a traditional prison but a sincere attempt to relieve and reform the poor on the margins of the overall relief system who could not be addressed by existing measures. Innes, "Prisons for the Poor: English Bridewells, 1555–1800," 42.

49. Thomas Adams, *Mystical Bedlam, or, The World of Mad-Men*, 75.

50. On the role of companies in the administration of city affairs, especially charity, see Rappaport, *Worlds within Worlds*, 190–93; Frank F. Foster, *The Politics of Stability*, 95; W. K. Jordan, *Philanthropy in England 1480–1660*, 86; Carroll, *Fat King, Lean Beggar*, 12.

51. Robert Wilkinson, *The Merchant Royal: A Sermon Preached at Whitehall before the King's Majesty*, C1v (emphasis added).

52. Quoted in Scott Cutler Shershow, "Work and the Gift," 99.

53. Rappaport, *Worlds within Worlds*, 189.

54. Stow, *Survey of London*, 671. See James F. Larkin and Paul Hughes, eds., *Stuart Royal Proclamations*, 1:20.

55. Stow, *Survey of London*, 678.

56. Henry Peacham, *The Compleat Gentleman*, Bb1v–Bb2r.

57. Foster, *Politics of Stability*, 99.

58. See Marcel Mauss, *The Gift: The Form and Reason of Exchange in Primitive Societies*, 72.

59. David Bergeron, *English Civic Pageantry, 1558–1642*, 263; Paster, *Idea of the City*, 125.

60. "Orazio Busino's Eyewitness Account of the Triumphs of Honour and Industry," trans. Kate D. Levin, in Thomas Middleton, *The Complete Works of Thomas Middleton*, ed. Gary Taylor and John Lavagnino, 1266–69.

61. Paster, *Idea of the City*, 125.

62. Thomas Dekker, *Troia-Nova Triumphans: London Triumphing*, A3v.

63. Ibid., B2v (original emphasis).

64. Ralph L. Rosnow and Gary Alan Fine, *Rumor and Gossip: The Social Psychology of Hearsay*, 87–88.

65. Samuel Rowland, *A Whole Crew of Kind Gossips, All Met to Be Merry*, A2r.

66. Thomas Dekker, *Lanthorne and Candlelight*, K3v; Peter Clark, *The English Alehouse: A Social History, 1200–1830*, 39–44.

67. John Taylor, *Taylor's Travels and Circular Perambulation*, B2v.

68. Tiffany Stern, "'On Each Wall and Corner Poast': Playbills, Title-pages, and Advertising in Early Modern London," 73.

69. Clark, *English Alehouse*, 130.

70. Thomas Thompson, *A Diet for a Drunkard*, 12–13, 19; Thomas Adams, *The Happiness of the Church*, 319.

71. Patricia Fumerton, "Not Home: Alehouses, Ballads, and the Vagrant Husband in Early Modern England," 500. See Theodore Leinwand, "Spongy Plebs, Mighty Lords, and the Dynamics of the Alehouse," 160.

72. William Cornwallis, *Essays*, L3v.

73. Dekker, *Lanthorne and Candlelight*, K3r.

74. "What a Justice of the Peace May Do," fol. 1. Huntington MS 17298, Henry E. Huntington Library, San Marino, California.

75. Clark, *English Alehouse*, 124–37.

76. Stephen Gosson, *Plays Confuted in Five Actions*, D3r–v, C7v.

77. Quoted in Gurr, *Playgoing*, 237.

78. Henry Petowe, *Londoners: Their Entertainment in the Country*, A4v–B1r.

79. Ian Archer, "Government in Early Modern London: The Challenge of the Suburbs," 135–36.

80. Greater Southwark, known officially as Bridge Ward Without, lacked membership on the London common council. Its alderman was not elected by the residents of Southwark but by Londoners north of the river, so its interests were probably inadequately represented in the municipal government's deliberations.

81. Herbert Morrison, *How London Is Governed*, 13; Geoffrey Cumberlege, *The Corporation of London: Its Origin, Constitutional Power, and Duties*, 27.

82. David Johnson, *Southwark and the City*, 114.

83. John Norden, *Speculum Britannie*, C3r.

84. Mullaney, *Place of the Stage*, 24.

85. Boulton, *Neighborhood and Society*, 263. See Archer, "Government in Early Modern London," 141.

86. Quoted in Ward, "Imagining the Metropolis," 26.

87. Gurr, *Shakespearian Playing Companies*, 55.

88. Chambers, *Elizabethan Stage*, 4:294–96.

89. Richard Dutton, *Mastering the Revels: The Regulation and Censorship of English Renaissance Drama*, 16, 142–63.

90. Ward, "Imagining the Metropolis," 32–33.

91. Philip Henslowe, *Diary*, 13.

92. Joseph P. Ward, *Metropolitan Communities: Trade, Guilds, Identity, and Change in Early Modern London*, 4.

93. Boulton, *Neighborhood and Society*, 68–70.

2. THE PUBLIC THEATRES AND THEIR COMMUNITIES

1. Quoted in Lawrence Manley, ed., *London in the Age of Shakespeare: An Anthology*, 142.

2. William Turner, *Turner's Dish*.

3. William Ingram, "The Globe Playhouse and Its Neighbors in 1600," 67–70; Phillip Norman, "The Accounts of the Overseers of the Poor of Paris Garden, Southwark," 68.

4. G. E. Bentley, "Records of Players in the Parish of St. Giles," 801.

5. Chambers, *Elizabethan Stage*, 1:181.

6. Ibid., 1:294.

7. Ibid., 1:300.

8. Ibid., 4:327–28.; J. P. Collier, ed., *Memoirs of Edward Alleyn*, 58.

9. G. E. Bentley, *The Jacobean and Caroline Stage*, 2:571.

10. Ibid., 6:215–16. We have reason to doubt the amount of these highway payments due to the extraordinarily large sum as well as the ambiguous wording of document itself. See William Ingram, "Playhouses Make Strange Bedfellows: The Case of Aaron and Martin," 124–25.

11. Collier, *Memoirs of Edward Alleyn*, 90; William Ingram, "'Neere the Playe Howse': The Swan Theatre and Community Blight," 56.

12. Collier, *Memoirs of Edward Alleyn*, 98–102. On Alleyn's activities in Bishopsgate, see Richard Tames, *Clerkenwell and Finsbury Past*, 6; on the loan to James, see

S. P. Cerasano, "Cheerful Givers: Henslowe, Alleyn, and the 1612 Loan Book to the Crown," 217–18.

13. Gurr, *Playgoing*, 66–67.

14. Ibid., 160–66. Although the third quotation refers to the Curtain, that theatre is compared with the Red Bull (which replaced it as the regular venue of Queen Anne's Men sometime after 1605) and the Fortune often enough to surmise that the latter two playhouses had garnered a similar reputation by the early seventeenth century. See Bentley, *Jacobean and Caroline Stage*, 6:133.

15. John Taylor, *All the Works of John Taylor the Water Poet*, 172. An undated petition from the 1590s from "the Lord Strange, his servants and players" appeals to the Privy Council for permission to play on the Bankside (at the Rose) in part *because of* the "great relief to the poor watermen there" offered by the playgoing traffic. The Globe therefore must have drawn the majority of its audience from people in the city within the walls who flocked there not just by ferry but also across London Bridge. See Carol Rutter, ed., *Documents of the Rose Playhouse*, 65.

16. Chambers, *Elizabethan Stage*, 2:406.

17. Eccles, *Rose Theatre*, 15.

18. See S. P. Cerasano, "The Patronage Network of Philip Henslowe and Edward Alleyn," 84–86.

19. Eccles, *Rose Theatre*, 16; Julian Bowsher and Pat Miller, *The Rose and the Globe: Excavations 1988–91*, 109.

20. Rutter, *Documents of the Rose Playhouse*, 65.

21. S. P. Cerasano, "Revising Philip Henslowe's Biography," 69.

22. J. P. Collier, ed., *The Diary of Philip Henslowe from 1591 to 1609*, xv.

23. Frederick G. Fleay, *A Biographical Chronicle of the English Drama, 1559–1642*, 1:117; Norman Nathan, "Is Shylock Philip Henslowe?" 164. For Collier, Fleay, and others, the sharer system adopted by Shakespeare's company ultimately triumphed over the impresario-driven model used by Henslowe's companies.

24. Bernard Beckerman, "Philip Henslowe."

25. S. P. Cerasano, "The Geography of Henslowe's Diary," 342. For Henslowe's dealings in Southwark, see Rutter, *Documents of the Rose Playhouse*, 5–7.

26. Fleay, *Biographical Chronicle*, 1:117.

27. Henslowe, *Diary*, 131, 9.

28. Neil Carson, *A Companion to Henslowe's Diary*, 33.

29. Gurr, *Shakespeare's Opposites*, 27.

30. Henslowe, *Diary*, 6–7, 9–13.

31. Gurr, *Shakespearian Playing Companies*, 66–75; Eccles, *Rose Theatre*, 39–44.

32. Thomas Nashe, *The Unfortunate Traveler and Other Works*, 116.

33. Chambers, *Elizabethan Stage*, 2:132.

34. For the story of the Swan and its owner, see William Ingram, *A London Life in the Brazen Age: Francis Langley, 1548–1602*, 101–233.

35. Herbert Berry, *Shakespeare's Playhouses*, 38; Irwin Smith, *Shakespeare's First Playhouse*, 56–58.

36. James Wright, *Historia Histrionica: An Historical Account of the English Stage*, B3r.

37. John Heath, *Two Centuries of Epigrams*, E3r–v.

38. Andrew Gurr, "The General and the Caviar: Learned Audiences in the Early Theatre."

39. John Webster, *The White Devil*, prologue.

40. Kempe, after dancing his way to Norwich, reappeared on the London stage a few years later with Worcester's Men, whose plays still gave scope to his brand of comedy. In a thinly veiled jab at his former troupe, Kempe refers to his detractors as "Shakerags" in *Nine Daies Wonder*. One character in John Cooke's *Greene's Tu Quoque*, named for Thomas Greene (an actor in Kempe's image), refuses to attend a play at the Globe because the "clown have [*sic*] [no] part," probably expressing the tastes of many playgoers: "I am nobody without a fool" (G2v). For a brief biography of Kempe, see David Wiles, *Shakespeare's Clown: Actor and Text in the Elizabethan Playhouse*, 23–42.

41. Wiles, *Shakespeare's Clown*, 43–45.

42. Gurr, *Shakespeare Company*, 69–74; Wiles, *Shakespeare's Clown*, 46.

43. Andrew Gurr, "The Authority of the Globe and the Fortune," 262–65.

44. Ann Jennalie Cook, *The Privileged Playgoers of Shakespeare's London*, 124.

45. Butler, *Theatre and Crisis*, 293–306. Cook herself is reacting to Alfred Harbage's championing of a popular audience in *Shakespeare's Audience* (1941). I would suggest that both sides of this debate are overly reductive in their attempt to posit a single audience for all Renaissance drama; hence my claim that we need to think of a variety of different audiences and audience conditions that held at different theatres. For a summary of the debate about early modern theatre audiences, see S. P. Cerasano, "Must the Devil Appear?: Audiences, Actors, Stage Business," 193–97.

46. Alvin Kernan, *Shakespeare, the King's Playwright*, 9; Anthony Dawson and Paul Yachnin, *The Culture of Playgoing in Shakespeare's England: A Collaborative Debate*, 42–44.

47. Gurr, *Playgoing*, 70. Where evidence survives of some noteworthy visitors to the Fortune and Red Bull, it is usually because the playgoer was either the perpetrator or the victim of some form of criminal activity in the playhouse yard. Revealingly, no reports of similar crimes are extant for the Globe. While I admit that this disparity might be due to a deficiency in the local records, it could be an indication of a livelier and more raucous environment at the northern theatres.

48. Gurr, *Shakespeare's Opposites*, 18–23.

49. John Russell Brown, *Shakespeare and the Theatrical Event*, 8.

50. See Mullaney, *Place of the Stage*, 49–50.

51. Southwark, by contrast, had a large transient population. Part of its appeal as a site of misrule must have been that it preserved the anonymity of those who participated in—and provided—its various entertainments. Some historians suggest that Southwark was often a temporary residence for newcomers to London before they became settled in trades and homes north of the Thames. See Boulton, *Neighborhood and Society*, 207.

52. Stow, *Survey of London*, 210.

53. Roger Finlay, *Population and Metropolis: The Demography of London*, 61. See also Rappaport, *Worlds within Worlds*, 64.

54. Larkin and Hughes, *Stuart Royal Proclamations*, 1:246.

55. Archer, *Pursuit of Stability*, 151–52.

56. Stow, *Survey of London*, 696.

57. Finlay and Shearer, "Population Growth and Suburban Expansion," 67; Ilana Ben-Amos, *Adolescence and Youth in Early Modern England*, 84; Ian Archer, "Material Londoners?" 184.

58. Quoted in Mark Thornton Burnett, "Apprentice Literature and the 'Crisis' of the 1590s," 50.

59. Gurr, *Playgoing*, 246, and *Shakespearian Playing Companies*, 215–16; Whitney, *Early Responses*, 190–91.

60. Heywood, *Four Prentices*, A3r.

61. Warrant from Charles Howard, Earl of Nottingham, 12 January 1599/1600. Rutter, *Documents of the Rose Playhouse*, 177.

62. Chambers, *Elizabethan Stage*, 2:435–38.

63. Henslowe, *Diary*, 66. This was not the last time Henslowe worked with Street. He employed the carpenter to build a new gateway to the Bear Garden in 1606. See Bowsher and Miller, *Rose and the Globe*, 109.

64. Henslowe, *Diary*, 120–21. See Vincent Landrow, "Henslowe's Relocation to the North: Playhouse Management in Renaissance London," 42–43.

65. Gurr, *Shakespeare's Opposites*, 6–7.

66. S. P. Cerasano, "'More Elbow Roome, But Scant Better Aire': The Fortune Playhouse and Its Surroundings," 70.

67. Knutson, *Playing Companies and Commerce*, 35–36.

68. S. P. Cerasano, "Edward Alleyn's 'Retirement' 1597–1600," 105; Gurr, *Shakespeare's Opposites*, 20.

69. S. P. Cerasano, *Relocating the Fortune Playhouse: A New History*, 8–11.

70. Beckerman, "Philip Henslowe," 19–34.

71. Rutter, *Documents of the Rose Playhouse*, 177–78; on Nottingham's influence over local JPs, see Gurr, *Shakespearian Playing Companies*, 231–32.

72. Rutter, *Documents of the Rose Playhouse*, 185–86. Rutter notes that organizing the community to sponsor this petition would have taken a considerable amount of work in canvassing local residents and hiring a scrivener, suggesting that residents were strongly in favor of the measure or that somebody, perhaps Alleyn himself, did much of the groundwork.

73. Gurr, *Shakespeare's Opposites*, 135.

74. Thomas Dekker, *The Pleasant Comedy of Old Fortunatus*, A4r.

75. Boulton, *Neighborhood and Society*, 62–65.

76. Stow, *Survey of London*, 301–16.

77. C1/582/18, National Archives (formerly Public Record Office), Kew, UK.

78. Stow, *Survey of London*, 318.

79. The Red Bull, like all playhouses, staged a variety of plays, making generalizations difficult and potentially misleading. Yet, judging by comments that mention that theatre, it quickly became known for its heroic plays and turgid acting style. For more on the repertory of this theatre, see Bayer, "Red Bull Playhouse"; and Astington, "Playing the Man."

80. Thomas Seckford (d. January 1587/1588), Henry's father, was "a Tudor arriviste." He was master of the Court of Requests and surveyor of the lucrative Court of Wards and Liveries. When he retired to Clerkenwell in the early 1580s, he became patron of cartographer Christopher Saxton. He was buried in Suffolk, where he endowed an almshouse in Clerkenwell for thirteen men to be maintained by income from his Clerkenwell holdings, one of which was undoubtedly the land upon which the Red Bull was built. Another powerful figure in the playgoing industry, Sir Edmund Tilney (the Master of the Revels under Elizabeth), resided at St. John's Gate in Clerkenwell. See Tames, *Clerkenwell and Finsbury Past*, 28.

81. Slater is not mentioned in any of the troupe's patents but was nevertheless an actor who toured with the company in the provinces. His claim to the property is dubious, because only Holland is mentioned in later disputes concerning the lease. Ingram, "Playhouses Make Strange Bedfellows," 123.

82. Bentley, *Jacobean and Caroline Stage*, 6:215; Eva Griffith, "New Material for a Jacobean Playhouse," 8.

83. Herbert Berry, "Building Playhouses, the Accession of James I, and the Red Bull," 67.

84. Pinks, *The History of Clerkenwell*, 12.

85. British Library Stowe MS 1047, fol. 208r; British Library Add. MS 37666, British Library, London, UK.

86. Norman Brett-James, *The Growth of Stuart London*, 214.

87. Peter Heywood, brother of the playwright, was employed as a justice of the peace in this facility.

88. Brett-James, *Growth of Stuart London*, 217–18.

89. Corporation of the City of London Record Office Remembrancia II, fol. 70, National Archives (formerly Public Record Office), Kew, UK.

90. A. L. Beier, *Masterless Men: The Vagrancy Problem in England, 1560–1640*, 43.

91. Stow, *Survey of London*, 483; see Philip Temple, ed., *South and East Clerkenwell*, 203.

92. Stow, *Survey of London*, 395; Guildhall MS 10597, Guildhall Library, London, UK.

93. Rappaport, *Worlds within Worlds*, 171–73.

94. Pinks, *History of Clerkenwell*, 2; Stow, *Survey of London*, 391; William Howitt, *The Northern Heights of London*, 36; Tames, *Clerkenwell and Finsbury Past*, 14.

95. John Wilson, *A Concise Account of St. John's Gate Clerkenwell*, 8–9.

96. Pinks, *History of Clerkenwell*, 3; Stow, *Survey of London*, 119; Anne Lancashire, "Multi-day Performance and the London Clerkenwell Play."

97. Stow, *Survey of London*, 118–23.

98. Taylor, *Taylor's Travels and Circular Perambulation*, A8r.

99. See, for instance, Bentley, *Jacobean and Caroline Stage*, 6:238; Cook, *Privileged Playgoers*, 137–38; Gurr, *Playgoing*, 170.

100. John Swinnerton's eldest son was named Thomas, but we cannot know if this was the player. Swinnerton is often accused of censoring Robert Taylor's *The Hog Hath Lost His Pearl*, performed at Whitefriars in February 1613/1614. Smith's dedication suggests that the mayor may have been more amenable to players than is commonly assumed.

101. Wentworth Smith, *The Hector of Germany*, A2r.

102. George Wither, *Abuses Script and Whipt*, D3v.

103. Thomas Tomkis, *Albumazar*, C4v–D1r.

104. Gurr, *Playgoing*, 246.

105. Bentley, *Jacobean and Caroline Stage*, 6:238. None of the other playing spaces described in such detail in this six-volume work warrant a similar treatment of their reputations.

106. Marta Straznicky, "The Red Bull Repertory in Print, 1605–60," 144; Tom Rutter, "Adult Playing Companies, 1603–1613," 86. I think that both of these claims are exaggerated. The market for printed plays does not seem to be a sufficient basis to speculate about their audience in performance. Heywood draws a firm distinction between the printed version of the *Iron Age* and the version played at the Red Bull. The playhouses certainly offered plays on similar themes and subjects, but their content and their style were modified to suit different audiences. The vast gulf between Shakespeare's take on the Trojan War in *Troilus and Cres-*

sida and Heywood's in the *Iron Age* suggests that the two playwrights had different classes of auditors in mind.

107. Bentley, *Jacobean and Caroline Stage*, 6:218. See Gurr, *Shakespearian Playing Companies*, 149.

108. Keith Sturgess, *Jacobean Private Theater*, 13.

109. Gurr, *Shakespearean Stage*, 144–45.

110. Thomas Dekker, *If This Be Not a Good Play, the Devil Is in It*, A3r–v.

111. Stow, *Survey of London*, 914–15.

112. This passage also highlights the enormous self-recognition that the physical structure of all the London amphitheatre playhouses would have forced on spectators. See Dawson and Yachnin, *Culture of Playgoing*, 94–97.

113. The epilogue to Shakespeare's *2 Henry IV* makes a similar move in an effort to drum up future business, promising that "our humble author will continue the story with Sir John [Falstaff] in it" (ll. 22–23).

114. Gurr, *Shakespeare's Opposites*, 2.

115. Stern, "'On Each Wall and Corner Poast,'" 57.

3. RELIGIOUS COMMUNITIES AT LONDON'S NORTHERN PLAYHOUSES

1. John Foxe, *Actes and Monuments of These Latter and Perilous Days*, q2v.

2. Henry Ainsworth, *Counterpoyson* (Amsterdam, 1608), ***3v, quoted in Jeffrey Knapp, *Shakespeare's Tribe: Church, Nation, and Theatre in Renaissance England*, 26.

3. John Robinson, *A Justification of Separation from the Church of England*, A2v.

4. *If You Know Not Me* was probably first staged by Queen Anne's Men at the Curtain and revived numerous times at the Red Bull and later at the Cockpit in Drury Lane. It was printed seven times before the theatres closed in 1642. *The Whore of Babylon*, despite a poor beginning, was successfully revived later in the decade and prompted the author to pen similar plays, such as Dekker's *If This Be Not a Good Play, the Devil Is in It* (1611) and Dekker and Massinger's *The Virgin Martyr* (1620). See Gurr, *Shakespearian Playing Companies*, 132, 247.

5. Susan Brigden, *London and the Reformation*, 394, 406; Foxe, *Actes and Monuments*, Mmm4r.

6. John Foxe, *Actes and Monuments* (1576 edition), Ooooo4r–v (emphasis added).

7. Quoted in Henry Foley, *Records of the English Province of the Society of Jesus*, 1:108.

8. Ibid., 107.

9. Obviously, numerous studies have dealt with the theatre within the context of the Reformation and charted the ways in which plays reflected on religious matters. Too often, however, studies which elegantly underscore the synergis-

tic interplay of drama, religious polemic, and early modern Londoners do so by focusing either on individual playwrights (Margot Heinemann, *Puritanism and Theater: Thomas Middleton and Opposition Drama under the Early Stuarts* [Cambridge: Cambridge University Press, 1980], on Middleton; Donna B. Hamilton, *Shakespeare and the Politics of Protestant England*, on Shakespeare; and James H. Sims, *Biblical Allusions in Marlowe and Shakespeare*, on Marlowe, to list but a few) or on sweeping ideological trends over the course of several decades (for example, Alan Sinfield, *Literature in Protestant England*, 106–28; Paul Whitfield White, *Theater and Reformation*; and Huston Diehl, *Staging Reform, Reforming the Stage* [Ithaca, N.Y.: Cornell University Press, 1997]).

10. Gurr, *Shakespearean Stage*, 216–20; Cerasano, "'More Elbow Roome,'" 73.

11. Stow, *Survey of London*, 289; see Brigden, *London and the Reformation*, 586.

12. The dissolution of this priory occurred much later than that of other monastic lands throughout England. During the reign of Mary (1553–1558) the buildings belonging to the former priory were repaired for the purpose of celebrating mass for the merchant-tailors and other London companies, and the order was not completely abolished until 1559. Pinks, *History of Clerkenwell*, 218–19.

13. Tames, *Clerkenwell and Finsbury Past*, 27.

14. *The Rat-Trap, or, The Jesuits Taken in Their Own Net*, A4v–B2v; see figure 5.

15. Foley, *Records of the English Province of the Society of Jesus*, 1:99–111. Account books indicate that annual expenses amounted to £227 10s 5d and that the books seized were valued at £400. See British Library MS 5506, fol. 67r, British Library, London, UK.

16. Foley, *Records of the English Province of the Society of Jesus*, 1:104.

17. John Stuart Blackie, *Messis Vitae*.

18. John Cordy Jeaffreson, *The Middlesex County Records*, 2:386; William Hardy, ed., *Middlesex Session Records*, 220.

19. Folger MS Y.c.123 (A–E), fols. b–c, Folger Shakespeare Library, Washington, D.C.

20. Stow, *Survey of London*, 313. See Warren R. Wooden, *John Foxe*, 11.

21. Peter M. Blayney, "John Day and the Bookshop That Never Was," 330–31; James Raven, *The Business of Books: Booksellers and the English Book Trade, 1450–1850*, 29.

22. Andrew Pettegree, "Day, John (1521/2–1584)"; Elizabeth Evenden, "Day, Richard (*b.* 1552, *d.* in or before 1606)."

23. Stow, *Survey of London*, 291.

24. John Andrews, *The Brazen Serpent*, B4v–C1r.

25. Simon Parret, in a 1582 letter, complains of "the foul paper and obscure print" of this inferior publication. See David Loades, ed., *John Foxe and the English Reformation*, 48–50. It seems that Day used the capital-intensive editions of 1563

and 1570 to generate the revenue necessary to make the 1576 edition readily available at a more reasonable price and in a slightly less unwieldy format.

26. One unique innovation consists in a table "to help the unlearned," in which the compilers "thought it good to set forth the plain numbers with Ciphers in algorithm, whereby they might understand the numbers better" (q9r). Here, for instance, a Roman numeral is given alongside its Arabic equivalent, leading to what many might consider the oversimplified explanation that "ii [the Roman numeral] = 2." The 1576 edition also introduces various readerly "helps" of its own, including a previously unpublished set of concordances for scriptural references and theological doctrines as well as an expanded index. Loades, *John Foxe and the English Reformation*, 62.

27. Foxe, *Actes and Monuments*, q1v.

28. John Gee, *New Shreds of the Old Snare*, D2r.

29. Ibid., D3v, C4v.

30. William Holbrooke, *A Sermon Preached at St. Botolph's near Aldersgate, the 26 of February 1609*, A7r–v.

31. For a discussion of these two different varieties of history plays, see Richard Helgerson, *Forms of Nationhood: The Elizabethan Writing of England*, 193–215.

32. Other candidates for the play's authorship include George Peele, with Dekker as a possible collaborator. The play was printed by Thomas Pavier in 1605.

33. Knapp, *Shakespeare's Tribe*, 32–37.

34. Thomas Jordan, *A Nursery of Novelties in Variety of Poetry*, C4r.

35. Kathleen McLuskie, *Dekker and Heywood: Professional Dramatists*, 41–42.

36. Thomas Heywood, *If You Know Not Me, You Know Nobody*, A2r, G3r. The play was first entered into the stationer's register on 5 July 1605 by Nathaniel Butter and published by him in 1605, 1606, 1608, 1613, 1623, 1632, and 1639; Thomas Pavier published editions in 1608 and 1610. Only the 1639 edition was authorized by Heywood. Nearly continuous reprinting throughout the reigns of James I and Charles I attested not only to the play's popularity but to the undiminished nostalgia for Elizabeth during that period. It is also likely, as Marsha Robinson notes, that many of these editions capitalized on current events such as the proposed Spanish Match in 1623 or the Laudian trial of William Prynne, Henry Burton, and John Bastwick in 1637. See Marsha S. Robinson, *Writing the Reformation:* Actes and Monuments *and the Jacobean History Play*, 164.

37. Foxe, *Actes and Monuments*, q1.

38. Ivo Kamps, *Historiography and Ideology in Stuart Drama*, 67–68.

39. Foxe, *Actes and Monuments*, GGGg4v.

40. John N. King, *English Reformation Literature*, 274.

41. See Katherine Eisaman Maus, *Inwardness and Theater in the English Renaissance*, 47–48.

42. Loades, *John Foxe and the English Reformation*, 29–30.

43. Webster suggests that it was partially the inclement weather which led to the play's dismal reception in February and March 1612, but he also says, in a prefatory note, that the audience at the Red Bull was not up to the intricate court dialogue. As many commentators have noted, the play's focus on subtle court intrigue and deception is anomalous in the Queen's Men's repertory during these years. John Webster, *The White Devil*, prologue.

44. Dieter Mehl, *The Elizabethan Dumb Show*, 89.

45. Foxe, *Actes and Monuments*, RRRRr4v.

46. John N. King, *Tudor Royal Iconography*, 110–13; see figure 7.

47. Alexandra Walsham, *Providence in Early Modern England*, 118–20.

48. Richard Day, *A Book of Christian Prayers*, *2v. Like the *Book of Martyrs* itself, *The Book of Christian Prayers* offers numerous aids to assist its readers in their devotional pursuits. It contains an extensive table to help readers easily find prayers on certain subjects and for various occasions. Typical of work printed by Day, it is richly illustrated with woodcuts that offer figural representations of the spiritual message embodied in each prayer.

49. Richard Mulcaster, *The Queen's Majesty's Progress through the City of London*, C2r.

50. Foxe, *Actes and Monuments*, RRRRr4v.

51. Ibid., RRRRr5r.

52. The Globe Theatre burnt to the ground on 29 June, during a performance of *Henry VIII*.

53. Gurr, *Shakespearian Playing Companies*, 367–69.

54. Gurr, *Shakespeare's Opposites*, 44.

55. David Cressy, *Bonfires and Bells*, 142–45.

56. Julia Gasper, *The Dragon and the Dove: The Plays of Thomas Dekker*, 63; Cyrus Hoy, *Introductions, Notes, and Commentaries to Texts in the Dramatic Works of Thomas Dekker*, 303; Susan Kranz, "Thomas Dekker's Political Commentary in *The Whore of Babylon*"; McLuskie, *Dekker and Heywood*, 52.

57. Gurr, *Shakespeare's Opposites*, 175.

58. William Barlowe, *The Sermon Preached at Paul's Cross the Tenth Day of November*, B3r; see Barbara K. Lewalski, Paradise Lost *and the Rhetoric of Literary Forms*, 50–51.

59. Patrick Collinson, *The Elizabethan Puritan Movement*, 26–27.

60. William Bailey, *A Rumor of Wars among the Times and Signs of Peace*, A4r.

61. Foley, *Records of the English Province of the Society of Jesus*, 1:204–5.

62. Andrews, *Brazen Serpent*, C8r.

63. According to Susan Kranz, the Catholic church and the Spanish nation are uneasily conflated throughout the play in order to preserve the opposition be-

tween true and false church and indict both parties in the Gunpowder treason. Kranz, "Thomas Dekker's Political Commentary," 273.

4. THE SPECTACLE OF HISTORY AT THE RED BULL

1. Thomas Dekker, *The Wonderful Year, Wherein Is Showed the Picture of London, Sick of the Plague*, D1r–D2v.

2. Thomas Dekker, *The Seven Deadly Sins of London*, A3r. For a review of the economics of London's neighborhoods over this period, see Archer, *Pursuit of Stability*, 149–54.

3. Thomas Heywood, *The Brazen Age*, L2r–L3v.

4. The plays in the cycle, all written by Thomas Heywood, included *The Golden Age* (ca. 1609), *The Silver Age* (ca. 1610–1611), *The Brazen Age* (ca. 1610–1612), and the two-part *Iron Age* (ca. 1612–1613). This popular quintet inspired at least one spinoff, *The Escapes of Jupiter*, staged nearly a decade later, possibly to coincide with a revival of *The Golden Age* and *The Silver Age*. The epilogue to *2 Iron Age* leaves ample room for potential future installments. The dating of these plays has been subject to considerable debate. Theatre historians have suggested that they are revivals and revisions of plays performed by the Admiral's Men in the 1590s. *Seleo et Olympo*, staged at the Rose in 1595, became the *Golden Age*; *1* and *2 Hercules* (1595) became *The Silver Age* and *The Brazen Age*. *The Iron Age* was an update of either the lost *Troy* (first performed on 22 June 1596), an unnamed Admiral's Men play about the Trojan story for which a plot fragment survives, or Dekker and Chettle's *Troilus and Cressida* (paid for by Henslowe in April 1599). The connection is tempting, given Heywood's affiliation with the Admiral's Men during those years and the mention of several stage properties that could be used in conjunction with the plays in an inventory of the Admiral's Men in March 1598. Because all the earlier playtexts have been lost, it is impossible either to verify or to disprove this hypothesis. For a discussion of the arguments both for and against these claims, see Ernest Schanzer, "Heywood's *Ages* and Shakespeare," 18–20; and John S. P. Tatlock, "The Siege of Troy in Elizabethan Literature, Especially in Shakespeare and Heywood," 699–726. If it is true, these earlier versions of the *Ages* would have represented some of Heywood's earliest work for the public stage. Regardless of their date of composition, it seems obvious that the plays were heavily revised and updated for performance at the Red Bull late in the first decade of the seventeenth century; the title page to *The Golden Age*, the first of the five to be printed (in 1611), advertises its popularity at that theatre. Most recent scholarly discussions of the play have also assumed these later dates. See McLuskie, *Dekker and Heywood*, 15; and George Reynolds, *The Staging of Elizabethan Plays at the Red Bull*, 182.

5. Thomas Heywood, *The Iron Age*, A4r.

6. Quoted in Butler, *Theatre and Crisis*, 181.

7. John Cooke, *The Two Merry Milkmaids*, A2r. For a typically disparaging summary of the reputation of this playhouse, see Bentley, *Jacobean and Caroline Stage*, 6:238–47.

8. Reynolds, *Staging of Elizabethan Plays*, 24; Gurr, *Playgoing*, 175.

9. F. P. Wilson, *The Plague in Shakespeare's London*, 17–19.

10. Thomas Lodge, *A Treatise of the Plague*, A2r.

11. *Lachrymae Londinenses, or, London's Tears and Lamentations*, B2r–v.

12. Dekker, *Wonderful Year*, D1r.

13. Charles Creighton, *A History of Epidemics in Britain*, 1:480.

14. Ibid., 1:493.

15. Dekker, *Wonderful Year*, C3r.

16. Thomas Pullein, *Jeremiah's Tears, or, A Sermon Preached in York-Minster upon Trinity Sunday, in the Year of Our Lord 1604*, E4r.

17. Taylor, *All the Works of John Taylor*, 59.

18. Lodge, *Treatise of the Plague*, A3v, C4r.

19. Dekker, *Wonderful Year*, D2v.

20. Anthony Anderson, *An Approved Medicine against the Deserved Plague*, A4v, B1v.

21. Thomas Hastler, *An Antidote against the Plague, or, A Salve for All Sores*, A6v–A7r (emphasis added).

22. T. C., *A Godly and Learned Sermon upon the 91st Psalm*, B7r.

23. Joan, the player's wife, writes in October 1603 (immediately after the worst of the outbreaks) that "my own self, your self, and my mother and the whole house are in good health." Henslowe, *Diary*, 297.

24. Herbert Berry, *The Boar's Head Playhouse*, 70. Browne's son William entered his father's profession (and his stepfather's when the widowed Susan Browne married the comedian Thomas Greene) and acted with Queen Anne's Men and its successor companies at the Red Bull until his death on 6 November 1634.

25. Leeds Barroll suggests that during the summer and fall of 1603 the entire troupe repaired to the home of one of the sharers, Augustine Phillips, in Mortlake in Surrey, where they were comfortably removed from the crowded and unsanitary conditions in London. During August 1604 they again left London, attending the constable of Castile as grooms of his chamber at Somerset House. Leeds Barroll, *Politics, Plague, and Shakespeare's Theater: The Stuart Years*, 112–22.

26. Gurr, *Shakespearian Playing Companies*, 322.

27. Barroll, *Politics, Plague, and Shakespeare's Theater*, 31–49, 173.

28. See Gurr, *Shakespeare Company*, 255. These extra court performances and the revenue generated from touring would have represented only about 6 percent of the money usually generated from public playing.

29. *The Stage-Player's Complaint*, 1, 6.

30. Barroll, *Politics, Plague, and Shakespeare's Theater*, chapters 4–6.

31. According to the general pattern extrapolated by Roslyn Knutson from the records contained in Philip Henslowe's *Diary*, a typical stage run for an initially successful play lasted for six months, during which the play was performed eight to twelve times. Popular plays frequently continued in the next playing season, doubling the number of performances and meaning that many plays were in continuous rotation for a year or more and were given at least twenty performances. Finally, a company's seasonal repertory was rounded out with revivals, consisting of tried selections from previous seasons, revisions of already produced plays, and "blockbusters" like *Tamburlaine* and *The Spanish Tragedy* that seemed to draw large audiences regardless of their age or the number of times they had been staged. Roslyn Knutson, *The Repertory of Shakespeare's Company*, 32–40.

32. Berry, "Building Playhouses," 69.

33. E. A. J. Honigmann and Susan Brock, *Playhouse Wills: 1558–1642*, 162–64, 191–94.

34. Copelia Kahn, *Roman Shakespeare: Warriors, Wounds, and Women*, 4; Bruster, *Drama and the Market*, 107–13; Heather James, *Shakespeare's Troy: Drama, Politics, and the Translation of Empire*.

35. In this work Heywood draws on the classics of Homer, Virgil, and Ovid, in addition to English renditions of this material, including Geoffrey Chaucer's *Troilus and Criseyde*, John Lydgate's *Troy Book* (1420), William Caxton's *Recuyell of the Histories of Troy* (1474, the first book printed in English), and the more recent *Peele's Tale of Troy* (1589).

36. Thomas Heywood, *The Second Part of the Iron Age*, E2v.

37. See Robert Hanning, *The Vision of History in Early Britain: From Gildas to Geoffrey of Monmouth*.

38. George Puttenham, *The Art of English Poesy*, 32–33. See R. G. Collingwood, *The Idea of History*, 57.

39. Phyllis Rackin, *Stages of History: Shakespeare's English Chronicles*, 18.

40. Ovid, *Metamorphoses*, A2v, A3r. This translation was reprinted in 1575, 1584, 1587, 1593, and 1603.

41. Heywood, *Iron Age*, A2r.

42. D. R. Woolf, *Reading History in Early-Modern England*, 26–27. During these years Philemon Holland also translated Livy, *Roman History* (1600), Suetonius, *History of Twelve Caesars* (1606), and Marcellinus, *Roman History* (1609); Lodge contributed a translation of *The Famous and Memorable Works of Josephus* (1602, reprinted 1609); and North's translation of Plutarch, first published in 1579, underwent four new editions in the early 1600s, including three in 1603 alone.

43. Plutarch, *The Lives of the Noble Grecians and Romans*, A3r.

44. Heywood, *Apology for Actors*, B3v.

45. Nashe, *Unfortunate Traveler*, 112–13.

46. Heywood, *Apology for Actors*, B3v.

47. Webster made his disparaging comments about the playgoers at the Red Bull in a prefatory note to *The White Devil*, printed by Nicholas Oakes in 1612.

48. Thomas Heywood, *The Silver Age*, B1r.

49. Heywood, *Apology for Actors*, C3v.

50. Edmund Gayton, *Pleasant Notes upon Don Quixote*, Mm3r.

51. Heywood, *Silver Age*, K2v, H4v.

52. Thomas Bilson, *The Survey of Christ's Sufferings for Man's Redemption and His Descent into Hades or Hell*, D3r.

53. Heywood, *Silver Age*, I4v–K3r.

54. Pullein, *Jeremiah's Tears*, B4v–C2v.

55. Alan R. Young, "Thomas Heywood's Pageants: New Forms of Evidence," 129–30. These ventures led him to collaborate with some of the best set designers and pageant makers in the business, including Inigo Jones and Gerard Christmas.

56. Bergeron, *English Civic Pageantry*, 240–41.

57. Thomas Middleton, "Epistle," in *The Roaring Girl*; Peter Heylyn, quoted in Bentley, *Jacobean and Caroline Stage*, 6:135.

58. Reynolds, *Staging of Elizabethan Plays*, 88–133.

59. McLuskie, *Dekker and Heywood*, 15.

60. Thomas Heywood, *The Golden Age*, G2r (stage direction). An equally spectacular battle occurs later in the same play between Tros and Saturn and their armies (I4v).

61. Heywood, *Brazen Age*, C1v. The intricacies of the latter scene are analyzed in Alan C. Dessen, *Elizabethan Stage Conventions and Modern Interpreters*, 3–5. Archery, which is obviously unusually difficult and dangerous to perform onstage, reappears in *1 Iron Age* when Paris shoots Achilles through the heel (I4r).

62. Whitney, *Early Responses*, 176. See John D. Cox, *The Devil and the Sacred in English Drama, 1350–1642*, 9–11.

63. Gayton, *Pleasant Notes*, B2r. We cannot tell with certainty if the butcher's actions came in response to Heywood's play at the Red Bull. We do know, however, that audiences sometimes reacted physically to productions at that playhouse and that the Red Bull's proximity to the cattle route along St. John's Street to Smithfield meant that it was convenient for butchers. See Reynolds, *Staging of Elizabethan Plays*, 10.

64. Gurr, *Shakespeare's Opposites*, 173.

65. Lily B. Campbell, *Scenes and Machines on the English Stage during the Renaissance: A Classical Review*, 126–30.

66. Aside from the Trojan Horse, many of the properties used in the *Ages* are

listed in an inventory compiled by Henslowe. They belonged at one time to the Admiral's Men, possibly for use in an earlier play recounting the Hercules story. It might have passed to the Queen's Men when their earlier incarnation (the Earl of Worcester's Servants) was playing at the Rose or the Curtain. Henslowe, *Diary*, 319–20; Lena Cowen Orlin, "Things with Little Social Life: Henslowe's Properties," 100.

67. Heywood, *Silver Age*, K2r; *Brazen Age*, A2r.

68. *1 Iron Age*, G4r. Reynolds documents all the uses of fireworks in the five *Ages*, eighteen in all (*Staging of Elizabethan Plays*, 171–72).

69. Alan C. Dessen and Leslie Thompson, *A Dictionary of Stage Directions of English Drama*, 39, 92–93.

70. Heywood, *Silver Age*, K1r. The infant, of course, is Dionysus.

71. Jean MacIntyre, *Costumes and Scripts in the Elizabethan Theatres*, 261. These effects seem to have been carried off without incident, because reports of any accidents or injuries that occurred onstage tend to survive in records of various kinds. Despite the use of so much fire, the Red Bull never burnt down, unlike the Globe and the Fortune.

72. Lawrence Manley, "Playing with Fire: Immolation in the Repertory of Strange's Men," 116.

73. Phillip Butterworth, *Theatre of Fire: Special Effects in Early English and Scottish Theatre*, 22–24.

74. Heywood, *Brazen Age*, H2r, I3v.

75. Heywood, *Iron Age*, A2r.

76. Heywood, *Golden Age*, A2r. On Heywood's apprehension at seeing the *Ages* come to print, and his anxieties about publication generally, see Douglas A. Brooks, *From Playhouse to Printing House: Drama and Authorship in Early Modern England*, 196–204.

5. THE CLERKENWELL RIOT AND ITS AFTERMATH

1. Christopher Beeston leased the buildings from John Best on 9 August 1616 for a 31-year period, beginning on 29 September. Queen Anne's Men debuted at the new house a few months later, perhaps after the Christmas 1616 court season. Bentley, *Jacobean and Caroline Stage*, 1:160–61.

2. Ibid., 1:161–62.

3. Ibid., 5:54. It is doubtful that any of the rioters were ever executed.

4. Ibid., 1:163.

5. Hardy, *Middlesex Session Records*, 220.

6. On the Catholics in this street, see Foley, *Records of the English Province of the Society of Jesus*, 1:205.

7. Bentley, *Jacobean and Caroline Stage*, 2:363–66. For a reevaluation of Beeston's

career as an actor and impresario, see Eva Griffith, "Christopher Beeston: His Property and Properties," 607–22.

8. Peter Burke, *Popular Culture in Early Modern Europe*, 37–41.

9. Roger B. Manning, *Village Revolts: Social Protest and Popular Disturbances in England, 1509–1640*, 192–95.

10. Stow, *Survey of London*, 75.

11. Harbage, *Shakespeare's Audience*, 107.

12. Ellesmere MS 6221, Henry E. Huntington Library, San Marino, California.

13. Edward Coke, *The Third Part of the Institutes of the Laws of England*, 176.

14. Huntington MS 17298, fol. 132, Henry E. Huntington Library, San Marino, California.

15. John Walter and Keith Wrightson, "Dearth and Social Order in Early Modern England," 112.

16. Manning, *Village Revolts*, 202–3.

17. This riot was not unique in having a strategic aim. Residents of Southwark, many of them apprentices, rioted in protest against price-fixing at the local market that resulted in a sharp reduction in the average price for foodstuffs. John Stevenson speculates that many riots of this kind probably occurred between 1585 and 1640. Stevenson, "The 'Moral Economy' of the English Crowd: Myth and Reality," 232.

18. E. P. Thompson, "The Moral Economy of the Crowd in the Eighteenth Century," 78. The notion of a moral economy is clearly related to social capital. The visibility of such an economy and the extreme lengths that individuals and groups went to defend it could hardly materialize in communities where a high degree of networking and interaction was not present.

19. Emily Cockayne, *Hubbub: Filth, Noise, and Stench in Early Modern England*, 161; see Paul Griffiths, *Lost Londons: Change, Crime, and Control in the Capital City, 1550–1660*, 99.

20. Keith Sturgess, *Jacobean Private Theater*, 15.

21. Cook, *Privileged Playgoers*, 218–20, 277–79.

22. O. Jocelyn Dunlop and Richard Denman, *English Apprenticeship and Child Labour: A History*, 61; Charles Wilson, *England's Apprenticeship, 1603–1763*, 17.

23. Jessica Browner, "Wrong Side of the River: London's Disreputable South Bank in the Sixteenth and Seventeenth Century," 43–44. See chapter 1 in this book.

24. Stow, *Survey of London*, 404.

25. Ibid., 407–8.

26. Butler, *Theatre and Crisis*, 113.

27. Taylor, *Taylor's Travels*, B1v.

28. Sturgess, *Jacobean Private Theater*, 16.

29. Francis Beaumont, *The Knight of the Burning Pestle*, 270.

30. Janette Dillon, *Theater, Court, and City: 1595–1610*, 43.

31. Quoted in C. J. Sisson, "The Red Bull Company and the Importunate Widow," 62.

32. Hardy, *Middlesex County Records*, 235.

33. Quoted in Bentley, *Jacobean and Caroline Stage*, 2:368.

34. Sturgess, *Jacobean Private Theater*, 28–29.

35. Thorstein Veblen, *The Theory of the Leisure Class*, chapter 4.

36. Harbage, *Shakespeare's Audience*, 22–23.

37. Chambers, *Elizabethan Stage*, 1:369. This figure also aligns with the court's practice of paying £10 for court performances to compensate for the loss of that day's profits. The court, out of generosity and gratitude, probably slightly overestimated a company's daily revenue.

38. My tentative calculations of the daily *maximums* at the Red Bull and the Cockpit accord with Smith's determination of the King's Men's 1610 daily *average* incomes at the Globe (£8 10s) and the Blackfriars (£15 15s). Irwin Smith, *Shakespeare's Blackfriars Playhouse*, 69. James Wright's *Historia Histrionica: An Historical Account of the English Stage*, a retrospective look from 1699 at the London theatres several generations earlier, indicates that "[t]he Blackfriars, cockpit, and Salisbury Court . . . were all three built almost exactly alike, for form and bigness" (7), suggesting that we can accurately extrapolate the economics from one to the other.

39. In the immediate aftermath of the riot, when one or both of its London houses were too damaged to play in, the troupe was forced to take the show on the road, an endeavor with which it had little experience and even less success. Although the company had toured sporadically during the summer throughout its history, activity in the provinces increased substantially from 1616 to 1618. In 1616 documents collected in the Records of Early English Drama (REED) volumes indicate that the troupe appeared in Norwich in March and again in May and throughout Sussex and Lancashire in October and November; the following year it again played in Norwich and Coventry in the summer and autumn. Gurr, *Shakespearian Playing Companies*, 331–34.

40. Jean E. Howard, *Theatre of a City: The Places of London Comedy, 1598–1642*, 70; Archer, *Pursuit of Stability*, 111–20.

41. William Rowley, *The Search for Money*, B1r.

42. Richard Barnfield, *Lady Pecunia, or, The Praise of Money*, B1r.

43. Ben Jonson, et al., *Eastward Ho!* 5.5.122–29.

44. Craig Muldrew, *The Economy of Obligation: The Culture of Credit and Social Relations in Early Modern England*, 278–81.

45. Although the original performance date is disputed, most commentators propose a date between 1621 and 1625. Alfred Harbage, *Annals of Early English Drama: 975–1700*, 112–13. During this period the company that had been Queen

Anne's Men was in transition. Queen Anne had died in 1619, and the troupe split into two allied companies, both under Beeston's management. Beeston now controlled Prince Charles's Men, allocated to the Cockpit, as well as the Revels company (also known as the Red Bull company), who stayed on in Clerkenwell. The two companies overlapped significantly. Perkins, Worth, and Cumber stayed behind at the Red Bull while the remaining sharers continued with Prince Charles's Men and later Queen Henrietta's Men at the Cockpit in 1625. After a very brief stint with the King's Men, Perkins appears on the lists of Queen Henrietta's company in 1625, along with other erstwhile members of Queen Anne's Men. Gurr, *Shakespearian Playing Companies*, 326–27.

46. Middleton, *Michaelmas Term*, 1.1.136.

47. Philip Massinger, *A New Way to Pay Old Debts*, 3.1.83, 2.3.55–56, 2.1.32–33.

48. Theodore B. Leinwand, *Theatre, Finance, and Society in Early Modern England*, 79–82.

49. John Blaxton, *The English Usurer*, H1v.

50. Leinwand, *Theatre, Finance, and Society*, 88.

51. Holland received one-seventh of the total receipts. This is significantly less than the share taken by other theatre owners. Henslowe received one-half of the takings of the galleries in his theatres, a much larger sum than Holland's seventh. In addition, Holland was responsible for normal "housekeeping" duties, including maintenance, ground rent, and taxes.

52. Charles W. Wallace, "Three London Theaters of Shakespeare's Time," 294.

53. All evidence suggests that Woodford was a man of ill repute. In addition to his questionable ethics during his career as a moneylender, he was cited by the Admiralty for piracy and by the Middlesex justices for passing counterfeit coin. William Ingram, "The Playhouse as an Investment, 1607–1614: Thomas Woodford and Whitefriars," 213, 228.

54. *Woodford vs. Holland*, Court of Requests, 10 James I.

55. It is not difficult to imagine that Holland would miscalculate the building's potential to turn a profit. He apparently was easily duped. Reynolds suggests that because Holland was "utterly unlearned and illiterate" he was easily and routinely taken advantage of in business transactions. Reynolds, *Staging of Elizabethan Plays*, 6.

56. *The Records of Early English Drama, Norwich*, ed. Sally-Beth MacLean, 145.

57. Gurr, *Shakespearian Playing Companies*, 324; Berry, "Building Playhouses," 69.

58. Honigmann and Brock, *Playhouse Wills*, 91.

59. Bentley, *Jacobean and Caroline Stage*, 1:158–60.

60. Sisson, "Red Bull Company," 61.

61. C/24/500, National Archives (formerly Public Record Office), Kew, UK.

62. Chambers, *Elizabethan Stage*, 2:238.

63. Gurr, *Shakespearian Playing Companies*, 324–25.

64. Pinks, *History of Clerkenwell*, 213.

65. Thomas Heywood, preface to Cooke, *Greene's Tu Quoque*, A2r.

66. Sisson, "Red Bull Company," 68.

67. The cost of converting the Red Bull to a full-time theatre is not known. Martin Slater claimed that it cost £500, but Holland's original instrument of incorporation would have raised only £450. Berry, "Building Playhouses," 67.

68. Chambers, *Elizabethan Stage*, 1:372. Queen Anne's Men's apparel and properties were probably near the upper end of this figure due to the sophisticated stagecraft that characterized performances at the Red Bull.

EPILOGUE

1. Bentley, *Jacobean and Caroline Stage*, 2:690.

2. Rick Bowers, "Players, Puritans, and 'Theatrical' Propaganda, 1642–1660," 463. Bowers himself recognizes that this interpretation of the theatre closure is reductive. Other scholars also have offered a more nuanced account of the 1642 ban. See, for instance, David Scott Kastan, *Shakespeare after Theory*, 201–20.

3. *The Actor's Remonstrance or Complaint for the Silencing of Their Profession and Banishment from Their Several Playhouses*, A2r–v.

4. Wright, *Historia Histrionica*, 8. Wright uses the old calendar. The event he is speaking of took place in 1649.

5. Francis Kirkman, *The Wits, or, Sport upon Sport*, A2v.

6. Quoted in Bentley, *Jacobean and Caroline Stage*, 6:326.

7. Even the fine of five shillings was relatively light compared to the £40 fine levied against Charles Cutts, a Westminster barber who attended a clandestine performance at one of the private houses. Bowers, "Players, Puritans, and 'Theatrical' Propaganda," 475.

8. Leslie Hotson, *The Commonwealth and Restoration Stage*, 51. Hotson's quip that the players might not have been safe from each other probably refers to the abundant swordplay and other dangerous action at the Red Bull.

9. Bentley, *Jacobean and Caroline Stage*, 2:571.

10. Kirkman, *Wits*, A2v; Bowers, "Players, Puritans, and 'Theatrical' Propaganda," 475.

11. William Van Lennep, "The Death of the Red Bull," 131. Old Marlovian favorites like *Tamburlaine* and the *Jew of Malta* were also performed at the Red Bull during the 1550s. See Hotson, *Commonwealth and Restoration Stage*, 45.

BIBLIOGRAPHY

PRIMARY MATERIALS

The Actor's Remonstrance or Complaint for the Silencing of Their Profession and Banishment from Their Several Playhouses. London: Edward Nickson, 1643.

Adams, Joseph Quincy. *Shakespearean Playhouses*. Cambridge, Mass.: Riverside, 1917.

Adams, Thomas. *The Happiness of the Church*. London: John Grismand, 1619.

———. *Mystical Bedlam, or, The World of Mad-Men*. London: George Purslowe, 1615.

Ainsworth, Henry. *Counterpoyson*. Amsterdam: G. Thorp, 1608.

Anderson, Anthony. *An Approved Medicine against the Deserved Plague*. London: Thomas Est, 1593.

Andrews, John. *The Brazen Serpent*. London: Thomas Thorpe, 1621.

Bacon, Francis. *The Advancement of Learning*. London: Henry Tomes, 1605.

Bailey, William. *A Rumor of Wars among the Times and Signs of Peace*. London: Blount, 1608.

Barlowe, William. *The Sermon Preached at Paul's Cross the Tenth Day of November*. London: Matthew Law, 1606.

Barnfield, Richard. *Lady Pecunia, or, The Praise of Money*. London: John Hodges, 1605.

Beaumont, Francis. *The Knight of the Burning Pestle*. Ed. Andrew Gurr. Berkeley: U of California P, 1968.

Bilson, Thomas. *The Survey of Christ's Sufferings for Man's Redemption and His Descent into Hades or Hell*. London: John Bill, 1604.

Blackie, John Stuart. *Messis Vitae*. London: Macmillan, 1886.

Blaxton, John. *The English Usurer*. London: John Norton, 1634.

Cicero, Marcus Tullius. *The First Book of Tully's Offices*. Trans. John Brinsley. London: H. Lownes, 1616.

Civil and Uncivil Life. London: R[ichard] Jones, 1579.

Coke, Edward. *The Third Part of the Institutes of the Laws of England*. London: M. Flesher, 1648.

Cooke, John. *Greene's Tu Quoque*. London: John Trundle, 1614.

———. *The Two Merry Milkmaids*. London: Bernard Alsop, 1620.

Cornwallis, William. *Essays*. London: John Brown, 1610.

Day, Richard. *A Book of Christian Prayers*. London: Richard Day, 1578.
Dekker, Thomas. *Dramatic Works*. Ed. Fredson Bowers. 4 vols. Cambridge: Cambridge UP, 1964.
———. *The Gull's Hornbook*. London: R. S., 1609.
———. *If This Be Not a Good Play, the Devil Is in It*. London: John Trundle, 1612.
———. *Lanthorne and Candlelight*. London: M. Parsons, 1638.
———. *The Pleasant Comedy of Old Fortunatus*. London: William Aspley, 1600.
———. *The Seven Deadly Sins of London*. London: Nathaniel Butter, 1606.
———. *Troia-Nova Triumphans: London Triumphing*. London: Nicholas Oakes, 1612.
———. *The Wonderful Year, Wherein Is Showed the Picture of London, Sick of the Plague*. London: Thomas Creed, 1603.
Foxe, John. *Actes and Monuments of These Latter and Perilous Days*. London: John Day, 1570.
Fulke, William. *Two Treatises Written against the Papists*. London: Thomas Vautrollier, 1577.
Gayton, Edmund. *Pleasant Notes upon Don Quixote*. London: William Hunt, 1654.
Gee, John. *New Shreds of the Old Snare*. London: Robert Mylbourne, 1624.
Goffe, Thomas. *The Careless Shepherdess*. London: Richard Rogers and William Ley, 1656.
Gosson, Stephen. *Plays Confuted in Five Actions*. London: Thomas Gosson, 1582.
Guazzo, Stefano. *The Civil Conversation*. London: Richard Watkins, 1581.
Hall, Joseph. *Contemplations on Principal Passages of the Holy Story*. London: H. L[ownes], 1614.
Hardy, William, ed. *Middlesex Session Records*. London: Guildhall, 1935.
Hastler, Thomas. *An Antidote against the Plague, or, A Salve for All Sores*. London: M. Flesher, 1625.
Heath, John. *Two Centuries of Epigrams*. London: John Windet, 1610.
Henslowe, Philip. *Diary*. Ed. R. A. Foakes and R. T. Rickert. Cambridge: Cambridge UP, 1961.
Herring, Francis. *Mischief's Mystery*. London: E. Griffin, 1617.
Heywood, Thomas. *An Apology for Actors*. London: Nicholas Oakes, 1612.
———. *The Brazen Age*. London: Nicholas Oakes, 1613.
———. *The Four Prentices of London*. London: I. W[right], 1615.
———. *The Golden Age*. London: William Barrenger, 1611.
———. *If You Know Not Me, You Know Nobody*. London: Nathaniel Butter, 1639.
———. *The Iron Age*. London: Nicholas Oakes, 1632.
———. *The Second Part of the Iron Age*. London: Nicholas Oakes, 1632.
———. *The Silver Age*. London, Nicholas Oakes, 1611.

Holbrooke, William. *A Sermon Preached at St. Botolph's near Aldersgate, the 26 of February 1609*. London: Elizabeth Burby, 1609.

Honigmann, E. A. J., and Susan Brock. *Playhouse Wills: 1558–1642*. Manchester: Manchester UP, 1993.

Honorable Company of Parish Clerks. *The True Copy of All the Burials*. London: John Windet, 1602–1609.

Jeaffreson, John Cordy. *The Middlesex County Records*. 3 vols. Clerkenwell: Middlesex County Records Society, 1886.

Jonson, Ben. *Four Comedies*. Ed. Helen Ostovich. London: Longman, 1997.

———, George Chapman, and John Marston. *Eastward Ho!* Ed. Michael Neill. New York: Norton, 1995.

Jordan, Thomas. *A Nursery of Novelties in Variety of Poetry*. London: n.p., [1665?].

Kempe, Will. *Kemp's Nine Daies Wonder*. London: Nicholas Ling, 1600.

Kirkman, Francis. *The Wits, or, Sport upon Sport*. London: n.p., 1673.

Lachrymae Londinenses, or, London's Tears and Lamentations. London: H. Holland, 1626.

Larkin, James F., and Paul Hughes, eds. *Stuart Royal Proclamations*. 2 vols. Oxford: Clarendon, 1973.

Lodge, Thomas. *A Treatise of the Plague*. London: Edward White, 1603.

Lupton, Donald. *London and the Country Carbonadoed*. London: Nicholas Oakes, 1632.

Manley, Lawrence, ed. *London in the Age of Shakespeare: An Anthology*. University Park: Penn State UP, 1986.

Marlowe, Christopher. *Doctor Faustus and Other Plays*. Ed. David Bevington et al. Oxford: Oxford UP, 1995.

Massinger, Philip. *A New Way to Pay Old Debts* (1633). Ed. T. W. Craik. New York: Norton, 1993.

Middleton, Thomas. *The Complete Works of Thomas Middleton*. Ed. Gary Taylor and John Lavagnino. Oxford: Oxford UP, 2008.

Montaigne, Michel de. *The Essays or Moral, Political, and Military Discourses of Lord Michel de Montaigne*. Trans. John Florio. London: Edward Blount, 1603.

Mulcaster, Richard. *The Queen's Majesty's Progress through the City of London*. London: n.p., 1558.

M[unday], A[nthony]. *Himatia Paleos: The Triumph of Drapery, or the Rich Clothing of England*. London: Edward Alde, 1614.

Nashe, Thomas. *The Unfortunate Traveler and Other Works*. Ed. J. B. Steane. Harmondsworth: Penguin, 1972.

Nobody and Somebody. London: John Trundle, 1606.

Norden, John. *Speculum Britannie*. London: n.p., 1593.

Ovid. *Metamorphoses*. Trans. Arthur Golding. London: William Seres, 1567.

Peacham, Henry. *The Compleat Gentleman*. London: Francis Constable, 1622.
Petowe, Henry. *Londoners: Their Entertainment in the Country*. London: Cuthbert Burby, 1604.
Plutarch. *The Lives of the Noble Grecians and Romans*. Trans. Thomas North. London: Richard Field, 1612.
Pullein, Thomas. *Jeremiah's Tears, or, A Sermon Preached in York-Minster upon Trinity Sunday, in the Year of Our Lord 1604*. London: William Jaggard, 1608.
Puttenham, George. *The Art of English Poesy*. London: Richard Field, 1589.
The Rat-Trap, or, The Jesuits Taken in Their Own Net. London: John Oakes, 1641.
The Records of Early English Drama. Ed. Sally-Beth MacLean et al. Toronto: U of Toronto P, 1976–.
Robinson, John. *A Justification of Separation from the Church of England*. London, 1610.
Rogers, John. *A Discourse of Christian Watchfulness*. London: William Jones, 1620.
Rowland, Samuel. *A Whole Crew of Kind Gossips, All Met to Be Merry*. London: John Dean, 1609.
Rowley, William. *The Search for Money*. London: Joseph Hunt, 1609.
Rutter, Carol, ed. *Documents of the Rose Playhouse*. 2nd ed. Manchester: Manchester UP, 2000.
Sanderson, Robert. *Ten Sermons Preached*. London: R. Dawlman, 1627.
Shakespeare, William. *The Norton Shakespeare*. Ed. Stephen Greenblatt et al. New York: Norton, 1996.
Sidney, Sir. Phillip. *The Defence of Poetry* (1587). Ed. J. A. Van Dorsten. Oxford: Oxford UP, 1966.
Smith, Wentworth. *The Hector of Germany*. London: Thomas Creed, 1615.
The Stage-Player's Complaint. London: Thomas Bates, 1641.
Stow, John. *A Survey of London . . . Enlarged by the Care and Diligence of A. M[unday] in the Year 1618, and Now Completely Finished by the Study and Labour of A. M[unday], H[umphrey] D[yson], and Others, This Present Year 1633*. London: Elizabeth Purslowe for Nicholas Bourne, 1633.
T. C. *A Godly and Learned Sermon upon the 91st Palm*. London: Edward White, 1603.
Taylor, John. *All the Works of John Taylor the Water Poet*. London: James Boler, 1630.
———. *Taylor's Travels and Circular Perambulation . . . with an Alphabetical Description of All the Tavern Signs in the City, Suburbs, and Liberties*. London: [A]ugustine [M]atthews, 1636.
Thompson, Thomas. *A Diet for a Drunkard*. London: Richard Bankworth, 1612.
Tomkis, Thomas. *Albumazar*. London: Nicholas Oakes, 1615.

Turner, William. *Turner's Dish of Lenten Stuff, or, A Galymaufery to the Tune of Watton Towns End*. London: [S. Stafford?] for J. W[right?], 1612.

Webster, John. *The Devil's Law Case* (1623). Ed. Elizabeth Brennan. New York: Norton, 1975.

———. *The White Devil* (1612). Ed. Christina Luckyj. New York: Norton, 1996.

"What a Justice of the Peace May Do." Huntington Manuscript 17298, 1627. Henry E. Huntington Library, San Marino, Calif.

Wilkinson, Robert. *The Merchant Royal: A Sermon Preached at Whitehall before the King's Majesty*. London: Edward Blount, 1615.

Wither, George. *Abuses Script and Whipt*. London: Francis Burton, 1613.

Wright, James. "Excerpta Quaedam." British Library Additional MSS 22608. British Library, London, UK.

———. *Historia Histrionica: An Historical Account of the English Stage*. London: William Hawes, 1699.

SECONDARY MATERIALS

Archer, Ian. "Government in Early Modern London: The Challenge of the Suburbs." *Proceedings of the British Academy* 107 (2001): 133–47.

———. "Material Londoners?" In *Material London, ca. 1600*, ed. Lena Cowen Orlin, 174–92. Philadelphia: U of Pennsylvania P, 2001.

———. *The Pursuit of Stability*. Cambridge: Cambridge UP, 1991.

Astington, John. "Playing the Man: Acting at the Red Bull and the Fortune." *Early Theatre* 9 (2006): 130–43.

Barish, Jonas. *The Antitheatrical Prejudice*. Berkeley: U of California P, 1981.

Barroll, Leeds. *Politics, Plague, and Shakespeare's Theater: The Stuart Years*. Ithaca: Cornell UP, 1993.

Bayer, Mark. "The Red Bull Playhouse." In *The Oxford Handbook of Early Modern Theatre*, ed. Richard Dutton, 225–39. Oxford: Oxford UP, 2009.

Beckerman, Bernard. "Philip Henslowe." In *The Theatrical Manager in England and America*, ed. Joseph Donohue, Jr., 19–62. Princeton: Princeton UP, 1971.

Beier, A. L. *Masterless Men: The Vagrancy Problem in England, 1560–1640*. London: Methuen, 1985.

———, and Roger Finlay, eds. *London 1500–1700: The Making of the Metropolis*. London: Longman, 1986.

Ben-Amos, Ilana. *Adolescence and Youth in Early Modern England*. New Haven: Yale UP, 1994.

Bentley, G. E. *The Jacobean and Caroline Stage*. 6 vols. Oxford: Clarendon, 1941.

———. "Records of Players in the Parish of St. Giles." *PMLA (Publications of the Modern Language Association)* 44 (1929): 789–826.

Bergeron, David. *English Civic Pageantry, 1558–1642*. Revised ed. Tempe, AZ: Medieval and Renaissance Texts and Studies, 2003.

Berry, Herbert. *The Boar's Head Playhouse*. Washington, D.C.: Folger Books, 1986.

———. "Building Playhouses, the Accession of James I, and the Red Bull." *Medieval and Renaissance Drama in England* 18 (2005): 61–74.

———. *Shakespeare's Playhouses*. New York: AMS P, 1987.

Blackham, Robert. *The Soul of the City: London's Livery Companies*. London: Low and Sampson, 1931.

Blayney, Peter M. "John Day and the Bookshop That Never Was." In *Material London, ca. 1600*, ed. Lena Cowen Orlin, 322–43. Philadelphia: U of Pennsylvania P, 2000.

Bonahue, Edward T. "Citizen History: Stow's *Survey of London*." *Studies in English Literature 1500–1900* 38 (1998): 61–85.

Boulton, Jeremy. *Neighborhood and Society*. Cambridge: Cambridge UP, 1987.

Bourdieu, Pierre. "The Forms of Capital." In *Handbook of Theory and Research for the Sociology of Education*, ed. John Richardson, 241–60. New York: Greenwood, 1986.

———. *An Outline of a Theory of Practice*. Trans. Richard Nice. Cambridge: Cambridge UP, 1977.

Bowers, Rick. "Players, Puritans, and 'Theatrical' Propaganda, 1642–1660." *Dalhousie Review* 67 (1988): 463–79.

Bowsher, Julian, and Pat Miller. *The Rose and the Globe: Excavations 1988–91*. London: Museum of London Archeology, 2009.

Brett-James, Norman. *The Growth of Stuart London*. London: Unwin, 1935.

Brigden, Susan. *London and the Reformation*. Oxford: Clarendon, 1989.

Bristol, Michael D. *Carnival and Theater*. London: Methuen, 1985.

———. "Shamelessness in Arden: Early Modern Theater and the Obsolescence of Popular Theatricality." In *Print, Manuscript, and Performance*, ed. Arthur F. Marotti and Michael D. Bristol, 279–306. Columbus: Ohio State UP, 2000.

Brook, Donald. *The Romance of the English Theatre*. London: Rockliff, 1945.

Brooks, Douglas A. *From Playhouse to Printing House: Drama and Authorship in Early Modern England*. Cambridge: Cambridge UP, 2000.

Brown, John Russell. *Shakespeare and the Theatrical Event*. London: Palgrave, 2002.

Browner, Jessica. "Wrong Side of the River: London's Disreputable South Bank in the Sixteenth and Seventeenth Century." *Essays in History* 36 (1994): 34–72.

Bruster, Douglas. *Drama and the Market in the Age of Shakespeare*. Cambridge: Cambridge UP, 1992.

Burke, Peter. *Popular Culture in Early Modern Europe*. Aldershot: Ashgate, 1994.
Burnett, Mark Thornton. "Apprentice Literature and the 'Crisis' of the 1590s." In *Patronage, Politics, and Literary Traditions in England, 1558–1658*, ed. Cedric Brown, 47–78. Detroit: Wayne State UP, 1993.
Butler, Martin. *Theatre and Crisis, 1632–1642*. Cambridge: Cambridge UP, 1984.
Butterworth, Phillip. *Theatre of Fire: Special Effects in Early English and Scottish Theatre*. London: Society for Theatre Research, 1998.
Calhoun, Craig. "Habitus, Field, and Capital: The Question of Historical Specificity." In *Bourdieu: Critical Perspectives*, ed. Craig Calhoun, Edward LiPuma, and Moishe Postone, 61–88. Cambridge: Polity, 1993.
Campbell, Lily B. *Scenes and Machines on the English Stage during the Renaissance: A Classical Review*. Cambridge: Cambridge UP, 1923.
Carroll, William E. *Fat King, Lean Beggar: Representations of Poverty in the Age of Shakespeare*. Ithaca: Cornell UP, 1995.
Carson, Neil. *A Companion to Henlowe's Diary*. Cambridge: Cambridge UP, 1988.
Cerasano, S. P. "Cheerful Givers: Henslowe, Alleyn, and the 1612 Loan Book to the Crown." *Shakespeare Studies* 28 (2000): 215–19.
———. "Edward Alleyn's 'Retirement' 1597–1600." *Medieval and Renaissance Drama in England* 10 (1998): 99–109.
———. "The Geography of Henslowe's Diary." *Shakespeare Quarterly* 56 (2005): 328–53.
———. "'More Elbow Roome, But Scant Better Aire': The Fortune Playhouse and Its Surroundings." *Indiana Social Studies Quarterly* 35 (1982): 70–84.
———. "Must the Devil Appear?: Audiences, Actors, Stage Business." In *A Companion to Renaissance Drama*, ed. Arthur Kinney, 193–211. Oxford: Blackwell, 2002.
———. "The Patronage Network of Philip Henslowe and Edward Alleyn." *Medieval and Renaissance Drama in England* 13 (2000): 82–92.
———. *Relocating the Fortune Playhouse: A New History*. London: Globe Occasional Papers, 2007.
———. "Revising Philip Henslowe's Biography." *Notes and Queries* 32 (1985): 66–73.
Chambers, E. K. *The Elizabethan Stage*. 4 vols. Oxford: Clarendon, 1923.
Clark, Ira. *Comedy, Youth, and Manhood in Early Modern England*. Newark: U of Delaware P, 2003.
Clark, Peter. *The English Alehouse: A Social History, 1200–1830*. London: Longman, 1983.
———. *English Provincial Society*. Sussex: Harvester, 1977.
Clark, Sandra. *Women and Crime in the Street in Early Modern Literature*. London: Palgrave, 2004.

Cockayne, Emily. *Hubbub: Filth, Noise, and Stench in Early Modern England*. New Haven: Yale UP, 2007.

Collier, J. P., ed. *The Diary of Phillip Henslowe from 1591 to 1609*. London: New Shakespeare Society, 1845.

———. *Memoirs of Edward Alleyn*. London: New Shakespeare Society, 1841.

Collingwood, R. G. *The Idea of History*. New York: Oxford UP, 1956.

Collinson, Patrick. *The Elizabethan Puritan Movement*. London: Jonathan Cape, 1967.

Cook, Ann Jennalie. *The Privileged Playgoers of Shakespeare's London*. Princeton: Princeton UP, 1991.

Cox, John D. *The Devil and the Sacred in English Drama, 1350–1642*. Cambridge: Cambridge UP, 2000.

Creighton, Charles. *A History of Epidemics in Britain*. 2nd ed. 2 vols. London: Frank Cassa, 1965.

Cressy, David. *Bonfires and Bells*. London: Weidenfield and Nicholson, 1989.

Cumberlege, Geoffrey. *The Corporation of London: Its Origin, Constitutional Power, and Duties*. Oxford: Oxford UP, 1950.

Davis, Tracy, and Thomas Postlewait, eds. *Theatricality*. Cambridge: Cambridge UP, 2003.

Dawson, Anthony, and Paul Yachnin. *The Culture of Playgoing in Shakespeare's England: A Collaborative Debate*. Cambridge: Cambridge UP, 2001.

Dessen, Alan C. *Elizabethan Stage Conventions and Modern Interpreters*. Cambridge: Cambridge UP, 1984.

Dessen, Alan C., and Leslie Thompson. *A Dictionary of Stage Directions of English Drama*. Cambridge: Cambridge UP, 1999.

Dillon, Janette. *Theater, Court, and City: 1595–1610*. Cambridge: Cambridge UP, 2000.

Dunlop, O. Jocelyn, and Richard Denman. *English Apprenticeship and Child Labour: A History*. London: Unwin, 1912.

Dutton, Richard. *Mastering the Revels: The Regulation and Censorship of English Renaissance Drama*. Iowa City: U of Iowa P, 1991.

Eccles, Christina. *The Rose Theatre*. New York: Routledge, 1990.

Evenden, Elizabeth. "Day, Richard (*b*. 1552, *d*. in or before 1606)." In *Oxford Dictionary of National Biography*, ed. H. C. G. Matthew and Brian Harrison, vol. 15, 584–86. Oxford: Oxford UP, 2004.

Farmer, Alan, and Zachary Lesser. "'Vile Arts': The Marketing of English Printed Drama, 1512–1660." *Research Opportunities in Renaissance Drama* 39 (2000): 77–165.

Finlay, Roger. *Population and Metropolis: The Demography of London*. Cambridge: Cambridge UP, 1981.

———, and Beatrice Shearer. "Population Growth and Suburban Expansion." In *The Making of the Metropolis: London 1500–1700*, ed. A. L. Beier and Roger Finlay, 37–59. London: Longman, 1986.

Fischlin, Daniel. "Theatre, Theory, and the Shaping Fantasies of Early Modern Criticism: A Review Essay." *Essays in Theatre* 15 (1997): 239–46.

Fleay, Frederick G. *A Biographical Chronicle of the English Drama, 1559–1642*. 2 vols. London: Reeves and Turner, 1891.

Foley, Henry. *Records of the English Province of the Society of Jesus*. 7 vols. in 8. London: Burns and Oates, 1877.

Foster, Frank F. *The Politics of Stability*. London: Royal Historical Society, 1977.

Fumerton, Patricia. "Not Home: Alehouses, Ballads, and the Vagrant Husband in Early Modern England." *Journal of Early Modern Cultural Studies* 32 (2002): 493–518.

Gasper, Julia. *The Dragon and the Dove: The Plays of Thomas Dekker*. Oxford: Oxford UP, 1992.

Griffith, Eva. "Christopher Beeston: His Property and Properties." In *The Oxford Handbook of Early Modern Theatre*, ed. Richard Dutton, 607–22. Oxford: Oxford UP, 2009.

———. "New Material for a Jacobean Playhouse." *Theater Notebook* 55 (2001): 5–23.

Griffiths, Paul. *Lost Londons: Change, Crime, and Control in the Capital City, 1550–1660*. Cambridge: Cambridge UP, 2008.

Gurr, Andrew. "The Authority of the Globe and the Fortune." In *Material London ca. 1600*, ed. Lena Cowen Orlin, 251–67. Philadelphia: U of Pennsylvania P, 2000.

———. "The General and the Caviar: Learned Audiences in the Early Theatre." *Studies in the Literary Imagination* 26 (1993): 7–20.

———. *Playgoing in Shakespeare's London*. Cambridge: Cambridge UP, 1987.

———. *The Shakespeare Company, 1594–1642*. Cambridge: Cambridge UP, 2004.

———. *The Shakespearean Stage, 1574–1642*. 3rd ed. Cambridge: Cambridge UP, 1992.

———. *Shakespeare's Opposites*. Cambridge: Cambridge UP, 2009.

———. *The Shakespearian Playing Companies*. Oxford: Oxford UP, 1996.

Hamilton, Donna B. *Shakespeare and the Politics of Protestant England*. Louisville: UP of Kentucky, 1992.

Hanning, Robert. *The Vision of History in Early Britain: From Gildas to Geoffrey of Monmouth*. New York: Columbia UP, 1966.

Harbage, Alfred. *Annals of Early English Drama: 975–1700*. London: Methuen, 1964.

———. *Shakespeare's Audience*. New York: Columbia UP, 1941.

Heath, John Benjamin. *Some Account of the Worshipful Company of Grocers.* London: C. Whittingham, 1864.

Heinnemann, Margot. *Puritanism and Theatre: Thomas Middleton and Opposition Drama under the Early Stuarts*. Cambridge: Cambridge UP, 1980.

Helgerson, Richard. *Forms of Nationhood: The Elizabethan Writing of England.* Chicago: U of Chicago P, 1992.

Hotson, Leslie. *The Commonwealth and Restoration Stage*. New York: Russell and Russell, 1962.

Howard, Jean E. *The Stage and Social Struggle in Early Modern England*. New York: Routledge, 1994.

———. *Theatre of a City: The Places of London Comedy, 1598–1642*. Philadelphia: U of Pennsylvania P, 2007.

Howitt, William. *The Northern Heights of London*. London: Longman and Green, 1869.

Hoy, Cyrus. *Introductions, Notes, and Commentaries to Texts in the Dramatic Works of Thomas Dekker*. 4 vols. Cambridge: Cambridge UP, 1978.

Ingram, William. "The Globe Playhouse and Its Neighbors in 1600." *Theatre Notebook* 2 (1984): 63–72.

———. *A London Life in the Brazen Age: Francis Langley, 1548–1602*. Cambridge, Mass.: Harvard UP, 1978.

———. "'Neere the Playe Howse': The Swan Theatre and Community Blight." *Renaissance Drama* 4 (1971): 53–68.

———. "The Playhouse as an Investment, 1607–1614: Thomas Woodford and Whitefriars." *Medieval and Renaissance Drama in England* 2 (1985): 209–30.

———. "Playhouses Make Strange Bedfellows: The Case of Aaron and Martin." *Shakespeare Studies* 30 (2002): 118–27.

Innes, Joanna. "Prisons for the Poor: English Bridewells, 1555–1800." In *Labour, Law, and Crime: An Historical Perspective*, ed. Francis Snyder and Douglas Hay, 42–122. London: Tavistock, 1987.

James, Heather. *Shakespeare's Troy: Drama, Politics, and the Translation of Empire*. Cambridge: Cambridge UP, 1997.

Johnson, David. *Southwark and the City*. Oxford: Oxford UP, 1969.

Jordan, W. K. *Philanthropy in England, 1480–1660*. London: Allen and Unwin, 1959.

Kahn, Copelia. *Roman Shakespeare: Warriors, Wounds, and Women*. New York: Routledge, 1997.

Kamps, Ivo. *Historiography and Ideology in Stuart Drama*. Cambridge: Cambridge UP, 1996.

Kastan, David Scott. *Shakespeare after Theory*. London: Routledge, 1999.

Kathman, David. "Grocers, Goldsmiths, and Drapers: Freemen and Apprentices in the Elizabethan Theatre." *Shakespeare Quarterly* 55 (2004): 1–49.

Kernan, Alvin. *Shakespeare, the King's Playwright*. New Haven: Yale UP, 1995.

King, John N. *English Reformation Literature*. Princeton: Princeton UP, 1985.

———. *Tudor Royal Iconography*. Princeton: Princeton UP, 1990.

Knapp, Jeffrey. *Shakespeare's Tribe: Church, Nation, and Theatre in Renaissance England*. Chicago: U of Chicago P, 2002.

Knutson, Roslyn. *Playing Companies and Commerce in Shakespeare's Time*. Cambridge: Cambridge UP, 2001.

———. *The Repertory of Shakespeare's Company*. Little Rock: U of Arkansas P, 1991.

Kranz, Susan. "Thomas Dekker's Political Commentary in *The Whore of Babylon*." *Studies in English Literature 1500–1900* 35 (1995): 271–91.

Lancashire, Anne. "Multi-day Performance and the London Clerkenwell Play." *Early Theatre* 9 (2006): 114–29.

Landrow, Vincent. "Henslowe's Relocation to the North: Playhouse Management in Renaissance London." *Theatre Survey* 38 (1997): 31–47.

Leinwand, Theodore B. "Spongy Plebs, Mighty Lords, and the Dynamics of the Alehouse." *Journal of Medieval and Renaissance Studies* 19 (1989): 159–84.

———. *Theater, Finance, and Society in Early Modern England*. Cambridge: Cambridge UP, 1999.

Lewalski, Barbara K. Paradise Lost *and the Rhetoric of Literary Forms*. Princeton: Princeton UP, 1985.

Loades, David, ed. *John Foxe and the English Reformation*. Aldershot: Ashgate, 1997.

MacIntyre, Jean. *Costumes and Scripts in the Elizabethan Theatres*. Edmonton: U of Alberta P, 1992.

Manley, Lawrence. "Playing with Fire: Immolation in the Repertory of Strange's Men." *Early Theatre* 4 (2001): 115–29.

Manning, Roger B. *Village Revolts: Social Protest and Popular Disturbances in England, 1509–1640*. Oxford: Clarendon, 1988.

Maus, Katherine Eisaman. *Inwardness and Theater in the English Renaissance*. Chicago: U of Chicago P, 1995.

Mauss, Marcel. *The Gift: The Form and Reason of Exchange in Primitive Societies*. Trans. W. D. Halls. New York: Norton, 1990.

McLuskie, Kathleen. *Dekker and Heywood: Professional Dramatists*. London: Macmillan, 1994.

Mehl, Dieter. *The Elizabethan Dumb Show*. Cambridge, Mass.: Harvard UP, 1966.

Minson, Stuart. "Public Punishment and Urban Space in Early Tudor London." *London Topographical Record* 30 (2010): 1–16.

Morrison, Herbert. *How London Is Governed*. London: People's UP, 1949.
Muldrew, Craig. *The Economy of Obligation: The Culture of Credit and Social Relations in Early Modern England*. New York: St. Martin's, 1998.
Mullaney, Steven. *The Place of the Stage*. Chicago: U of Chicago P, 1988.
Nathan, Norman. "Is Shylock Philip Henslowe?" *Notes and Queries* 193.2 (1948): 163–65.
Norman, Phillip. "The Accounts of the Overseers of the Poor of Paris Garden, Southwark." *Surrey Archeological Collections* 16 (1901): 55–107.
Orgel, Stephen. *Impersonations: The Performance of Gender in Shakespeare's England*. Cambridge: Cambridge UP, 1996.
Orlin, Lena Cowen. *Locating Privacy in Tudor London*. Oxford: Oxford UP, 2007.
———. "Things with Little Social Life: Henslowe's Properties." In *Staged Properties in Early Modern English Drama*, ed. Jonathan Gil Harris and Natasha Korda, 99–128. Cambridge: Cambridge UP, 2002.
Paster, Gail Kern. *The Idea of the City in the Age of Shakespeare*. Athens: U of Georgia P, 1985.
Pearl, Valerie. "Change and Stability in Seventeenth-Century London." *London Journal* 5 (1979): 1–34.
Pettegree, Andrew. "Day, John (1521/2–1584)." In *Oxford Dictionary of National Biography*, ed. H. C. G. Matthew and Brian Harrison, vol. 15, 596. Oxford: Oxford UP, 2004.
Picard, Liza. *Everyday Life in Elizabethan London*. New York: St. Martin's, 2003.
Pinks, W. I. *The History of Clerkenwell*. London: Charles Herbert, 1881.
Putnam, Robert. *Better Together: Restoring the American Community*. New York: Simon and Schuster, 2003.
———. *Bowling Alone: The Collapse and Revival of American Community*. New York: Touchstone, 2000.
Rackin, Phyllis. *Stages of History: Shakespeare's English Chronicles*. Ithaca: Cornell UP, 1990.
Rappaport, Steve. *Worlds within Worlds: Structures of Life in Seventeenth-Century London*. Cambridge: Cambridge UP, 1984.
Raven, James. *The Business of Books: Booksellers and the English Book Trade, 1450–1850*. New Haven: Yale UP, 2007.
Reynolds, George. *The Staging of Elizabethan Plays at the Red Bull*. New York: MLA, 1940.
Robinson, Marsha S. *Writing the Reformation*: Actes and Monuments *and the Jacobean History Play*. Aldershot: Ashgate, 2002.
Rosnow, Ralph L., and Gary Alan Fine. *Rumor and Gossip: The Social Psychology of Hearsay*. New York: Elsevier, 1976.

Rutter, Tom. "Adult Playing Companies, 1603–1613." In *The Oxford Handbook of Early Modern Theatre*, ed. Richard Dutton, 72–87. Oxford: Oxford UP, 2009.
Schanzer, Ernest. "Heywood's *Ages* and Shakespeare." *Review of English Studies* 11 (1960): 18–28.
Shershow, Scott Cutler. "Work and the Gift." In *Money and the Age of Shakespeare*, ed. Linda Woodbridge, 97–112. New York: Palgrave, 2003.
Sims, James H. *Biblical Allusions in Marlowe and Shakespeare*. Gainesville: U of Florida P, 1966.
Sinfield, Alan. *Literature in Protestant England*. London: Croom Helm, 1983.
Sisson, C. J. "The Red Bull Company and the Importunate Widow." *Shakespeare Survey* 7 (1954): 57–68.
Smith, Irwin. *Shakespeare's Blackfriars Playhouse*. New York: New York UP, 1964.
———. *Shakespeare's First Playhouse*. Dublin: Liffey Press, 1981.
Stern, Tiffany. "'On Each Wall and Corner Poast': Playbills, Title-pages, and Advertising in Early Modern London." *English Literary Renaissance* 36 (2006): 57–89.
Stevenson, John. "The 'Moral Economy' of the English Crowd: Myth and Reality." In *Order and Disorder in Early Modern England*, ed. Anthony Fletcher and John Stevenson, 218–48. Cambridge: Cambridge UP, 1985.
Straznicky, Marta. "The Red Bull Repertory in Print, 1605–60." *Early Theatre* 9 (2007): 144–56.
Sturgess, Keith. *Jacobean Private Theater*. New York: Routledge, 1987.
Tames, Richard. *Clerkenwell and Finsbury Past*. London: Historical Publications, 1999.
Tatlock, John S. P. "The Siege of Troy in Elizabethan Literature, Especially in Shakespeare and Heywood." *PMLA (Publications of the Modern Language Association)* 30 (1915): 673–770.
Temple, Philip, ed. *South and East Clerkenwell*. Survey of London Vol. 46. New Haven: Yale UP, 2008.
Thompson, E. P. "The Moral Economy of the Crowd in the Eighteenth Century." *Past and Present* 50 (1971): 76–136.
Unwin, George. *The Guilds and Companies of London*. London: Allen and Unwin, 1908.
Van Lennep, William. "The Death of the Red Bull." *Theatre Notebook* 16 (1962): 126–34.
Veblen, Thorstein. *The Theory of the Leisure Class* (1899). New York: Penguin, 1976.
Vincent, Susan. *Dressing the Elite: Clothes in Early Modern England*. Oxford: Berg, 2003.

Wallace, Charles W. "Three London Theaters of Shakespeare's Time." *University Studies* 9.4 (October 1909): 287–356.

Walsham, Alexandra. *Providence in Early Modern England*. Oxford: Oxford UP, 1999.

Walter, John, and Keith Wrightson. "Dearth and Social Order in Early Modern England." In *Rebellion, Popular Protest and the Social Order in Early Modern England*, ed. Paul Slack, 108–28. Cambridge: Cambridge UP, 1984.

Ward, Joseph P. "Imagining the Metropolis in Elizabethan and Stuart London." In *The Country and the City Revisited: England and the Politics of Culture, 1550–1850*, ed. Gerald Maclean, Donna Landry, and Joseph P. Ward, 24–40. Cambridge: Cambridge UP, 1999.

———. *Metropolitan Communities: Trade, Guilds, Identity, and Change in Early Modern London*. Stanford: Stanford UP, 1997.

Weimann, Robert. *Shakespeare and the Popular Tradition in the Theater* (1978). Trans. R. Schwartz. Baltimore: Johns Hopkins UP, 1987.

White, Paul Whitfield. *Theater and Reformation*. Cambridge: Cambridge UP, 1993.

Whiting, Robert. *Local Responses to the English Reformation*. New York: St. Martin's, 1998.

Whitney, Charles. *Early Responses to Renaissance Drama*. Cambridge: Cambridge UP, 2006.

Wiles, David. *Shakespeare's Clown: Actor and Text in the Elizabethan Playhouse*. Cambridge: Cambridge UP, 1987

Wilson, Charles. *England's Apprenticeship, 1603–1763*. 2nd ed. New York: Longman, 1984.

Wilson, F. P. *The Plague in Shakespeare's London*. Oxford: Oxford UP, 1927.

Wilson, John. *A Concise Account of St. John's Gate Clerkenwell*. London: Langham Chambers, 1869.

Woodbridge, Linda, ed. *Money and the Age of Shakespeare: Essays in New Economic Criticism*. Houndmills and New York: Palgrave Macmillan, 2003.

Wooden, Warren R. *John Foxe*. Boston: Twayne, 1983.

Woolf, D. R. *Reading History in Early-Modern England*. Cambridge: Cambridge UP, 2000.

Yachnin, Paul. *Stage-Wrights: Shakespeare, Jonson, Middleton and the Making of Theatrical Value*. Philadelphia: University of Pennsylvania Press, 1996.

Young, Alan R. "Thomas Heywood's Pageants: New Forms of Evidence." *Research Opportunities in Renaissance Drama* 30 (1988): 129–45.

INDEX

STUDIES IN THEATRE HISTORY & CULTURE

Actors and American Culture, 1880–1920
By Benjamin McArthur

The Age and Stage of George L. Fox, 1825–1877: An Expanded Edition
By Laurence Senelick

American Theater in the Culture of the Cold War: Producing and Contesting Containment
By Bruce McConachie

Classical Greek Theatre: New Views of an Old Subject
By Clifford Ashby

Czech Theatre Design in the Twentieth Century: Metaphor and Irony Revisited
Edited by Joseph Brandesky

Embodied Memory: The Theatre of George Tabori
By Anat Feinberg

Fangs of Malice: Hypocrisy, Sincerity, and Acting
By Matthew H. Wikander

Fantasies of Empire: The Empire Theatre of Varieties and the Licensing Controversy of 1894
By Joseph Donohue

French Theatre Today: The View from New York, Paris, and Avignon
By Edward Baron Turk

Jews and the Making of Modern German Theatre
Edited by Jeanette R. Malkin and Freddie Rokem

The Making of Theatrical Reputations: Studies from the Modern London Theatre
By Yael Zarhy-Levo

Marginal Sights: Staging the Chinese in America
By James S. Moy

Melodramatic Formations: American Theatre and Society, 1820–1870
By Bruce A. McConachie

Meyerhold: A Revolution in Theatre
By Edward Braun

Modern Czech Theatre: Reflector and Conscience of a Nation
By Jarka M. Burian

Modern Hamlets and Their Soliloquies: An Expanded Edition
By Mary Z. Maher

Molière, the French Revolution, and the Theatrical Afterlife
By Mechele Leon

The Most American Thing in America: Circuit Chautauqua as Performance
By Charlotte M. Canning

Othello and Interpretive Traditions
By Edward Pechter

Our Moonlight Revels: *A Midsummer Night's Dream* in the Theatre
By Gary Jay Williams

The Performance of Power: Theatrical Discourse and Politics
Edited by Sue-Ellen Case and Janelle Reinelt

Performing History: Theatrical Representations of the Past in Contemporary Theatre
By Freddie Rokem

The Recurrence of Fate: Theatre and Memory in Twentieth-Century Russia
By Spencer Golub

Reflecting the Audience: London Theatregoing, 1840–1880
By Jim Davis and Victor Emeljanow

Representing the Past: Essays in Performance Historiography
Edited by Charlotte M. Canning and Thomas Postlewait

The Roots of Theatre: Rethinking Ritual and Other Theories of Origin
By Eli Rozik

Shakespeare and Chekhov in Production: Theatrical Events and Their Audiences
By John Tulloch

Shakespeare on the American Yiddish Stage
By Joel Berkowitz

The Show and the Gaze of Theatre: A European Perspective
By Erika Fischer-Lichte

Stagestruck Filmmaker: D. W. Griffith and the American Theatre
By David Mayer

Strange Duets: Impresarios and Actresses in the American Theatre, 1865–1914
By Kim Marra

Textual and Theatrical Shakespeare: Questions of Evidence
Edited by Edward Pechter

Theatre and Identity in Imperial Russia
By Catherine A. Schuler

Theatre, Community, and Civic Engagement in Jacobean London
By Mark Bayer

Theatre Is More Beautiful Than War: German Stage Directing in the Late Twentieth Century
By Marvin Carlson

Theatres of Independence: Drama, Theory, and Urban Performance in India since 1947
By Aparna Bhargava Dharwadker

The Theatrical Event: Dynamics of Performance and Perception
By Willmar Sauter

The Trick of Singularity: *Twelfth Night* and the Performance Editions
By Laurie E. Osborne

The Victorian Marionette Theatre
By John McCormick

Wandering Stars: Russian Emigré Theatre, 1905–1940
Edited by Laurence Senelick

Writing and Rewriting National Theatre Histories
Edited by S. E. Wilmer